CRIME WAVE

REPORTAGE AND FICTION FROM THE UNDERSIDE OF L.A.

JAMES ELLROY

ARROW

Published by Arrow Books in 1999

13 5 7 9 10 8 6 4 2

"Hush-Hush", "Tijuana, Mon Amour" and "Hollywood Shakedown" are works of
fiction. Names, characters, businesses, places and incidents in those stories are the
product of the author's imagination or used fictitiously. Any resemblance to actual
events, locales, or persons, living or dead, is entirely coincidental

All of the pieces in this collection were published in *GQ* magazine: "Out of the
Past" (Nov. 1993), "My Mother's Killer" (Aug. 1994), "Sex, Glitz, and Greed: The
Seduction of O. J. Simpson" (Dec. 1994), "The Tooth of the Crime" (July 1995), "Bad
Boys in Tinseltown" (Oct. 1997), "Hollywood Shakedown" (in 2 parts, Nov. /Dec.
1997), "Body Dumps" (in 2 parts, Mar. /Apr. 1998), "Hush-Hush" (Sept. 1998),
"Let's Twist Again" (Nov. 1998), "Glamour Jungle" (Dec. 1998), and "Tijuana, Mon
Amour" (in 2 parts, Feb. /Mar. 1999).

First published in the United Kingdom in 1999 by Century

Arrow Books Limited
20 Vauxhall Bridge Road, London, SWIV 25A

Random House Australia (Pty) Limited
20 Mfred Street, Milsons Point, Sydney,
New South Wales 2061, Australia

Random House New Zealand Limited
18 Poland Road, Glenfield
Auckland 10, New Zealand

Random House South Mrica (Pty) Limited
Endulini, 5a Jubilee Road, Parktown 2193, South Africa

Random House UK Limited Reg. No. 954009

A CIP catalogue record for this book
is available from the British Library

Papers used by Random House UK Limited
are natural, recyclable products made from wood grown in
sustainable forests. The manufacturing processes conform to
the environmental regulations of the country of origin

ISBN 0 09 927999 1

Printed and bound in Norway by
AIT Trondheim AS

To
Curtis Hanson

CONTENTS

INTRODUCTION

by Art Cooper, Editor-in-Chief, *GQ*

It was love at first sight. I first met James Ellroy in the fall of 1993 at The Four Seasons restaurant, a midtown Manhattan mecca for publishing poobahs where lunch for two can easily exceed the advance for a first novel. The first word James uttered was "Woof!"—and thus did the Demon Dog of American Literature enter my life and *GQ's*. In the five years since, James has contributed some of the finest journalism and fiction we have published, and all of it is included in this volume. Contrary to the convention that writers make their names in magazines before turning to books, James was at the top of his game as a novelist when he decided to try magazine writing.

James is a big man with a big voice and a big personality. Those who don't know him well find him intimidating. So do those who know him well. And he is fearless as a Doberman, which I discovered early on when we were trying to decide on a perfect story. Having admired his *The Black Dahlia*, I acknowledged my own fascination with Hollywood murders of the '40s and '50s. The conversation went something like this:

ME: You know, some Miss Idaho goes to Hollywood to be a star, doesn't make it, works as a cocktail lounge waitress or a hooker, and winds up horribly and mysteriously murdered. JAMES: Well, I'm obsessed by an unsolved murder. My mother was murdered when I was 10. She had been drinking in some bar and left with a guy. They found her body on an access road by a high school. She had been strangled. They never found who did it. ME (*excitedly*): That's it! Write your obsession. Reinvestigate it. Write it.

Right away. JAMES: Yes, Godfather. (He calls me Godfather all the time. I like it. It makes me feel well-tailored.)

I didn't find out until a couple of years later that James went immediately from my office to visit with his agent, Nat Sobel, a wise, compassionate man on every occasion but this one. Art wants me to write about my mother's murder, said James. Don't do it, advised Nat. It will dredge up a lot that I don't think you want to confront. I'm gonna do it, said the Doberman. The article, "My Mother's Killer," appeared in our August 1994 issue and was one of the most widely praised magazine pieces of that year. James later expanded the piece into his bestselling memoir *My Dark Places.*

I am not alone in thinking that everything that James has written, indeed his very essence, has been shaped by the murder of Geneva Hilliker Ellroy. He acknowledges as much when writing of her in "My Mother's Killer": "The woman refused to grant me a reprieve. Her grounds were simple: My death gave you a voice, and I need you to recognize me past your exploitation of it." James inscribed my copy of *My Dark Places* "She lives!"

Accompanying the article there was a photograph of James just after he has been told of his mother's death. Look at his eyes. They are shocked, uncomprehending. Raised by his father, a rakish "Hollywood bottom feeder" (James's words), who did or did not "pour the pork" to Rita Hayworth, James grew to be a teen punk, a peeping tom and a petty thief who broke into houses to sniff women's panties. He filed away, in his mind, everything he saw when he was strung out on drugs or drunk on cheap booze or spending nine months in local lockups—nightmarish, photographic visions that would fuel his noirish fiction.

These complex tales of Los Angeles's seamy underside provide the truest social history of the city in the 1940s and '50s, an era of "bad white men doing bad tings in the name of authority." Ellroy's stories are as dense as an overcrowded prison, but his syncopated style is deceptive: short, staccato, often alliterative bursts. But they are not riffs. Each muscular sentence follows the next and orderly advances the plot. His protagonists are deeply wounded men on both sides of the law, scarred and corrupted by what they have seen.

James had achieved a reputation as the best American hard-boiled crime writer when his novel *L.A. Confidential* was turned into a critical and commercial hit movie, which happily introduced him to a much larger audience. He writes about that experience here in "Bad Boys in Tinseltown." In this volume, too, are three short fictions that continue where *L.A. Confidential* ended: "Hollywood Shakedown," "Hush-Hush," and "Tijuana, Mon Amour." James reprises Danny Getchell, the cannily corrupt star writer of *Hush-Hush* magazine, who has the grisly goods on almost everyone in Tinseltown and will blackmail anyone to obtain exclusive dirt. Ellroy gleefully dips in the muck his band of merry miscreants, including Jack Webb, Mickey Cohen, Frank Sinatra, Lana Turner, Johnny Stompanato, Dick Contino, Sammy Davis Jr., Oscar Levant, and Rock Hudson. There is a raunchy ring of verisimilitude, a truly bizarre believability, to the way Ellroy makes them behave.

Two years ago I hosted a dinner party at The Four Seasons for another '50s icon, 71-year-old Tony Curtis, who arrived wearing a ruffled white shirt, a tuxedo jacket without lapels, a medal from the French government on his chest, and his stunning 26-year-old, 6'1" girlfriend, Jill Van Den Berg, on his arm. James was there as were Tom Junod, who had written a brilliant profile of Curtis for *GQ*, and an editor whose name will come to me in a moment. When I suggested that Tony be seated away from the other diners, James thought it would be better if he sat near them. James, of course, was right. All evening, middle-aged suburban matrons fawned over Tony, pleaded for his autograph, touched him, told him he was the handsomest movie star ever.

We drank some surpassingly good wine, laughed a lot, and listened raptly to Tony and James, back and forth like a shuttlecock, tell ribald tales of Hollywood in the '50s. It became clear to me that no one alive knows more than James about that particular time in that particular place. He seems to know everything about the famous, the near-famous, and the infamous. Especially their penis size. His novels, like his conversation, abound with references to it. Some of his characters are "hung like a donkey," others "like a cashew." Why he is so obsessed is best left to Freudians, but for Ellroy, more than any other writer, anatomy is truly destiny.

Ellroy's destiny was to be a moralist. But he doesn't ride his moralism like some hobbyhorse. When he is outraged by some wrongdoing, he gets really juiced. Shortly after O. J. Simpson committed the double-slash of ex-wife Nicole and her friend, Ron Goldman, I asked James if he'd write an essay on the Crime of the Century. Yes, indeed, he replied. The result made the hair on the back of my neck stand up. "Sex, Glitz, and Greed: The Seduction of O. J. Simpson" is a passionate, powerful piece that skewers Simpson and the horrific Hollywood celebrity culture that spawned him. Several months ago, James was in moral high dudgeon again, this time outraged at Bill Clinton's sexual dalliance with Monica Lewinsky and his rather bizarre pronouncement that a blow job really isn't sex. James was itching to rip Bubba, and I, perhaps unwisely, declined.

This white-hot morality and a singular narrative gift aside, I think James has become one of the finest writers of our time because he is the most disciplined scrivener I have ever known. He rises early and spends 10 hours every day writing. He has never been blocked. He seems always to be juggling a novel, short fiction, and his magazine work. Astonishingly, he has never missed a deadline. He possesses the concentration—and the confidence—of a cat burglar; the outline of his novel-in-progress runs 343 pages.

Genius has its rewards. Ellroy now commands advances robust enough to dine regularly at The Four Seasons. Last October he flew from his home in Kansas City to New York where, resplendent in black tie (James is some bespoke dandy), he accepted *GQ*'s Man of the Year Award for Literature, for which he was selected by our ferociously intelligent readers. The two previous winners are Norman Mailer and John Updike. Mr. Mailer and Mr. Updike should feel flattered.

PART ONE

UNSOLVED

BODY DUMPS

I

DETECTIVE DIVISION/HOMICIDE BUREAU/LOS ANGELES
COUNTY SHERIFF'S DEPARTMENT (EL MONTE PD
ASSISTING). VICTIM: SCALES, BETTY JEAN. DOD: 1/29/73.
DISPOSITION: MURDER/187 PC. FILE #073-01946-2010-
400 (UNSOLVED)

I

The victim was a 24-year-old white female. She lived at 2633
Cogswell, El Monte. The city was downscale. The racial mix was
white trash and low-rent Latin.

The victim was married to William David Scales—a 26-year-
old white male. They had a 4-year-old daughter and a 3-month-
old son. The victim was unemployed. Her husband installed
insulation.

8:00 P.M. Monday, 1/29/73:

The victim leaves her apartment. She's alone. Her stated intention: to deposit some checks at a bank night drop and shop at
Durfee Drugs and Crawford's Market. She takes off in her husband's Ford pickup. Scales stays home. He watches the kids and
checks out the *Laugh-In* TV show.

The bank is a block from the market. Durfee Drugs is one mile west. Their apartment sits equidistant.

It's a tight local spread. Scales figures his wife will be gone one hour.

9:00, 9:30, 10:00. No Betty Jean. The baby wants food. Scales feeds him and slaps on fresh diapers. He's ticked off and worried. He's working on pissed off and scared. He starts running abandonment tapes.

Betty left me and the kids. Betty *stuck* me with the kids. Betty's got a boyfriend. They're at his place or a bar or a motel. They're bopping at the Nashville West.

He calmed down. He switched tapes. Betty needs some time by herself.

To unwind. To cut loose. To visit her girlfriends.

He called Connie, Terry, and Glenda. They said they hadn't seen Betty. He ran tapes from 10:30 to midnight. He called the El Monte PD and the California Highway Patrol. He described his truck and his wife. He asked about car wrecks.

No go:

Your truck was not involved in any reported collisions.

He ran crash tapes to 2:00 A.M. He called the El Monte PD back. He got another No. The desk man said sit tight and wait by the phone.

He tried to sit tight. The tapes kept spinning. He left his kids alone and walked by Crawford's Market and the Nashville West. They were closed. He didn't see his wife or his truck. He walked home. He called the girlfriends again. He got three more No's. He fell asleep on the couch and woke up at 5:30. He called Betty Jean's dad in Corona. Bud Bedford said he hadn't seen or heard from Betty Jean. He said he'd shoot up to El Monte.

Bill Scales and Bud Bedford connected. They drove by Durfee Drugs, the bank, and the market. They did not see Betty Jean or the truck. They drove to the El Monte PD. They filed a missing-persons sheet. Scales said his wife was devoted. She wasn't a runaround chick. She didn't smoke dope or chase men. She wouldn't just split unannounced.

The cops told Scales and Bedford to sit tight. Don't think car wrecks or abductions. We're legally constrained until your wife is gone forty-eight hours. Think car wrecks or abductions then.

Bill Scales thought it now. Bud Bedford thought it. They did not sit tight.

They drove the #10 Freeway east/west. They drove the 605 north/south. They stopped at gas stations. They talked to attendants. They described Betty Jean and the truck. Scales got a bug up his ass. He knew his wife was kidnapped. He *knew* the guy stopped to gas up.

More *No's*. *No's* straight across. No Betty Jean/no truck.

Bedford went home. He'd divorced Betty's mother years back. He had to break the news and say it don't look good.

Scales stuck the kids with a baby-sitter. He borrowed a car and went at the freeways systematically. He hit gas stations. He flashed a snapshot of Betty. He got a straight run of *No's*.

Wednesday, 1/31/73:

The missing-persons investigation kicked in pro forma. An APB went out. A Teletype detailed the truck and Betty Jean Scales:

WF/DOB 3/6/49, 5'4", 115, brown hair, brown eyes. Last seen wearing a red-pink top, brown Levi's, and white tennis shoes.

1:30 A.M. Thursday, 2/1/73:

An El Monte PD unit spots the truck. It's parked in the lot at Vons Market. The location: Peck Road and Lower Azusa. The location: two miles north of 2633 Cogswell. The location: 2.5 miles north of Durfee Drugs, the bank, and Crawford's Market.

A patrolman impounds the truck. He tows it to a yard in South El Monte. He talks to a clerk at Vons Market. The clerk says the truck was in the lot at least forty-eight hours. He noticed it around 4:00 A.M.—Tuesday, 1/30.

Eight hours after Betty Jean left her apartment.

The El Monte PD contacts Sheriff's Homicide. The Scales thing vibes murder. Deputy Hal Meyers and Sergeant Lee Koury drive to the tow yard.

They examine the truck.

In the bed: metal scaffolds, a milk crate, an empty cardboard box, a leather tool holder, a matching belt, and a length of rope. In the cab: three bottles of baby formula in a small box. A purse, a white bra, white panties, one left-foot white tennis shoe, and a pair of brown Levi's.

The box is on the floor. The clothes are stacked beside it.

Koury and Meyers look under the seat. They find the matching shoe. A key ring is tucked inside. They note a blood spot on the canvas.

On the seat: a red-pink sweater. Distinct bloodstains. A toolbox on the step by the passenger door. Blood spotted.

More bloodwork:

Smears on the seat back. Spatters on the inside of the passenger door. Drops on the step near the toolbox.

Koury called the crime lab and told them to send out a crew. Meyers opened the purse. He found cosmetic items, three checks made out to William D. Scales, Betty Jean Scales's ID, and a checkbook. The last check logged in: $9.71, to Durfee Drugs, 1/29/73. Meyers checked the box on the floor. He found a cash-register receipt for $9.71. Koury called the EL Monte PD and told them to contact the husband.

The lab crew arrived. A print man dusted the truck inside and out. He found no latent prints. He found wipe marks on the steering wheel and dashboard. A man scraped blood samples and cut a swatch out of the seat back. He found a long brown hair congealed in a blood smear.

1:30 P.M., 2/1/73:

Koury and Meyers meet Bill Scales at the El Monte PD. Scales recounts his wife's Monday-night plans. He runs down his own actions and describes his marriage as stable.

3:30 P.M., 2/1/73:

Koury and Meyers drive to Durfee Drugs. They interview a clerk named Gloria Terrazas. Mrs. Terrazas ID's a photo of the probable victim and says she came in about 8:30 Monday night.

She purchased some baby formula and paid by check. She came in and left alone. She behaved in a normal fashion.

4:00 P.M., 2/1/73:

Koury and Meyers drive to Crawford's Market. They grill the people working Monday night. They flash a photo of the probable victim. They say, "When was the last time you saw her?" They get a straight consensus: She did not come in Monday night.

It looks tight and local. The probable victim leaves her pad and drives to Durfee Drugs. She never gets to Crawford's or the bank. Her deposit-ready checks are still in her purse. It looks like a snatch. The guy grabs her outside Durfee Drugs or en route to the bank and Crawford's. He hijacks the truck. He dumps her and dumps the truck at Vons Market. The truck was in the lot from 4:00 A.M. Tuesday on.

Or it's the husband.

6:00 P.M., 2/1/73:

Koury and Meyers meet Bill Scales at the tow yard. Scales ID's his truck and the items in the bed. He points to the empty box. He says his staple-bat is missing. It's very heavy. Maybe the guy beat his wife to death with it.

Koury and Meyers look at Scales real close.

Scales looks in the cab. He spots some gravel on the floor. He extrapolates.

Some clown kidnapped his wife. He beat her to death with his staple-bat and dumped her in the Irwindale pits.

It's a good theory.

Koury and Meyers make Bill Scales as one cold motherfucker.

The Irwindale gravel pits ran northeast of El Monte. They bordered the 605 Freeway. They covered twenty-four square miles. They fused with flood-control basins and brushland.

The pits ran fifteen to 150 feet deep. Paved roads connected them. Street access was cake. You could pull off east-west thoroughfares and drive right in.

The pits looked psychedelic. Scoop cranes hung over them all day and all night. Rainfall turned the pits into tide pools. Water collected and receded at a very slow rate.

Heavy rain hit L.A. that winter. The pit floors were submerged. The pit line began 1.5 miles east of Vons Market.

The Scales thing vibed body dump. The cops figured she was down in the pits.

Friday, 2/2/73:

A search team goes in. Deployed: one Sheriff's helicopter, ten deputies, three El Monte PD men, and three Sheriff's Homicide men. The chopper flies low. The cops kick through wet gravel all day.

Saturday, 2/3/73:

The search resumes. Deployed: one chopper, seven deputies, two El Monte PD men, four Sheriff's Homicide men and 103 horsemen from the Sheriff's Mounted Posse. The search area is greatly expanded. It covers El Monte, Baldwin Park, Irwindale, Azusa, Arcadia, and unincorporated parts of L.A. County.

The chopper flies low. The walking cops wear hip boots. The horses buck knee-high water. A storm hits at 3:00 P.M. The search is called off.

The storms continued. Big rain on Sunday and Monday. The search was postponed indefinitely. They had to let the water recede.

Koury and Meyers called it a snatch, rape, and kill. They leaned on registered sex offenders. They logged in zero suspects.

They door-to-doored by Durfee Drugs and Vons Market. They tapped out. Nobody saw anything. They interviewed the probable victim's father, mother, stepfather, stepmother, and brother. The father and mother ragged the husband:

He's a lowlife. He's a tyrant. He's a cold son of a bitch. Bud Bedford says it flat out: He killed Betty Jean.

Wednesday, 2/7/73:

Bill Scales is summoned to the Sheriff's Crime Lab. Sergeant Ben Lubon administers a polygraph test. Koury, Meyers, and an El Monte PD man observe.

Lubon calls the result conclusive. The subject has no guilty knowledge of his wife's disappearance and possible death.

The Scales job stalled out. No body and no workable crime scene. Koury and Meyers caught fresh murders. The new jobs demanded full-time work. The rain came and went. The pits were full of stagnant water.

3:30 P.M. Sunday, 2/25/73:

A perimeter road near a big pit mined by Conrock-Durbin. A five-gallon can on the side of the road.

A security guard stops his car and picks up the can. His dog jumps out of the car and runs into the pit. The guard whistles. The dog barks and ignores the command. The guard walks to the edge of the pit and looks down.

She was nude. She was faceup at the bottom of the pit. The staple-bat was fifty-seven inches from her left hand.

She was badly decomposed. Immersion had intensified the decomp. Maggots had eaten her eyes and most of her membranous tissue.

Her skull was caved in. Her hair fell out as she decomped. Maggots swarmed inside the cranial vault.

Matted hair on the business end of the staple-bat.

A dozen cops hit the crime scene. They grid-searched the pit. A chopper flew over. A photo deputy shot some wide-angles.

The grid search tapped out. Zero: dirt, rocks, mud, and gravel. A deputy coroner requisitioned the body.

He performed a postmortem. His stated cause of death: blunt-force trauma and resultant skull fractures. His semen smear turned up inconclusive. The vaginal membranes were waterlogged and badly decomposed.

Everyone knew who she was. They tagged her Jane Doe #10 anyway. They needed a formal ID.

They ID'd her off dental charts:

Betty Jean Bedford Scales. Born 3/6/49. Probable date of death: 1/29/73.

. . .

Koury and Meyers worked the case part-time. They checked recent sex assaults with suspects at large. Their geographic focus: El Monte/Baldwin Park/Irwindale.

12/16/72:

2:00 A.M. The Baldwin Park Post Office. 220 PC—Assault with Intent to Commit Rape.

A white youth accosts a 44-year-old white female. He shoves her into her car at knifepoint. He rips off her bra, pulls down her pants, and fondles her buttocks. The victim screams. The suspect flees on foot.

12/17/72:

3:45 A.M. The all-night laundromat at 4428 Peck, El Monte. 220 PC—Assault with Intent to Commit Rape.

A male Latin accosts a 56-year-old white female. She works at the laundry and another laundry four blocks away.

The suspect tries to push her into a storeroom. He states, "I want pussy! I want pussy! I don't want to rob you!" The victim pulls a safety pin off her coat. She stabs the suspect. The suspect screams and runs out the door. The victim calls the El Monte PD. A patrol team responds. She tells them: "I saw the same man at two o'clock this morning. He cruised by my other laundry and looked in the window."

1/4/73:

1:00 A.M. The all-night laundromat at 4851 Peck, El Monte. 207 PC—Kidnapping, 261 PC—Rape, 245 PC—Assault with a Deadly Weapon, 10851 CVC—Grand Theft/Auto.

A male Latin accosts a 26-year-old white female. He saps the victim. He forces her into her car and takes the wheel. He drives out the 605 Freeway, the 210 Freeway, and Highway 71. He stops on a side street and orders the victim out. He marches her into a brush field. He rapes her and forces her to orally copulate him. He marches her to her car and drives her back to El Monte. He forces her out of the car at Cherrylee and Buffington. He tells her he'll leave the car at Cherrylee and Peck.

The suspect leaves the car at that location. He wipes down the steering wheel and dashboard.

2/2/73:

1:45 A.M. Lower Azusa and Peck, El Monte. 314.1 PC—Indecent Exposure.

A male Latin accosts a 36-year-old white female. The victim is standing by a bus bench. The suspect displays his penis. He states, "I can't sleep tonight because I can't get anyone to fuck."

The victim yells. The suspect walks away. A passing patrol car stops him. The suspect is carrying three pornographic books. The titles are *Husband and Friend*, *A Widow's Hunger*, and *Cocker Conqueror*.

The suspect was arrested. He was grilled on the laundromat jobs. He was exonerated.

The laundromat freak was still out there. His assaults preceded the Scales snatch by forty-two and twenty-five days. Vons Market was one hundred yards from 4428 Peck.

Durfee Drugs was two miles south. The killer grabbed the Scales woman at 8:30 P.M. The laundromat freak worked the late shift. He didn't quite vibe for the Scales job.

The post-office assault preceded the Scales snatch by forty-three days.

Koury and Meyers worked fresh murders. They stopped checking sex-assault sheets.

3/8/73:

7:15 P.M. Baldwin Park Post Office. 207/286/288A PC—Kidnapping, Sodomy, Oral Copulation.

A white youth accosts a 17-year-old white female. He flashes a knife and forces her to drive to a nearby park.

The area is secluded. The victim parks in the lot. The suspect forces her into the backseat and orders her to disrobe. She complies. The suspect gets in the backseat. He pulls down his pants and fondles the victim's genitalia.

He gets an erection. He partially penetrates the victim's anus. He forces her to orally copulate him. He masturbates and ejaculates on the victim's chest. He tells her to get dressed. She complies. He marches her into the park and orders her to take off her clothes. She complies. The suspect grabs her clothes and flees on foot.

3/13/73:

9:35 P.M. Food King Market. 14103 Ramona, Baldwin Park. 242 PC—Battery.

A white youth accosts a 25-year-old white female. He opens the passenger door of her car. He grabs the victim and tears her jacket. The victim pulls free. She runs from the car. The suspect flees on foot.

3/14/73:

7:15 P.M. Lucky Market. 13940 Ramona, Baldwin Park. 207/220 PC—Kidnapping/Attempt Rape.

A white youth accosts a 29-year-old white female. He opens the driver's-side door of her car. He flashes a knife and says, "Slide over." The victim complies. The suspect takes the wheel and drives out of the parking lot. The victim asks him to state his intentions. The suspect says, "I'm going to make love to you."

The suspect drives southeast. He stops at a red light. The victim tries to jump out. The suspect accelerates. The victim grabs the car keys. The suspect says, "Put them back or I'll kill you." The victim does not comply.

The car decelerates. The victim jumps out. The suspect jumps out. A struggle ensues. The victim grabs the suspect's knife and stabs him in the arm. The suspect flees on foot. The victim retrieves her car and drives to the Baldwin Park PD.

She reports the incident. Officer Henry Dock takes notes. She describes her assailant and the knife wound she inflicted. She's cut and scratched. Officer Dock drives her to Hartland Hospital. A doctor treats her cuts and scratches.

Sergeant J. Morehead calls Officer Dock at Hartland. He says a knife-wound patient is there now. He matches the victim's description of her assailant.

The victim observes the knife-wound patient surreptitiously. She ID's him 100%.

He's 17. He's blond and skinny and acne afflicted. He goes to high school and lives with his parents.

Officer Dock arrests the kid. A doctor treats his wound. Officer Dock transports the kid to the Baldwin Park Station. A detective interviews him. The kid is released to his parents. A 207/220 charge pends.

The Baldwin Park PD contacts Sheriff's Homicide. They lay out the kid and his MO. They make him as a suspect in one rape and three attempt-rape priors. Koury and Meyers are working fresh cases. They don't key on the kid for the Scales job.

4/23/73:

1:30 P.M. Durfee Drugs, El Monte. 220 PC—Assault with Intent to Commit Rape.

A white youth accosts an 18-year-old white female. The victim is sitting in her car. The driver's-side door is open.

The suspect appears at the door. He grabs the wheel and tells the victim to move over. The victim says no. The suspect restates his demand. The victim screams. The suspect puts one hand on her mouth and sticks one hand down the front of her bra. The victim digs in and pushes her weight against him. The suspect flees on foot.

4/25/73:

The kid is arrested and charged with the 4/23 assault. He turned 18 on 4/12. He's a culpable adult now.

Four prior victims ID him. He's held at the Temple City Sheriff's Station. A station detective contacts Koury and Meyers. They interview the kid about the Scales job.

The kid says he doesn't recall the rape and attempt rapes. He says he suffers blackouts. He snapped out of blackouts twice and found himself messing with women. He has problems with women. He's been seeing a shrink since his first bust on 3/14. He could have done things in blackouts.

The kid consents to a polygraph test. Sergeant Ben Lubon administers it.

The kid denies killing Betty Jean Scales. He denies the rape and attempt rapes that the victims made him for. He says he was never at Durfee Drugs. Sergeant Lubon calls the test "inconclusive."

6/12/73:

Koury and Meyers reinterview the kid. He denies killing Betty Jean Scales. He says he was never at Durfee Drugs. Koury and

Meyers press on the Scales job. The kid invokes his right to silence.

The kid remained in custody. He was convicted for his 3/14 attempt rape. His sentence: an open-ended stretch of Youth Authority time.

The Scales file was marked UNSOLVED. It was the second unsolved homicide in El Monte history. It followed another body dump by fifteen-plus years.

The victim was named Geneva Hilliker Ellroy. She was my mother.

2

It was 6/22/58. The killer dumped my mother on a road next to Arroyo High School. He may have killed her there. He may have killed her at another location. It went down early Sunday morning. The road was a local tryst spot. It met established standards for short-term concealment. Street access was good. Shrubs cut down the street view.

The killer raped her or had consensual sex with her. He strangled her with a cotton cord and her right nylon stocking. He dumped her in an ivy patch. She was fully clothed and disheveled.

SHERIFF'S HOMICIDE FILE #Z-483-362 (EL MONTE PD ASSISTING)

The cops traced her Saturday night.

She left the house at 8:00 P.M. She was alone. She drove to the Five Points strip in El Monte. She checked out Mama Mia's Pizza—"like she was looking for someone." She was seen at the Manger Bar. She was alone.

10:30 P.M. Saturday, 6/21/58:

My mother and a swarthy white man dine at Stan's Drive-In. They sit in his car—a '55 or '56 Olds.

11:15 P.M., 6/21/58:

My mother and the Swarthy Man hit the Desert Inn—a night-club that caters to Okies and middle-aged drunks. A blonde woman walks in with them. The three drink, dance, and talk. They leave at midnight.

2:30 A.M. Sunday, 6/22/58:

My mother and the Swarthy Man hit Stan's Drive-In again. They're alone. They sit in his car. The Swarthy Man has coffee. My mother has a late snack.

10:10 A.M., 6/22/58:

Pedestrians spot my mother's body.

It's tight and local.

The house is 1.5 miles from Five Points. The pizza joint and bar are just south. Stan's Drive-In sits at the hub. The Desert Inn is seven blocks west. The dump site is 2.8 miles northwest.

My parents were divorced. I spent that weekend with my father. I didn't see my mother walk out. I didn't panic at her absence or fear that she'd never return. I was 10 years old. I didn't know the term "body dump." I did not endure a rain-prolonged deathwatch or view my mother's decomposed remains.

I was a cold little kid. I hated and lusted for my mother and went at her through postmortem surrogates. I buried her in haste and burned flames for other murdered women. My mother's death corrupted and emboldened my imagination. It liberated and constrained me concurrently. It mandated my mental curriculum. I majored in crime and minored in vivisected women. I grew up and wrote novels about the male world that sanctioned their deaths.

I ran from my mother. I put years and miles between us. I ran back to her in 1994. I was 46 years old. Fate intervened. It sparked a confrontation.

A friend called me. He said he was writing a piece on unsolved murders in the San Gabriel Valley. It would spotlight the Sheriff's Unsolved Unit. My friend would see my mother's file and know things that I didn't know.

The call announced an opportunity. I could see my mother's file.

My friend set me up on a hot blind date. I didn't know that I would take an epic fall for my mother.

I saw the file. I read the reports and saw my mother dead at Arroyo High School. It was shocking and revelatory. I knew that her death shaped my curiosity and gift for storytelling. It was long-standing knowledge. It was coldly reasoned and mock-objectified. I sensed the full weight of it now. I sensed that it carried a debt of recognition and homage. I sensed that I came out of her in a way that superseded all ties of shared blood. I sensed that I *was* her.

A Homicide detective showed me the file. His name was Bill Stoner. He was 53 years old and set to retire. He had thirty-two years on the Sheriff's. He broke the Cotton Club Case and the Mini-Manson Case and worked on the Night Stalker Task Force. He worked Homicide for fifteen years.

Stoner impressed me. I appraised him as he appraised me. I glimpsed a powerful and orderly intellect. I sensed that he balanced a vital compassion against strict levies of judgment. I sensed that he could teach me things.

Stoner retired from active duty. He remained on the Sheriff's reserve force and retained his full cop status.

I decided to reinvestigate my mother's homicide. I asked Stoner to help me. He agreed.

The investigation spanned fifteen months. I stayed in L.A. and worked with Stoner full-time.

We studied every paper scrap in the file. We contacted the surviving witnesses. We hypothetically reconstructed my mother's final movements 10,000 times. We installed a toll-free tip line and logged hundreds of worthless tips. We stalked the Swarthy Man extrapolatively.

Was he a salesman passing through El Monte? Did he book racetrack bets at the Desert Inn? Did the Blonde work with my mother or frequent the same cocktail bars?

We extrapolated. We targeted local lifers and retoured the late

'50s. We combed the San Gabriel Valley. We hit El Monte, Baldwin Park, Irwindale, Duarte, Azusa, Temple City, Covina, West Covina, and Rosemead. We stalked my mother back to Chicago and rural Wisconsin. We found people who knew her sixty years ago.

We did not find the Blonde or the Swarthy Man. We heard the oral history of bumfuck L.A. County. People told us intimate things. I mimicked Stoner's inquisitor's stance and learned when to talk and when to listen. I was a voyeur/observer with a vindictive streak in deep camouflage. Cops liked me because I knew I wasn't one of them and didn't want to be. They liked me because I loved and hated along their lines of rectitude.

Bill Stoner became my closest friend. Our commitment ran bilateral and exceeded the investigation. Our worldviews meshed and expanded to encompass two distinct visions. We discussed crime for hours running. Bill told cop stories. I described my petty-crime exploits and county-jail stints twenty years back. We laughed. We satirized macho absurdity and admitted our complicity in perpetuating it. Bill gave me things. He empiricized L.A. crime. He embellished it with great verve and let me place my mother in context.

We talked about her. We did not defer to her status as a murder victim or my mother. We bluntly discussed her alcoholism and bent for cheap men. We followed the evidentiary track of her life and charted the detours. We shared a genderwide and wholly idealized crush on women. We were indictable coconspirators in the court of murder-victim preference. Bill reveled in the luxury of a sustained investigation with a probable dead suspect and negative outcome. It let him live with the victim and explore her life and honor her at leisure.

The investigation faded out. The Swarthy Man became less relevant. We targeted a killer and amassed facts on his victim. I wanted to write a book and give my mother to the world. I wanted to take what I learned about her and portray my arc of recognition and love.

I wrote *My Dark Places* in seven months. I went at it with deliberate intention. I spilled the most sordid facts of my mother's life and did not cite mitigation. I did not want people to think that I loved her in spite of her unconsciousness and erratic and negligent acts. I wanted people to know that I loved her because of them—and that my debt of gratitude derived from the fact that she was precisely who she was—and that the specific components of her ambiguously defined psyche and her sexual hold on me all contributed to shape and save my life.

My Dark Places was a best-seller and a critical success. I booktoured in America and Europe. Bill Stoner joined me in France and L.A. We took camera crews to El Monte. We showed them Arroyo High and the spots where the Desert Inn and Stan's Drive-In stood. I summarized my mother's story 6,000 times. I reduced it to comprehensible sound bites. I gave her to the world in a spirit of passion and joy.

The book sparked a string of worthless tips. Bill checked them out. I went home to Kansas City and researched my next novel.

My mother stayed with me. She stormed my heart at unpredictable times. I welcomed her insistent presence.

I couldn't give *My Dark Places* up. I didn't want to give it up. I toured for the paperback edition. I gave more readings and more interviews and took my mother public again. I told her story with undiminished passion. The repetition did not wear me down. I went home wanting more. I went home wanting something new and altogether familiar.

I missed Bill.

I missed the law-enforcement world and my observer role.

I missed El Monte.

I lived there for four months in 1958. I left the day my mother died. I stayed away for thirty-six years.

It was hot, smoggy, and dusty. Rednecks and wetbacks reigned. My father called it "Shitsville, U.S.A."

My mother died and scared me west to my father and Central L.A. Her ghost kept me out and pulled me back.

Arroyo High was still Arroyo High. My old house was still standing. Stan's Drive-In was gone. The Desert Inn was Valenzuela's Restaurant.

I reembraced my mother in the town that killed her. El Monte was our prime communion zone. My first visits scared me. Sustained contact wiped the fear out. Bill and I made friends with the cops and the man who owned my old house. We dined on the spot where my mother danced with her killer. We ate at Pepe's across the street and jived with Oscar De La Hoya.

I love El Monte now. El Monte is the pure essence of HER.

I wanted to give El Monte the power to shock and drive me again. I wanted to take my mother's lessons and consciously address a murdered woman. I wanted to find a workable case and write about it.

Bill was still a Homicide reserve. He told me he was scanning old files for DNA submission. The captain ordered a big file review. DNA was a hot new ticket. A lot of old unsolveds might be solvable now.

I pitched my plan. Bill liked it. I asked him to check his review files for El Monte unsolveds.

He called me back and said he found a body dump. It was just as tight and local as the Jean Ellroy case.

3

I booked a hotel room near Bill's place and flew out to Orange County. I holed up with the Scales file overnight.

It looked like my mother's file. Crime-scene shots and Teletypes and reports stuck in a blue notebook. Paper scraps and a tape cassette: Bill Scales's first interview.

I played the tape.

Scales spoke slowly and carefully. He described his wife's disappearance and a recent motorcycle race in the same tone. He lived to race. He should have won a trophy last week. He couldn't grab his bike and look for Betty last Monday. His bike was not street legal.

I studied a stack of ID photos. Betty Jean Scales alive: a prim woman with long hair and granny glasses. I studied the crime-scene shots. Betty Jean twenty-seven days dead: a bloated mannequin and insect repository.

I studied the perspective shots. The pits looked like moon craters. I pictured local acidheads grooving on the landscape.

I read the crime-scene and lab reports. I took notes. I found an odd notation:

"Vic's sweater. Stain O+—non-secretor."

Odd:

I thought the line referred to a semen stain. Some men secrete identifiable blood cells in their ejaculate; some men do not. "O+—non-secretor" was a non sequitur.

I read the missing-persons report. I recognized locations.

My mother shopped at Crawford's Market. We lived two blocks west of Peck Road. Arroyo High flanked Lower Azusa. Betty Jean vanished en route to Five Points.

I read the sex-assault reports. I cleared the laundromat freak. He worked late nights and north El Monte exclusively.

The kid vibed HOT suspect.

He was convicted for one attempt rape. Four other rape/attempt rape/abduction victims ID'd him as their assailant. He assailed his consummated victim in dark seclusion. Betty Jean was last seen at Durfee Drugs. The kid worked at a print shop two blocks away. His last alleged assault occurred at Durfee Drugs on 4/23/73.

I called Bill. He cosigned my assessment and urged me to remain circumspect. We shouldn't lock in on suspects. We should sift evidence and refrain from prejudicial conclusions.

He reminded me:

This was now an official Sheriff's/El Monte PD investigation. I was to look, listen, and ask questions judiciously.

Bill said he had calls in to Koury and Meyers. They both retired to Missouri. We had to get their assessments. I mentioned the secretor notation. Bill said we should go by the property vault and retrieve the evidence bags. The victim's clothing had to be screened for semen stains and conflicting bloodstains. That was the standard pre-DNA procedure.

I filled in the hypothetical blanks.

The kid allegedly ejaculated on his 3/8 victim. He might have done the same thing with Betty. He might have wiped his penis with her sweater, panties, or bra. The coroner's semen smear turned up "inconclusive." The victim's vaginal membranes were badly decomposed. DNA procedures did not exist in 1973. DNA-certified semen stains can be compared to cell scrapings taken from present-day suspects. The crime lab could lift cells off Betty's clothing. The crime lab could run the kid's DNA. The lab could determine the presence or absence of DNA with absolute certainty. Fabrics retain DNA cells indefinitely.

I mentioned Bill Scales and vaginal drip from normal inter-course. Bill Stoner said we had to find him and take a blood sample or a mouth scrape. We had to differentiate his fluid cells. He said the stain placements were crucial. Normal leakage would pool at the crotch of the victim's panties. If the killer wiped himself with the panties, the stains would be wide and diffuse.

I slept poorly that night. I tossed and transposed the file statistics of Betty Jean and my mother. I knew I'd blitz the next day with coffee and pure brain energy.

I did.

Bill and I drove to El Monte. We found our key locations and ran straight routes between them.

2633 Cogswell: small bungalows and dirty kids in diapers. Durfee Drugs: a small corner store with wraparound parking. Crawford's Market: gone. The bank: gone. Vons Market: a big corner store with a big parking lot.

The gravel pits: a skyscape of scoop cranes and rock piles. Fenced-in access roads and Keep Out signs.

I went through the file and checked addresses.

The kid lived at 14335 Ramona. The 3/13 and 3/14 assaults occurred at 14103 and 13940.

We drove by the locations. The old structures were gone. Shopping centers had replaced them.

The Baldwin Park Post Office: still in its old location. Walking distance to the kid's apartment. The gravel pits and Vons Market: walking distance for a kid jacked up on fear and adrenaline.

We drove to the El Monte PD. We talked to Chief Wayne Clayton and Assistant Chief Bill Ankeny.

They remembered the Scales case. Ankeny said the husband was their first hot suspect. He didn't remember the kid or the laundromat freak. Clayton said they popped a rape-o around the same time. A Latin guy sandbagged a girl by some railroad tracks. A witness scared him off as he forced the girl to strip. He was grilled and cleared on the Scales job.

Clayton said he'd help us any way he could. We stood outside his office and bullshitted. I looked down the hallway. My mind wandered. I walked down that hallway the first time in June '58. Thirty-nine years had intervened. I was still obsessed and hungry at the cusp of 50.

Bill and I drove to Sergeant Tom Armstrong's office. Armstrong ran the El Monte PD's Internal Affairs Unit. He worked out of a PD adjunct building.

Bill ran down the Scales case. Armstrong keyed on the kid. He said he'd request full paper on him. Bill said full was essential. We had to know him before we tried to find him.

Bill grabbed Armstrong's phone and called Joe Walker. Joe is a civilian crime analyst. He knows computer search systems. He helped us locate people in my mother's case.

Bill laid out the kid. Joe said he'd find him—dead or alive.

Bill and I drove to Sheriff's Homicide. Bill ran a DMV check on William David Scales. He hit. Scales was fifty-one years old now. He lived in Rancho Cucamonga.

Close. A straight shot through the San Gabriel Valley.

Bill said Valley folks never strayed far. I said the Valley was a fucking life sentence. Bill said, "For you it is."

. . .

The evidence vault adjoined the Sheriff's Academy. Evidence bags were stored on shelves stacked twenty-five feet high. The vault looked like an airplane hangar. Two dozen shelves ate up most of the floor space. Technicians accessed them with forklifts.

It was my second visit. I viewed the evidence from my mother's case the first time.

I'd touched the stocking and the cotton cord that killed her. I put the dress she died in to my face and caught a trace of her perfume.

Bill requisitioned the Scales bag. A technician found it. We examined it in a small room next to the vault.

The red-pink sweater, the panties, the bra. Separate items in separate envelopes.

Bill filled out a routing form and placed the items in a cardboard box. I didn't touch them. They looked like cheap stuff purchased at Sears or JC Penney. They smelled like dust and old synthetics.

We dropped the items off at the Sheriff's Crime Lab. A serologist named Valorie Scherr logged them in. She explained DNA in a wholly precise and stupefyingly soporific manner.

Scherr said the prescreen would take ten days. They had to identify semen or other fluids first. The amount did not matter. DNA could be successfully typed off a single cell. Dissipation might factor in. The event occurred twenty-four years ago. The stains might have eroded during storage.

Scherr gave Bill eight swab sticks and containers. She said he should tell the husband to scrape the inside of his mouth vigorously.

She advised a backup procedure.

They might not have a valid victim sample. He should try to locate the victim's parents or a sibling and take scrapings from them. This would help identify the victim's DNA.

Bill grabbed Scherr's phone and called Sheriff's Homicide. A colleague tapped the DMV computer. He got a hit on Bud Bedford. His last known address: a trailer park in Fresno.

Bill got his number from Fresno information. He called him and stated his business. Bedford agreed to be interviewed. He said he'd submit a cell sample. He said his ex-wife was still in Fresno. He gave Bill her number.

Bill called her. She said she'd cooperate.

We broke it off for the day. I went back to my hotel room and stared at a picture of Betty Jean smiling. I sensed that things went stray for her—beyond her already low expectations. I wanted to know how they stood on the night she died.

We door-knocked Bill Scales. He stepped out of a time warp and let us into his house.

He was tall and rangy and an old 51. His voice matched the voice on the interview tape down to subtle inflections.

Bill stated our business and stressed that he was not a suspect. Scales said he'd help all he could. Bud Bedford still thought he did it. Bud had Bill Scales's own daughter convinced.

The house was small, neatly tended, and starkly underfurnished. We sat down at a dinette table.

Scales described the night of 1/29 unsolicited. His eyes flicked on and off Bill's gun. His account tallied with his taped account of 2/1/73. He ran it down deadpan. Bill interposed questions. Scales answered them and jumped back to his basic narrative. He rolled over for authority figures. I knew it was a long-term practice.

I said, "Tell us about Betty Jean."

Scales said she was a dingbat. She was mousy, easygoing, and submissive. She talked a mile a minute like a true nutcase. Simple tasks flummoxed her. She didn't know how to do things.

He said "dingbat" dead cold. I used to call my mother a drunk and a whore the same way.

I didn't say, Why did you marry her then? Scales gave us the narrative version.

He met Betty in late '67. He was living in Bell Gardens. She was living in Downey. Her father set her up in a pad. He found Betty in bed with a boy and cut off his support abruptly.

Betty was going to high school then. Bill Scales moved in with her. He got her pregnant and married her. Their daughter, Leah, was born in October '68. They moved to El Monte in '71. He raced motorcycles and hung insulation. Betty worked on the assembly line at Avon cosmetics and quit to be a full-time mother. They had a son. He was 3 months old when Betty died. Leah married a guy named Baker. They had two kids. Leah was fat. She blamed her obesity on her father and her mother's death. He had a second family and raised Leah and her brother with them. Leah did not appreciate it. Betty's parents hated him and encouraged her to hate him.

Scales said that second marriage folded. He gave us a quick rundown on the details.

His candor was praiseworthy and appalling. He impressed me as a control freak with a dark self-knowledge learned the hard way. He cut his losses and lived inside rigid boundaries. His subtext was all male pride and self-pity.

He gave us his daughter's phone number. He said he'd give us a cell scrape. He said he didn't remember the last time he had sex with Betty. She was on the Pill. He didn't wear rubbers. The sperm on her panties might turn out to be his.

He looked like an Okie transplant and employed perfect grammar. He set out to refute his roots every time he opened his mouth.

He said Bud Bedford sicced a P.I. on him back in '73. The guy tailed him to a siding job in Temecula.

Bill said, "How did Bud and Betty get on?"

Scales said, "Not well." Her brother said they were feuding right before Betty died.

Bill said, "Where's the brother now?"

Scales said, "He died of AIDS."

We door-knocked Leah Scales Baker. She let us in and sat on a couch between us.

The apartment was small and overfurnished. I heard kids back in the bedrooms. The husband sat on the living-room floor and observed the interview.

Leah Baker was prepared. Bill called ahead and stated our purpose.

He introduced me. I smiled. He said my mother was a murder victim. It fell flat. Leah Baker looked right through me. She said her mother's death destroyed her life.

Bill asked her if she remembered her mother. Leah said hardly at all. Bill laid out a riff on DNA and said we had a promising suspect. Leah started in on her father.

He was mean. He was nasty. He belittled her in front of his family. She locked herself in closets and gobbled cookies to spite him.

Bill said he was cleared back in '73 and was not a suspect now. Leah said she had dreams. Her father was hitting a faceless figure. She watched him. She was wearing a white nightgown. Her grandfather said she used to wear a nightgown like that as a child.

Bill said, "Did your father beat you?" Leah said, "Maybe." She had these memory gaps. She could not recall large blocks of her childhood.

Bill tried to ask a string of questions. Leah talked over him.

Her father ridiculed her. Her stepmother and stepbrother teased her. They tried to tease her out of being fat—but she stayed fat anyway.

Bill asked her if she'd like to see her mother's case solved. Leah started back on her father. Bill clenched up. So did I. Victimhood was a summons to exploit and explore. Love the one you lost only if they deserved it.

Know your dead. Learn how you derive and diverge from them.

Leah said her father was the key suspect. She didn't know her mother was murdered for years. Her father hid the fact. That was suspicious. That meant he was hiding things. Her grandfather said he saw the apartment the day after her mother vanished. The place was a mess. Clothes were scattered around. Her baby brother sat in a pool of urine.

Bill said, "Your father passed a polygraph test."

Leah shrugged.

I asked her where she got her information.

Leah said, "My grandfather."

I asked her if she ever read newspaper accounts.

Leah said, "No."

Bill gave me his "more questions?" look. I shook my head.

Bill thanked Leah. I said we might clear this thing. It might help her get on with her life.

Leah looked right through me.

I dropped Bill off and drove back to my hotel. I stretched out on the bed and turned the lights off. I dropped their male surnames and ran with Betty Bedford and Geneva Hilliker.

Not doppelgängers. Not symbiotic twins. Inimical personalities and antithetical souls.

My mother drank Early Times bourbon. She fucked cheap men and cut them off if they cloyed or messed with her solitude. She got pregnant in '39 and aborted herself. She rammed literacy and the Lutheran Church down my throat and made me grateful as a middle-aged man.

Betty fell into things. My mother hid out in El Monte. She lived out the dreams and crazy expectations that drive bright and beautiful women. Betty hid out in El Monte. It was a good place to live the lie that life was hunky-dory.

Two Jeans.

My mother went to nursing school and shortened Geneva to Jean. She was 19. It was 1934.

She could shoot men down with stern words or a look. She wanted sex on her own sweet and unconscious terms. She knew how to say no.

She said yes, no, or maybe that night. She didn't sense danger. She could have walked away from the drive-in. She had options that Betty Jean didn't. Her unconsciousness made her passively complicit. Betty Jean went to the drugstore and bought baby food. Her life ended nineteen years short of my mother's.

I wanted to find the piece of shit who killed her and fuck him for it.

Bill called first thing in the morning. He said he just got off the phone. He talked to Tom Armstrong, Joe Walker, and Lee Koury.

They traced the kid. He was serving three-to-life. He got out on parole in '75. He stayed out two years and went down behind a fresh rape.

AND:

Koury said the kid almost confessed to the killing. He almost gave it up at his polygraph test. He said, "My dad's got heart trouble. This would really kill him."

II

4

I replayed the words from L.A. to Fresno. Koury and Meyers made the kid for the Scales snuff. The kid was 42 now. He was locked down at the California Men's Colony. He fell behind a kidnap-rape in Bakersfield. Tom Armstrong just received a full report.

Bakersfield was a hundred miles from Fresno. Bill was from Fresno. Betty Jean's parents lived in Fresno.

We drove up in Bill's car. We took Bill's father along. Angus Stoner was 86. He knew Kern County. Kern County was all new to me.

Dirt fields and shack towns. Wind and dust and a big flat sky.

Angus supplied travel notes. He identified orchards and harvesting contraptions. He talked up his hobo adventures, circa 1930.

He picked walnuts and grapes. He slept in boxcars. He poured the pork to numerous women. He cut a wide indigent swath. Butch queers rode the rails then. They dogged his handsome ass. He kicked their asses good.

Bill and I laughed. Bill called Kern County "El Monte North." I called it "Dogdick, Egypt." We were white-trash postgrads. Disorder and poverty scared us. We trashed it with postgrad license. We were like blacks calling each other "nigger."

The kid did Youth Authority time, and he got paroled. He split the San Gabriel Valley. He pulled a postgrad rape here in Kern County.

We hit Fresno at dinnertime. It was too late to hit Betty's parents. We booked three hotel rooms and ate at a chain coffee shop. Angus reprised his travelogue. I drifted in and out of it. I had the kid in my brain-sights.

Bud Bedford lived in a trailer park between two freeway ramps. His trailer was small and dirty inside and out.

He lived with his long-term girlfriend and a small, bug-eyed dog. The dog perched on his wife's lap and showed Bill his teeth. He stared at Bill and sustained a low growl throughout the whole interview.

Bill and I flanked Bud Bedford. Bill laid out the investigation and emphatically cleared Betty's husband. Bud Bedford stared at a neutral point between us. He sucked on a cigar stub and took the smoke in deep. His girlfriend stared at him. The dog stared at Bill.

Bedford was seventy-something. His hands twitched. His face twitched. He looked frail and nihilistically inclined. A good blast of cigar smoke could debilitate or kill him.

He did not react to Bill's pitch in any discernible manner.

I said, "Tell me about Betty Jean."

Bedford said, "She was a good girl and a good mother."

I said, "What else can you tell us?"

Bedford said, "She shouldn't have got mixed up with Bill Scales."

I backed off. My questions were taking me nowhere. I wanted perceptive or passionate answers. I wanted to know if Betty Jean still lived in her father's mind and if he fought to keep her there.

Bill took over. He asked specific questions and let Bedford ramble. I listened for signs of fatherly love in the mix.

He broke up with Betty's mom when Betty was 8 or 9. They fought some custody battles. She got Betty first. He got her second. Bill Scales married her. Bill was plain no-good. He was scared that Bud would get custody of the kids he had with Betty. He hid them with his sister so Bud couldn't see them. Bud hired a private eye. He wanted to get the goods on Bill Scales. The P.I. infiltrated a bike gang Scales allegedly rode with. Bud paid him $500. The guy took his money and never turned up shit.

Scales was no outlaw biker. He was an amateur motorcycle racer.

The monologue winded Bedford. His voice broke a few times. I didn't know if he was fighting emotion or exhaustion. I didn't know if he was reliving the loss of his daughter or the weight of his hardscrabble years.

I didn't bring up my murder story. I tried to get some empathy going with Betty Jean's daughter and got nowhere. That interview went nowhere. I didn't want a repeat here.

Bud Bedford hated Bill Scales. It felt like a property beef. He ceded his daughter to the man who he thought killed her or let her die. Ownership infractions. Bud set Betty up in her own pad and cut off the rent when he caught her in bed with some guy. Bill Scales assumed ownership then.

Bill got out his mouth swabs and explained the procedure. Bud Bedford put his cigar down and rinsed his mouth with water. He took a swab and ran it all over his gums.

I thanked the Bedfords and walked to the door. The dog growled at me.

Betty's mother was named Lavada Emogene Nella. She lived in a board-and-care home in middle-class Fresno.

Bill called ahead. Mrs. Nella and her companion met us. We sat down in the dayroom. Old people on walkers pushed by.

Mrs. Nella was attractive and perfectly groomed. She was young and fit by rest-home standards.

Her eyes darted and latched onto fixed targets and went blank while she retained eye contact.

I said, "Tell me about Betty Jean."

Mrs. Nella called her daughter a "chatterbox" and a "home-body" and a "sweet-natured girl" who "only wanted to be a good wife and mother." Things tended to confuse Betty Jean. She was outgoing and shy at the same time. She relied on other folks to make her decisions.

Bill mentioned Betty's marriage. Mrs. Nella said it was difficult. Bill Scales was cold and dictatorial.

Bill mentioned physical abuse. Betty Jean's daughter described her dad as hard and domineering. That accusation dominated her interview.

Mrs. Nella said no. Bill Scales didn't need to hit. He had Betty under his thumb without resorting to violent behavior. He controlled Betty with his knowledge of how much she loved him.

I said, "He didn't kill her."

Mrs. Nella said, "Oh, I knew that. The police cleared him back when it happened."

Bill said we had a hot suspect now. We might be able to close the case officially.

Mrs. Nella lit up. Her eyes slipped into focus.

Her companion showed me some press clippings. I read an L.A. *Times* piece from March '73. It described the escalating murder rate in El Monte. The ironic postscript: The Scales case was the first unsolved murder since "Jean Elroy in 1956."

They misspelled my mother's name. They got the year of her death wrong. It pissed me off more than it should have.

Mrs. Nella gave us a cell scraping. She said she never got to say good-bye to Betty. The police said she was too far decomposed.

We drove back to El Monte. Tom Armstrong got the fiie from the Bakersfield PD and let us read through it.

The kid's name was Robert Leroy Polete Jr. His last name was pronounced *Po*-lay. He married Vonnie in April '76. He entered the United States Navy in September '76. He completed basic training. He was assigned to the Naval Air Station in Lemoore, California. Lemoore is near Bakersfield and Fresno.

Polete was arrested on 2/8/77. The charges:

FELONY, IN FOUR COUNTS, TO WIT: RAPE, 261 PC/KIDNAPPING, 209 PC/ROBBERY, 211 PC/ORAL COPULATION, 288A PC.

2/4/77:
Polete leaves Lemoore air station. His intention: to visit his wife in Hacienda Heights. Hacienda Heights is in the San Gabriel Valley.

Polete has $5. It won't get him out of Kern County. He buys a $4 bus ticket. He lands in Bakersfield at 8:25 P.M.

He doesn't know what to do. He wants to see his wife. She's about to be evicted from her apartment. He's nursing a grudge. The navy should have stationed him down in L.A.

Polete walks around the bus depot. He contemplates a purse snatch and rejects the notion. If he grabs a purse in the depot and buys a ticket south, the cops will bust him right here.

He leaves the depot. He walks by the Pacific Telephone Building. He spots a woman. He follows her to a '74 Honda Civic.

The woman gets in the car and pulls out. The driver's-side door is unlatched. Polete opens it. He places a knife against the woman's neck and says, "Move over or you're dead."

The victim says, "You can have my car if you let me out." Polete says, "Don't give me any lip." The victim slides into the passenger seat.

Polete drives a short distance northwest. He pulls into a parking lot and stops the car. He tells the victim to crawl into the backseat and undress.

The victim complies. Polete tells her to lie on her stomach. The victim complies. Polete ties her hands behind her back. He uses her bra, her panties, and a swimsuit top.

Polete orders the victim to turn over and sit up. She complies.

Polete gets into the backseat. He kisses her and fondles her genitalia. He sticks two fingers in her vagina and sticks the same two fingers in her mouth.

He orally copulates the victim. He rapes her. He wipes his penis with the victim's clothing.

He goes through her purse. He finds $7 in change. He says, "You sure are rich." The victim says she's got another $6 in bills.

Polete steals the money. He drives to a dark field off the Rosedale Highway. He marches the victim sixty-five yards in and orders her to sit down. The victim complies. Polete scatters her clothes out of sight.

He tells the victim not to leave for ten minutes. He says, "I know where to find you." He tells the victim not to call the cops—because he's got her ID and he's got friends who'll get her if anything happens to him. He says he'll drop the car off in Fresno. If anything happens to him or the car, his insurance will take care of it. He says, "I'm sorry, but I had to do this. I've been treated badly."

Polete drives off. The victim finds her clothes and walks to a gas station. She calls her father. Her father calls the Bakersfield PD and reports the incident.

Polete drives to Hacienda Heights. He spends the weekend with his wife. He returns to Lemoore air station early Sunday night.

Tuesday, 2/8/77:

Polete calls the victim's mother—collect. He uses the phone in his office.

The victim's mother does not accept the call. Polete gives her a call-back number and ID's himself as "Security Officer Johnson." He says he has information on her daughter's car.

Polete hangs up. The victim's mother calls the victim. The victim calls the Bakersfield PD. She talks to Detective J. D. Jackson. She says a "Security Officer Johnson" called her mother. The man implied her car was somewhere at Lemoore air station. He left a number: (209) 998-9827.

Detective Jackson calls the number. Polete answers. Jackson

asks him about the car. Polete says Johnson is handling it. Jackson says he'd like to talk to him. Polete says Johnson is out. Jackson tells him to secure the car. Polete says he will.

Jackson talks to his supervisor. They've got a lead on the missing car in the 2/4 rape. The supervisor calls Lemoore. He contacts the chief of security. The chief tells him that Airman R. L. Polete told him the following story:

Polete was hitching back to the station last Sunday night. A man in a Honda Civic picked him up. The man pulled a knife. He told Polete that he stole the car from a woman in Bakersfield. He told him to call her on Tuesday and make sure she got the car.

Polete balked. The man gave him a phone number for the woman's mother. The man stole Polete's ID papers. They showed his address in Hacienda Heights. The man said he'd better comply—or his wife would have problems.

Detective Jackson and Detective J. L. Wheldon drove to Lemoore. They questioned Airman Polete. He strongly resembled their victim's description. Polete told them his hitchhiking story. Jackson and Wheldon poked holes in it. They read Polete his Miranda rights. Polete started sobbing. He said he stole the Honda. He described the events preceding the theft.

From the Bakersfield PD report:

Polete said he had to see his wife. He needed bus fare. He was stuck in Bakersfield. He figured he'd snatch a purse.

He saw this girl. He pulled his knife and jumped into her car. He stated his intention: to drop her off someplace safe and split with the car.

He drove off. Polete said the girl came on to him. She rubbed his leg up near his crotch. He said, "Don't do that, I'm married—all I want is the car."

The girl said, "If you're going to take the car, you might as well take everything." She groped him again. She said, "Let's pull over somewhere—get in the backseat and do it."

Polete said he'd do it—"if she promised to leave him alone." The girl got in the backseat and took all her clothes off. They drove to a dark field.

The girl pulled him into the backseat. She started kissing him. She asked him to give her some head. Polete refused. The girl said she wouldn't make him do it.

They had intercourse. Polete got back in the front seat. The girl said, "You said you were going to leave me off somewhere. Let's go."

Polete dropped the girl off on the other side of the freeway. He found $5 on the floorboard and took it. He drove down to Hacienda Heights.

Jackson and Wheldon booked Polete on four felony counts: 261, 209, 211, and 288A. The victim viewed a mug shot spread and identified him. Jackson and Wheldon got a warrant and searched Polete's locker. They found the clothes the victim said Polete was wearing.

The prelim was held on 3/1/77. Polete was held to answer for the 261 and 209 charges.

He went to trial on 7/5/77. He pleaded guilty. His lawyer said he should. His lawyer thought he could get him tagged as an MDSO—a Mentally Disordered Sex Offender.

His lawyer thought he could get him some state-hospital time. His lawyer miscalculated.

The judge gave Polete the maximum sentence. Two terms prescribed by law—to run consecutively. The court transcript stated:

"I think he is a serious menace to the people of this community and any other community that he would live in. I want to make sure that he doesn't get out for a long, long time."

I went through the rest of the file. Polete was denied parole in '83, '92, '93, '94, and '96.

Three to life. Two consecutive terms. Twenty years and four months inside. It was unknown why Polete was denied parole.

Bill and I discussed it. Bill's take: Polete fucked up inside or was recognizably psycho and unable to con the parole board.

He was locked down at CMC. He couldn't hurt women there.

It wasn't enough. He was up for parole late in '98.

. . .

The DNA prescreen flopped. They found blood on the victim's sweater and no semen on her panties. The next step: to examine the rest of the garments for semen.

The result derailed Bill's plan of attack. He needed a verified semen stain. The lab could run it against Bill Scales's DNA. A negative hit would indicate unidentified ejaculate. Bill could take that result and get a search warrant. The warrant would empower him to extract a fluid sample from Robert Leroy Polete.

We discussed options. Bill said it boiled down to a face-to-face talk. He would interview Polete.

We went back to the file. We wanted to make sure we didn't overlook a single bit of data. We pulled odd note sheets and found new names to run. We got one positive hit.

John Fentress rode bikes with Bill Scales. He joined the El Monte PD in '73. His wife knew Betty Jean.

We met him at the El Monte Station. I said, "Tell me about Betty Jean."

Fentress said she was talkative and mentally slow. She was totally in love with Bill Scales. Scales was the boss. Betty went along with the program.

Betty struggled with her marriage. He doubted if Scales ever hit her.

Bill and I went back to the file. We reviewed the physical evidence and hypothetically reconstructed the crime.

Bloodstains on the truck seat. Small drips and spatters inconsistent with the victim's massive head wounds. Hypothetical conclusion: Polete or the unknown assailant did not transport the body to the gravel pits. The seat would have been badly bloodstained if he drove the body any good distance. It all went down in the truck.

He kidnapped her. He hijacked the truck. He drove her to the gravel pits. He assaulted her and killed her there and dumped her immediately.

Hypothetically:

She's nude. He raped her on the seat. He orders her out of the truck. She refuses. She thinks he intends to take her somewhere and kill her.

He's standing outside the truck. He grabs the staple-bat. He tries to pull the victim out of the cab. She resists. She's facedown. He hits her on the back of the head and caves her skull in.

He pulls her out of the cab. Her head brushes the seat back and passenger door and leaves stains. He throws her into the pit.

A sound hypothesis. In sync with aspects of Polete's MO. Suitable for other unknown suspects.

Bill called the prison. He arranged to interview Robert Leroy Polete. I felt the case veer toward a dead-end metaphysic.

I knew that static level intimately. It defined my mother's case.

Knowledge did not equal provability. Faulty memories spawned misinformation. Hypothetical renderings imposed logic on chaotic events and were rarely confirmed by firsthand accounts. Evidence was misplaced. Witnesses died. Their heirs revised and retold their stories inaccurately. Consensus of opinion seldom equaled truth. The passage of time and new perpetuations of horror deadened the reaction to old horror. Victims were defined as victims exclusively.

I was able to deconstruct my mother's victimhood. I gathered an ambiguous array of facts and sifted them through reminiscence and my will to claim and know her. I had memories and personal perception to guide me. My witnesses supplied me with diverse testimonial lines. I was able to discredit or credit them from an informed perspective. I was able to establish the extent to which my mother's free will raged and smeared the ink on her own death warrant.

Betty's death defied deconstruction. Her witnesses defined her unambiguously. I reluctantly bought their consensus. I wanted to accumulate odd bits of data and credit Betty with a bold streak or a secret mental life. I did not want to form her in my mother's image or remake her as anything but who she was. I only wanted proof that she'd lived more. I wanted it for her sake.

The dead-end metaphysic blitzed my shot at my mother's killer. We never approached a live suspect.

We had a live suspect now. We had knowledge *and* a shot at provability.

5

10:20 A.M. Thursday, 11/20/97:

> THE CALIFORNIA MEN'S COLONY AT SAN LUIS OBISPO.
> SERGEANT BILL STONER REPRESENTING SHERIFF'S
> HOMICIDE. DETECTIVE GARY WALKER REPRESENTING EL
> MONTE PD. THE SUSPECT: INMATE ROBERT LEROY POLETE
> JR. PRISON #B84688.

The interview was held in a small administration office. A window overlooked the prison yard. Bill Stoner sat at a desk. Inmate Polete sat in a chair directly in front of him. Gary Walker sat to the side of the desk and faced Inmate Polete diagonally.

Bill Stoner's first impression of Inmate Polete:

"He looked soft. He was about thirty pounds heavier than his '73 arrest statistics. He had a paunch, and his body wasn't toned. His hair had receded in front. He looked like a blond surfer kid who didn't take care of himself as he got older. He didn't look in any way menacing."

Stoner and Walker identified themselves. They said they were investigating a 1973 murder. Inmate Polete was a suspect then. They read Inmate Polete his Miranda rights.

Inmate Polete waived his right to have a lawyer present. He said he knew the murder they meant. He took a polygraph test in '73 and passed it. The test guy asked him some questions about this woman's murder.

Stoner said he *did not* pass the test. The result was "inconclusive."

Inmate Polete explained. He said the cops asked questions about the other cases before he took the test. The cops asked him about the murder. He got scared and confused. He said, "Yes, I did it," out of fear and frustration.

Koury and Meyers had not stated that he made a flat-out admission. They said he got right to the brink and retreated.

"My dad's got heart trouble. This would really kill him."

Inmate Polete insisted that he *did* pass the test. Stoner told him that he *did not.*

Detective Walker asked Inmate Polete to describe his life in 1973. Inmate Polete said he worked in his dad's print shop. They lived behind the shop. Him, his dad, his mom, and his kid brother.

He went to Sierra Vista High School. He played the cymbals and the sousaphone in the school band. He went to the Pentecostal Church at Five Points in El Monte and dated the minister's daughter. He worked at C&R Printing part-time.

Bill Stoner's second impression of Inmate Polete:

"He was getting agitated, because he knew we weren't going to just go away. He came off more and more juvenile emotionally. He had a 17-year-old personality and attitude stuck in the body of a 42-year-old man."

Inmate Polete said his DNA was on file with the state. It would prove he did not kill that woman. He was very emphatic.

Inmate Polete said he only did two crimes total. He was trying to reach out. He thought no one cared about him.

Stoner asked him which two crimes he meant. Inmate Polete said the Bakersfield thing and that thing with the woman who stabbed him. The women did not understand. He just wanted to be held and loved.

Stoner contradicted him. Stoner told him that he sodomized a teenage girl on 3/8/73. The assault occurred in Baldwin Park. The victim identified him.

Inmate Polete denied the assault. He said someone else copped out to that case.

No one else copped out to that case.

Stoner read from a Baldwin Park PD report. It was dated 3/20/73. A Baldwin Park PD detective stated:

Robert Leroy Polete admitted the kidnap/rape of 3/8/73.

Robert Leroy Polete admitted two other attempted abductions. The dates: 2/16/72 and 3/13/73. He wasn't tried for the crimes.

Stoner asked Inmate Polete to explain the report. Inmate Polete said he did not commit those crimes. He could not explain the report.

Stoner read from a Temple City Sheriff's report. It was dated 4/25/73. A Sheriff's detective stated:

Robert Leroy Polete said he blacked out while watching girls at the shopping center on Durfee and Peck. He woke up back at C&R Printing, one and a half blocks east. He was sweaty. He could not recall what he had done. A woman identified Robert Leroy Polete. She told detectives he assaulted her in front of Durfee Drugs. The event occurred at 1:30 P.M., 4/23/73.

Stoner asked Inmate Polete to explain the report. Inmate Polete said the facts were wrong. He never told anybody he blacked out that day. He was never at Durfee Drugs.

Stoner read from a Sheriff's Homicide report. It was dated 4/25/73. Deputy Hal Meyers stated:

Robert Leroy Polete said that he suffers from blackouts. He cannot recall any of the assaults that he was accused of. He snapped out of blackouts twice and found himself hurting women. He said he may have done things that he cannot recall.

Stoner asked Inmate Polete to explain the report. Inmate Polete said he never committed crimes during blackouts. The only crime he committed as a kid was that thing with the woman who stabbed him. The only crime he committed as a grown-up was that Bakersfield thing.

And:

He felt guilty about the Bakersfield thing and turned himself in at the air base.

And:

He knew why he blacked out. It was anger at his father. His father used to beat him with his fists and a belt.

And:

He was never alone when he went into blackouts.

And:

If he did cop out to some crimes, it was just to anger his parents. *Stoner did not say, "You never turned yourself in." He did not ask Inmate Polete how he knew what he did in blackouts. He did not challenge his "I was never alone" statement. He was letting his lies accumulate. He'd contradict them at the right moment.*

Stoner asked Inmate Polete how he got along with girls and women. Inmate Polete said he got along with them fine. Stoner mentioned an old file note. It stated: Polete told a cop that fourteen girls beat him up in the seventh grade. His girl troubles started then.

Inmate Polete said he never had girl troubles. Fourteen boys beat him up—not fourteen girls.

And:

He knew why that thing happened with that woman who stabbed him. It was because his mother was contemplating suicide. He was mad at her because she wanted to leave him. He just wanted to be loved and held.

And:

He knew why that thing in Bakersfield happened. He was mad at his father. He was having marital problems on top of his thing with his dad. He wanted to prove he could still perform sexually.

Bill Stoner's third impression of Inmate Polete:

"He had a defensive and poorly reasoned answer for everything. I couldn't tell if he believed his lies or not. I got some details on his parole hearings before the interview. Polete never took responsibility for his Bakersfield rape and continued to state that the victim came on to him. He wasn't smart enough to feign simple remorse in order to get out of prison."

Stoner switched gears. He mentioned Betty Jean's children. They grew up with no mother.

Inmate Polete started sobbing. Stoner thought they might be getting close. Walker asked Inmate Polete if he'd like to give it up.

Inmate Polete stood up. He wiped his eyes and balled his fists. He looked flat-out scary.

He yelled at Stoner and Walker. He said he didn't kill anybody. He said the interview was over as of now.

The interview was terminated at 12:30 P.M.

Bill called me. He described the interview in significant detail. I asked him if he thought Polete killed her. He said yes. I asked him if Gary Walker agreed. He said yes.

I asked Bill what he planned to do next. He said he wanted to talk to some people and brace Polete with more information.

12/1/97:

Bill Stoner calls the Beaverton, Oregon, PD. He talks to Lieutenant Jim Byrd. Lieutenant Byrd worked Baldwin Park PD in 1973.

He remembers Robby Polete. He calls him a "choirboy rapist." He tells Stoner that Polete admitted the entire series of assaults that he was initially accused of. Polete supplied details to substantiate his admissions. Polete said he was admitting the crimes because he did them. He tried to shift the blame to his victims. He said they all came on to him.

Stoner brings up the 3/8/73 case. Polete contends that someone else copped out.

Lieutenant Byrd says no. Another man was arrested that night—but the victim exonerated him immediately.

Stoner asks why Polete was never charged with the 3/8 crimes: Kidnap/Sodomy/Oral Copulation.

Lieutenant Byrd says the victim moved out of state. Her parents didn't want her to testify and relive her ordeal in court.

And:

Lieutenant Byrd attended a hearing on Polete's attempt-rape case. He observed Polete and his father outside the courtroom.

The father was dispensing advice. He told Robby to say that the woman who stabbed him came on to him first.

12/2/97:

Bill Stoner calls Roger Kaiser—Baldwin Park PD, retired. Kaiser remembers Robby Polete and his father.

Polete Senior was the treasurer of the Baldwin Park Little League. League officials accused him of embezzling league funds. The case was settled out of court. Polete Senior made restitution.

12/4/97:

Bill Stoner calls the music director for the Baldwin Park school district. The man supervised the Sierra Vista High School band in 1973.

He remembers Robby Polete. Robby was scatterbrained, undependable, and a lot of talk that never turned into action. Robby and his brother were very afraid of their father.

12/8/97:

Gary Walker calls the former pastor of the Pentecostal Church of God in El Monte. The man does not recall Robby Polete. He doubts that his daughter dated him.

Walker talks to the pastor's wife. She recalls Robby Polete and his brother.

They went to her husband's church. Sometimes the boys would walk. Sometimes she and her husband would give them a ride. The pastor and his wife had two girls at Sierra Vista High School then. They didn't socialize with Robby or his brother outside of school or church. She knew that Robby was arrested back in '73. It surprised her. He didn't seem to be a violent boy.

Stoner ran checks on Polete's ex-wife, parents, and brother.

The father was dead. The mother and brother were living in Oregon. He couldn't locate Polete's ex-wife—Vonnie Polete. He found a Bakersfield file note that surprised him.

Robert Polete and Vonnie Polete were undoubtedly divorced. Polete had remarried.

8/12/87:

A woman named Lori M. Polete writes to the Kern County courthouse. She identifies herself as Robert L. Polete's wife. She requests a copy of his 1977 court records.

She was living in Oregon then.

Bill held off on the mother and brother. He put the wives aside. He wanted to brace Robby first.

Thursday, 12/11/97:

THE CALIFORNIA MEN'S COLONY AT SAN LUIS OBISPO. SERGEANT BILL STONER REPRESENTING SHERIFF'S HOMICIDE. DETECTIVE GARY WALKER REPRESENTING EL MONTE PD. THE SUSPECT: INMATE ROBERT LEROY POLETE JR. PRISON #B84688.

The interview was held in a parole-hearing office. Stoner and Walker sat at the long end of a T-shaped table. Inmate Polete sat at the T end.

Bill Stoner's first impression of Inmate Polete:

"He was scared now. But I could tell he was curious. He wanted to know what we had."

Stoner went in calm and slow. He told Polete that they checked out his exoneration claims. They talked to two Baldwin Park detectives. Both men said his claims were untrue. The 3/8 victim moved out of state and declined to testify. No one else was arrested or charged with those crimes. Polete admitted his guilt in '73. Both detectives said so. The 3/14 attempt rape was the most prosecutable case. The 12/16, 3/13, and 4/23 cases were not as viable. Prosecutors liked to present concise cases. He got lucky that way.

Inmate Polete said the 3/14 case was bogus. The so-called victim was bogus. He said she had a thing with one of the cops.

Stoner mentioned Inmate Polete's alleged blackouts. Stoner said he had obtained Polete's juvenile records and wanted to discuss some discrepancies.

Inmate Polete blew up. He balled his fists and yelled at Stoner and Walker. He said the interview was over. They had no right to look at his juvie file.

And:

He had an alibi for the night of the murder. He was at a church-fellowship thing. The whole congregation would back up his claim.

The Pentecostal Church of God was across the street from Crawford's Market. Betty Jean Scales vanished en route to Crawford's.

Inmate Polete was very upset. Stoner did not ask the obvious questions:

How do you recall your actions on a given night twenty-four years and eleven months ago? What made that night so auspicious or so horrible or so traumatic that you will remember every detail for the rest of your life?

Inmate Polete walked out of the room. The interview was terminated at 1:00 P.M.

6

Bill said it hit him hard. It hit Gary Walker simultaneously.

The church and Crawford's Market. Polete's market-snatch MO. Subsequent assaults at the Food King and Lucky Market. The alibi that played like an admission.

Bill said it hit him hard. He told me a story to dramatize the impact.

He worked a case years back. A body dump in Torrance. A white male victim.

They ID'd him. His roommate was a carpet layer.

They took him to lunch. The man was not a suspect.

They took him to his apartment. They wanted to talk some more. They needed his take on the victim.

They walked in the door. Bill saw a brand-new carpet on the living-room floor.

And:

He *knew* that the man killed the victim right there. He knew that he'd find washed-out blood spots under the carpeting.

He found them. He confronted the man. The man confessed.

That was a fresh case. This was an old case. Instinctive knowledge never equals provability. Circumstantial confirmation buttresses instinctive knowledge and increases its evidentiary value.

12/15/97:

Bill Stoner calls the church pastor's daughter. She says she never dated Robby Polete. She never saw him with other girls. She saw him at school. She saw him at church youth groups.

12/16/97:

Bill Stoner calls the former youth-group leader. She does not recall Robby Polete. Youth-group meetings were held at the church on Sundays, Mondays, and Thursdays. They ran from 7:30 P.M. to 9:30 P.M.

1/29/73 was a Monday. Betty Jean Scales was last seen at 8:30 P.M.

Bill checked out C&R Printing. The 1973 owner still owned the shop.

He remembered Robby Polete. Polete's dad owned a shop in Baldwin Park. Robby worked at C&R sporadically. He did his dad's loan-out jobs.

Bill went through old work sheets and time cards. He had to see if Robby worked on 1/29/73.

The work sheets and time cards only went back to 1979. The man tossed his older records to save shelf space.

The dead-end metaphysic.

Bill found Lori Polete. He interviewed her. He interviewed Robby's mother and brother.

The brother didn't have much to say. He and Robby ran with different crowds. The mother said Robby couldn't have killed Betty Jean. She said she had ESP. She would have known if Robby killed some woman. She almost killed herself a long time ago. She saw a preacher on a TV show. He convinced her not to do it.

Lori started out as Robby's pen pal. She thought Robby would be paroled soon. She wised up after a while. She figured out that Robby never wised up to himself. He never took responsibility for his own actions. He couldn't survive out of prison.

The dead-end metaphysic has an evidentiary upside. Complex procedures take time. Positive results can strike out of nowhere.

The sheriff's crime lab found a stain on Betty Jean's Levi's. The technician said it *might* be a semen stain. The identification procedure is still in progress.

The dead-end metaphysic has a psychic upside.

Frightened people lose their fear over time. Guilty people divulge information injudiciously. Compliant people wise up to the people who exploit them. Tired people fold and betray their secrets.

People relinquish. Intransigent detectives wait and stay poised to listen. They hover. They eavesdrop. They prowl moral fault lines. They assume their victims' and their killers' perspectives and live their lives to stalk revelation.

In the matter of Betty Jean Scales, white female, DOD 1/29/73:

Bill Stoner will continue. Sheriff's Homicide and the El Monte PD will extend their investigation. Stoner will remain fixed on Robert Leroy Polete. He will not succumb to bias. He will retain an objective eye for leads that might subvert his opinion that Polete killed Betty Jean Scales. He stands by ready to address the California State Parole Board in the fall of '98.

He will portray Polete as a remorseless predator with good predatory years left and the will to perpetuate his rage. He will state his opinion that Polete should be kept in prison for the rest of his life. He will tell the story of women savaged in anger and self-pity. He will pray for a receptive parole board. He will draw strength from his dead going in. Tracy Stewart. Karen Reilly. Bunny Krauch.

Killed by men known and unknown.

Add Betty Jean Scales and Geneva Hilliker Ellroy. Add me as Stoner's chronicler. Add my insurmountable debt and his professional commitment. Add the need to know and serve that drives us both. Factor in the core of sex that drives us toward these women.

Bill Stoner will continue. I will continue to tell his story. Our collective dead demand it.

March, April 1998

MY MOTHER'S KILLER

I thought the pictures would wound me.

I thought they would grant my old nightmare form.

I thought I could touch the literal horror and somehow commute my life sentence.

I was mistaken. The woman refused to grant me a reprieve. Her grounds were simple: My death gave you a voice, and I need you to recognize me past your exploitation of it.

Her headstone reads GENEVA HILLIKER ELLROY, 1915–1958. A cross denotes her Calvinist youth in a Wisconsin hick town. The file is marked "JEAN (HILLIKER) ELLROY, 187PC (UNSOLVED), DOD 6/22/58."

I begged out of the funeral. I was 10 years old and sensed that I could manipulate adults to my advantage. I told no one that my tears were at best cosmetic and at worst an expression of hysterical relief. I told no one that I hated my mother at the time of her murder.

She died at 43. I'm 46 now. I flew out to Los Angeles to view the file because I resemble her more every day.

The L.A. County Sheriff handled the case. I set up file logistics with Sergeant Bill Stoner and Sergeant Bill McComas of the Unsolved Unit. Their divisional mandate is to periodically review open files with an eye toward solving the crimes outright or assessing the original investigating officers' failure to do so.

Both men were gracious. Both stressed that unsolved homicides tend to remain unsolved—thirty-six-year-old riddles deepen with the passage of time and blurring of consciousness. I told them I had no expectations of discovering a solution. I only wanted to touch the accumulated details and see where they took me.

Stoner said the photographs were grisly. I told him I could handle it.

The flight out was a blur. I ignored the meal service and the book I had brought to kill time with. Reminiscence consumed five hours—a whirl of memory and extrapolatable data.

My mother said she saw the Feds gun down John Dillinger. She was 19 and a nursing-school student fresh off the farm. My father said he had an affair with Rita Hayworth.

They loved to tell stories. They rarely let the truth impinge on a good anecdote. Their one child grew up to write horrible crime tales.

They met in '39 and divorced in '54. Their "irreconcilable differences" amounted to a love of the flesh. She majored in booze and minored in men. He guzzled Alka-Seltzer for his ulcer and chased women with an equal lack of discernment.

I found my mother in bed with strange men. My father hid his liaisons from me. I loved him more from the gate.

She had red hair. She drank Early Times bourbon and got mawkish or hellaciously pissed off. She sent me to church and stayed home to nurse Saturday-night hangovers.

The divorce settlement stipulated split custody: weekdays with my mother, three weekends a month with my father. He rented a cheap pad close to my weekday home. Sometimes he'd stand across the street and hold down surveillance.

At night, I'd douse the living-room lights and look out the window. That red glowing cigarette tip? Proof that he loved me.

In 1956, my mother moved us from West Hollywood to Santa

Monica. I enrolled in a cut-rate private school called Children's Paradise. The place was a dump site for disturbed kids of divorce. My confinement stretched from 7:30 A.M. to 5 P.M. A giant dirt playground and a swimming pool faced Wilshire Boulevard. Every kid was guaranteed passing grades and a poolside tan. A flurry of single moms hit the gate at 5:10. I developed a yen for women in their late thirties.

My mother worked as a nurse at the Packard Bell electronics plant. She had a boyfriend named Hank, a fat lowlife missing one thumb. Once a week she'd take me to a drive-in double feature. She'd sip from a flask and let me gorge myself on hot dogs.

I coveted the weekends with my father. No church; sleepover studs, or liquored-up mood swings. The man embraced the lazy life, half by design, half by the default of the weak.

Early in 1958, my mother began assembling a big lie. This is not a revisionist memory—I recall detecting mendacity in the moment. She said we needed a change of scenery. She said I needed to live in a house, not an apartment. She said she knew about a place in El Monte, a San Gabriel Valley town twelve miles east of L.A. proper.

We drove out there. El Monte was a downscale suburb populated by white shitkickers and pachucos with duck's-ass haircuts.

Most streets were unpaved. Most people parked on their lawns. Our prospective house: a redwood job surrounded by half-dead banana trees.

I said I didn't like El Monte. My mother told me to give it time. We hauled our belongings out early in February.

I traded up academically: Children's Paradise to Anne Le Gore Elementary School. The move baffled and infuriated my father. Why would a (tenuously) middle-class white woman with a good job thirty-odd miles away relocate to a town like El Monte? The rush-hour commute: at least ninety minutes each way. "I want my son to live in a house": pure nonsense. My father thought my mother was running. From a man or to a man. He said he was going to hire detectives to find out.

I settled into El Monte. My mother upgraded the custody

agreement: I could see my father all four weekends a month. He picked me up every Friday night. It took a cab ride and three bus transfers to get us to his pad, just south of Hollywood.

I tried to enjoy El Monte. I smoked a reefer with a Mexican kid and ate myself sick on ice cream. My stint at Children's Paradise left me deficient in arithmetic. My teacher called my mother up to comment. They hit it off and went out on several dates.

I turned 10. My mother told me I could choose who I wanted to live with. I told her I wanted to live with my father.

She slapped me. I called her a drunk and a whore. She slapped me again and raged against my father's hold on me.

I became a sounding board.

My father called my mother a lush and a tramp. My mother called my father a weakling and a parasite. She threatened to slap injunctions on him and push him out of my life.

School adjourned for summer vacation on Friday, June 20. My father whisked me off for a visit.

That weekend is etched in hyper-focus. I remember seeing *The Vikings* at the Fox-Wilshire Theatre. I remember a spaghetti dinner at Yaconelli's Restaurant. I remember a TV fight card. I remember the bus ride back to El Monte as long and hot.

My father put me in a cab at the depot and waited for a bus back to L.A. The cab dropped me at my house.

I saw three black-and-white police cars. I saw my neighbor Mrs. Kryzcki on the sidewalk. I saw four plainclothes cops—and instinctively recognized them as such.

Mrs. Kryzcki said, "That's the boy."

A cop took me aside. "Son, your mother's been killed."

I didn't cry. A press photographer hustled me to Mr. Kryzcki's toolshed and posed me with an awl in my hand.

My wife found a copy of that photograph last year. It's been published several times, in conjunction with my work. The second picture the man took has previously never seen print.

I'm at the workbench, sawing at a piece of wood. I'm grimacing ear to ear, showing off for the cops and reporters.

They most likely chalked my clowning up to shock. They couldn't know that that shock was instantly compromised.

The police reconstructed the crime.

My mother went out drinking Saturday night. She was seen at the Desert Inn bar in El Monte with a dark-haired white man and a blonde woman. My mother and the man left the bar around 10 P.M.

A group of Little Leaguers discovered the body. My mother had been strangled at an unknown location and dumped into some bushes next to the athletic field at Arroyo High School, a mile and a half from the Desert Inn.

She clawed her assailant's face bloody. The killer had pulled off one of her stockings and tied it loosely around her neck post-mortem.

I went to live with my father. I forced some tears out that Sunday—and none since.

My flight landed early. L.A. looked surreal, and inimical to the myth town of my books.

I checked in at the hotel and called Sergeant Stoner. We made plans to meet the following day. He gave me directions to the Homicide Bureau; earthquake tremors had ravaged the old facility and necessitated a move.

Sergeant McComas wouldn't be there. He was recuperating from open-heart surgery, a classic police-work by-product.

I told Stoner I'd pop for lunch. He warned me that the file might kill my appetite.

I ate a big room-service dinner. Dusk hit—I looked out my window and imagined it was 1950-something.

I set my novel *Clandestine* in 1951. It's a chronologically altered, heavily fictionalized account of my mother's murder. The story details a young cop's obsession: linking the death of a woman he had a one-night stand with to the killing of a redheaded nurse in El Monte. The supporting cast includes a 9-year-old boy very much like I was at that age.

I gave the killer my father's superficial attributes and juxtaposed them against a psychopathic bent. I have never understood my motive for doing this.

I called the dead nurse Marcella De Vries. She hailed from my mother's hometown: Tunnel City, Wisconsin.

I did not research that book. Fear kept me from haunting archives and historical sites. I wanted to contain what I knew and felt about my mother. I wanted to acknowledge my blood debt and prove my imperviousness to her power by portraying her with coldhearted lucidity.

Several years later, I wrote *The Black Dahlia*. The title character was a murder victim as celebrated as Jean Ellroy was ignored. She died the year before my birth, and I understood the symbiotic cohesion the moment I first heard of her.

The Black Dahlia was a young woman named Elizabeth Short. She came west with fatuous hopes of becoming a movie star. She was undisciplined, immature, and promiscuous. She drank to excess and told whopping lies.

Someone picked her up and tortured her for two days. Her death was as hellishly protracted as my mother's was gasping and quick. The killer cut her in half and deposited her in a vacant lot twenty miles west of Arroyo High School.

The killing is still unsolved. The Black Dahlia case remains a media cause célèbre.

I read about it in 1959. It hit me with unmitigated force. The horror rendered my mother's death both more outré and more prosaic. I seized on Elizabeth Short and hoarded the details of her life. Every bit of minutiae was mortar with which to build walls to block out Geneva Hilliker Ellroy.

This stratagem ruled my unconscious. The suppression exacted a price: years of nightmares and fear of the dark. Writing the book was only mildly cathartic; transmogrifying Jean to Betty left one woman still unrecognized.

And exploited by a master self-promoter with a tight grip on pop-psych show-and-tell.

I wanted her to fight back. I wanted her to rule my nightmares in plain view.

The Homicide Bureau was temporarily housed in an East L.A. office complex. The squad room was spanking clean and cop-antithetical.

Sergeant Stoner met me. He was tall and thin, with big eyes and a walrus mustache. His suit was a notch more upscale than his colleagues'.

We had a cup of coffee. Stoner discussed his most celebrated assignment, the Cotton Club murder case.

The man impressed me. His perceptions were astute and devoid of commonly held police ideology. He listened, carefully phrased his responses, and drew information out of me with smiles and throwaway gestures. He *made me* want to tell him things.

I caught his intelligence full-on. He knew I caught it.

Talk flowed nicely. One cup of coffee became three. The file rested on Stoner's desk—a small accordion folder secured by rubber bands.

I knew I was stalling. I knew I was postponing my first look at the pictures.

Stoner read my mind. He said he'd pull the worst of the shots if I wanted him to.

I said no.

The file was a mishmash: envelopes, Teletype slips, handwritten notes and two copies of the Detective Division Blue Book, an accumulation of reports and verbatim interviews. My first impression: This was the chaos of Jean Ellroy's life.

I put the photograph envelope aside. Penal-code numbers and birth dates jumped off the Teletypes.

The DOBs ran from 1912 to 1919. The codes designated arrests for aggravated assault and rape.

My mother left the bar with a "fortyish" man. The Teletypes deciphered: requests for information on men with sex-crime priors.

I read some odd notes. Minutiae grabbed me.

The Desert Inn bar: 11721 East Valley Boulevard. My mother's '57 Buick: license KFE 778. Our old house: 756 Maple Avenue.

I read the names on the front of the Blue Book. The investigating officers: sergeants John Lawton and Ward Hallinen.

The squad room lapsed into slow motion. I heard Stoner telling people that Bill McComas had aced his surgery. I spotted two full-size sheets of stationery with memo slips attached.

Early in 1970, two women wrote Homicide and informed "To Whom It May Concern" that they believed their respective ex-husbands murdered Geneva Hilliker Ellroy. Woman Number One stated that her ex worked at Packard Bell and had had affairs with my mother and two other women there. The man "behaved in a suspicious fashion" in the weeks following the killing and hit her when she pressed him about his whereabouts on the night of June 21. Woman Number Two said that her ex-husband harbored a "long-standing grudge" against Jean Ellroy. My mother refused to process a workers' compensation claim that the man had proffered, and his resentment sent him "off the deep end."

Woman Number Two included a postscript: Her ex-husband torched a furniture warehouse in 1968 to avenge a dinette-set repossession.

Both letters read vindictively sincere. Both were respectful of police authority. Memorandums indicated that the leads were checked out.

One detective interviewed both ex-husbands. He concluded that the allegations were groundless and that the women did not know each other and thus could not have colluded.

A relatively obscure homicide. Two disturbingly similar accusations—*unrelated* accusations—eleven and a half years after the crime.

I examined the Blue Book. The reports and interview transcripts lacked a continuous narrative line. I scanned a few pages and realized that my basic knowledge of the case was sufficient to make odd bits of data cohere.

The crime-scene report was logged in mid-book. The first El Monte cop to respond reported that "the victim was lying on her back at the side of the road. There was dry blood on her lips and nose. The lower part of the victim's body was covered with a woman's coat. The victim was wearing a multi-colored (blue and black) dress. A brassiere appeared to be around the victim's neck."

Further examination reveals:

The brassiere is really a stocking.

A necklace strand rests under the body.

Forty-seven individual pearls are scattered nearby.

The coroner arrives. He views the body and points out bruises on the neck. He thinks the woman was strangled with a window-sash cord or clothesline. Drag marks on the woman's hips indicate that she was killed elsewhere and brought to this location.

The investigation commenced. My memory filled in Blue Book continuity gaps.

No identification was found on the body. The El Monte Police Department called in the Los Angeles County Sheriff's Detective Bureau.

Radio bulletins went out. The dead woman's description was flashed Valley-wide.

Our neighbor Mrs. Kryzcki responded. She was brought to the county morgue and identified the body. She said Jean Ellroy was a fine lady, who did not drink or date men.

My mother's car was discovered parked behind the Desert Inn. Bar employees were detained at El Monte police headquarters.

They identified my mother from a snapshot that Mrs. Kryzcki provided. Yes, the woman came in last night. She arrived alone about eight o'clock and later joined a man and a woman. Said man and woman were not regular patrons. None of the staff had ever seen them before.

The man was a swarthy Caucasian or a Mexican. He was about 40 years old, thin, between five feet nine and six feet tall. The woman was white, blonde, and in her late twenties. She wore her hair tied back in a ponytail.

No one heard them exchange names. A waitress recalled that a regular named Michael Whitaker had several drinks with the dead woman and two unknowns.

A waitress supplied more names: every *known* patron in the bar Saturday night. Sergeants Hallinen and Lawton checked the El Monte PD arrest docket and learned that Michael Whitaker was picked up for plain drunk at 4 A.M.

The man, 24, was spotted on foot near Stan's Drive-In. He sobered up in the El Monte drunk tank and was released at 9 A.M.

The known patrons were brought in and questioned. Several remembered seeing my mother with the Swarthy Man and the Blonde. None of them had ever seen my mother before. None of them had ever seen the Swarthy Man or the Blonde.

Michael Whitaker was brought in. Hallinen and Lawton questioned him. A police stenographer recorded the interrogation.

Whitaker's memory was booze-addled. He couldn't recall the name of the woman he was currently shacked up with. He said he danced with my mother and hit her up for a Sunday-night date. She declined, because her son was coming back from a weekend with his father.

Whitaker said the Swarthy Man told him his name. He couldn't remember it.

He said my 43-year-old mother looked "about 22." He said he got "pretty high" and fell off his chair once.

He said he saw the Swarthy Man and my mother leave together at about 10 P.M.

The Swarthy Man told Whitaker his name. This supported my long-held instinct that the murder was not premeditated.

A waitress confirmed Whitaker's account. Yes, Michael fell off his chair. Yes, the redhead left with the Swarthy Man.

Hallinen and Lawton retained a sketch artist. Desert Inn patrons and employees described the Swarthy Man. The artist drew up a likeness.

The drawing was circulated to newspapers and every police agency in Los Angeles County. The Desert Inn crew examined thousands of mug shots and failed to identify the Swarthy Man.

Officers canvassed the area around Arroyo High School. No one had noticed suspicious activity late Saturday night or Sunday morning. Hallinen and Lawton interrogated a score of local cranks, perverts, and career misogynists.

No leads accumulated. No hard suspects emerged.

On Wednesday, June 25, a witness came forth—a Stan's Drive-In carhop named Lavonne Chambers. Hallinen and Lawton interviewed her. Her testimony—recorded verbatim—was precise, articulate, and perceptive. Everything she said was new to me. Her statement radically altered my take on the crime.

She served the Swarthy Man and my mother—*on two different occasions*—late Saturday night and early Sunday morning. She described my mother's dress and mock-pearl ring. She described the Swarthy Man's car: a '55 or '56 dark-green Olds. She said the sketch was accurate and ID'd the man as white, not Latin.

They arrived at 10:20, shortly after their Desert Inn departure. They "talked vivaciously" and "seemed to have been drinking." The man had coffee. My mother had a grilled cheese sandwich. They ate in the car and left a half hour later.

Miss Chambers worked late that night. My mother and the Swarthy Man returned at 2 A.M.

He ordered coffee. He seemed "quiet and sullen." My mother was "quite high and chatting gaily." The man "acted bored with her."

Miss Chambers said my mother looked "slightly disheveled." The top of her dress was unbuttoned, and one breast was spilling out.

Sergeant Hallinen: "Do you think they might have had a petting party?"

Miss Chambers: "Maybe."

They left at 2:45. Jean Ellroy's body was discovered eight hours later.

I turned to the autopsy report. The coroner noted signs of recent intercourse. My mother's lungs were severely congested, presumably from years of heavy smoking.

She died of ligature asphyxiation. She sustained several blows to the head. Her fingernails were caked with blood, skin, and beard fragments.

She fought back.

I opened the photo envelope. The first stack of pictures: detained and exonerated suspects.

Cruel-looking men. Rough trade. White trash with a vengeance. Hard eyes, tattoos, psychopathic rectitude.

I recognized Harvey Glatman, a sex killer executed in 1959. A note said he passed a polygraph test.

The second stack: miscellaneous photos and wide-angles of the crime scene.

My father, circa 1946. A notation on the back: "Vict's ex-husband." A faded snapshot: my mother in her teens. The man beside her? Probably my German-immigrant grandfather.

Arroyo High School, 6/22/58. Santa Anita Road and King's Road—a football field with jerry-built goalposts. Those right-hand-corner X marks: the curbside bushes where they found her. The topography lacked perspective. Every detail hit my eyes as too small, and unequal to the central myth of my life.

I looked at the pictures of my dead mother. I saw the stocking around her neck and the insect bites on her breasts.

Lividity had thickened her features. She did not look like anyone I had ever known.

I knew it wasn't over. I knew my hours with the file constituted an ambiguous new start.

I left the squad room and drove to El Monte. The years then to now had been cruel.

I clenched up. It felt like something had to hit me at any second. I kept expecting a migraine or a bad case of the shakes.

New prefab houses had aged and split at the joints. Smog obscured the San Gabriel peaks.

The Desert Inn was gone. A taco hut replaced it. The El Monte PD building had been razed and rebuilt.

Anne Le Gore School remained intact. Gang graffiti on the walls provided an update.

Stan's Drive-In was gone. My old house had been face-lifted past recognition.

Arroyo High School needed a paint job. The playing field needed a trim. Weeds grew thick all around the X-marked spot.

The town had compressed. Its old secrets had subsided into the memories of strangers.

Stoner told me Sergeant Lawton was dead. Sergeant Ward Hallinen: 82 years old and living outside San Diego.

I called him and explained who I was. He apologized for his failing memory and said he couldn't recall the case. I thanked him for his efforts thirty-six years ago. I remembered a cop who gave me a candy bar, and wondered if it was him.

It wasn't over. The resolution felt incomplete.

I canceled a dinner date and willed myself to sleep. I woke up at 3 A.M.—unclenched and sick with it.

Conscious thoughts wouldn't process. I went down to the hotel gym and slammed weights until it hurt.

Steam and a shower helped. I went back to my room and let it hammer me.

New facts contradicted old assumptions. I had always thought my mother was killed because she wouldn't have sex with a man. It was a child's coda to horror: A woman dies fending off violation.

My mother made love with her killer. A witness viewed post-coital moments.

They left the drive-in. He wanted to ditch this desperate woman he fucked and get on with his life. The combustion occurred because she wanted more.

More liquor. More distance from the Dutch Reformed Church. More self-abasing honky-tonk thrills.

More love 16,000 times removed in desiccation.

I inherited those urges from my mother. Gender bias favored me: Men can indiscriminately fuck women with far greater sanction than women can indiscriminately fuck men. I drank, used drugs, and whored with the bravado of the winked-at and condoned. Luck and a coward's circumspection kept me short of the abyss.

Her pain was greater than mine. It defines the gulf between us. Her death taught me to look inward and hold myself separate. That gift of knowledge saved my life.

It wasn't over. My investigation will continue.

I took a new gift away from El Monte. I feel proud that I carry her features.

Geneva Hilliker Ellroy: 1915–1958.

My debt grows. Your final terror is the flame I touch my hand to. I will not diminish your power by saying I love you.

August 1994

GLAMOUR JUNGLE

I
The Crime

SHERIFF'S HOMICIDE FILE #Z-961-651. DATE: 11/30/63.
LOCATION: 1227½ NORTH SWEETZER AVENUE, WEST
HOLLYWOOD. VICTIM: KUPCINET, KARYN (NMI),
W/F/22/DOB 3/6/41.

The place:
A courtyard complex off the Sunset Strip.
The victim:
A drug-addicted and eating-disordered actress-dilettante.
The crux of the major-case commitment:
Money and prestige. The victim's father had very large pull.
Saturday, 11/30/63. 7:00 P.M.:
Mark Goddard enters the courtyard. His wife waits in the car.
Mark Goddard is a TV actor. Marcia Goddard is Karyn Kupcinet's best friend.

They're worried about her. She had dinner at their house Wednesday night. She acted very weird.

Her eyes were pinned-out. She said she took a Miltown. She told them a crazy story.

She said she found a baby on her doorstep. The cops came and took him away. The story was wholly fantastic.

Goddard walked up to Karyn's apartment and knocked on the door. He saw a light on inside. He got no answer. He tried the door. It popped open.

Goddard got scared. He went back to the car and brought Marcia up. They entered the apartment. The TV was on. The sound was down low.

They saw a body on the couch. It was nude and stretched out facedown.

Marcia screamed. Mark ran to the manager's apartment. The manager called the West Hollywood Sheriff's Station.

The dispatcher radioed a patrol car. The manager grabbed a neighbor with some medical skills. The man entered the apartment and confirmed the victim was dead.

The patrol cops arrived. They examined the victim and noted signs of decomp. Fluids dripped from the mouth, nose, and eye sockets. The purge had turned her face blue-black.

The patrol cops talked to Mark and Marcia Goddard. They observed the immediate scene.

They noted:

"Several magazines lying on the porch outside the deceased's front door, dating to 11/28/63. Immediately inside the front door and approximately 18″ from the west end of the couch was an overturned glass container with numerous cigarettes inside and sixteen Kent cigarettes strewn about the floor at the end of the couch. A white metal coffee maker (pot) was lying on its side approximately 10 feet north of the couch. The television was observed to be playing at a moderate volume on Channel 4. A lamp table on the east wall of the living room was observed to have the lower drawer standing open, and a coat-closet door was open in the northeast corner of the living room. The bedroom was observed to have numerous articles of clothing and bedding strewn about the floor, and three dresser drawers were standing open. The rear door was observed to be secured from the inside with a hook-and-eye type fastener."

The patrol cops talked to Mark and Marcia Goddard. They revealed:

Karyn was a close friend. They met her in '61. Her father was Irv Kupcinet. He was a columnist and TV host in Chicago. "Kup" was big-time. He was "Mr. Chicago."

They saw Karyn Wednesday night. She said she saw a shrink. The shrink said she was in bad shape. Karyn was seeing an actor named Andy Prine. Andy costarred on the *Wide Country* show. The romance was dead. Karyn was very depressed.

8:45 P.M.:

Sheriff's Homicide arrives. Representing the squad: Lieutenant George Walsh, Sergeant Bobby Chapman, Sergeant Jim Wahlke.

They talked to Mark and Marcia Goddard. They observed the immediate scene.

They noted:

"Location consisted of a living room, an attached dining area, kitchen, hallway, one bedroom and bath.

"A red bathrobe was observed on an overstuffed chair on the east side of the living room. This bathrobe appeared to have been taken off and placed in the chair in a disorderly fashion. . . .

"The living room closet door was observed to be open. Expensive items of clothing, including a mink stole, were immediately visible. Other items, such as a pair of women's shoes and a teddy bear, were also observed lying on the floor in the vicinity of the doorway leading into the hall, bathroom, and bedroom."

Dirty dishes in the kitchen sink. Three coffee cups. An empty cake box on a hallway book stand. A serving knife on top of it.

An orderly bathroom. A negligee on a hanger. A brassiere on the left side of the washstand.

The bedroom:

Twin beds shoved together. Disheveled sheets and bedcovers. On the beds:

One nightgown, one shower cap, one hairbrush, one towel, one red-checked blouse.

A dressing table. A bath towel wadded up on a chair. A pile of women's clothes on the floor.

Chapman and Wahlke searched the apartment. They found a weird book. It was open to a very weird page. The text said you should dance in the nude to free your inhibitions.

They checked the medicine chest. They found thirteen pill jars. They read the fill dates on the labels.

Miltown, Amvicel, Thyroid Extract, Modaline, Desoxyn.

Miltown was a trank. Desoxyn was a diet pill/upper. Two fifty-pill Desoxyn scripts were refilled last Monday. Forty-eight pills and thirty-three pills were gone. A twenty-five-pill Modaline script was refilled on Tuesday. Eight pills were gone. A fifty-pill Amvicel script was filled on Monday. Six pills were gone. A hundred-pill Desoxyn script was filled on 11/9. The hundred pills were gone.

Chapman called the victim's parents in Chicago. They took it hard. They said they'd fly out in the morning.

10:30 P.M.:

Division Chief Floyd Rosenberg and Captain Al Etzel arrive. Two photo cops show up. They shoot the pad and the victim's body. Lieutenant Walsh finds a handwritten note.

For me—

I feel self-conscious about this, like I'm going to have to get approval on it eventually. (Approval it is—or you're doomed to insignificance). Everything I've done, supposedly being myself and with the promise of anonymity, I do *for* approval . . . knowing . . . "this'll get 'em." "They'll love me for this" and "They'll say nice things behind my back."

I guess I've been searching for an identity too desperately . . . seized the nearest image; whether David and doing things <u>his</u> way and <u>pointedly</u> not <u>compromising</u> with my traditional way—and using it vs. my parents—snubbing my nose at their way. Always hate to be with them after a lengthy visit with "current" boyfriend and their families—guilt—I guess. Trying to show them I can be something. Always faking it. Never tapping my own resources. Afraid of—what? Me or that there won't be anything.

I'm no good. I'm not really that pretty. My figure's fat and will never be the way my mother wants it. I won't let it be what she wants. How stupid. I want to be slim and she loves me and wants me to be slim—intellectualization doesn't mark.

Why must I be so alone. Have I fallen that short of my ideal? Why does my image of me have to be so aesthetic and perfect? What's the use of living with nothing to believe in? Have faith in? Where's the security—or habit or order—oh shit—what good is that going to do? What happens to me— or my Andy? Why doesn't he want me? Why? There's no GOD.

There's nothing only phony motives, selfish egoists, self-less people, fat heads and drunks, and I want out.

I like President Kennedy, Bertrand Russell, Theodore Reiks, Peter O'Toole, Sydney J. Harris, Albert Finney.

I just care about now who gives a shit about 10 years from now. (there won't be any with Andy—maybe that's it.) If only I had a reason. No one needs me—or cares to need me. They're right. I'm bored and I'm a doll at first, then a phony and fake. I feel like "they" owe me a life. Like all my failings are their fault. . . . I dare them to make me happy. How immature and childish—I know.

Chapman and Wahlke let the Goddards go home.

The press arrived. They caught the dead-body call off a police-band broadcast. Chapman and Wahlke made them stand in the courtyard. They revealed the victim's name and ID'd her father. The reporters dispersed and phoned in their stories.

The coroner's investigator arrived. He removed the victim's body and took it to the L.A. County Morgue. Dr. Harold Kade performed the autopsy.

Rubberneckers jammed up the courtyard. The victim's phone rang. Chapman grabbed it.

The caller said his name was Bryan O'Byrne. He said he heard a radio bit on Karyn. He knew Andy Prine. He said he'd try to find him and bring him to the West Hollywood Sheriff's Station.

Rosenberg, Walsh, and Etzel drove back to Homicide. Chapman and Wahlke locked up the apartment. They drove to the West Hollywood Station.

Three men arrived. They said they heard a radio spot and rushed right down.

Their names:

Robert Hathaway—white male/age 24. William Mamches—white male/age 23. Edward Rubin—white male/age 22.

They knew the victim and Andy Prine. Rubin and Hathaway saw Karyn last Wednesday night. They left her pad at 11:00 P.M.

She fed them coffee and cake. They split after *The Danny Kaye Show*.

Chapman and Wahlke told the guys to come back later. They'd have to submit full statements.

3:00 A.M.:

Chapman and Wahlke drove down to Homicide. They called Dr. Kade. He said they had a murder.

His stated cause of death:

Manual strangulation. The victim's hyoid bone was fractured.

The only *visible* trauma was neck trauma. The decomp wiped out all possible signs of face trauma.

The probable time-of-death: late Wednesday P.M. or early Thursday A.M.

Chapman and Wahlke told Etzel and Rosenberg. Etzel called Sergeant Ward Hallinen and Sergeant Roy Collins. He assigned them to the Kupcinet case.

Chapman and Wahlke called the captain of the Sheriff's Metro Squad. The captain called Deputy Jim Boyer and Deputy Sam Miller. He told them to work the Kupcinet case full-time.

Chapman and Wahlke went back to the victim's apartment. A print team arrived and dusted all four rooms. A backup crew arrived. They bagged bedding, towels, sofa cushions, and clothing.

7:00 A.M., Sunday, 12/1/63:

Chapman called Mark and Marcia Goddard. Wahlke called Hathaway, Mamches, and Rubin. They arranged a string of interviews at the West Hollywood Station.

The Karyn Kupcinet case was twelve hours old.

The witnesses showed up. A stenographer transcribed their statements verbatim.

Bryan O'Byrne found Andy Prine and brought him in. Chapman and Wahlke braced him first. The interview began at 7:45 A.M. and ended at 8:54.

Prine was 27. He said he met Karyn last December. She got a gig on his show. They started dating. He got Karyn pregnant last summer. Mark and Marcia Goddard took her to T.J. She got an abortion there.

Chapman asked Prine where they stood lately. Prine said it was "minimized." He didn't want to marry Karyn. He wanted to date other chicks. Karyn was into their thing more than he was.

Wahlke asked Prine if his buddies ever came on to Karyn. Prine said, "No." Wahlke asked Prine if Karyn would fight off a rape-o. Prine said, "Yes." Wahlke asked Prine if Karyn slept around. Prine said, "No."

Wahlke asked Prine if Karyn had any enemies. Prine said some nut sent them both hate notes.

It started last summer. The notes were made up from magazine clips. The nut placed them by his door and Karyn's. The nut knew when they were home and when they were out.

Karyn got a dozen dirty phone calls. He got some weird hangups. He took the notes to the LAPD. They told him not to sweat it. Stuff like that happened to minor celebrities.

Wahlke asked Prine when he last saw Karyn. Prine said they went to Palm Springs last weekend. Earl Holliman and his chick went with them. Earl was on *Wide Country*.

The Kennedy snuff bummed them all out. They decided to hit the Springs and catch some rays. They left Friday night and got back Sunday night. He dropped Karyn off at 8:00 P.M. He never saw her again.

Wahlke asked Prine when he last talked to Karyn. He said they talked twice on Wednesday—11/27.

She called him about 6:00 P.M. They discussed the baby that someone dumped on her doorstep. He went out that night. He took an actress chick to a movie. They saw *A Streetcar Named Desire*. They went out for a drink. He dropped her off at her pad. He went home and called Karyn. It was 11:30 or 12:00. Karyn said the cops took the baby away.

Wahlke asked Prine if he caused Karyn's death. Prine said, "No." Wahlke asked him if he'd take a polygraph test. Prine said, "Yes."

Chapman and Wahlke braced Edward Rubin. The interview began at 9:07 A.M. and ended at 10:03.

Rubin was a "free-lance writer." He shared a pad in Beverly Hills. He used to live next door to Andy Prine. Bill Mamches and Bob Hathaway shared the pad now.

Chapman asked Rubin if he had sex with Karyn. Rubin said, "No." Chapman asked Rubin how long he knew her. Rubin said, "Five months."

Chapman asked Rubin about the Karyn-Andy thing. Rubin said Karyn loved Andy more than Andy loved her. Chapman asked Rubin about Wednesday night. Rubin laid it out.

He walked over to Karyn's pad. He got there around 8:30. They talked for an hour. Karyn got antsy and went for a walk. She ran into Bob Hathaway. She brought him back up. She served cake and coffee. They all watched TV.

Karyn mentioned the baby she found. Chapman asked Rubin if he thought she made up the story. Rubin said, "Possibly."

Karyn dozed with two guys right there. He walked her into the bedroom and watched her get into bed. He watched TV with Bob. They split. They walked down to the Raincheck Room. They spent fifteen or twenty minutes there. They walked to Bob's car and drove to Bob and Bill's place. They got there about 11:30. Bill was asleep. They watched a flick on TV. Andy Prine showed up a half-hour later. They gabbed until 3:00 A.M. Andy lived next door. He dropped by a lot. Long bullshit sessions were common. Andy said he went to a rodeo. He went to Grassari's Bar right after.

Rubin's statement contradicted Prine's. Prine said he took a chick to a movie.

Wahlke asked Rubin if Andy had a bad temper. Rubin said, "He is usually very calm." Wahlke asked Rubin if he ever saw Andy perform violent acts. Rubin said, "No." Wahlke asked Rubin if he'd take a polygraph test. Rubin said, "Yes."

Chapman and Wahlke braced Bob Hathaway. The interview began at 10:15 A.M. and ended at 10:34.

Hathaway was a part-time actor. He confirmed Rubin's Wednesday night run-through.

Karyn was restless and tired. That baby-on-the-doorstep thing had her wheels spinning.

Wahlke asked Hathaway if he ever hit on Karyn. Hathaway said, "Never." Wahlke asked him about Karyn and Andy. Hathaway said they were on-again, off-again.

He confirmed Rubin:

Andy said he went to a rodeo that night.

Wahlke asked Hathaway if Andy was a violent guy. Hathaway said, "No." Wahlke asked him if he'd take a polygraph test. Hathaway said, "Yes."

Chapman and Wahlke braced Bill Mamches. The interview began at 10:40 A.M. and ended at 10:54.

Mamches was a part-time actor. He said he knew Karyn casually. He never went out with her. He never hit on her. Andy never bragged about the sex they had. Andy wasn't an evil cat. He chased broads. He wasn't a one-woman man. Karyn was a one-man woman.

Chapman asked Mamches if he'd take a polygraph test. Mamches said, "Yes."

Chapman and Wahlke braced Marcia Goddard. The interview began at 11:20 A.M. and ended at 11:52.

Chapman asked Mrs. Goddard if Karyn made up tales. Mrs. Goddard said, "Yes." Chapman asked her if the baby tale was typical. Mrs. Goddard called it an extreme example. Her husband called the hospital and learned that Karyn lied.

Chapman mentioned Karyn's pill use. Mrs. Goddard called it excessive.

Karyn left her house at 8:30 P.M. Wednesday. A cab picked her up. Karyn didn't drive. She took cabs everywhere. She said she'd call Marcia later. She never called her again.

Chapman asked Mrs. Goddard how Karyn looked last Wednesday. Mrs. Goddard said her lips seemed numb. Her voice was funny. She moved her head at odd angles.

Wahlke asked Mrs. Goddard to name Karyn's old boyfriends. She mentioned David Wallerstein. He was an old family friend. He lived in Pomona now. He loved Karyn. She didn't love him. She didn't think of him as a love interest.

Chapman asked Mrs. Goddard to describe Karyn's morals. Mrs. Goddard said, "I couldn't say." Chapman asked her if Karyn slept around. Mrs. Goddard said, "Not that I know of." Wahlke asked her if she'd take a polygraph test. Mrs. Goddard said, "Yes."

Chapman and Wahlke braced Mark Goddard. The interview began at 12:00 P.M. and ended at 12:19.

Goddard had a costar gig on *The Bill Dana Show*. He knew Karyn for two-plus years. His wife's parents knew her parents.

Wahlke brought up Andy Prine. Goddard said he liked him. He was a good actor. He was a straight-ahead guy. Wahlke asked Goddard if Karyn loved Andy more than Andy loved her. Goddard said, "Yes." Wahlke asked him if Andy ever hit Karyn. Goddard said, "No, sir, never."

Goddard said Karyn was blitzed Wednesday night. He confronted her. She put an arm around him and cried.

Wahlke asked Goddard if Karyn was a dick tease. Goddard said, "No." Wahlke asked him if he'd take a polygraph test. Goddard said, "Yes."

Irv Kupcinet showed up at Karyn's apartment. He brought his lawyer along. Captain Etzel and Chief Rosenberg briefed them. Deputy Boyer and Deputy Miller arrived. Rosenberg told them to canvass the neighborhood.

Prine, Rubin, Mamches, and Hathaway took polygraph tests. All four were judged inconclusive. Chapman and Wahlke reinterviewed Prine and Rubin. Prine said the bull session went down Tuesday night. Rubin said it went down Wednesday. Chapman and Wahlke called the actress chick. She partially confirmed Prine's statement.

She ran into Andy at Grassari's Tuesday night. He said he just went to the rodeo. They made a date for Wednesday night. The date went down like Andy said it did.

Chapman and Wahlke ran a string of checks. They ran Prine, Rubin, Hathaway, and Mamches. They came back clean—no wants, no warrants, no rap sheets. Chapman and Wahlke ran a check on Karyn Kupcinet. She came back dirty. The Pomona PD popped her for petty theft. The bust occurred on 11/10/62.

She boosted some stuff from a store. She got a fine and three years' probation.

Hallinen and Collins found David Wallerstein. He was covered for the victim's estimated time-of-death.

The print men filed a report. They found prints for the victim and Edward Rubin. They found a few unknown sets.

Boyer and Miller canvassed the courtyard and the adjoining buildings. They asked about suspicious shit Wednesday night and Thursday morning.

1227¼ North Sweetzer—nothing. 1227 North Sweetzer—zilch.

1223½ 1225, 1235 D-2, 1229½, 1221½, 1223½, 1229, 1233 A-1, A-2, and B-1—nothing.

Miller hit 1223¼. The female tenant snitched off the guy who lived below Karyn.

His name was David Lange. He did something weird. It happened Sunday evening—12/1/63.

He walked into the woman's pad uninvited. He said he walked up to Karyn's door on Friday. It was unlocked. He jiggled the knob—but didn't go in. He ran into some cops last night. He didn't tell them the exact truth.

Boyer and Miller looked for Lange. They couldn't find him.

1229—nothing. 1223 and 1221¼—vacant. 1231¼—nothing. Eight tenants unavailable or out of town.

Andy Prine turned over the notes he got. Chapman and Wahlke sent them to the Crime Lab.

On 4 × 6 plain white paper:

> WANT YOUR HOT BODY. ONLY TAMPAX WILL STOP
> YOUR FERTILITY PROBLEM.

On 6 × 10 plain white paper:

> YOU WILL NEED PROTECTION. BEN CASEY CAUGHT
> MESSAGE FOR YOUR BEAU. YOU HAVEN'T MUCH TIME
> FOR DREAMS.

On 4 × 6 plain white paper:

> FORGET FAME AND ROMANCE WITH AGING GLEN
> FORD. DEVIL MUST KILL YOU.

On 5 × 7½ lined paper:

> YOUR LADY NEEDS SURGERY SUDDENLY. EXPECT TO
> GET BAD BREAKS WHEREVER YOU GO. YOUR RICH
> BEAUTY HAS NO TIME.

On 4 × 6 plain white paper:

> ARE YOU GOING TO LATIN AMERICA OR FLORIDA?
> LET YOUR BEAUTIFUL VIRGIN BECOME LONESOME
> AND SO EASY TO MAKE. BET K KUP TASTES AS GOOD
> AS IT LOOKS. BLOW.

On 6 × 10 plain white paper:

> YOU ARE THE CERTAIN GIRL TO DIE.

On 4½ × 7½ lined paper:

> YOU MAY DIE WITHOUT NOBODY. WINNER OF
> LONELINESS WANTS DEATH UNTIL SOMEONE
> SPECIAL CARES.

The words were clipped from movie magazines. They were secured with Scotch tape. A lab crew searched the victim's apartment. They found the magazines that were used.

A print man dusted the words under the tape. He found Karyn Kupcinet's prints.

She sent the notes to Andy Prine—and herself.

Chapman and Wahlke talked to Andy Prine's ex-wife. She laid Andy out as a no-good motherfucker.

He was volatile. She heard that he strangled a cat. Their cat disappeared. Maybe Andy snuffed him.

Chapman and Wahlke reinterviewed Prine. He said he never snuffed any cats. He said he had the Tuesday vs. Wednesday thing straight. He went to the rodeo Tuesday. He went out with the actress chick Wednesday. The bull session had to be Tuesday. He went straight home Wednesday night and called Karyn.

Chapman and Wahlke talked to Rubin and Hathaway. They said they might have fucked up. The talkathon might have been Tuesday.

Chapman and Wahlke braced Karyn and Andy's friends. Hallinen and Collins braced them. The consensus: Karyn and Andy were headed for Splitsville. Chapman and Wahlke braced Andy on that. He said he kept things cooool. He liked to ball her on his own terms.

Prine said Karyn stalked him in taxis. She hid out at his pad once. She caught him with another woman.

Chapman and Wahlke braced Earl Holliman. He dittoed Prine's account of their Palm Springs weekend.

Boyer and Miller stuck a note on David Lange's door. They told him to call Sheriff's Homicide. A Narco cop called Chapman and Wahlke. He said he got a tip on Lange.

A woman snitched him off. She said Lange called her on 12/1/63. He said he knew Karyn. He said, "I killed her, you know."

David Lange was 27 years old. He was a script reader. The actress Hope Lange was his sister. Hope Lange used to date Glenn Ford. Glenn Ford knew Andy and Karyn. Andy had Thanksgiving dinner at Ford's house.

Lange showed up at the West Hollywood Station. Chapman and Wahlke braced him.

He said he didn't kill Karyn. He told that woman he did. He was just kidding.

He knew Karyn. He liked her. Andy Prine introduced them. That tenant woman lied. He did not knock on Karyn's door that Friday. He did not say he lied to the cops.

A cop knocked on his door the night they found the body. He was in bed with a girl. He blew the cop off and went back to bed.

Lange laid out his actions for 11/27 and 11/28.

He had dinner at Natalie Wood's house. He arrived at 7:00. He left at 11:30. Arthur Loew and Bob Jarris were there. He went to Bob's place. He drank a bit. He got "rather high." He went home at 12:30. He went to bed. He got up at 9:00 A.M. Thursday.

He never balled Karyn. He never tried to.

Chapman and Wahlke asked him who he balled lately. Lange named two starlets. Lieutenant Walsh and Wahlke called the woman who snitched Lange off. She said she balled Lange once. Chapman and Wahlke called the two starlets. They both said they balled Lange once. One starlet said Lange pissed her off. He told her she gave him the clap. It was bullshit. She knew she was clean.

Lange balled the other starlet at his pad. It was Saturday night—11/30/63.

Somebody knocked on the door. Lange got up and talked to him. He did not come back and tell her that his friend Karyn was dead.

Lange said he'd take a polygraph test. Chapman and Wahlke drove him downtown. Hallinen and Collins braced him. He said he lied to Chapman and Wahlke.

That chick told it straight. He tried Karyn's door that Friday. But:

He didn't go in. He didn't see Karyn—dead or alive.

Lange said he had a recent bout of the clap. He got it from this starlet he balled. He went to a doctor and fixed himself up.

Lange took a polygraph test. The result was judged inconclusive.

Chapman and Wahlke checked their autopsy notes. Doc Kade took a vaginal smear. He found a leukorrhea discharge.

They had it tested. It was decomposed. They couldn't compare it to the test smear that Lange's doctor took.

Prine and Lange remained major suspects. The inconclusive polygraphs meant everything and nothing. Some cops bought polygraph tests. Some cops thought they were bullshit. A bunch of guys at Sheriff's Homicide thought it wasn't even a murder.

The victim was a hophead. They found her nude. They found that "dance-in-the-nude" book. She might have danced and stumbled around. She might have made that big mess. She might have tripped and clipped her hyoid bone on a chair. She might have crawled up on the couch and died. She might have passed out on the couch and choked on her own puke. She might have purged the dope in her system as she decomped. Doc Kade was a juicehead. They hauled him out of bed and put him to work at 2 A.M. All he found was a broken hyoid. He might have snapped it himself.

The L.A. papers played up the case. It got some national ink. The Hollywood angle brought out the perverts and freaks.

12/4/63:

A man calls Sheriff's Homicide. The starlet killer is stalking this girl he knows. Some cops brace her. She's scared. A guy tried to choke her last October. He hangs out with a fag.

Some cops found the guy. *He* was a fag himself. He said he choked the bitch accidentally. He said he never met Karyn. He said he might have met Andy Prine. The cops wrote him off as a nut.

12/7/63:

A "Script Supervisor" calls Sheriff's Homicide. An actress friend got a weird phone call. A guy said, "You know what happened to Karyn, and you are going to be next."

The actress used to date Andy Prine. Her current squeeze knew Andy and Karyn.

Chapman and Wahlke braced the squeeze. He said he met Karyn in '61. He said he got popped for shoplifting once.

He stole some Ex-Lax at a Thrifty Drugstore. He didn't mean to steal it. He didn't want to buy the shit from a lady clerk. Chapman and Wahlke wrote him off as a nut.

Hallinen and Collins got a tip. A snitch snitched off an actor named Rick Bache.

Bache killed himself on 11/30. Dig it. It might tie in to the Kupcinet snuff.

They checked it out. It was straight out of *Lolita*.

Rick Bache was hot for a 15-year-old-girl. He wanted to marry her. Her mother disapproved. Bache offed himself. Hallinen and Collins braced his friends. They all said he never knew Karyn. Hallinen and Collins wrote him off as a perv.

Tips came in. It was 99.9 percent freak stuff. Everybody was a would-be actor or part-time actor and full-time shitbird. They printed everybody. They ran their prints against the unknown prints at the crime scene. Nothing matched.

They braced Andy Prine repeatedly. He cooperated. He stuck to his story.

They checked the weirdo file at West Hollywood Station. They zeroed in on a well-known peeper. They checked him out and wrote him off. He only peeped the gash in his own building.

Chapman and Wahlke talked to Glenn Ford. He liked Andy Prine. Andy was a righteous dude.

They talked to Andy Prine's ex-girlfriends. They logged in a consensus.

Andy was tender. Andy was sensitive. Andy got more ass than a toilet seat.

More tips. More bullshit. A gang rape or a gang bang at Karyn's old apartment. The date: 4/19/64.

It began at the Raincheck Room. The alleged victim was a movie extra.

She got bombed at the Raincheck. The new guy in Karyn's pad got bombed. They went back to the pad. Six or seven cats joined them. The new guy said, "This is where Kupcinet was murdered and every time I think of it, I get sick to my stomach."

The woman said six or seven guys raped her. The guys said she put out. Chapman and Wahlke reviewed the occurrence. They leaned toward the gang-bang scenario. They braced the new tenant guy. They wrote him off as a homicide suspect. They wrote him off as a rape-o and gang-bang participant.

More bugs blew into the light. Walter Winchell crashed the case and tried to hoist his career out of the toilet.

He showed up at Sheriff's Homicide on 6/25/64. He told a wild story.

It featured Andy Prine's ex-wife and her cat, "Calhoun." It involved Vince Edwards on the *Ben Casey* show. It involved J. Edgar Hoover and the "Syndicate." The cat was the star. Andy's ex said Andy offed the motherfucker. The backup cast: a female private eye, an armed robber, and two guys on death row at Big Q.

Eight detectives probed Winchell's story. The old cocksucker hounded them and made them dance to his tune.

He set up interviews and hosted dinners at Chasen's. He laid on the meager remnants of his charm. He choreographed a freak show and made the cops join in interactive.

He wasted hundreds of police man-hours. The final report ran 8,000 words. The narrative line was incomprehensible.

The case dragged on. It retained a priority status. The Kupcinet family applied pressure.

Essee Kupcinet believed in psychics. She urged the cops to employ them. They accommodated her.

1/23/65:

A psychic named Hans Holzer jumps in. He hypnotizes a woman named Maxine Bell. Mrs. Bell assumes the soul of Karyn Kupcinet. She zooms back to her last night on earth.

Karyn's guests split. Andy comes over. He gets mad at Karyn. He hits her. He bombs out of the apartment.

Karyn takes a shower. She towels herself off. A white male sneaks into her pad. He calls Karyn a bitch. He chokes her and places her on the couch.

The man was 55 years old. He stood five-six to five-eight. He had silver-gray hair and blue eyes.

1/26/66:

Boss psychic Peter Hurkos weighs in. He groks Andy Prine as the killer. He groks David Lange as the backup suspect. Hurkos met Prine and Lange at Glenn Ford's house. Karyn said she'd fuck up Andy's career if he left her. Hurkos calls that the murder motive.

1/31/66:

A female psychic fondles Karyn's jewelry. She gets a brain-storm.

It was a contract hit out of Chicago. The killer looked Jewish or Italian. He had dark hair and a broad forehead.

The psychic shit went nowhere. They discontinued it. They re-interviewed most of the key witnesses. They pressed the case all the way through '66.

They went at Andy Prine. They braced him on 11/2/66. Bobby Chapman and Lieutenant Norm Hamilton went at him hard.

Prine stuck to his story. Chapman tried to shoot it down. He pressed one theory—hard.

It's 11/27/63. Andy drops off the actress chick. He doesn't try to fuck the actress chick. He wants to break it off with Karyn—for keeps. He goes to her pad. Things escalate. Karyn dies in the process.

Prine stuck to his story. He didn't try to fuck the actress chick. He wasn't that hard up for cooze. He didn't want to cut off Karyn. He dug her as a sometime thing. She never said she'd fuck up his career. The bad publicity fucked him. That was the only way he got fucked.

11/14/66:

Edward Rubin calls Sheriff's Homicide. He changes his story substantially.

It's 11/27/63. He leaves Karyn's place. He's with Bob Hathaway.

They go to the Raincheck Room. Bob takes off alone. Rubin meets two chicks. He can't remember their names. They drive him home. They've got a '57 Austin-Healey. He asks one chick for a date. She turns him down. She's leaving for New Mexico U in the morning.

Bobby Chapman tried to verify the story. He couldn't get a line on the chicks.

Strange:

Rubin did not recall the chicks three days after the crime. He recalled them three years later.

12/7/66:

Chapman braces Bob Hathaway. He refutes Rubin's revised statement. He revises his own statement substantially.

He said the big bull session was a big non sequitur. Andy never dropped by and stayed that long.

12/14/66:

Chapman braces Edward Rubin. He dittoes Hathaway. It did seem strange that Andy stayed that long.

The case dragged on. A lot of the cops thought it wasn't even a murder. Bobby Chapman transferred out. Bobby Morck and Vince Bogdanich got the case. Morck thought it wasn't a murder. Bogdanich wasn't sure. They checked out leads anyway.

Bogdanich braced David Lange on 7/23/68. Lange stuck by his '63 story. He refused to take a second polygraph test—on advice of legal counsel. Bogdanich thought he was a viable suspect.

The leads trickled out. They worked other jobs. They worked the Kupcinet job as tips materialized. They braced David Lange on 9/17/69.

Lange had a gig at Paramount. Morck and Bogdanich braced him at his office. He cooperated. They asked him if he'd take another polygraph. Lange said he'd talk to his lawyer.

His lawyer called the boss at Sheriff's Homicide. He said: Mr. Lange would *not* take another polygraph test.

The Karyn Kupcinet case was five years, nine months, and twenty-three days old. It was a freak show and a heartache. A woman got lost in the uproar.

2
The Victim

It was Kup's town. The funeral was Kup's Show.

The heavies turned out. Governor Kerner, aldermen, Mayor Richard J. Daley. They rode at the front of the car-line. Karyn's friends rode at the back.

12/4/63:

Temple Sholom on the Gold Coast. Adios, Karyn—it was too damn brief.

Fifteen hundred people. Major coverage. A big egalitarian spin.

Ward heelers weep. Hoodlums hurl tears into their hankies. Hipsters hobnob with hackies and schvartze waiters from the Pump Room.

It's a mob scene. It's a mitzvah for a media man and his movie-mad daughter. It plays nine days after the JFK entombment.

Andy Prine did not attend the service. Rabbi Louis Binstock emceed. He praised Karyn. He said she was "high above the stage, with her warmth of manner and a glow in her eyes."

An all-star lineup lugged the casket out to the hearse. Among them: ex-Chicago Bears quarterback Sid Luckman.

Karyn closed strong. She would have dug the show.

She was Irv and Essee K.'s first child. They named her Roberta Lynn and called her "Cookie." Their son, Jerry, was born three years later.

Essee came from money. Irv came from zilch. He played pro football. He called Bears games on radio and TV. He wrote for the *Chicago Sun-Times*. He hosted *Kup's Show*—a gabfest with real legs.

Kup lobbed softballs in his column. People loved him. He

loved the Joe Blow Chicagoan impersonally. He loved celebs for real.

Essee loved celebs and culture. She took Cookie and Jerry to ballets and stage shows. She doted on Cookie. She said she should be an actress. She pushed her that way. Cookie bought the program.

Essee stressed beauty and thinness. She got Cookie some child-model gigs.

Cookie loved drama. She loved to act. She loved Kup's World.

It was glamorous. It was who you knew and who blew who. It was ringside seats and a special guest for dinner every night. Cookie dropped names like most kids dropped vowels.

She went to the Francis Parker School. She excelled at kid theatrics. She got summer-stock gigs in and around Chicago. She played the tomboy role in a boffo rendition of *Picnic*.

She finished high school. She went to Pine Manor College for a year and a half. She played leads and second leads in school shows. She put on a little weight. She took it off and put it on again. She moved to New York City in '60.

She gained weight and lost weight. She never got fat. It was all crazy shit in her head.

She changed her name to Lynn Roberts. A plastic surgeon reshaped her chin.

She lived off money from home. She auditioned and got a few gigs. She gained weight and lost weight. She got depressed. She dropped "Lynn Roberts" and renamed herself "Karyn Kupcinet."

Kup was tight with Jerry Lewis. Jerry liked Karyn. He offered her a bit part in his flick *The Ladies' Man*.

Karyn flew out to L.A. She dug it and decided to stay.

Essee's mother moved out and played chaperone. They found a pad on Hollywood Boulevard. Essee set Karyn up with Mark and Marcia Goddard. Kup set her up with A-list contacts.

Karyn started a new datebook on 3/9/61. She recorded her

weight in most entries. She got a nose job on 5/16. She weighed 115½ pounds.

"Awake during operation. AGONY. Felt needles, cutting, *everything!*"

Karyn thought her new nose looked like a pig snout. Other people disagreed.

5/29/61. In Vegas with Kup and Essee:

"Nose *much* better!" "So many compliments!" Warren Beatty: "You're so beautiful." Eddie Fisher: "Thought you were Liz."

5/27/61:

"I'm pretty! So happy!"

Karyn got a guest shot on *Hawaiian Eye.* Bob Conrad was "a doll." "*Me*—so-o complimented!"

Karyn auditioned. Karyn went to brunch, lunch, and dinner. Karyn shopped and got her hair done. Karyn got her weight down to 113½.

She got a series gig on 7/25. The show starred Gertrude Berg. It was called *Mrs. G. Goes to College.*

She started work on 8/2. Her weight stood at 114. The director said she had a "wild body." Karyn played a kooky college kid.

Karyn worked. Karyn hung out at P.J.'s and the Crescendo. Karyn ate at Linny's and the Hamburger Hamlet. Karyn shopped at Jax and Saks.

8/17/61:

Gertrude thought she wore too much makeup. "Everyone around there makes me nervous."

8/18/61:

"Gertrude impossible. Finally—got my close-up and took four or five takes. Couldn't get damn thing straight."

9/11/61: 113 pounds. 9/12/61: "Hardly ate at all!" 9/15 and 9/16/61: "Ate & ate."

10/4/61: The *Mrs. G.* pilot airs. 109 pounds, "My hair darling—lots of compliments." 10/15/61: 116 pounds. "Ate 3 Danish," "Eating too much."

Karyn logged male compliments. Karyn logged male encounters. She met men. She kissed them. They got schizzy and blew her off. 10/22/61: 110 pounds, "No one *calls* me." 10/28/61: 114½ pounds. "Eating too many sweet rolls."

Karyn worked on the Berg Show and tried out for other gigs. She went out on bad dates and hung out with her girlfriends. She went to twist clubs and movie premieres.

1/23/62: 121 pounds. "I look too heavy; yet everyone calls me beautiful." 2/1/62: 117 pounds. "Everyone noticed my weight loss." 2/5/62: 125 pounds. "Stayed in bed. Ate. Feel so draggy & tired." 2/15/62: 121 pounds. "Took pills." "Looked gorgeous." 2/16/62: "Woke up very dopey (after 3 sleeping pills). Groggy." 2/19/62: "Slept late," "Bought 'Leen' tablets."

The Berg Show was cancelled. Karyn went on unemployment. Kup and Essee sent her money. Her grandmother moved back to Chicago.

3/22/62: 123 pounds. "Got to lose at least 10 lbs. by April 8! Only 17 days."

3/29/62:

"I'm beginning to discover who I am! My convictions & 'image' are getting clearer. I know I'm happiest following the pattern of sophistication, than one of girlish appeal."

Karyn got a guest shot on *The Red Skelton Show*. Skelton to Karyn, 4/2/62: "3 people said you were prettier than Liz Taylor."

More auditions. More pills. More brunches, lunches, and dinners.

Two brief love affairs. Summer stock in Chicago—*Sunday in New York*. The Annie Sullivan role in *The Miracle Worker* at the Laguna Beach Playhouse. Good reviews and a run below 115.

10/1/62:

"Woke up feeling slightly nauseous & groggy. Hallucinations, inferiority complex, aching limbs, stiff neck, (surely liver damage) resulted from pills."

10/8/62: "Cried myself to sleep." 10/9 to 11/10/62: doodles and incomplete notations. 11/11/62: "Continuous hysteria. Deepest depression ever." 12/3/62: "*Wide Country*—6:00 A.M. call (location)." 12/4/62: "Andy Prine—doll!" 12/6/62: 105 pounds. "Andy. 'Raincheck.'" 12/9/62: "Andy." 12/11/62: "Andy." 12/12/62: "Look thin." 12/13/62: "Andy." 12/18, 19, 20, 21, 22: "Andy"—and no other notations.

Karyn flew to Chicago for Christmas. 12/28, 12/31 and 1/1/63: "Andy called—'I love you.'"

It was all Andy now.

1/17/63: "Met Andy for lunch. He was attentive." "*Wide Country*—Andy was *brilliant*, I was an *EXTRA*. Felt depressed." 1/20/63: "Andy—aloof." 2/5/63: "Tense & anxious over Andy's attitude." 2/11/63: "Me tense, blurred vision. To Dr. Getzoff (pills) with Andy." 2/19/63: "Must maintain my own identity; not become his door-mat. So useless."

3/25/63: "Andy picked me up 5:30. Lovely love—ate at DuPar's—Back & lovely love." 4/9/63: "Eating *much too much*." 4/11/63: "I love Andy Prine." 5/21/63: "12 P.M.—Dr. Kroger. Gave me weight capsules. Finally get a 'lift.' Appetite's inhibited." 5/30/63: "Andy distant—me terribly possessive and weak."

Karyn tanked auditions. Karyn shopped and ate and saw shrinks. 6/21/63:

"At his house; found out about Cheryl H. & B. Scott. Awful! 'I don't want to see you tonight either.' I went over. Got in. Came back later—HYSTERICS."

6/27/63: "Getting my self-respect back. I'm stronger." 6/30/63: "Oh Andy, lovely, lovely." 7/1/63: 134 pounds. "Beginning today—I starve!" "Dr. Krohn prescribed Desoxyn." 7/8/63: 124 pounds. "Dr. Krohn, 1:30 P.M. (Figure's looking better.) Andy: 'It excites me to hurt U a little.'"

Karyn learned she was pregnant. Mark and Marcia took her down to T.J. 7/9/63: "Like a nightmare. This can't be happening to me." 7/10/63: "Oh God—I don't know what to do. Called Dr. Estrada (call back after noon)."

7/11/63: "Called Dr. Estrada again. Getting used to the idea." Karyn got an abortion on 7/12/63. "Traumatic. Glad it's over. Relief after nightmare." She returned to L.A. "Andy considerate & attentive." "Knots, gas—like cramps. Andy made soup."

7/25/63: "I'm so happy. How long can it last?" 7/30/63: "Andy with Anna. Me watched from hedge. Awful. Nightmares."

Karyn stopped auditioning. Karyn cut down her social contacts. 8/15/63: "I must not be possessive—sweet."

8/17/63:

"Really *MAD* at the Son of a Bitch. For the first time, I really dislike Andy. He shows no consideration or understanding & he humiliates me." 8/18/63: "How dare he not make one concession or show any feelings?"

8/20/63: "So humiliated by Andy's lack of interest." 8/27/63: "Feel like I'm about to explode!" 8/28/63: "Eating *too* much!"

Karyn stepped up her social contacts. Karyn moved to the Monterey Village Apartments. A heat wave scorched L.A. Karyn got a shot on *Perry Mason*.

10/29/63:

"Andy acting ugly. Complete indifference. Scene at his house. I'm hysterical."

11/1/63: "No Andy—spyed on him." 11/2/63: "Went to his house—selfish, independent, inconsiderate & thoughtless. Never gives & unpenetrable." 11/4/63: "I hid in attic; then sat outside in cold for 2 or 3 hours. Wish I were dead." 11/8/63: "Dr. Kroger—cried in his office." 11/9/63: "Eating all day & night." 11/10/63: "Can't stand it—I'm losing reality." 11/11/63: "Call Andy—sex." 11/15/63: "2:00 P.M.—Kroger. Happy & *up*. Wore pink skirt—Admiring looks."

11/22/63: "President assassinated."

11/23/63: "Palm Springs."

11/25/63: "Ate to oblivion."
11/27 or 28:

DEAD

The datebook ended five weeks short of New Year's. A sheet was clipped to the back.

Karyn jotted down some book titles. They were psychoanalytic texts.

Beside them:

A list of all the men she'd slept with.

3
Karyn Redux

They entombed her in a Jewish cemetery. They honored her with classy endowments.

Two Karyn Kupcinet Theaters. A Karyn Kupcinet Gallery. A Karyn Kupcinet Scholarship.

Kup and Essee kept her name out there. No one knows how they defined her death and rush to self-destruct. No one knows how many what-ifs and might-have-beens they indulged over cocktails.

Karyn died moments after a freeze-frame. The camera's in tight. She's all passion and disorder. A close-up sends out an implication: She could go anywhere now.

It might be true. It might be a wishful conceit. She left a list of books and a list of men as her last will and testament. It might have marked a step toward self-knowledge. It might have been a Band-Aid to cover her wounds until her shitheel lover called. She had a fierce heart and no will to moral judgment. Her compulsive componentry was common to young women. She carried her own strain of a plague. It hadn't been identified yet. The time impinged her. Her shrink cosigned her rebop and tapped Kup's bankbook. She didn't get the gender-role thing. She didn't know that women took it up the shorts systematically. She didn't know that the precept could spark a will to change. She had the juice to grasp the concept. She might have found the guts to go with it and burned her old life to the ground. She was just a kid. She didn't know shit from Shinola. She labored under a shroud. She thought showbiz was real.

It was the Kupcinet family blessing and curse. It started with Kup. He passed it on to Karyn and Jerry.

Jerry turned 19 the month Karyn died. He loved the visual arts. He wanted to forge a Kupcinet life on the other side of the camera.

He went to Bradley U and Columbia of Chicago. He studied photography. He graduated and shot pix for *Playboy*. He shot stills for the Chicago stage run of *Hair*.

He became a TV cameraman and director. He directed segments of *A.M. Chicago* and *Good Morning America*. He married a woman named Sue Levine. They had a son and a daughter.

Jerry got a gig on *The Richard Simmons Show*. He moved his family out to L.A. It was '81. His daughter was nine years old. Her name was Karyn Ann Kupcinet.

Essee called it reincarnation. Kup said he almost agreed. The blessing and curse hit a third generation.

Karyn Two didn't look like Karyn. It was all inside. The Karyns bubbled and churned. They lived to please and lived to perform. Essee pushed Karyn Two the same way she pushed Karyn. She pushed her to act and stay thin.

Karyn Two went to Parker School in Chicago. She hung out at the Karyn Kupcinet Gallery. She pretended that they named the place after her.

She knew her Aunt Karyn died young. She knew somebody killed her. Nobody fed her more details. She felt no urge to learn more.

Jerry moved his brood out to L.A. Karyn Two grew up on Karyn's old turf.

She gained weight and lost weight. Food was a punishment. Food was a reward.

She went out on kid auditions. She got a few TV and stage parts. She played Helen Keller in *The Miracle Worker*. She was a high-school freshman then.

She kept a journal. She wrote a play called *The Porcelain Doll*. It was all about a weight-obsessed girl. She writes her thoughts in a journal. She dies young. Her best friend finds the journal and reads it.

Karyn Two acted. Karyn Two gained and lost weight. Karyn Two had a nice boyfriend.

The boyfriend went to the Film Academy library. They kept files on professional performers. He asked to see the file on Karyn Two. The clerk gave him the file on Karyn.

The file freaked him out. He skimmed it and called Karyn Two. She went to the library and read the file cover to cover.

She copied down most of the data. She studied it. She flew to Chicago and looked through Karyn's belongings. Kup and Essee kept twelve boxes.

Karyn Two dug through them. She read Karyn's datebooks. She read fan-mag stories on Andy Prine. She started writing journal entries to her aunt.

She caught the psychic-twin bit full-on. She caught the ugly belief in appearances that took Karyn down and tossed it straight back at herself. She saw herself as Karyn reborn. She got stone fucking obsessed.

She reread Karyn's datebooks. She ran "what-if" and "might-have-been" riffs. She dreamt about Andy Prine.

She loves him. She trusts him. He loves her. He does not act like a shitheel or a killer.

The dreams drove her crazy. Maybe Karyn sent them. Maybe she wanted to absolve Andy. Maybe she was glad that he killed her. Her life was horrible. Maybe death was a treat.

She finished high school. She went to UCLA. She auditioned. She got commercial gigs and guest shots on soaps. Rejections killed her. She felt like the '62 Karyn. Her OBSESSION ate her alive.

She wrote to a dead woman. She reread her last words and hoarded the details of her life. She kept Karyn's purse. She fondled her wallet and dried-out cigarettes.

She was born in '71. She never knew her aunt. She knew she had her mad blood in her veins.

She turned 20. She got a steady gig on *The Young and the Restless*. She played a pregnant crackhead. She had ratted hair and wore ripped jeans. She cried on cue every day. They shot the show at Beverly and Fairfax. The Monterey Village Apartments stood a mile or so northwest. Andy Prine's ex-wife worked on the show.

Karen Two loved the work. She loved the whirl that went with it.

Parties and clubs. Access to exciting people. Accommodators and sycophants. Insider status in an insider town. Limos and drugs. Weak, sexy men. Kup's World—updated and revised for a youth market.

She fell into it. It subsumed her dialogue with a dead woman and thinned out her mad blood.

The pace kept her weight down. Cocaine helped. Hallucinogens undermined her monomania.

She ran through soft and self-obsessed men. "Actors." "Musicians." Studs who ran long on looks and "Potential." Her affairs burned out in similar patterns. The studs revealed themselves fast. Karyn Two possessed good antennae. She majored in Karyn One and minored in Andy Prine and David Lange. She started to put it all together. She built a generational thesis. She connected the dots back to 1963.

It came to her slow. The L.A. scene tempted and diverted her. She put it together over good time.

Mad blood shared. Gifts locked within. P.J.'s and the Crescendo. The Rainbow and the Roxy. Desoxyn and hallucinogens. Weak men and skinny bodies to make them love you. Would-be actors and actors. The actors' psyche as defined by some actor-savant: "My only regret in life is that I'm not somebody else."

She put it together slow. Andy Prine types distracted her. She put it together over good time. She made the connections and sealed and severed the bond all in one go.

She walked.

4
Reopening

Karyn Two went by "Kari" now. She was four years out of L.A.

She married a stable guy named Brad. She owned a candle store in Chicago. She put down her bad L.A. habits. She surmounted her eating disorder and maintained a stable and slender weight.

Karyn saved her. The obsession still owned her. She flew out to L.A. to see the murder file.

She spent a week at the Homicide Bureau. She went through the file. Sergeant Bill Stoner studied it with her. Stoner retired in '94. He spent fourteen years at Sheriff's Homicide. He remained on the active Reserve.

Kari wanted to rework the case herself. The file provided her with insights and data on the key players. She wanted to find them and interview them.

I met Bill and Kari for dinner. We hogged a booth at the Pacific Dining Car. We discussed the case for three hours.

The consensus at Sheriff's Homicide: Andy Prine and David Lange remained viable suspects—*if* it was a homicide to begin with.

Karyn probably took eighty-one Desoxyns inside forty-eight hours. She might have built up a tolerance. The collective dose might not have fazed her. It might have caused dizziness and heart cramps.

Hathaway and Rubin revised their statements three years after the fact. Rubin recalled minute details out of nowhere. Hathaway altered the whole tone of his first statement.

Doc Kade was dead now. He did an autopsy shortly after his Kupcinet job. He allegedly told a colleague, "At least I didn't break the hyoid bone on this one!"

Kade had an erratic reputation. Some cops braced him on the hyoid bone back in '66. He stuck to his original statement.

He filed his initial report on 12/1/63. He noted a hemorrhage inside the throat. It buttressed his alleged finding on the hyoid bone.

Forensic glitches. Inconsistent statements. Advanced decomposition and incomplete toxology. Screwed-up witnesses in a screwed-up milieu. Exponential possibilities resultant.

Kari's puzzle to ponder. Her world to explore.

I juxtaposed Karyn and Kari. I melded their features and framed a tight close-up. I captioned it while the image held.

Karyn owned a gene for survival. She didn't get the chance to outgrow her silly fucking dreams.

December 1998

PART TWO

GETCHELL

HUSH-HUSH

L.A. *TIMES*, JUNE 5, 1998:

TURNER-STOMPANATO LOVE LETTERS
TO BE AUCTIONED

Smith & Kleindeinst, the Beverly Hills auctioneers, announced today that they will sell the late actress Lana Turner's love letters to reputed hoodlum Johnny Stompanato at their August 16 auction in Century City. A Smith & Kleindeinst spokesman said that the letters were consigned to them by a source who prefers to remain anonymous. There are a total of 14 letters, dated between October 9, 1957, and March 12, 1958. They will be sold as a block purchase.

The Turner-Stompanato liaison occupies a prominent place in Los Angeles criminal history. Their violent relationship culminated on the evening of April 4, 1958, when Cheryl Crane, Miss Turner's 14-year-old daughter by the late restaurateur Steve Crane, came to her mother's aid and stabbed Stompanato to death. No criminal charges were filed against Miss Crane. She was sent to a youth treatment facility for psychiatric evaluation and care.

The Smith & Kleindeinst spokesman said that bidding for the letters will most likely begin in the "mid-six-figure" range.

The Advocate, JUNE 6, 1998:

SCANDAL-SHEET WRITER
IN CRITICAL CONDITION

Daniel "Danny" Getchell, 68, editor-in-chief and head writer for the infamous *Hush-Hush* scandal magazine of the 1950s and early 1960s, was admitted to Cedars-Sinai Medical Center last week. An undisclosed source at the center revealed that Getchell is in the "final, deadly throes" of a "severe brain tumor."

Hush-Hush and the other scandal sheets of the era—*Confidential, Whisper, Rave, Lowdown,* and *Tattle*—waged a collective smear campaign against gays and lesbians and accomplished it with vicious outing tactics. Innuendo and intimidation were their most commonly applied methods, and their goal was titillation at any human price. The scandal sheets destroyed the lives of many gay and lesbian Americans, and *Hush-Hush* was arguably the worst of the lot.

Benjamin Luboff, ex-*Whisper* writer and author of the mea culpa memoir *Scandal-Rag Scourge,* described Danny Getchell as "viciously single-minded in his fast-buck pursuit of naming homosexual names" and "pathologically driven by a sadistic urge to out gays." When asked to comment on Getchell's hospitalization, Luboff replied, "What can I say? I wish no person—straight or gay—a painfully protracted death, but the world will be a better place without Danny Getchell."

A hospital source said that Getchell is under intensive around-the-clock care and would not be able to answer a list of questions submitted by *The Advocate.*

Cheryl Crane did not shank Johnny Stompanato, and I don't have a fucking brain tumor. And I always gave the fags I fragged a chance to buy their stories back.

And you won't believe the shit I've got on Ben Luboff.

The brain-tumor bit is a smoke screen smoked by a hospital flack. I'm ensconced in a secret Cedars ward built from an old bomb shelter. I'm sunk subterranean with sixty-three male patients and sixteen doctors set to vanquish our virus. They'll hypocritically ignore the Hippocratic oath and sell their cure exclusively to the rich. I'm selling everything I own to buy bed space at twenty grand a day.

I've got AIDS. The worst thing about having it is having it. The fact that people think you're a fag runs a close second.

I'm not a fag. I'm a junkie with a 40-year-old monkey on my back.

Reliable rejuvenations ruined me. I periodically purge my putrefied system with black-market blood transfusions. I bought some Desert Storm surplus blood back in '91. It dried out my sex drive, downsized my red-blood count, and devastatingly deep-sixed me into total devolution.

Or somebody poisoned me on purpose.

Maybe a minor miscreant I maligned in May '61. Possibly a punk I pilloried as purple-tinged a loooong time ago. Perhaps a perpetrator with a perfect sense of poetic justice.

I'm pulsatingly paranoid now. I'm a hemophiliac homophobe and a crucifiable Christian abed at the Gay Roman Inn.

I see six of my scandal-rag scapegoats hooked up to hydration machines. They strategically strafe me with hate in their eyes. They huddle within hailing and hurting range and haunt me as I hatch this harangue in the Hush-Hush *style.*

I've got a sharp shiv shoved under my bed. I've got the guardedly gay-friendly tale that you're about to get. I'll pander to pederastic pride or hurl some hurt in the spirit of the Hush-Hush *holocaust.*

The gonif three gurneys down is staring straight through me. I can't place him in my backlog of blackmail and bad juju. I'm going to cut him out of my thoughts and concentrate on my story while I can still alliterate alluringly.

I

The debilitating dirt drought of Spring, '58.

It hindered, hampered, and hog-tied *Hush-Hush*. It forced us to print presumption as veracity verified. It forced me to misconstrue old morgue memos and pass them off as fresh scandal skank.

JACKIE GLEASON FIGHTS FOOD FIXATION AT FAT FARM OUTSIDE PHILLY! JOHNNIE RAY MAULED IN MEN'S-ROOM MISADVENTURE! STARLETS STATE STEVE COCHRAN TOPS TAPE AS TINSELTOWN'S MR. KINGSIZE!

Bum bits and rumor retreads. Libelous liabilities and lightning rods to lasso lewd litigation. Unprovable assertions to attract unremitting heat in an unenlightened climate.

Maureen O'Hara keestered *Confidential* last year. The mag maligned her and said she groped a guy at Grauman's Chink. She sued successfully. *Confidential* detailed Dorothy Dandridge's dipso descent. She sued successfully. Monkey see, monkey do: A chain of chimps sued *Hush-Hush*. Our current courtroom count stands at 0-and-3. We're mainlining monetary liens and moving toward Bankrupt Boulevard and Moribund Mesa. We're taking it up the ass bad.

We've dramatically downscaled our dimensions. We moved into a dumpy building down from the downtown dog pound. The doped-out dentist down the hall drives my new crew crazy. I cut my old crew loose to cover court costs and slapped up some fresh slaves from the Salvation Army. They're all dry drunks with the shimmy-shimmy shakes. Dental-drill noise drips through the walls and drills its way under their skin. They drop type trays and drizzle glue all over my pasteup plates.

Our circulation has circled down to the scandal-rag cellar. *Whisper* was whispered to top our toll by ten figures per month. Ben Luboff scammed skank for *Whisper*. I hated him. I owed his bookie brother two big on Basilio-Robinson. Ben bought bonus buzz-dirt off me and bought down my debts with his brother sometimes. I hated to humble *Hush-Hush* and humiliate myself—but I had to now.

I looked around the office. A dry drunk dropped a cigarette and scorched a scalding shot primed for pasteup:

Lezzie Lizabeth Scott with a loin-lapping look at Linda's Little Log Cabin on Lankershim Boulevard.

Shit—

It was time to pound the pavement proactive. I walked down the hall and wiggled into Dr. Dave Dockweiler's chair.

Dave said, "How long?" I said, "Forty-eight hours straight." Dave jacked joy juice into a spike and found a vividly viable vein in my left arm.

He said, "Three good ones too hot to print. I'm going to an American Legion smoker tonight." I concocted a commie conspirator's clique and twisted a fist to twang my target vein.

"Paul Robeson is pouring the pork to Pat Nixon. I swear this is no shit. He's got her hooked on that big roll of tar paper he's packing, and she's leaking him all of Tricky Dick's secrets, and Robeson's feeding them to the Kremlin, and they're feeding them to Senator John F. Kennedy, who's going to run against Dick in '60. This is no shit, I swear to you. Oh, and Sammy Davis Jr. is fucking Mamie Eisenhower. I swear to you, Dave, this is no fucking shit."

Dave spanked his spike on my vividly violet vein. "You swear this is no shit?"

"This is no shit, Dave, I swear to you."

Dave bit the bait and shook his head and let my shit sift into his system. He shot me up with his shit and watched me shift up to the stars.

I went into orgasmic orbit. I spun past *Sputnik* and jived with Jesus himself. I jumped back to Earth and jumped out of the chair like a jacked-up jungle bunny.

I fly on methamphetamine moored in male hormones and a multivitamin mix. Here's why scandal sheets fly:

People are ambivalently amped up on celebrities. They wildly worship them. They aim their adolescent adulation at them and get bupkis back. It's depressingly disassociative. It's idiotic idolatry. Fan magazines fan the flames of fatuous fancy and reinforce the fact that your favorite stars will never fuck you. Scandal rags rip that reinforcement and deliriously deconstruct and deidolize the idols who ignore you. It's revisionistic revenge. It reduces your unrequited lovers to your own low level of erratic erotics. It rips the rich and regal and guns them into the gutter beside you. It fractiously frees you to love them as one of your own.

I was flying on high-grade meth and a high-faluting head full of *Hush-Hush* homilies. I hit Hollywood hopped-up to dish dirt and dig my way out of debt.

Every bartender, bouncer, B-girl, busboy, and B-movie bimbo in town has his hand out to *Hush-Hush* or whispers to *Whisper* or tattles their tails off to *Tattle*. I tripped a path through my tipsters and said, "How's tricks?" I locked in the following lowdown:

Howard Hughes had a hard-on for a high-yellow hooker named Dusky Deelite. Rin Tin Tin ripped Lassie into renal distress at a recent kiddie roundup. Mickey Cohen can't afford to keep Candy Barr. Candy's starring in stag flix and moving a mountain of Mary Jane. Mickey's tapped out and tapping his old legbreakers for loans. Johnny Stompanato stood Mickey up at the Statler and stiffed him on a long-term debt. Lana Turner was lamenting the loss of Lex Barker. Stompanato stomped into her life. He bullies her and beguiles her into long bouts of bury the brisket. Lana now lisps, "Lex who?"

Bob Mitchum mauled a mulatto mama at a niggertown niteclub. Porfirio Rubirosa pulled out his pud at a Bel-Air bash for Bill Bendix. Rock Hudson humps prodigiously pretty call-service boys. He gets them from a sweaty swish carhop at Delores's Drive-In. Lenny Bruce is handing up hopheads to the Sheriff's Narco Squad.

The Rin Tin Tin riff rated zero. The Mitchum mishigaas might be milkable and make for a good miscegenation piece. Stompanato was stale stuff—*Confidential* cornholed him three months back. I'd played up Porfirio's pud and Howard Hughes's hooker hungries already. Ben Luboff wouldn't bite for that batch.

But he'd bite for the boffo bit on Rock Hudson.

Ben wanted to ram Rock out of the closet. He wanted to push

him past the Pink Curtain and parade him around in a purple peignoir. Every scandal scribe wanted to skewer and scupper the Rock. He was the hunky height of the homo heap. *Hush-Hush, Whisper, Rave*—we all got cloyingly close to the clasp on the closet door. But pugnacious publicists grabbed at our greed, bought our stories back, and heaped us with heat on their other homo clients. The Rock remained ramrod erect—just past the Purple Passage.

Ben Luboff hogged a back booth at Googie's twenty hours a day. Tipsters trucked in and tossed him tidbits. I bopped back to his booth and blew out a blast of bravado.

"I owe your brother two Gs. Take care of it and slip me an item for the May issue, and I'll give you the Rock."

Ben belched bicarbonate of soda. Bubbles bipped off his lips. He looked disturbingly drawn and dyspeptic. The dirt drought had drained him dry.

He nudged me a napkin. I pulled out my pen and wrote down my rap on Rock and the sweaty swish. Ben Scripto scrawled his own napkin note. We noodled our notes across the table simultaneously.

His read:

"Don Jordan (top welterweight contender) running string of wetback maids as hookers out of the Luau."

MOONLIGHTING MEXICAN MAIDS MAKE FOR MISCHIEVOUS—

Ben noshed my napkin note and blew me a big bicarbonate kiss.

2

The Luau:

A tiki-torchlit restaurant rendezvous on Rodeo Drive. A mecca for movie-biz mavens and Beverly Hills business boys.

Big booths and baroque backlighting. Tricked-up tropical trappings. Rambunctious rum drinks and rumaki sticks at the bamboo bar.

A polyurethane Polynesian paradise—with peekaboo posts perched behind wall panels by the bar and the ladies' too.

Steve Crane owned the Luau. Steve loved to lurk and look. He voyeur-vamped the joint every night.

Steve owed me. I bought him out of a blow-job beef back in '54. Ben Luboff tried to trap him with a 16-year-old San Quentin quail. Steve let me lurk in peeper perpetuity.

I was lurked out behind the ladies' lav. My peephole post provided a prime view. I saw Helen Hayes hitch up her hose. I saw the Misty June Christy crimp a crisp twenty and crib coke up her nose. I ducked down a dark panel passage and peeped out a peephole right behind the bar.

Dreamy drunks adrift in demerara rum. Don Jordan fretting a frosted fruit frappe. Demonic Don from the Dominican Republic—a maladroit mulatto now in moonlight mode with a melange of Mexican maids.

Donkey Don: rumored to reach twelve inches. Devil Don: rumored to run a right-wing death squad back in the D.R. A ripe recent rumor: Mickey Cohen owned a prime piece of Don's prize-fighting percentage.

I bored my eyes in on the bar. Don downed his daiquiri and doodled up his napkin. Three wetback wenches wiggled up to him.

Luscious Latinas pulling out va-va-va-voom volts. A stellar stable too starkly dark to strike up biz in Steve Crane's lily-white Luau.

Steve stuck to a strict B-girl Bill of Race Rights. Negro: Nyet, nein, no, not at my place. White: Welcome, what will you have? Latin: Light-skinned Lupes and Lucitas only.

Something was twisted two twirls off.

It hit me:

Two twists in twin frocks fresh out of Frederick's of Hollywood. Pulchritudinous—but not pulsingly so. The supreme señorita: languidly lissome in Lana Turner's light blue gown from last month's Oscar show.

Lana Turner:

Steve Crane's ex. Movie-star mama to Steve's starstruck daughter, Cheryl. Steve was still starved for Lana's lewd love. Steve

couldn't stomach thoughts of Johnny Stompanato sticking it
to her.

I panted and peeped out my peephole. A methamphetamine
breath mist glazed up the glass. I wiped it off and watched a waiter
walk up to the mass magnifica mama.

He passed her a piece of paper. Don Jordan passed his other
prosties Mickey Mouse–size Minox minicameras.

What the fuck—

The main mamacita mainlined her way out of the bar. I
peephole-patched a path through the main passageway and kept
her within peeping range. She walked out to the back parking lot
and stepped over to Steve Crane. Steve was poised by a powder
blue Packard Caribbean.

I pushed out a passageway panel and pulled myself into a storeroom. I pushed aside some rum crates and pried open a window.
Whisper-close: Steve and the stark dark stunner.

I loitered. I lurked. I lolled my head below the window ledge
and listened.

Steve said, "—come on, you know the deal. Don can run you
and the other girls out of here, but only—"

The girl said, "Pleeeese, Mr. Crane. I don't know what joo want
me to say."

Steve said, "Don't play coy, Yolanda. We've been through this
before."

Yolanda said, "Well, all right, but joo should say exactly what
joo—"

"Does Johnny ever hit Lana or Cheryl?"

"No, he just yells at them. It eeesn't very nice, but—"

"Are you still mailing the letters that Lana writes him?"

"Well, yes . . ."

"Love letters, right?"

"Well . . . I don't . . ."

"Yolanda, you told me that she dips the letters in perfume, and
you saw her drop in curly little hairs when she sealed the
envelopes."

Man-o-Manischewitz! What a pussy-whipped provocateur and masochism-mangled motherfucker!

Yolanda said, "Please, Mr. Crane. I don't like to—"

"Yolanda, I want you to give me the next letter that Lana gives you."

"No. No, no, no, no no. I cannot do that to Miss Lana."

Steve—stern, strong, and strident-voiced now: "I only let you and the others work out of here because you give me information. Don wouldn't like it if I eighty-sixed you."

Yolanda, fetchingly firm and faultlessly focused: "I cannot betray Miss Lana, as long as Mr. Johnny does not hurt her or Miss Cheryl."

Steve, resoundingly resigned and ripped with regret. "Well . . . shit . . . okay . . . for now, at least. But I just want to protect Lana from herself, and I want you to promise me that you'll let me know if Johnny ever puts a hand on her or Cheryl. You see, I've got a gangster buddy who hates the son of a bitch."

Yolanda, a mellifluous madonna: "Oh, yes, I will. I care about Miss Lana and Miss Cheryl just as much as joo do."

Mickey Cohen hated Johnny Stompanato. Mickey was the meshugenah mouseketeer on the L.A. mob scene. Mickey had a minor cut of Don Jordan's contract and not much else. Mickey was too Minnie Mouse to stand up for Steve and stomp out Stompanato—and I started to smell money in the mix.

I could steal the steamy Lana letters. I could sell them to Steve or some lascivious Lanaphile. I could lube-job Ben Luboff and lay a few lackluster excerpts on him for big bread. I could proudly print the whole tumescent text in *Hush-Hush*.

The truth is my moral mandate. Dirt digs define my devotion to that difficult discipline. "Disillusionment Is Enlightenment"— some pundit popped that platitude and clipped a clear chord in my soul. I live to edify, entertain, enlighten, and enforce moral standards. It all entails enterprising entrapment. I'm a zealous First Amendment zealot. I contentiously contend that scandal skank scores free free speech to its fullest extension. I set tricky traps to track down the truth. My methedrine-mapped mandate makes it all morally sound.

I got Stompanato's stats from the West L.A. White Pages. I called his number and nailed a nigger maid. She said, "Mr. Johnny be back soon," and, "I just be leavin' myself." She sounded like some shine in *Song of the South*.

I bopped up to Benedict Canyon and buried my Buick coupe behind some bushes off Beverly Drive. I beat feet a block to Johnny's boss bunker: a big all-glass A-frame.

Lavishly landscaped and lit up light at 1:00 A.M. Wide windows to wiggle your eyes at and high hedges to hide behind. Peeper Paradise and Voyeur Valhalla.

Motherfuck—

The mail slot slid straight into the front French doors. I couldn't lift a latch and liberate Lana's love letters.

I hid behind a hydrangea hedge. I bored my beady browns into a big picture window ten feet away. Johnny Stomp stomped into sight. Don Jordan jiggled up and joined him.

They yelled and yowled at each other. They paced paths around the parlor and poked themselves in the pecs. Popped *P*s popped off the plate-glass window—but I couldn't pick out particular words.

Jordan pulled a passel of pix out of his pockets and fanned them full. I popped up and peered through the plate-glass powerfully hard. I saw darkroom-dipped photos still wet with developing doo. Interior shots: bountiful bedroom suites with balconies and wide walk-in closets.

My brain went bim, bango, bingo:

Don Jordan's moonlight maids with Minox minicams. Wetback women hooked in as hookers. Luau-lounging B-girls brought to Brentwood and Beverly Hills. Papa pops the girls to the pad while Mama meanders in Miami or mingles at her Monday mah-jongg club. The girls pop perspective pix and juke them back to Jordan. Jordan jukes them to some big bad burglary man. Jordan juked Yolanda into the plan. Johnny yanked Yolanda's chain, scammed the skinny on Demon Don's designs and demanded a cut. Yolanda lounged around the Luau in Lana Turner's low-cut gown. Still-torching Steve Crane recognized it. He yipped, yelled, and yodeled at Yolanda. He demanded that she double-agent for him. Yolanda agreed to dump domestic dirt on Lana and Johnny.

Stompanato stamped his feet. Jordan jabbed his chest. They stepped back and countermanded the course of a counterproductive contretemps. They smiled. They commandeered a couch. They pored over their pix and penciled a map on a piece of paper.

I hunched down and hunkered back to my hedge. I smelled Methedrine popping out of my pores—mixed with the musk of MONEY.

I needed names. I could B&E Johnny's pad and boost a burglary list. I could bug the pad and bug Demon Don's digs. I could tap their telephones and tape their talks and wire up the wetback wenches. I could impersonate an Immigration agent and intimidate them. I could contact the feckless fools that they fucked and feed them an ultimatum: Feed me in five figures, or I'll tell your wife who you fucked one freaky Friday night.

Oooooh, Daddy-o!!!!! I was digging it all, delirious!

I hauled back to the *Hush-Hush* office. I had to hook my hands on a boss batch of bug shit.

The office was occupied. My crew was crapped out on the floor. They were blasted, blitzed, blotto, zilched, zorched, and zombified. They'd gone off the wagon en masse.

They got tanked on Tokay and T-Bird. They got stinko on Sterno and got wiped out on White Port. Short-dog bottles shifted and shimmied on every spare inch of floor space.

I checked my equipment chest. All my bug mikes were bunched up, broken, frayed, frazzled, and fucked. My condenser cords were stripped and striated down to mere strips. My diode dials were ripped, rusted, and ratched to shit.

FUCK—

I had to find a freelance bug freak and co-opt him into my conspiracy. That meant pitching him a prime piece of my potential payout.

FUCK—

I called Freaky Fred Turentine. His wife said he was working for *Whisper* tonight. I buzzed Buddy "Bug King" Berkow. His wife said Ben Luboff just brought him in on a big bug job. I called Voyeur Vance Vanning. His wife said he was out on a wire job for *Whisper.* He left her a late-nite number: a pay phone at Wilshire and La Cienega.

It all congealed and constellated.

My tip to trap homo hunk Rock Hudson. The sweaty swish at Delores's Drive-In. Ben Luboff poised to scale the Purple Parthenon.

3

It had to be huge. Three bug boys at twenty bucks an hour boded big. My bet: Ben wanted bug bits on the bun-boy biz—to buttress his hit on hunky Rock Hudson. He'd set some phone-tap traps and bug baits on the sweaty swish carhop and develop some derogatory dish on Delores's Drive-In. A prick-tease prelude to priapic Rock and some prick-happy call boy.

I had to see it. It beckoned as big as the Bikini Atoll atom-bomb blast. A bifurcated motive bolstered my urge to merge with the moment. I wanted to boost a batch of Buddy Berkow's bug gear for *my* gig.

I whizzed down to Wilshire and La Cienega at warp speed. I whipped by Delores's Drive-In and dug all the dirty details.

The 2:00 A.M. tumult. Late-nite L.A. out for burgers, borscht, and bagels. Beatniks and beaten-down benny-heads in battered Bonnevilles. Cholos in chopped-down Chevys riding on cheater slicks.

Carhops rolling roisterous on roller stakes. All mincy males laid out in lacy lounge wear. Buddy Berkow's bugmobile back by the men's room. Beside it: Voyeur Vance Vanning's van. Freaky Fred Turentine wolfing french fries at an inside counter.

I whipped back to Wilshire and parked. I brought my beady

browns up against my Bausch & Lombs and went into ocular orbit.

Dig:

Sweat beads bipping off the brow of that too-tall carhop topping off the tape toward 6'8". A sweaty swish with the shakes: His tray twitched and twisted and almost toppled two twin-cheeseburger plates.

He fed the food to two Filipinos in a Ford Fairlane. He flitted back to a little shack lit by floodlights. He stood by the door and chain-smoked two Chesterfield Kings.

Envy entered my heart. An enlightened sense of entitlement entered my soul. A cosmic course of covetousness covered my whole being.

This gig should be MINE. I was the scandal-scamming, skinny-skimming scopophiliac king. The scopophiliacal scope of this gig screamed GETCHELL!

I alakazammed to Allah, genuflected to Jesus, and called out to that cat the kikes call God. I said I'd keester communists and bash ban-the-bombers, and dig up dirt on that dowager dyke Eleanor Roosevelt. I'd donate dough to a Moslem mosque. I'd put in with Pat Boone, wear white buck shoes, and warble at a Billy Graham Crusade. I wouldn't print my piece on Rabbi R. R. Ravitz and that Hebrew-school Hannah he humped last Hanukkah.

I shut my eyes. I gave the God guys time to get together and go for my deal. I could feel them finagling the fine points. Divine deals demand deliberation.

I opened my eyes. Ben Luboff bopped in front of my binoculars. He slid the sweaty swish a C-note and slid into the shack alone. The swish sashayed up to a lavender Lincoln and leaned in.

Ben bribed the too-tall brunser. That meant he didn't want to roust his racket. The gig developed different dimensions—maybe divinely deigned.

I latched my lenses on the Lincoln and locked my eyes in hard. I saw hunky Rock Hudson hand up a handful of hard cash.

All praise to Allah! Joy to Jesus! *Hush-Hush* hosannahs to the Hebrew God!

Rock locked his Lincoln, ditched the drive-in, and joyfully jay-walked straight across Wilshire. He walked up to the front of the Fine Arts movie house and made with a wicked wolf whistle.

A winsome wolf whistle whisked back his way. A muscular man-child meandered out of a moonbeam and leaned in the lobby doorway.

Rock, you rambunctious rump ranger—

Rock loped into the lobby. The kid locked them in. They disappeared near a dark candy counter.

I blew out of my Buick and flew around the Fine Arts fast-footed. I saw blue lights blink at the back of the building upstairs. I shimmied up a shaky drainpipe and shagged myself onto a ledge. I undulated through an unlocked window and heard Rock ulu-lating.

I landed on a lopsided pile of film cans. I pitched forward and pulled myself up. I peeped through a pebble-glass door and saw shadows shifting down a short hallway.

I fast-footed it out of the film-storage room. I saw flickery flits of light flick out from below two doorways. I ducked down the dark hall. Shifty shadows shot up from the door slits. I crept up on them and got down in a crab-crawl crouch. I slid one eye up against the door slits.

I saw a punk cameraman with a Panflex porta-cam packed into a pod-shaped peephole. Next door: Rock and the monster-hung man-child making meat-mangling motions on a light-colored couch with the lights on. Motherfucker: minuscule mini-mikes taped to a tall table lamp!

I flew back to the film-storage room. I rapidly reshimmied down that drainpipe. I whizzed across Wilshire, looped around La Cienega, and ducked down an alley behind Delores's Drive-In. I vaulted a vine-covered fence, veered past Vance Vanning's van, and vibrated up to that shitty little shack that the sweaty swish had swayed by.

The drive-in was deep in a late-nite lull. I spotted six sleds snouted into snack-serving slots. I looked left and wrapped my eyeballs right. I didn't see the sweaty swish or Ben Luboff. I saw Vance Vanning and Buddy Berkow buzzing logs in their bug vans.

I fearlessly faced the shack door. I nervously knocked and locked my loins to fight a scandal-skank war of some scope. Nobody answered. I wiggled the door open and walked in uninvited.

A lousy little all-linoleum office. Disinfectant stench, a dirty desk, and a doily-covered chair.

A closet.

A preciously apropos prop and a prime hideout hole.

I hid in the closet. I hunched myself up and heaved for breath. Methedrine-mad minutes marched by. I sweated and swore out a warrant on Ben Luboff's hide.

I heard the outer door open and shut. Furtive footsteps and vague voices. I peered through a pint-size pinhole in the closet door. I saw Ben Luboff and the sweaty swish.

Perspiration poured over the pinhole and voided my view. I locked my eyes shut and listened.

Ben said, "You know, it's ironic. I've been hearing about your service for years, but it took a tip from fucking Danny Getchell to get me to contact you."

The sweaty swish said, "Choice chicken, doll. The best boys in the West, and a good rep for discretion."

Ben said, "Yeah, and that's why the Rock buys all his extracurricular tail from you."

The sweaty swish said, "The Rock ain't nothin' but a hound dog. He's got a perfectly *gorgeous* lover at home—an art director at Metro—but he's got to roll around with every Tom, Dick, and Harriet he can find—with the emphasis on *Dick*."

Ben said, "You've never forgiven him, have you? He broke your heart, and that's what makes this deal so sweet for you."

The sweaty swish said, "Truer words never spoken, doll. And godddd, it was torture selling boys to him."

Ben said, "Vengeance is sweet, baby-cakes. You get your shot at the Rock, I get mine at the schmendrick Getchell."

In your faigeleh-finagling dreams, you fucking—

The sweaty swish said, "You're sure we can't get hurt on this?"

Ben said, "Nix. My camera guy set up a breakaway set at the Fine Arts. If the Rock takes the fuzz back there, they won't find the room he told them about. It was all strictly clandestine. My camera guy let your boy in the theater, and none of the theater chumps know that any of this happened."

The sweaty swish said, "Vengeance is mine, sayeth both of us."

Ben said, "Especially me. See, I gave Getchell that tip on Don Jordan's whore racket, and I called Don and clued him in that Getchell was onto his biz. Now, Don Jordan is a bad hombre to fuck with. He killed lots of guys in the Dominican Republic, and he's tight with this spic gang—the Apaches—out in Boyle Heights. I think it's safe to say that Danny Getchell's days are numbered."

I swirled sweat off my face and popped an eye up to the pint-size pinhole. Ben said, "And look, call it penance. I've done a shitty thing by exposing our kind of people, but now I'm doing all of us a mitzvah by taking Getchell out."

"Penance"? "*Our* people—"?

Ben leaned in and kissed the sweaty swish on the lips. He said, "Later, Lover," and languidly loped out the door.

I crashed out of the closet—crazily out of control. The sweaty swish saw me. He swirled and swung a switchblade out of his pocket.

He pirouetted and pounced. I closed the closet door, swiveled, and swung it at him. His switchblade swiped wood. He swung off balance. I swatted at his knife hand and kicked him in the kidneys and the *cojones*.

He clipped the closet door. I clotheslined him and claimed his knife off the floor. I clamped down on his neck and kicked out his legs and laid him out on the linoleum.

I pinned him prone and swicked sweat beads off his beak with my blade. I said, "Sing, shitbird."

He coughed and caught some breath. He hemmed, hawed, and

hummed in hyperventilation. He stopped and stared at me. He got hip to the hard hophead hate I had for him and put it all out prestissimo.

"It all went down today. You tipped off Ben to my operation, which he'd heard rumors about for years. Ben told me you'd ratted me out, but why blow a potentially sweet partnership when we could work breakaway-bedroom jobs and snag some big people? I wanted to put some hurt on Rock, and Ben and I both wanted to nail you for all the gay folk you've messed with."

I leaned in laceratingly low. "So this was a scandal squeeze on the Rock. Pay, or see yourself in *Whisper*."

The sweaty swish said, "Yes." I said, "How much were you going to squeeze him for?" The sweaty swish said, "Twenty-five G's."

I leaned in lower and laughed. "Rock doesn't have it. I heard he took a bath on a real estate deal."

The sweaty swish swung a sweet smile at me. "Then look for the Rock on the cover of the June 1958 issue of *Whisper*."

WHISPER WINS WICKED WAR OF WORDS! THE HUSH-HUSH HEGE-MONY WIPED OUT WITH A WHIMPER!

I blinked. The sweaty swish blindsided me blindingly fast.

He landed a left on my lips. He ratched a right to my chin. A knee bit my balls and bounced me backward.

The sweaty swish swung to his feet. I flattened myself to the floor, grabbed his two fat Florsheims and watched him fly back where he'd been. He landed on linoleum, lurched upright, and laughed. I lobbed my knife and lanced him in the larynx.

4

I punked out and panicked. I left the sweaty swish larynx-lashed and laid out in lurid state. I ran from the hellacious homo-cide.

I popped up to my pad off Pico. I saw a pack of pachucos parked outside. Mean Mexicans in mohair shirts and mohawk haircuts. Machismo-mangled minions. Don Jordan's homicidal *hermanos*.

I hauled to the *Hush-Hush* office. I hit on a horrific scene out of Hieronymus Bosch.

Heaps of *Hush-Hush* dirt files tossed and torched to Cinder City. Scandal skinny scorched and dumped into dust piles. Art sheets shivved and shorn to shit. Type trays trashed and chairs chopped into chop suey.

My crew:

Bruised, contused, confused, and ripped from a raid on Dave Dockweiler's dope stash.

Dawn.

I dashed back to Delores's Drive-In and dipped by at a safe distance. I drove one-handed and drilled the dive with my Bausch binoculars.

Cops—a bevy of bulls from the Beverly Hills PD. Two guys swinging the sweaty swish onto a sheet-shrouded stretcher. A biiiig bull bracing Ben Luboff—nellyingly nervous and limp-wristedly lily-white now. Shit shaking inside the shack—drones dripping print powder on the symbiotically symbolic closed closet door. Checking it out: Chief Clinton Anderson.

I fought a fit of foul fucking fear: I fondled that door and forgot to wipe my prints.

I buzzed by the BHPD Building. By the back door: two bulls and Buddy "Bug King" Berkow. Buddy looked beat on. I knew the bulls had bopped him with beaver-tail saps.

I bombed my Buick out of Beverly Hills. I ran my radio for random newscasts. KMPC coughed up crap on Croatian commies and switched to a swift bit on the sweaty swish.

A commentator called it a suicide. Clinton Anderson confirmed the call conclusively.

I was prespiringly perplexed and pulsatingly puzzled. I sent up guarded thanx to my guardian angel and dipped the dial to the BHPD band.

"All BHPD units only, APB on Daniel Douglas Getchell, G-E-T-C-H-E-L-L, white male, 28, 6'1", 180, brown and brown, driving a 1953 Buick Skylark, license G-B-D, 882. Be advised, BHPD units only, approach and bring to station."

What?—a pristinely private bulletin to bag me. A BHPD exclusive—to swing with the sweaty swish "suicide."

I felt bad boogie bopping my way. I bombed to Burbank and breezed by Brad's Auto Dump. I boosted fresh plates off an old Oldsmobile and placed them over my plates. I plowed back to L.A. and mainlined myself to the L.A. *Times* morgue.

I felt intertwined intrigues interdicting me. I played a *Hush-Hush* hunch and read reports on recent Beverly Hills burglaries.

Six—slickly slotted from late '57 to last week. Ulceratingly unsolved. Salivatingly similar stats: bedroom boosts while Mama and Papa went out to separate parties. Large losses and no standard talk of stakeouts to bag the B&E bad boys.

Bad BHPD boogie bopping my way? Twisted twirls and circles circumscribing me—

I popped to a pay phone and called Steve Crane. I told him to light out to the Luau lickety-split.

I beelined to Bedford Drive in Beverly Hills. I Bausch & Lomb'd Lana Turner's backyard. I saw Johnny Stompanato jump on Lana and lash out with limitlessly lewd language. Lana lashed back. She julienned Johnny with jive on his jilt-happy gigolo ways. She spritzed spite. She shot shit at him shamelessly. She pounced on his pint-sized penis and his wicked welterweight dupe Don Jordan. She called him a guinea gangster and said he poured the pork to her Mexican maid with his poquito pee-pee. She said he pandered and pimped her and got her gussied up in her own Givenchy gown.

Some show. A bracing breakfast bash on beautiful Bedford. Dig the all-star audience, perched on their porches with pancakes and poached eggs:

Dino, Duke Wayne, Walt Disney, wolfing Wheaties. That white-haired wimp on *The Webster Webfoot Show*.

Steve Crane said, "So I'm letting Don Jordan run girls out of here. So Yolanda Paez brings me back the latest on Lana and Johnny. So what? You want to write the story up, great. But it's the last you'll ever peep out of my peepholes."

The Luau was listlessly still. Steve opened up early to meet me. My meth jolt was melting down. I mixed a mammoth martini to remagnetize it.

"I think Johnny crashed Jordan's whore racket and lured Yolanda into it. And I think the girls are the advance team for a burglary angle that Johnny and Jordan are working."

Steve stirred his planter's punch and braced his back into the bar. "I'm sure there's lots of angles in this thing. Yolanda told me the girls are hooking so they can bring their families up from Mexico and that Jordan will smuggle them across the border, get them kitchen jobs, and take a cut of their pay. I can't complain. He's promised me three dishwashers off his next run."

I said, "Don's a fucking sweetheart."

"Yeah, and he may be the next welterweight champ. I heard he's fighting Honeybear Akins in the fall."

"And Mickey Cohen's got a piece of his contract."

"Right, which is not exactly a news flash."

"Does Mickey have some truck with Don?"

"He can calm him down and get him to call off some of his crazier stunts. Why?"

I gulped Gilbey's and Vermouth. "Nothing, but let me run some names by you. Jack Hanson, Chick Nadell, James B. Harris, Ted Jaffe, Russ Pearce—"

Steve stopped me. "All Luau regulars, all men with big fucking money."

I said, "All burglary victims that Don and Johnny's girls picked up here, all married men too embarrassed to cop to the fact that they let whores into their pads and got B&E'd as a result."

Steve said, "Jesus fucking Christ." I said, "No—Daniel Douglas Getchell. And listen—Johnny and Don are operating a bit too freely in Beverly Hills. Can you throw some light on that?"

Steve drained his drink and munched a Maraschino cherry. "Clinton Anderson's got a regular john thing going with Yolanda. He met her here, and she told me that Johnny knows all about it."

Circling circles. Puzzle pieces popping into place.

Chief Anderson chewed up Ben Luboff at Delores's Drive-In. Ben blew the word: He'd dished me dirt on Don Jordan's doings. The Chief charged him to silence. The print pros took my prints off the closet door. The Chief chewed things over and decided not to swear out a warrant on the sweaty swish homo-cide. The Chief wanted to check me out up close and clip me—I might be *Hush-Hush* hip to his yen for Yolanda. I might make him as a Mexican whoremonger and Stompanato stooge.

Steve made himself a massive mai-tai. He said, "Lana, it was so gooooooooood with you, baby."

I said, "Call Yolanda. Tell her I can get her a permanent green card, if she beds a guy who doesn't like girls."

I was *Hush-Hush* hot. I was warrant-wanted and baited by a BHPD bounty. I traded my boss Buick for a busboy's boogied-out wheels. A real congo coach: coon maroon paint matched to matted mink seats. I left the Luau in lieu of a new hideout hut.

I rocked up to the Rock's pad on Roscomare Road and rang the bell. Rock opened up—regal and righteously razzed off in a royal blue kimono. I caught sight of a kimono-clad cutie behind him—a pretty punk pouting into page two of today's paper.

Rock ripped into me. "You're getting bold, Danny. I usually find you going through my garbage or trying to crawl in my bedroom window."

The playmate flipped me the finger. I blew him a bitchy kiss and latched a look on his *Herald-Express*. Wow! A sharp shot of the sweaty swish sheet-shrouded and dead.

Rock reripped me. "An old friend of mine killed himself last night, and I'm in no mood to fuck around with a lowlife like you."

I deflated his diatribe. "I'm moving in with you. You're going to hide me out, so I can fuck Ben Luboff for fucking me, and fuck him for fucking you with that kid you fucked at the Fine Arts last night."

Rock rocked, rolled, listed, lurched, and landed in my arms.

I moved in. I moved out of my Methedrine mode with Miltown and Macallan scotch. I made machinations to save myself and rescue the Rock.

I called Mickey Cohen. I tipped him to Candy Barr's barrage of shit behind his back and begged him to call off Don Jordan. Mickey tossed a tantrum and told me he'd try. I called in a cautiously coded note to Clinton Anderson. I told the Chief's chief chump to check this: I chomp at the chance to be the Chief's chief informant—and I need to stay alluringly alive. Let's talk later— I've got lots of lovely dirt to drop on the BHPD.

Steve Crane did his duty and duped Yolanda Paez into my plan to play out here at Rock's playpen. Said plan: to plant Yolanda and Rock in the sack and sock in a prank prowler call to my plant with the LAPD. The plant plants calls to his private press contacts— prowler prowls at Rock's Roscomare rancho right now! Black-and-whites bomb to Bel-Air! Reporters run to Rock's ranch! I fire shots out a back bedroom! Cops kick the door in and find Rock and his Mex mama fucking feverishly! Reporters find them and flood them with flashbulb flares! I sell my pre-shot sex shots to Randy Rothstein at *Rave* and Terry Tompkins at *Tattle*. Ben Luboff gets skinned alive and scooped by the scoop of the scopophiliac century: ROCK HUDSON IS STRAIGHT!

I yanked Yolanda to the playpen and played her through rehearsals with the richly reluctant Rock. The Rock's live-in lover took it all horrifically hard. He drank himself into dramatic hysterics and hurled hate hexes at me in a slithery and scintillating silence. I had constellated his self-contempt and crisply crystallized it. He hated himself for his love for hunky hound dog Hudson. He'd sweated the sweaty swish story out of the Rock. Rock's call-boy carousing blistered and blackened his heart. He was afraid that Rock would renounce his rump-happy ways with a real revisionistic yen for Yolanda. He blamed all this multiplied mishigaas dead on me.

Rock promised to drop some graft gelt and glom Yolanda a green card. Yolanda laid out some lurid Lana-Johnny tales of late. Lana and Johnny were wrapped in a ripe roundelay of sex and self-hatred. Brazen brawls and licentious language. Lana was ready to cut the cord and juke Johnny out of her life. Yolanda said she'd pay prime pop to liberate her love letters. I called Lana and laid out a deal. I said I'd latch onto the letters. She said she'd lure Johnny to her lair and call Yolanda at Rock's rancho. I'd run to Johnny's pad and pounce on her packet of purple prose then.

I set the date for the prowler-prowl press gig: 4/4/58.

Good Friday. A good day to crucify and crush the rumor that Rock ran the Greek way. A good way to resurrect him and hail him as heterosexual.

We waited. We worried details. Rock and I belted bonded bourbon and bullshitted our way down to D-Day.

Rock psyched me out and psychoanalyzed me. I told him about my chickenshit childhood in Chillicothe, Ohio. I told him how my meshugenah mom mistreated me. She only let me read one book: a thick thesaurus. Rock bestowed a bourbon-bombed benediction on me. I told him that *Hush-Hush* would always run and rag him as a raging pussy hound. I think we might have hugged once—but don't tell anyone.

8:10 P.M., Friday, 4/4/58. The lilac-colored carpet on Rock's living-room floor.

Rock jumped out of his jockey shorts. Yolanda yanked off her dress and stamped herself with the stations of the cross. I bored my eyes in on her and buzzed the fuzz.

My cop buddy caught the call. "Los Angeles Police Department. Sergeant Helgeland speaking."

I said, "Prowler at 841 Roscomare, Bel-Air. Shots fired." I hung up, hauled upstairs, and smoked two Smith & Wesson rounds out a rear window. I heard the live-in lover boohoo and beat his fists on the bed he bounced on with the Rock. I bounced back downstairs and went big-time bug-eyed.

It was supposed to be a faux-fuck. It wildly and willfully wasn't. Rock had Yolanda priapically pinioned. She had her eyes shut. She couldn't catch Rock surreptitiously centered on a male-centerfold spread.

The phone rang. Yolanda yelped and rocked off of Rock. She said, "It is Good Friday. I have a premonition." She pounced on the phone. I perched by the earpiece and heard what she heard—hissingly *Hush-Hush*.

"Johnny . . . hitting me . . . I'm so afraid. . . ."

Yolanda wrapped herself in Rock's robe and ran out the door. She ran to Rock's lavender Lincoln and raised rubber. I ran out and tailed her in my coon coach. We passed a big bevy of black-and-whites rolling toward Rock's rancho.

We bombed to Bedford Drive in Beverly Hills. We lashed into Lana Turner's house sixteen seconds apart. We bombed up to an upstairs bedroom. I froze in the doorway and caught a frightful freeze-frame frisson:

Lana—terrified, tear streaked. A teenage girl—shiny eyed, in shock, and scared shitless. Johnny Stompanato staring at the knife Yolanda just jammed in him.

That's the real story: off the record, on the Q.T. and very Hush-Hush.

I latched onto Lana's letters late that night. I leaked two to Ben Luboff and bought Rock back into the closet. I closed the closet door on Ben's big toe. I told him to clear me with Clinton Anderson or I'd clip him for that sweet smack he swung on the sweaty swish.

He capitulated and kowtowed and called me back. He passed me a cautiously codified Anderson aside.

I know where you were Good Friday. Y.P. going south. Let's go with the public version.

A deal went down behind BHPD doors. Anderson could not afford to yank Yolanda and push her public and stamp her for the Stompanato snuff. The Chief chiseled out a deal and chilled himself out of trouble and chipped Cheryl Crane into a chump child charge. Lana let it go down. Anderson addressed her with a big bag of dirt he took from Terry Tompkins at Tattle. *Lana liked to lez with Lila Lee once in a soft sapphic moon. Terry had a pack of Polaroids.*

Don Jordan decided to let me live. He decisioned Honeybear Akins and wore the welterweight crown for fifteen fat months. Benny "Kid" Paret mugged him and took his title in May 1960. Some male-

factors mugged him for real and murdered his mulatto ass in the mid-'90s.

Yolanda moved back to Mexico. Hollywood had its hooks in her. She transcended the tragedies of her life and triumphed as a snuff-film auteur.

Steve Crane crapped out in '85. Those lavish Luau liquor libations lopped out his liver.

The live-in lover left the Rock for Liberace. He maliciously maintained that I turned Rock straight—despite a massive mountain of definitive data that conclusively contradicted him. Rock and I remained friends. I pressed his preposterous straight credentials in Hush-Hush and herded him to a herbalist when I heard he had AIDS. Potent potions prolonged Rock's life for a small parcel of time. My current prognosis is presumably much better.

I want to LIVE. I want to lay out the scopophiliac scope of my life in a NON—mea culpa manner. I want to slap myself in serial form all over GQ. I've got an artful array of dirt on Art Cooper—the editor-in-chief. I've extorted him into publishing this piece. I've got dirt to illegitimize Ilena Silverman—Art's most artful editor. They'll print what I tell them to.

I talked to my doctors today. My red-blood count is oscillating optimistically up. I might make it to the moment that they dig up and discover a cure.

The gonif three gurneys down is still staring at me. He's looking more and more familiar. He's tripping out of the tableaux that I just tantalizingly tattled. I've got him on the tip of my tongue.

Right there. Right—

The Rock's lachrymose live-in lover. The cuckolded kid who cursed me back in—

He made me make him. He made a geriatric jump in my direction. He's got a hypodermic full of hyper-hazy, health-hazarding shit. He wants to reinfect me and get his revenge on the Rock.

I grabbed the sharp shiv shoved under my bed.

September 1998

TIJUANA, MON AMOUR

I lashed the live-in lover and left him for dead. A night nurse noted his absence and noticed his knees nudged under my bed. She hauled him out. She hydrated him. She tricked up a transfusion and blasted him with black-market blood.

She saved his life. She convinced a kangaroo court to convict me of Assault on an AIDS Ward. She trumped up a tribunal and jerry-rigged a jury. She found five fags and fed them facts on my fag-fragging Hush-Hush heyday. They banished me to a basement stuffed with stacks of old newspapers.

Doctors dip by and drizzle my IV drip. Pill pushers pump me with potions. A homophobic herbalist hops by and hails me as his heterosexual hero. I regale him with riotous riffs on scandal scores and outrageous outings. We ponder my plight as a fag-fragger plowed with the HIV plague.

I mope most mornings and meander most afternoons. I drag my IV drip and stumble. I study the stacks of old newspapers and notice my name now and then. I bop back to better times. I relive my reign as a nihilist knight and dream draconian.

Los Angeles Herald-Express, June 3, 1955:

MONAHAN KILLERS EXECUTED
AT SAN QUENTIN·

At 10:00 this morning, Barbara Graham, John "Jack" Santo, and Emmett Perkins, the convicted slayers of Burbank widow Mabel Monahan, went to their deaths in the gas chamber at San Quentin State Prison.

The executions capped a frantic series of appeals and phone calls to Governor Goodwin J. Knight. Governor Knight rejected last-minute pleas to save the lives of the convicted killers and sent them to their deaths for the 1953 murder. Santo wept and squealed as he was dragged to the gas chamber. Perkins and Miss Graham submitted to their punishment stoically. Miss Graham asserted her innocence a few moments before she was put to death. Los Angeles County Prosecutor J. Miller Leavy, who successfully tried the case, called her statement "poppy-cock. Barbara Graham was just as guilty as her murderous cohorts, and she was justly punished for her grievous transgression."

On the evening of March 9, 1953, Santo, Perkins, Miss Graham, and two men named John True and Baxter Shorter broke into Mabel Monahan's house, convinced that she was harboring $100,000 belonging to a gambler nephew. True and Shorter looked on in horror as Perkins, Santo, and Miss Graham pistol-whipped Mrs. Monahan in an effort to get her to reveal the location of the money. Mrs. Monahan told them that there was no cache of money, a statement which was proven to be true. Enraged, Santo, Perkins, and Miss Graham beat Mrs. Monahan to death.

John True voluntarily surrendered and turned state's evidence. Baxter Shorter disappeared before Santo, Perkins, and Miss Graham were apprehended. It is assumed that Santo and Perkins killed him to ensure his silence.

Santo and Perkins were suspected of having committed several other robbery-murders in northern California, dating back to 1951. Miss Graham was a narcotics addict and former prostitute. Her good looks and steadfast protestations of her innocence gained her a sympathetic audience among the general public and a small sector of the press. Before Miss Graham, Santo and Perkins's trial, rumors of police-DA's Office "dirty tricks" aimed at finagling a confession from Miss Graham surfaced. Deputy DA Leavy called the rumors "Poppy-cock. Every attempt that the DA's Office and members of the Los Angeles and Beverly Hills Police Departments made in order to get Miss Graham to recant her preposterous allegations of innocence were entirely legal and aboveboard."

The bodies of the three convicted killers will be shipped to undisclosed locations for burial.

LOS ANGELES MIRROR, DECEMBER 17, 1955:

PAYOLA PROBE IN WORKS
HEADED FOR GRAND JURY?

A confidential source within the Los Angeles District Attorney's Office told *Mirror* reporters that members of the Beverly Hills and Los Angeles Police Departments, along with the Los Angeles County Sheriff's Office, are conducting a probe into "Payola": The practice of bribing radio announcers, or "disc jockeys," into giving certain recordings preferential amounts of playing time on their programs.

The probe will allegedly focus on KMPC disc jockey Flash Flood and his treatment of Linda Lansing's current 45-RPM single, "Baby, It's Cold Inside." Flood (the former Arthur John Beauchamp) has been playing the novelty song at least sixteen times a day since the record was released on October 11. When asked to comment on this, Flood told a *Mirror* reporter: "What can I say? I dig the side, and I dig Linda Lansing, and nobody's paid me to dig either one. And I dig all the publicity I've been getting, because it's boosted my ratings way up, but I don't dig all the heavy treatment I've been getting from the fuzz, although I do dig all the heavy names that are getting caught up in this thing."

Linda Lansing (the former Hilda Claire Wassmansdorff) is the look-alike younger sister of actress Joi Lansing (the former Joyce Wassmansdorff), costar of *The French Line* and *Son of Sinbad*. "Baby, It's Cold Inside" was Miss Lansing's debut recording, and it was written for her by acclaimed songsmith Sammy Cahn. Miss Lansing is chiefly known as the model and pitchwoman for Teitelbaum Furs in Beverly Hills, and her "gimmick" is performing advertisement jingles, fur-clad, on Tom Duggan's weekly gabfest on Channel 13. She recently appeared as a singer at the Igloo Club in Long Beach and the Trianon Bowling Alley lounge in South Gate, but both engagements were considered unsuccessful. Flash Flood told the *Mirror*: "I dug Linda's act at both venues. I dig the way she sells a song, and I dig it that she wears short fur coats and nothing else as her trademark. Frankly, I dig Linda the most, but that doesn't mean I took payola to spin her side."

The Los Angeles District Attorney's Office does think that someone has paid Flood to promote "Baby, It's Cold Inside." Prosecutor J. Miller Leavy told the *Mirror*; "We think we're dealing with payola, pure and simple, and several police agencies are looking into it for us." Sergeant Robert Duhamel of the Beverly Hills Police Department confirmed Deputy DA Leavy's statement.

"Where there's smoke, there's fire," Duhamel told the *Mirror*. "And our investigation is turning up some prominent people."

Duhamel refused to comment on which "prominent people." The *Mirror* went to Danny Getchell, editor in chief and head writer for the notorious scandal magazine *Hush-Hush*. Getchell claimed that his piece in the December issue, "Payola Pantheon! Sex-Sational Sinatra and Luscious Linda Lansing Linked!" sparked Deputy DA Leavy's probe. Getchell told the *Mirror*: "I got a tip that Frank Sinatra was paying Flash Flood to promote Linda Lansing's song, and I confirmed that tip to my satisfaction and wrote it up in the December issue. That's all I'll say. I'll never feed your newspaper any hot leads that I could publish in my magazine. You can't blame me for that, can you?"

Deputy DA Leavy and Sergeant Duhamel would not comment on Mr. Getchell's assertions. Frank Sinatra and Linda Lansing could not be reached for comment. Flash Flood told the *Mirror:* "I don't dig Danny Getchell. He's a parasite passing himself off as a journalist. I dig Sinatra and I dig Linda Lansing. And dig this: I think Skip Towne (a rival disc jockey and the former Sol Irving Moskowitz) tipped off Getchell to louse up my career. Payola, schmayola. What we've got here is freedom of speech run amok. You can dig that, can't you?"

Skip Towne could not be reached for comment. Danny Getchell told the *Mirror:* "I stand by my piece in *Hush-Hush,* and I condemn Flash Flood's accusations as libelous and communistic. Freedom of speech should always serve as a search for the truth, and the truth is my moral mandate."

1.

Sin-sational Sinatra:

A macho-maimed mama's boy and pussy-whipped putz. A punk with a pack of pit dogs to rough up recidivistic reporters.

Skip Towne skimmed me the skinny: Frank flipped Flash Flood five grand to flip that song and hitch it up the Hit Parade. Impishly implied: Linda Lansing lanced Frank's libido and pulled him around by the pud. Payola payoffs and poontang—perennial poop for *Hush-Hush.*

Sinatra sent me a nice note:

"Danny, how could you? The Pacific Dining Car parking lot, 10:00 A.M. Thursday. You know it will go worse if I have to send the boys out to find you."

The Boys:

Freelance freaks out of Frisco. Greaseballs who grovel and suck up to Sinatra. Discipline dispensers hot to hurl some hurt and rack up ringside seats for Frank's next stand at the Statler.

Frank hates *Hush-Hush*. *Hush-Hush* hates him. I published a piece on his private doc and his prick-enlargement procedure. His pit dogs pounced on my Packard and blew it up on publication day.

"10:00 A.M., Thursday."

I deconstructed my dilemma. I contemplated compliance and concocted countermeasures. I strategized. I stripped the strait I was in down to strict essentials. I decided to frame Frank in the name of free speech.

8:30 A.M., Thursday, 12/21/55.

I bopped by Ben Hong's herb hut in Chinatown. I bought a bushel of Belladona Bulbs and a mound of man-eating Ma Huang. *Hush-Hush* pushes panaceas and hopped-up health highballs to hipsters and high-school kids. We pitch potency pills and cancer cures on our back pages and ship the shit out of a shack behind the Shangri-Lodge Motel. It's legal and lethal in the long run. A loyal league of losers laps it up. Belmont High hopheads buy our Bitter Burdock Buds in bulk and bounce off to Cloud 9 in class.

I needed to nail a big bag of boo. Ben Hong heard me out. He said Bob Mitchum was moving Maryjane to move out of debt with the Mob. I buzzed Bob and blitzed him with a bit of blackmail bait: that bleached blonde who blew you in the Hialeah bleachers was really a high-class drag queen. Bob stuttered, sputtered, and spat out, "What do you want?" I said, "Drop some stuff on me."

Bob kowtowed and consented. I popped out to his pad in Pacific Palisades and glommed a glassine-wrapped glob of righteously resinous reefer. I stoked up a stick in my Studebaker and stood on the gas. I mainlined my way downtown.

I flew like a flipped-out flamingo. I flapped my wings and wafted back to earth on West 6th. I popped by the Pacific Dining Car parking lot.

I slipped by in slow motion. I slid my eyes into slits. I reconnoitered—reefer wracked and wrapped in a marijuana mushroom cloud.

I saw sin-sational Sinatra sipping a midmorning martini. He was lounging by a lilac Lincoln. Two lethal-looking lapdogs were perched on a Pontiac Coupe. They laughed and lapped up every line Sinatra launched their way. They were maladroit mastiffs on a mission to maul for their master. Their snouts were snagged and snared cloyingly close to his ass.

The parking lot was packed. The Pontiac was penned between a Buick and a boss Bonneville. I could undulate in and out unseen.

I bipped down the block. I stashed my Studebaker off the street and bebopped back on foot. Sinatra had his goons in stammering stitches. Stale stuff: the story of Come-San-Chin, the Chinese cocksucker.

They didn't see me. I dipped down and duck-walked into the lot. I popped up to the Pontiac and whipped my bag of boo in a wind-wing.

I whizzed out of the lot. I winged down the street and wiggled into a phone booth. I dipped a dime in the slot and slid a call to Sergeant John O'Grady.

O'Grady:

Grandstanding and greedy. A gratuitous need to grab grasshoppers and hurl himself into the headlines. He popped Art Pepper for pot and bagged Bob Mitchum on a boo bounce back in '48. He hauled in Hedda Hopper's hophead son just last week.

He picked up. "Narcotics, O'Grady."

I said, "Getchell, bearing gifts."

"I'm listening. You've got three seconds to catch my attention."

I said, "The Pacific Dining Car parking lot. Frank Sinatra's goons and an ounce of shit on the floorboard of a green Pontiac."

"When?"

"*Now.*"

"Is Sinatra there?"

"You can't miss him. He's the skinny guy with the voice."

. . .

I loped back to the lot and breezed up brazen. Sinatra saw me. The lapdogs licked their lips. I saw a big guy in the backseat of the lilac Lincoln.

Sinatra slid on slick black sap gloves. They were wickedly weighted with dollops of double-ought buck. They packed a well-known wallop.

The lapdogs leered at me. A mean-looking Mexican busboy sidled out a side door. He balanced a monster martini on a mono-grammed tray.

The lapdogs laughed at me. The Mex marched up and made mealy-mouthed "Si, Señor" sounds. Sinatra popped his patent-leather fingers. The Mex made a suck-ass sound and sunk down submissive. Sinatra snapped his fingers and snared the martini.

He said, "You're prompt." He looked at his lapdogs. He said, "He's prompt, Boys." The lapdogs laughed. The Mex sneered and snickered. I snuck a look at the Lincoln. The big guy in the back-seat kept his back to me.

I popped up to the Pontiac coupe. I said, "How's tricks, Frank? Your mother still doing her act with the mule?"

Sinatra sizzled and simmered. Steam stormed out his ears and stung me. He made mincy fists. His martini glass shot into shrap-nel shards.

The lapdogs got lanced. The Mex got minor-league mangled. They shook shards off their shirts and popped puzzled eyes at Il Padrone. The punk patriarch palpitated and pissed in his pants. Dig the dip on those gorgeous gabardines!

I said, "I talked to Ava, Frank. She said you were hung like a cashew. I'm running it on the March cover. 'Sexy Songster Packs Pint-Sized Pecker, Gorgeous Gardner Sez.'"

Sinatra fumed and fueled himself into a fugue state. He stut-tered, stammered, slobbered, slathered, and came off catatonic. His heart hammered. Buttons shot off his shirt and sheared me in the shins.

The lapdogs lurched at me. The Mex made machismo-like motions. An LAPD narc ark arced into the lot.

Everybody froze—frustrated and fright-fraught.

John O'Grady jumped out. His paunchy partner piled out and paused by the passenger door. The lapdogs listed and almost landed in my lap. Glare glowed and shimmered off their shoulder-holster straps.

Badges—a shiny Sheriff's shield and a BHPD button.

O'Grady said, "LAPD. Nobody move. Nobody say a fucking word."

I looked at the lilac Lincoln. I made the big boy in the back. Sergeant Bob Duhamel—Beverly Hills PD.

A payola prober propped up in a prime suspect's sled.

?????

The paunchy partner popped over to the Pontiac. He popped the passenger door and picked up the bag of boo. O'Grady said, "Who's this belong to?"

Sinatra went knock-kneed and passed another passel of piss.

The Mex moaned mumbo jumbo and muttered, *"Mierda, mierda."*

The lapdogs whipped their coats wide. Sun shafts shot off their shields.

O'Grady ogled them. His eyes shot shield to shield. He said, "Tell me what we've got here, and make it convincing. And tell me why Frank Sinatra just wet his pants."

The lapdogs lowered their eyes. I felt their brainwaves broiling. They brought their eyes up bright and brutally bristling. They slung them slow at the Mex.

Lapdog #1 said, "We're working an inter-agency gig. Mr. Sinatra's gotten some death threats because of that payola thing, and we're bodyguarding him."

Lapdog #2 said, "Uh . . . yeah, and Pancho there tried to sell Mr. Sinatra some weed, but Mr. Sinatra said no, so Pancho planted the shit in my car, 'cause . . . uh . . . he thought it was Mr. Sinatra's car."

Pancho popped puddles of sweat. It poured off his pompadour. He stood there stunned and stamped himself with the Stations of the Cross. He dribbled and drizzled sweat. He dropped his tray. It popped to the pavement pulse-poundingly LOUD. Instantaneous instinct: four cops reached for their revolvers and ripped off short-range shots.

They pincushioned Pancho and poured through him. They powderburned him and poleaxed him and parted his pompadour down to his palate. Bullets bounced off his bones and belt buckle and shot back at the shooters. Richochets ripped the paunchy partner and notched his nose off his face. I cringed, crawled, crapped my pants, and ran—

2

I stashed my Studebaker at a storage garage. I walked to Wilshire and Western and hot-wired a Hudson Hornet straight off the street. I had to hide out. I watched the cops whack that wetback and wipe out one of their own. I spawned a spectacular fuckup and got a cop killed. I mandated my own murder—and maybe much more.

The fuzz would fuck me to cover up their snuff snafu. Sinatra would seek to silence me and humble *Hush-Hush*. Payola played in and percolated at the periphery.

I humped my Hudson Hornet to Hollywood. I hauled by Hal's Auto Dump and traded plates with a Triumph TR2. I tripped through Trancas Canyon and tricked a path through the trouble I was in.

Skip Towne shot me the shit on Flash Flood. I flaunted it in *Hush-Hush*. My prize prose prompted the payola probe and pissed off priapic Sinatra.

Sinful Sinatra sought the scent of sex citywide. His loyal lap-dogs doubled as blasphemous bloodhounds. They sniffed for snatch and snagged willing wenches out of waitress gigs and what-have-you. They latched onto Linda Lansing at a lezbo cathouse.

Luscious Linda—Joi Lansing's curvy kid sister. Lounge Lizard Linda—a low-rent lollapalooza living off lesbian love. A merce-nary mama now in moonlight mode in mink-coat TV ads.

Linda switch-hit and once swung with lip-smacking lez Lizabeth Scott. Late-breaking lowdown: Liz still torched for their torrid love. Linda's pay-for-play delight: delirious and delectable 3-ways. The *latest* late-breaking lowdown:

Sex-sational Sinatra—the thrill-seeking Three-Way King. He finds Linda Lansing and lures her to his lair. She throws him into the throes of three-way ecstasy. Mama mia—one man and two women waxing way out and wicked! Linda lassos Frank's libido and lays down the law: no more triad tricks until you make me a star! The King cons Sammy Cahn and has him hatch "Baby, It's Cold Inside." The tune tantalizes and titillates and ties in to Teitelbaum Furs. The King corners Flash Flood and flimflams him and flips him a flotilla of cash. Flash is floored. He flips a tepid tune and leads Linda Lansing into the Payola Pantheon.

Skip Towne skimmed me that scandal skank. It buttressed a boss back story—but left me with big questions:

Bob Duhamel—BHPD. A cop co-opted to the payola probe. His BHPD buddy and some Sheriff's shill. Three cops caught up in shady and shameful shit with shaky Frank Sinatra.

?????

I flew by Flash Flood's flat in Flintridge. Fuck—Flood's Fleetwood sedan and a fleet of cop cars framed out front.

Look—the lapdogs last seen popping shots at Pancho the Piñata. Beside them—Bob Duhamel, BHPD.

Call it a Cop Conspiracy. Cop to the cost of the contretemps you created. Crawl out of the crap crashing down on you and live to launch libel again.

I chanted that malevolent mantra. I charted a course to charm, cheat, chisel, and THRIVE.

Laura's Little Log Cabin:

A Mecca for mannish muff-munchers and fawnlike femmes as fair game. A rustic rendezvous for rapacious diesel dykes.

Loin-lapping Liz Scott's happy hunting grounds.

I walked in wary. She-wolves shot me shitty looks. My rabid rep preceded me and pried a pack of boss babes off of bar stools. I devastated and decimated the room.

I located Liz. She was waxing weepy into a whiskey sour. I nudged into her naugahyde booth and nabbed some cocktail nuts.

Liz said, "Help yourself. They're free."

I lit a Lucky out of Liz's pack. Liz laughed low and languid.

"You're scum, Danny. You're a tidal wave of karmic filth and dissension. I wouldn't fuck you if I was desperate and you were a beautiful woman."

Liz looked luscious on her last cover shot: LEZBOS LOLL AT LOG CABIN, LAPD TELLS HUSH-HUSH.

I popped a pineapple piece out of her drink and poured it down my parched throat. Liz lit a Lucky and laid a lungful of smoke in my face. I coughed up cocktail nuts and pineapple pulp.

"You're a disease that they haven't invented a name for, Danny. You're lower than cancer."

I tingled. Titillation tickled me. I groaned and grew a hard-on.

I said, "I always thought we might have clicked and had a swinging thing, if you had different predilections."

Liz laughed light and lilting. "On the planet Pluto, baby. Sometime around the twelfth of never, but only if you dressed in drag."

Ooooh, Daddy-o! She was turning me on, tumescent!

I sucked my cigarette down to a cinder. Liz laughed licentious. A jukebox jerked on. Linda Lansing lilted out: "Baby, It's Cold Inside."

Liz lowered her head and laid out a lake of tears. I said, "Linda's headed for shitsville, Sweetie. You know the drill on payola. Sinatra's too big to prosecute, and Flash Flood will turn State's. They'll make it look like Linda paid him to play her song, and she'll take the fall."

Lonely Liz looked at me. Bar light lit up her tear tracks and tributaries. I knew she had a handle on some hot stuff to help me—*very* Hush-Hush.

She winced and wiped her face. She whipped down the rest of her drink and chewed the cherry. She sucked the stem and stared at me. Her orbs sent me into orgasmic orbit.

She said, "You want information on Linda. You'll pay for it if you have to, and you're going to try to convince me that anything

I tell you won't hurt her. You know that I'll give it to you if you're convincing, so be convincing and get out, or I'll send a 300 pound butch with brass knuckles over to kick your ass out of my life."

Astoundingly astute. Breathtaking brevity and bravado.

I said, "I'll plant a piece that you're straight in *Hush-Hush*. I'll leave you alone forever. I'm in trouble with the payola thing myself, and I won't write a fucking word about Linda."

Liz looked me over loooooooooong. She lit another Lucky and licked a loose leaf off her lip.

Oooooh, Daddy-o! Save me from this sapphic siren!

"All right, Danny. One time and one time only. Linda told me she'd put in some innings with Frank, going back to '52. She said she had some dirt on him, and she used it to get him to bribe Flash Flood into playing her song."

The '52 bit bit a big hole in Skip Towne's skinny. He laid Linda and Frank out as a fresh item.

I said, "Where's Linda now?"

Liz said, "I don't know. I saw her a week ago, right after they announced the probe, and she said something about making a run to Tijuana for Al Teitelbaum."

I liberated a Lucky and lit it. Liz lifted a leather key fob and let it list on one long finger.

"2104 Berendo, off of Los Feliz. She was renting the place, and I made duplicates on the sly."

I snared the keys and snapped my fingers. I winked and whistled a whiff of "One for My Baby." Liz laughed loud and let me know I was a loser.

"You're not Frank, Danny, so don't even try. And I wouldn't fuck you if you had a sex change and came out Rita Hayworth."

I looped back to Los Feliz and ran my radio dial en route. Ring-a-ding—a ripe news report.

". . . and here's more on the shootout at the Pacific Dining Car parking lot, which left a marijuana-peddling Mexican busboy and one LAPD officer dead."

Static stung my ears. I ditzed the dial and diminished it. The newsman said, "The busboy was identified as Juan Ramon Pimentel, age 24, an illegal alien. He was the number one supplier of marijuana in the Los Angeles area and was the focus of an interagency investigation involving the LAPD, the Beverly Hills PD, and the Los Angeles County Sheriff's Department. Pimentel was cornered in the parking lot, pulled a gun, and fired at four officers. He killed LAPD Sergeant Richard D. Jackson, was fatally wounded by the officer's return fire, and . . ."

Static browned out the broadcast. I breezed by Brewster's Newsstand on Bronson and bought a *Herald-Express*. Huge headlines: HEROIC COPS IN GUN BATTLE! TWO DEAD!

I pored over the piece. It was officious obfuscation—doggedly dissembled with a profoundly pronounced pro-cop prejudice. Page 2 pix: John O'Grady posed with BHPD bimbo Bob Duhamel and the two police pitdogs.

Jive on the "Joint Police Venture." Delirious demonization: "Dope Kingpin Pimentel." Obviously and ominously omitted in his omnipresence: wicked witness Frank Sinatra.

Two cloyingly close and collusive columns down:

DA TO DROP PAYOLA PROBE.

A dozen desultory lines. A perfunctory paragraph. "Lack of Evidence" and "Deemed Insufficient"—insinuating innuendo in my book. Unconscionably unmentioned: Lewd Linda Lansing and triad trick Sinatra. One paltry pic: Demon DA J. Miller Leavy—leaning into Bad Bob Duhamel. A captivating caption: "Deputy DA Leavy and Sgt. Duhamel also worked together on the celebrated Barbara Graham case."

No mention of ME.

My payola piece prompted the probe. *My* marijuana machinations mandated a massacre. *I* was undeniably uniquitous and ignominiously ignored.

I shivered, shook, and almost shit my pants. My pulse pounded paranoically hard. I'd crusaded for truth in a Christlike fashion and crossed some invisible line. Call me crucifiable. The newspaper neglected to name my name and thus nailed me now for negation. The world wanted me dead. I violated the venal and vindicated their victims. I sodomized silly celebrities and fragged and framed them as frail. I vandalized their vulturelike souls and sold them as soulless on newsstands nationwide. I modeled myself on Mahatma Gandhi and moved beyond that motherfucker in my quixotic quest for the truth. I triumphed over trials that would mash most men to mush. I delivered disillusionment as dystopian dish and entertained, edified, and enlightened. I was a spiritual spearhead—like that spook who sparked the Montgomery Bus Boycott. *Hush-Hush* outhustles the Bible—at least in L.A.

I was the journalistic Jesus about to get justifiably Judas'd.

3

I bought a bottle of bonded bourbon. I bombed myself out of my martyrdom mode and looped by Linda Lansing's lair lickety-split.

I rapidly reconnoitered. I bipped around Berendo and cruised cross streets. I noted no cop cars. I hid my Hudson Hornet behind a hydrangea hedge and popped up to the pad.

It was a mock Moorish mosque in miniature. Minarets, mauve awnings, and mesquite fronds out front. I let myself in. I slipped a light switch, slammed the door, and slid into a slaughterhouse.

The stomach-stinging stench of flayed flesh. Matted hair and maggot mounds on a mauve rug. Blood blips on white walls and windowpanes.

Linda Lansing laid out flat on the floor. Slashed and sliced in a slit-leg gown. Sharp shiv marks and sheared tissue torn out in striated strips. Blonde hair blossomed into a blood slick.

Ten fingertips torn to the tendons and burned to the bone. A hot plate hooked into a wall switch. Scorched skin caught in the coils.

I rocked, rolled, reeled, and retched on the rug. I made myself memorize the murder scene.

Overturned ottomans and sofas stabbed into stuffing. Paintings pulled off walls and cut to confetti. Bookcases bumped to the floor and stomped to a stack of stale sticks.

Bad burns on the body. Scorch-scarred skin. Cigarette circles. A batch of butts blended into a blood pool.

Torment-inducing torture. Infernally inflicted. My inference: the inflictors intended to induce Linda Lansing into laying out something of interest. She rigorously resisted and refused to give IT up. IT was not information. Call IT concealable. The inflictors invaded the house with the intent to find where IT was. They went at it impulsively and impetuously. The implosive implication: IT was still here.

I looked at Linda Lansing. I blew the corpse a kiss. My memory snapped me snapshots of Linda alive and alluring and announced an anomaly. The live Linda ran lithe. The corpse ran reduced Rabelaisian.

I nudged my noggin out of necrophile notions. I bopped to a back bathroom and made for the medicine chest. I pillaged pills and concocted a chemical cocktail.

Sexy Secobarbital and devilish Dexedrine. Miltown to mellow them out. A bracing Bromo-Seltzer to bring the brew to a boil.

I licked up my elixir and chased it with a Chesterfield King. It chugged into me and detonated a depth charge. I deliberately and determinedly deep-sixed the house.

I tore up ten rooms. I upended umpteen underwear drawers. I whipped up wall-to-wall carpets and filleted fine furniture down to fabric debris. I deconstructed daybeds, divans, and doily-draped dressers. I drained drainpipes and cleaned out clothes closets and shivved behind shelves. I beat the basement walls with a baseball bat and bored into a hot little hidey-hole.

Inserted inside:

A packet of pix. Glorious glossies surreptitiously shot in Sinemascope.

Linda Lansing boffing boss butch Barbara Stanwyck. Steamy Stanny—still hot stuff.

Linda loin-locked with Lana Turner. Woo! Woo! Salivatingly sapphic!

Linda tasting tough Tallulah Bankhead. Tallulah—too much!

Linda limb-linked on a lavender bedspread. Buck naked beside Barbara Graham and Al Teitelbaum.

Sinful synergy. Pervasive perversion. A tricky trio trapped on filthy film.

A confounding connection.

A furtive fur merchant. A murder victim and a murderess who graced the green room at San Quentin. A connection to confront: Bob Duhamel did duty on the Barbara Graham case.

I pored over the pix. I stared at them and steamed them up. I dripped drool on Linda Lansing—lezzed out and lithe. A dyke-chotomy: her corpse ran corpulent.

?????

Perched by the pix:

A loose-leaf ledger. Latin names listed in left-hand columns. Five-figure moneymakings mapped to the right.

Martinez, Madragon, Marquez—Mex monickers. Tostado, Trejo, Tarquez—taco-heads all. Pellicar, Peja, P. Pimentel—

Whoa now, wait—

Juan Pimentel—the pincushion/piñata at the parking lot. The make-believe marijuana maven. The bad-luck busboy and scandal scapegoat.

?????

I packed the pix behind some pipes and laid the ledgers under a layer of loose linoleum. I beat feet to the back bedroom and bored through a bunch of books I'd flung to the floor. Va-va-voom—the *Variety Directory* for 1954.

I leafed to the *L*s and found "Lansing, Joi."

"Actress. B. 4/6/28, Salt Lake City."

I leafed to "Lansing, Linda."

"Singer. B. 5/21/30, Salt Lake City."

I looked at the Lansing listings. I perused two publicity pix. They blended blonde. They blurred and blossomed blissfully as near-identical twins.

"Nice stuff. I had the better one, so I should know.'"

A vivid voice—low and lezlike.

My hackles hopped. I hurled myself around and hoped for the best. I hitched eyes with Deputy Dot Rothstein.

Dildo dyke. Sheba the Sheriff's She-Dog at the Women's Jail downtown. A yenta with a yen for young cooze. A Large Marge in a man's suit.

I came on cooooool. "You look good, Dot. You make me wish I was a woman."

Dot shot me a boot to the balls. I belched bile and bounced to my knees. Pain pounded me.

Dot said, "Stay there. I like my women in that position."

I stood up straight and strong. I flipped Dot the finger. She bent it back and bit it to the bone.

Pain:

Lavishly localized. Bopping off my bit bone to my balls. Pillaging my pill-headed haze.

Dot said, "Did you kill her?"

I blotted blood on my blue blazer. "No, did you?"

Dot handed me a hankie. "I loved her, sweet cakes. We had an occasional thing going, and we were making money together."

I hankied up my hurt hand. "How?"

"I was pimping her to some politicians who could do the Sheriff's Department some good."

My pain pianissimoed. The Miltown mix was melting it mellifluously.

Dot said, "She was shaking down Frank Sinatra. She shot him some sex, then threatened to turn him off if he didn't get her song some big play."

Nix, nyet, and no way. Liz Scott shared some shakedown shit with me and laid it out large on Linda. Viably verbatim:

"She'd put in some innings with Frank, going back to '52."/"She had some dirt on him, and she used it."

Dot stared at me—stock still and stoic. "Care to tell me what you were thinking? And what you know about all this?"

I shrugged like I didn't know shit from Shinola. Dot said, "They killed the wrong woman. That's Joi in the living room. I know Linda's body on an intimate level, and that isn't her. Joi always ran chubbier than Linda, and she had a key to the place. And if Linda's smart, which she is, she'll gorge herself on hot fudge sundaes and impersonate her sister until all this blows over."

My synapses snapped to attentive attention. A theory threaded through my head.

Juan Pimentel—the parking lot pincushion/piñata. P. Pimentel—the piñata's padre or partner or hellacious *hermano*? Liz Scott, volubly verbatim: "Linda was making a run to Tijuana for Al Teitelbaum."

Teitelbaum: pornographically portrayed in Linda Lansing's love pix. Tijuana: sinfully situated a beat below the border. Joi Lansing: luridly lashed to linguine by Mexican marauders—bad-boy bandidos who botched their job and bagged the wrong bitch—because they only spoke Spanish.

Dot said, "Your wheels are turning. You're thinking up some kind of angle, and you're wondering where I fit in."

I shot her a shit-eating grin. "I'm wondering what you know about a cop named Bob Duhamel, and a run to T.J. that Linda might be making for Al Teitelbaum."

"Duhamel," ditzed Dot—she dipped her shoulders disingenuously.

"I don't know that cop you mentioned, but I do know that you were there when they took out that spic this morning, and I know that Al T.'s broke, and he's staging a fake fur heist to get some insurance money, and Linda was going to run the furs down to T.J. for him."

My wheels whizzed, shirled, whipped, and—

"Look, Danny. We're both in this, but you're in it *bad*. That said, I have to say that fifty Gs to the right people and some smear jobs in *Hush-Hush* could set you right."

—wiggled like a whacked-out whirlybird.

I said, "Give it to me. Straight, no chaser."

Dot delivered. "Teitelbaum doesn't know who the fake heist guys will be. Linda set the scam up, and all Al knows is the time and date—6:00 P.M. on the twenty-seventh. All you have to do is beat the heist guys to the punch, move the furs to T.J., and bring me the money. Linda will be too busy playing her big sister to fuck with you."

SCANDAL SCRIBE SCRAPS CAREER AND CAREENS INTO CRIME! BOFFO BURGLAR SAYS, "MAKE MINE MINK!" AND MOVES TO MEXICO!

I said, "Who do I dump the furs on?"

Dot said, "The Chief of Police in T.J. His name's Pedro Pimentel."

4

I hid out at a hip hutch in Santa Monica Canyon. I crawled to Crazy Chris Isherwood and begged for a bed.

Christlike Chris shot me shelter at his shitty little Shinto shrine. Crafty Chris issued the invite and predicated it on a promise:

Don't hump me in *Hush-Hush*. Don't spin your spotlight on my homo hijinx. Don't condemn my combination kick-pad/ashram and ridicule the residents. Don't publish that picture of me with a lip lock on Liberace.

I smiled smug. I crossed my heart to Chris and Christ Himself and issued an insincere promise. I hauled in my Hudson Hornet and my hop from Ben Hong's herb hut.

The ashram was a dope den and a lavender lovenest. My rambunctious roommates:

Aldous Huxley—addled on absinthe, pickled on peyote, and looped on a loony Lysol called lysergic acid diethylamide.

Bogie Bogart—battling the Big C with voodoo vows and peach-pit potions.

Oscar Levant—levitatingly lost in laudanum and Lowenbrau lager.

Sammy Davis Jr.—jigaboo-juked for pouring the pork to a white wench who went out with Walter Winchell. Winsomely COONfidential: Winchell sent some wops out to whack Sammy.

Last—but not loin-longingly least:

Three masochism-mauled marines marked for molestation.

Deserters seeking shelter from the Shore Patrol. Prime prey for Creepy Chris.

I moved in and made time to map out my mink misadventure. I lounged around in limbo.

I lapped up laudanum with Levant and got high on hashish with Huxley. Chris crystallized Ben Hong's herbs and cooked up anti-cancer cocktails for Bogie. I watched nightly newscasts and notched nerve-wracking news.

Skip Towne and Flash Flood—flattened by a fly-by-night who flipped a two-ton truck. Flash Flood's Fleetwood: torched to toast in Topanga Canyon. Rival DJs riding *together*? Make that murder in my magazine.

No news on lush Linda Lansing and the Moorish Mosque Massacre. No poop on the payola probe and priapic Sinatra. Call that collective collusion.

I called my cop contacts. I picked up poop on Pedro Pimentel. One baaaad beaner. The taco-phile Tojo of T.J.

He controlled the corrupt cop corps. His cops copped coin off incarcerated inmates run in on random charges. Pedro pried their property loose. He violated their virgin daughters and made them vice vixens at the Va-Va-Voom Club. He kicked their less comely kids into cardboard casas and coerced them to work in his sweatshops. They moonlighted as wistful waifs and charmed chump change out of cheerful gringos.

Pedro Pimentel owned a clap clinic and the Club Diablo—an adoringly adorned adobe hut that housed hermaphrodites and the best burro act in Baja. Pedro Pimentel smuggled smut. Pedro Pimentel pummeled pinkos and castrated Castroites out of Cuba. Pedro Pimental made nice to Nazis named at Nuremburg and assured them asylum.

Pedro Pimentel fenced furs.

My cop contacts dispensed more dish.

Juan Pimentel was Pedro's pedophile brother. Juan bopped out of Baja behind some child-snuff snafu. Pedro put him in touch with Bad Bob Duhamel—BHPD. Bad Bob made Wicked Juan his sneaky snitch. Wicked Juan worked at the Pacific Dining Car—

a front to frame his sniveling snitchwork. Bad Bob went way back with delightful dyke Dot Rothstein. They engaged in an entrapment scheme to screw Barbara Graham—wigged out in the women's jail.

Barbarous Barb was gorgeous gash and one good actress. She maintained that she didn't murder Mabel Monahan. Demon DA Miller Leavy found her fetching. He feared that she'd move the men on the jury to mush. Leavy dished up a plan to discredit her and divvied it out to Dot and Bad Bob.

They went underground. They unearthed some underworld untermenschen and unleashed them on Barbarous Barb. They handed her handy alibis for 3/9/53. She bit and said she'd buy them if they bought her out of the shit. The untermenschen shot her the shaft and strode straight to Miller Leavy. Leavy levied the alibi bit against Barb. It chewed her up and helped him chalk up a convincing conviction.

My cop contacts contradicted Diabolical Dot. She'd dissembled and said she didn't know Duhamel. The Barbarous Barb bit bit my brain and ditzed me to distraction. Did it play in to payola and sin-tillating Sinatra?

The riddle wracked my dope-diddled head. It lanced me as I laid low and lived it up in limbo.

I ran reefer-ripped ripostes with Sammy Davis. Sammy was one sick Sambo. Maryjane made him mean-minded. He ran race riffs like a mau-mau motherfucker. He teed off on ofay oppression and segued to sepia self-hate and slick slavemaster Sinatra.

Annihilating anecdotes:

Frank frags Sammy at a Mob meet in Miami. Sammy sings for made Mafia men. They make him step like Stepin Fetchit and feed him fettuccine with the Cuban kitchen crew. Frank frees Sammy and eggs him into an encore: "No-Count Nigger Me."

Sammy slips the schnitzel to Miss Schlitz Beer at a backstage bash for Sinatra. Sissified Sinatra sincerely thinks that he had first dibs. His chauffeur shanghais Sammy. He shunts him to Sheboygan, Wisconsin, and snouts him into a snowstorm in his snapbrim hat and skintight skivvies.

Sinatra stomps onstage as Sammy creams the crowd at the Crescendo. Sammy blows a bluesy ballad and lights an L&M to look cool. The crowd cracks up. Sinatra signals a waiter. The waiter wings a watermelon up onstage. The crowd craps its pants. Sammy laughs to look like he's loving it. Frank freezes him out and wilts the room with "Willow Weep for Me."

I spritzed my spin on Sinatra. Sammy succumbed to its succulence and sucked up to me. We sulked ourselves silly and sunk into a Sinatra-phobe Abyss.

We hexed him with hellish hate. We shivved him with a Shinto curse that Crazy Chris cooked up. We defaced and dart-boarded all his album covers and ratched the records inside. We worked ourselves into a frenzy—frankly frantic and Francophiliacal. The fragrance of Frankincense froze us—and freed me to act.

I said, "Help me steal some furs and run them down to T.J."

Sammy said, "Yes, Big White Bwana."

I said, "Call Frank. Make like you don't hate him, and put out some peace feelers for me."

Sammy said, "Yes, Sahib."

We surreptitiously surveilled Teitelbaum Furs. We sat in Chris's Chrysler and sunk down to the dash. We wore distinct disguises.

I played a Shinto shaman. Dig it: a multicolored monk's robe and sharp shades to shield my eyes. Sammy posed as a pachuco in peg pants and a cheap cholo chirt.

We restlessly reconnoitered Rodeo Drive. We learned the layout. We laid lazy eyes on the fur shop and watched two lowlifes in a late-model Lincoln loop around it themselves.

They looked larcenous. They looked lizardlike. They loop-the-looped and licked their lips and surveilled every surface in sight.

They surveilled serpentlike. We surveilled them serviceably. They lizard-lunched at Linny's Delicatessen. We noshed knockwurst at the next table and tallied their talk for two days.

The lizards loved liver and onions. They ordered it and ooh-la-la'd and went over their plans plenty loud. They conclusively confirmed Demon Dot: the heist would hatch at 6:00 P.M.—12/27.

We suspended our surveillance on Christmas Eve. Christlike Chris threw a party to praise the Prince of Peace.

Bogie got bombed on his peach-pit potion and peppermint schnapps. He chugalugged it and chanted Chinese chants to beat the Big C. Huxley hooked down hallucinogens. He held forth and heaped judgment on Jesus. He praised that prize prick Pontius Pilate and his "Paranoid Paradigm." It pissed off Oscar Levant. Oscar opted to ossify some "Existential Eggnog." He tossed in herbs, hash hunks, and Hungarian wine. The shit sheared Crazy Chris. He spouted aphorisms and spun around aphrodisiacal. The marines lurched from his libidinous assaults and went AWOL.

Sammy stayed stone sober and steamed over satanic Sinatra. He reissued his old indignities in insistently intimate detail and insisted that I listen. He flogged and flayed his own flesh bare. He catalogued catastrophic cruelties and cringed at his own compliance. He christened his crucifier the "Christmas Anti-Christ" and called him on Chris's phone.

Sammy crawled to the creep. He cradled the phone and crossed himself. He would have waved wolfsbane if he'd had it.

He said, "Frank says he'll meet you. You pick the time and place."

I said, "The motel by the Club Diablo. Midnight on the twenty-seventh."

Sammy mumbled into the mouthpiece. I mused on my moment to meet Satan on his own torrid turf.

5

We went in well armed. We masqueraded as marines and made it a military maneuver.

The marines marked for molestation left some shit at the shrine. We draped ourselves in their dress blues and packed their PX-pilfered pistols. I hid my Hudson Hornet and hot-wired a Vauxhall van. Monster masks made us menacing and marked us as men not to mess with.

I went in as the Wolfman. Sammy crept in as the Creature from the Black Lagoon. We moved our minkmobile into the back lot and barged in the back door.

5:46 P.M.

Fourteen minutes to filch furs and fill up the van. Fourteen minutes to fuck the fur-filchers already assigned to the job.

We monster-minced down a mink-lined hallway. We froze by the freezer vault. Al Teitelbaum latched eyes on us and laughed long and loud.

He howled and heaved for breath. He broke a sweat and swatted his legs. He swayed and pointed to a pile of pelts on the freezer floor.

He hocked into a hanky. He said, "Go, you fershtunkener furmeisters. Go, before I die of a fucking coronary."

Sammy popped the pelts into a large laundry bag. I shot my eyes into the showroom. I scanned scads of sensational sables and choice chinchillas and magnificent minks. Our paltry pile of pelts paled in considered contrast.

Teitelbaum said, "Hit me once, tie me up, and get out of here. Your theatrics are wearing me thin."

I pulled my piece and pistol-whipped him to pulp. I decimated his dentures. Blood dripped on my dress blues.

Teitelbaum tipped into dreamland. I dropped him in the freezer and gagged him with a gorgeous gaggle of furs. Sammy gloated and glared at the ofay oppressor. He muttered mau-mau musings and metamorphosed into the Creature from the Coon Lagoon.

5:51 P.M.

Sammy lugged the laundry bag back to the Vauxhall van. I shifted into overdrive and shot through the shop.

I manhandled minks and moved them out fast. I stole stellar stacks of stoles. I glommed glorious globs of glistening fur and furnished the van tip to tailpipes. I made myself a millionaire in one machination and emancipated Sambofied Sammy.

5:57 P.M.

I lashed up a last stack of stoles. The real robbers ripped through the *front* door—*rápidamente*.

I froze. Sammy froze by the freezer. The real robbers shared a "Shit" look. They shook their eyes around the showroom—shabbily shorn and sacked.

They whipped out Walter PPK's and popped me point-blank. My stack of stoles absorbed their ammo. The Creature from the Coon Lagoon crouched and pulled his piece. Six rounds ripped the real robbers and ratched them into a raccoon-coat rack.

We wrapped the bodies in raccoon and rolled them under a rug. Sammy dug the scene and dubbed it a "Massacre in Mink."

We moved our minkmobile to Mexico—mucho fast. Sammy negrofied Sinatra songs and arced them out a cappella.

He verse-vilified Sinatra and lynched him with licentious lyrics. He sang scatological scat and scoffed at Frank the freewheeling freak. He excoriated and exorcised his ex-slavemaster extemporaneously.

"Fly me to the moon, with my guinea goons, I ejaculate a little quick, some say I come too soon! In other words, hold my gland!"

"It's a quarter to three, all I feel is hate and bad self-pity. So set 'em up, Joe, 'cause Ava left me for a well-hung Negro."

"Come fly with me, come fly, come fly away! We'll abuse some squares in our Vegas lairs and pretend that we're not gay!"

Sammy ripped, rocked, roiled, rolled, and resurrected his nappy-headed niggerhood. We sidled south as psychopathic sidekicks.

We rolled into a rest stop and stripped to our street clothes. We cruised south, crossed the border, and tipped into Tijuana.

Dig:

Sweaty swarms of tattered toddlers tackling tourists and latching onto them leechlike. Syphilitic sailors cliqued up outside clap clinics. Punks peddling pot and peyote plants in plain sight. Vandals vending vibrating dildos and donkey show tix. Starving peons stretched out on the street from stark starvation. Punks picking their pockets and plucking their teeth out with penknives. Hermaphroditic he-shes huddled in haphazard hordes. A chain of chancre-sored chiquitas chipping by a chop suey joint. Spiffy spic cops in natty Nazi jackboots and jet-black outfits on every corner.

Oooooh, Daddy-o! I was digging it all, desensitized!

We dipped by the Club Diablo. Dig the nifty neon sign: a little Lucifer with high horns and a trident-trimmed dick.

11:37 P.M.

We checked into the cheesy Chinchinagua Motel and chatted up the manager. He was one choice cholo. I fed him some chump change and scammed some scalding skinny.

A "Mr. Duhamel" called and confirmed his room reservation. He and his "friend Frank" would be by and bop to their back bungalow by midnight.

I laid a mink coat on the Mex motherfucker. He muttered "Madre mía" and groveled ground-low. Sammy grabbed him and laid down the law: pass us your passkey to the back bungalow and let the chumps check in. Don't mention the boss banditos who just bought you off.

The Mex murmured, "Sí, sí" and passed us a passkey. We bipped to the back bungalow and bopped in unbidden. I wiggled a wall switch. Light leaped on and launched cockroach convoys out of control.

They bug-scuttled, buzzed, and bounced off the bed. They flip-flopped and flew off the floor. They crawled and crunched like ripe Rice Krispies under our feet.

11:48 P.M.

We reloaded our revolvers. Sammy syphoned a syringe full of Lysol-like lysergic acid. I juked out to the van and juked back with jumper cables.

We clipped the lights off and climbed into a closet. Cockroaches flipped off the floor and flew into our mouths. We gagged and hacked ourselves hoarse. We reflex-retched and bit the bastards into puslike pulp. We spat out roach residue and heard a rumble—right by the bungalow door.

A V-8 voom. Tire treads grinding gravel. Vigorous voices. A key-in-door cacophony. THE Voice: "Some fucking dump. And check those bugs on the dresser."

A barrel-chesty baritone: "I'll check the closet. Maybe there's some spray."

I scooped up a scad of roaches and got ready to rock. Sammy popped into a pile-driver pose. The closet door swung and swept outward.

I bug-bombed Bob Duhamel. Bugs buzzed into his mouth and dive-bombed down his throat and crawled all over his crew cut. Sammy slammed him in the slats and slipped his gun from his hip holster.

Bad Bob flailed and flapped his hands. He belched bug bile and gurgled goo. He hit the floor hard. Sammy slipped a beavertail sap off his belt and bopped him in the balls. I unhooked his hand-cuffs and hitched his hands behind his back.

Sinatra watched it all wicked wise. He swirled a martini and swayed sweet to some bedazzled beat. He blew smug smoke rings coooooolly concurrent. Frigidaire Frank—the hip hero and ad for greasy grace under pressure.

He said, "What have we got here, the Lone Ranger and Tonto? What's shakin', kemo sabe?"

Bugs bopped out of Bad Bob's mouth. Sammy slapped slivers of tape across it and muffled him mute. I slipped the syringe out of Sammy's shirt pocket and watched shimmering shit shoot up the shaft.

Sinatra said, "Are you clowns on the junk? Sambo, I'm shocked, and I may just have to snitch you off to the NAACP."

I laughed and lunged at him. We collided. I got martini-mottled and smoke-smacked. I grabbed a grip of greasy hair and tore off Frank's toupee. Frank squealed. I squeezed his neck and nailed my needle into a vibrating vein. I pushed the plunger and jacked jungle juice in his jugular.

Sammy said, "You're in for a wild ride, Paisan."

I tossed Freon Frank on the frayed bedspread. Bugs sidled on his Sy Devore suit. Frank was fricasseed, french-fried, and fresh out of cool. I froze the moment in my mind.

Sammy juked the jumper cable cords out to Frank's Lincoln and whipped the hood wide. He leaned on the gas. He bolted the blue hooks to the battery box. Sparks spit out. I slid the cords under the door slit and shut us in torture-tight. Sammy tore the tape off Bad Bob's mouth. I ran the red hooks right under his eyes.

Sparks spun out and spanked him. They sizzled and singed and browned his brows.

Frank said, "I am personal friends with many well-placed men in La Cosa Nostra."

Bad Bob said, "You wouldn't dare."

I hitched the hooks to his hands and hurled him some horse-power. He vibrated to V-8 volts and flapped on the floor.

I unhitched the hooks and watched him undulate. I said, "All of it. No lies and no omissions."

Bad Bob shook with the shimmy-shimmy shock-induced shakes—and flew with a flinty, "Fuck you."

I anchored the hooks to his ankles. Bad Bob buckled and bent back and did a spectacular spine-spin.

I unhooked the hooks. I heard him ululate. His pelvis popped. His legs lashed. He spasm-spun and spit sparks.

Sammy said, "Dig it!" He was hopped up on honky hate. He looked like that jigaboo Jomo Kenyatta.

Freon Frank was frazzled in fright. The acid was assimilating assiduously.

Bad Bob yipped and yelled, "All right!"

I bent low. Bad Bob blurted and blubbered at me. His tongue and teeth palpitated off his palate and pried out words prestissimo:

"Linda blew everything when she shook down Frank to get her song some play—then Skip Towne got hip to it and tipped you off—and you wrote your piece in *Hush-Hush*—and Miller Leavy read it and figured that Frank's name would give him some fucking marquee value—and he could get a probe going—but then he

learned what Linda really had on Frank and got fucking scared—
and I don't know what that was, but . . ."

Leavy and Bad Bob bopped back to the Barbara Graham case.
Dot Rothstein ran with them. Liz Scott scoffed at the skinny that
Linda and Frank were fresh stuff. She tattled the truth to me. She
said, "Linda and Frank had innings going back to '52"/"Linda had
some dirt on him, and she used it."

Barbaric Barb murdered Mabel Monahan. The date of doom:
3/9/53.

?????

I bent down to Bad Bob's level. I waved my cable hooks. I
caught a wiff of scorched skin.

"Does the dirt that Linda has on Frank pertain to the Barbara
Graham case?"

Bad Bob nodded No and went knock-kneed. My internal lie
detector measured him as mendacious. I hitched my hooks to his
nose.

He danced. He did the Voltage Voom and the Convoluted
Convulsion. He did the Stultified Stomp and the Sinful Sizzle
and the Gyroscope Gyration. He did the Tijuana Termination
Tango—

I unhitched the hooks.

Bad Bob blubbered, blathered, and bled. I renamed him
Rudolph the Red-Nosed Reindeer.

Sammy said, "Dig it!"

Frank squirmed and squealed, "Mommy!"

Bad Bob almost bought it. I couldn't kill him yet. He played
into my Pedro Pimentel plan.

I said, "Lay out the rest of it."

Bad Bob noodled his nose on the floor and fluffed out a follical
flame. He flipped away from me and laid it out largo:

"Linda Lansing runs shakedowns on politicians in L.A. with
Dot Rothstein. Pedro Pimentel—the Police Chief down here—
he bankrolls them. The spic we shot in the parking lot was Pedro's
kid brother—he was a plant at the Dining Car—but I didn't know
that. Lots of lawyers and politicians eat at the Car and talked

around him because they thought he didn't speak English—and Miller Leavy picked up lots of tips that way. Getchell you fuck—you pulled that fucking reefer number and fucked things up—and Frank fucked things up by insisting that we kick your ass at the Car—and I don't know where Linda is—and her and Dot are into all kinds of shady shit—and all this started because we didn't want Linda to spill what she had on Frank—and I came down here to frost you out and frost things out with Pedro 'cause we killed his fucking brother by accident and . . . and . . . we . . . tr-tr-tr . . ."

His traumatized transmission trailed off into trills. He passed out from aftershock affliction.

He didn't know that Linda Lansing slid off to Slice City. He didn't label Linda as an heistress hot to move millions in mink. He refused to reveal the ripe revelation now ripping me:

Frantic Frank and Barbaric Barb.

?????

Frantic Frank squirmed and squealed, "Mommy!" His eyes: blurred blue and dialated from diethylamide.

Sammy said, "Dig it!"

Frank Sinatra:

Uncontrollably uncool. Umbilically unattached and hopelessly unhip from here to Hoboken.

He moaned for his mama. He mewed for his Mafia mentor "Momo" Giancana. He pounded his pillows and petitioned Raymond L. S. Patriarca—the prize prick with the Providence Mob.

Sammy tortured and tormented him. Sammy shanked him for the shit he shot his way. Sammy shucked him on his wives and the way they wanted it wild and blasphemously black. Frank moaned for mama and made mea culpa motions and put out papist pleas to Pope Pius.

I dipped over to the Diablo Club. I downed some Dos Equis and bought some boss burro âct artifacts. A cook cooked me up some cat-meat carnitas to go. A burro handler hipped me to Pedro Pimentel's private number.

I called the taco-phile Tojo of T.J. and told him I had Teitelbaum's furs. I tantalized him and told him I took down ten times Linda Lansing's take. Tojo told me to meet him tomorrow. I said I'd slide by his slave camp and move in my mountain of mink. Tojo told me he'd measure the mound and meet me with mucho money.

I moseyed back to the motel. Frank was moaning for mama. Sammy was making like the Marquis De Mau-Mau. I booted Bad Bob into the bathroom and fed him the cat-meat carnitas. He went at it carnivorously. I didn't want him to die. I had to toss him to Tojo before he purchased a pass on Pancho the Pedophile.

I loped out to the lilac Lincoln and ran the radio. I latched onto an L.A. station and lucked out on a late-nite newscast. No news: nothing on the massacre in mink or lashed Linda Lansing. My bet: Bad Bob's boys in the BHPD buried it all. I could buy out of my bind and wave bye-bye with a big bundle of cash.

Noxious night air noodled my noggin. Some thread in my theories thrashed and threatened to lash my logic on the Linda Lansing end. My brain broiled. My mind misfired. I couldn't cook a contradiction up in context.

I noxiously night-dreamed. I ran the radio dial and got reverential with Rachmaninoff. I pictured a perfect world.

I deliver the dough to Dot Rothstein and pay off my perfidies. I pop down to Paraguay and purchase a palace and some peons. I instigate indentured servitude. I install myself as El Jefe. I spawn the spic *Hush-Hush—Husho-Husho* en Español. El Presidente Strongman Stroessner stridently defends me. I defame the democratic-minded devils out to oust him. I slather slander in a land with no libel laws. I lance libidinous Latins and lynch leftist losers in print. I pride myself as a prime anticommie. I hobnob with nervous Nazis assimilated in Asunción. I hump their half-spic/half-nordic, radically race-mixed and ravishing daughters. I spot a special Hush-Hush Hilda. She hatches a hole in my heart. I build the Berchtesgaden West as our love lair. We breed a brood of bright little Getchellites. I give them thick thesauruses on their first birthdays.

Oooooh, Daddy-o! I was digging it all, dystopian!

I bopped back to the bungalow. I freeze-framed Frigidaire Frank—

He was beaming bemused and be-bop beatific. His blue eyes blazed and blended with fabric flecks on his shiny sharkskin suit. He bowed and bestowed a benediction.

"I forgive you your transgressions, for I have been to the high mountaintop. I am the way and the truth and the life. Walk with me and you shall not walk alone."

Sammy said, "That acid shit misfired. The motherfucker thinks he's Jesus."

6

Tojo's burritofied Buchenwald:

Five football fields under a tortilla-tamped tin roof. A sunken sun magnet in the middle of a massive mesa. Nine hundred niños broiled brown. Bright-eyed brats brought in to sew serapes and loom lacework and shear sheet metal into shiny souvenirs for burro show sharpies. Labor by lathe, loom, and laundry press. Stoop work at standing stations. Slaves slotted down fifty rows roamed by rough boys with bullwhips and Bulgarian machine guns.

Kiddie casas off cattycorner. Corrugated cardboard—courtesy of Carl's TV in Carlsbad, California.

Facing Maladroit Mesa:

A barbed-wire bordered baby White House built to 1/10 scale. Righteous replication. Exquisite external detail. A lush lawn that led down to Slave City.

The lawn did double duty as an unpaved parking lot. I pulled up behind a beanerized Buick and a frijolified Ford. I felt felicitously fit and joyfully jingoistic. Tojo was flying a flag. His lusty little Lucifer was trimmed in tricolored lace. I flipped him a salacious salute.

The joint was jumping jackrabbit high.

A bonaroo buffet boded by the barbed-wire boundary. Bullwhips bit bullet-loud. Mangled muchachos moaned and mewed, "Mamacita!" Blackshirted blowhards lounged on the lawn and swicked switchblades into the grass.

I vipped out of the van. I hauled Bad Bob out by the hair. Sammy made a mountain of mink and moved it onto the lawn. The Juke Box Jesus was rope-wrapped and mouth-muted and mummified in mink. He could suffer and suffocate. He could vegetate in the van. He didn't play in my plan.

Sammy sealed him in safe and soundless. A blackshirt blizzard hit the Mink Matterhorn.

They reveled and rolled like dogs in the dirt. They mauled mink and salivated on sable. They grabbed and grass-stained and chewed up choice chinchilla.

A shadow shot over Mink Mountain and shaded in shiveringly. Pedro Pimentel—the tostadofied Tojo and menudoized Mussolini.

A spiffy spic. A blackshirted blackguard with blackhead pits and bad teeth. A jackbooted jackal not to jive with.

He said, "Stop."

The blowsy blackshirts stopped and stood at attention.

He turned to me. "Mr. Getchell?"

I said, "In the flesh." I hair-hauled Bad Bob over to him.

"He killed your kid brother. I'm giving him to you as a get-acquainted bonus."

Bad Bob boohooed and begged for his life. Pimentel pulled a pistol and popped him in the pineal gland. He sheared off six more shots and shaved his crew cut down to a crease.

Sammy said, "Dig it!"

Pimentel reholstered his heater. "You look like the American entertainer, Sammy Davis, Jr."

I said, "That's 'El Negrito.' He's a torpedo for a nigger mob in South L.A."

Sammy said, "What's shakin', Jefe?"

Pimentel patted his paunch. "Quite a remarkable resemblance. Come, I will give you a tour before we eat."

We whipped through the White House. The façade was fetching and faithful to our founding fathers' design. The inside was lusciously Latinate and refreshingly revisionistic.

The rooms resembled rat-traps on Route 66. Jefe housed his hermanos herd-style. They bunked in six-bed bunkers hung with burro act artwork. Dingo dogs and Dobermans dashed down the halls and defecated dolorously.

They lived in the Lincoln Bedroom. The Lincoln portraits were painted by Pedro Pimentel. El Jefe altered Abe and changed him to a cholo in a '52 Chevy.

The dog den opened into the Oval Office. The lewd little Lucifer leered on a lusciously loomed lavender rug. A heavy-hung hound was humping a chewed-up Chihuahua. A Pekingese was pissing on Pedro Pimentel's papers.

The Rose Room stood in as a stall for the stars at the classy Club Diablo. Dig the hip heaps of hay! Dig the trough tricked up with the devil dick design! Dig the donkeys dozing in postcoital peace!

The Roosevelt Room was a gun range. The John Adams Room adjoined it at a rigid right angle. It was Pedro Pimentel's private party pad.

A faux fur–flocked floor. Sheet-shrouded walls to smother with smut films projected prick-primingly. Presidential artwork by El Jefe:

Abigail Adams on dowager dyke Eleanor Roosevelt. Pat Nixon knob-noshing FDR—wigged out in his wheelchair.

Oooooh, Daddy-o! Save me from this pixilated Picasso!

We bopped out to the buffet behind the barb-wire fence. We feasted in full view of the slave kids. El Negrito and I flanked El Jefe. Bloated blackshirts blipped down and joined us.

Mink Mountain moldered in the sun. Flies flitted on the fur and flew off. A blowsy blackshirt brought me 500 Gs in a mink moneybag. I pitched Pimentel my plan to pop down to Paraguay and seek Paradise. He said he'd set me up with Strongman Stroessner.

We ate with unique utensils. We stabbed our meat with stilettos and tore our tortillas with Texas toad-stickers. We shivved shiny apples and swacked at our sweetbreads with switchblades. We slung slivers of food over the fence at the slaves. They slathered and scrapped over scraps. Blackshirts blasted them with their bullwhips and bullied them back to work.

El Jefe held forth—on himself. He ran down his rackets like a rabid raconteur. He shared shit on his shakedown scam and said he stored his blackmail bait in the basement of the Club Diablo. He raved about Dot Rothstein and lavished praise on Linda Lansing. He said he'd loooove to chuck his chorizo on Linda the next time he laid up in L.A. He'd looooove to jab Joi Lansing, too.

My brainwaves broiled, bristled, and brought forth that contradictory connection.

Joi Lansing—lashed to lo mein in Linda Lansing's L.A. lair. My take: Tojo sent two taco heads up to lash Linda and pry a priceless SOMETHING off the premises. The spics spoke no English. They butchered the wrong bimbo.

But—

Tojo talked like he loooooved Linda. Like he'd love to loooove her AGAIN. Like he didn't think she got shanked to Shiv City. He said he'd love to jab Joi Lansing—like he didn't know she got mashed to mulch by mistake.

Which proved the priceless SOMETHING had to be SOMEWHERE.

?????

We stabbed steaks with our stilettos. We shucked oysters with our shivs. We toasted Tojo. We drank to a dreary drumroll of dictators and despots. Tojo twirled a little Lucifer key ring—and clipped a clear chord in my head.

We toasted Bad Boy Batista. We toasted Patriarch Perón. A blackshirt blasted to his feet and blanched brown to bright white.

He said, "Hay-soos Christo." Elegant echoes eddied behind the barbed wire. Wasted waifs whispered:

"Hay-soos Christo."

"Hay-soos Christo."

"Hay-soos Christo."

The whispers whipped into worshipful wails. Blasphemous blackshirts blew the blessing out in synergistic sync. I stood up stunned and stung by the fragrance of Frankincense.

The Juke Box Jesus. Re-resurrected in Rayban shades and a wild white sheet. Re-toupeed and regal in lizard loafers and a crazy crown of thorns whipped up from wires and widgets and White House whatnots.

He walked our way. He waved a transistor radio vandalized from the van. "Ave Maria" ate up the air—off the album "All-Time Hits" by Craig Crawford's Christian Chorale.

He walked our way. He oozed optimum oomph. Juke Box Jesus outworks God at the Galilee Lounge in Las Vegas. He slid on his slick lizard loafers and lurched levitatingly.

He sliced and sluiced our way. He wiggled on wet grass. He warbled, "I grant you your freedom!"

Nine hundred niños went nuts. They stampeded—stigmata stained and hurled by the Holy Spirit.

They gored the guards. They tore at them with the tools they toiled with. They beat them with ball-peen hammers and hacked them with sheet-metal shears. They bullwhipped them and machetified them with machine-gun fire. They barged into the barbed-wire barrier barbarically strong. They ran though it razor-wracked and idolatrously indifferent.

Sammy said, "Dig it!"

The fence flew up and flattened the buffet table. Two dozen blackshirts went down wire whipped and barbed in the balls. Tojo took it all in. He stood trenchantly transfixed. He put his pistol to his teeth and tripped the trigger. I dodged whizzing wires and picked his pockets. I lifted the little Lucifer key ring.

Machine-gun fire torqued the table and tore it to tidbits. My mink moneybag was flayed to fur flecks. My half-million got bullet-burned and scrip-scrapped and devalued to a micro-dime on the dollar.

I vaulted up to the van. Sammy ran up *rápido*. Stigmata-stung muchachos stuck machine guns in the air and mowed down malevolent spirits. A group gravitated up to Mink Mountain. My stole stash was stripped to strings by stray bullets.

Sammy said, "Dig it!"

I sought out Savior Sinatra. I saw him swaying sweet in his sharp shades and sheet. He was smiling smug and smoking a cigarette. He was righteously and re-resurrectedly cooooooooool.

7

I lost my mink and my money. My psycho sidekick succumbed to the Savior and re-Sambofied himself resurrectionally.

I remained a Hush-Hush heretic and hauled to T.J. I left Juke Box Jesus and his jig John the Baptist at their cut-rate Calvary. Frank was serving up the Sermon on Mex Mountain. Ring-a-ding—nine hundred niños noncomprehending. No way for them to grok and groove "Clip Me, Clyde" and "Baby, You're Knocking Me Numbsville."

Dig it, distinct:

It didn't matter. The motherfucker made magic and charmed children into mass murder.

I dipped up to Club Diablo. I stashed my van by some burro stalls and stood by the basement door. I tried Tojo's keys. Number two tickled the lock and let me in.

I latched it behind me. I swicked on a wall switch and laid some light in. A long corridor led to a crud-crusted crawl space.

The corridor reeked of cordite and caustic chemicals. I coughed and caught sight of hipbones and hair-hanks in a hardened heap. Blood blips and flesh flaps flared out flat on the walls.

Tojo's torture chamber.

Quivering quiet upstairs. No delighted donkeyphile dementia. The club might be closed. Tojo's minions might have caught word on the coup at Calvary.

I walked wary. I crept into the crawl space. I skivved my way through skeletons and scooted through scorched scalps. I squealed and squirmed into another hipbone-heaped hallway.

I saw a dust-covered door. I ratched keys into a rusty lock. Key number three tumbled the tumblers. I tumbled into a tunnel-like enclosure.

Shelves shot floor to flat ceiling. Film cans filled them up. Tape strips were stuck to the edges. Date designations blipped out in black block print.

Bolted to the back wall: a rust-ratched movie magnification machine.

The cans were crammed in chronologically. The dates dipped back to 1936. I started there and shot my eyes shelf to shelf.

I hit 3/9/53. The date distracted me. I got dizzy. My memory mailed me a message: the Mabel Monahan murder.

I pulled out the film. I slid a slice under the slide on the movie magnifier. I looked in the lens. I thrilled to the throes of the Three-Way Supreme.

Freon Frank Sinatra.

Avid Ava Gardner.

Barbaric Barbara Graham.

Surreptitiously shot shakedown shit. An extortion extravaganza. The blackmail blight of all time.

I fed film and sliced it under the slide. I shared the sheets with a shimmering cast and spun under their spell. I popped a posthumous pardon on Barbaric Barb.

She didn't murder Mabel Monahan. She had an all-star alibi for 3/9/53. Linda Lansing learned about it. She shook down Freon Frank and had him pay her off with payola. Bad Bob and Demon Dot—in league with Devil DA Leavy on the Graham case. His conviction: contaminated by the contents of the film can. Call it a cause célèbre—the can could lay L.A. law enforcement laughing-stock low—Leavy pulled the plug on the payola probe for that reputation-ruining reason.

It ALL congealed and constellated. A special spark spoke to my spirit. Call it the Sermon on Mount Monahan.

Barbaric Barb the martyred madonna.

Who refused to rat off Frigid Frank and Avid Ava as her alibi. Who died in deference to the deification confirmed at the cut-rate Calvary.

Who jumped off the jury and did not Judas the Juke Box Jesus.

8

The kiddie coup went commie. The cops quelled it quicksville.

I filched five film cans and trawled T.J. for Jesus and Jungle John. I hit some hot spots and ran up against the Red Revolt in retreat.

Malnutrition-mauled muchachos moped down the main drag. They lurched and lisped leftist slogans. They slung empty machine guns and stumbled with the weight—withered waifs who wasted their wad at the White House.

They staggered and stumped for pickled plantains on every plate. They lashed out at laissez-faire labor laws and slandered slavery. They sideswiped soldiers and sailors. They agitated against Uncle Sam. They propagandized prostitutes. They chanted and chastised the cholos who made Mexico great. They beat their balls into an uproar and ran out of Red rancor. They hit the street from heat stroke one by one.

The local cops let them run raucous and run out of steam. They didn't muscle them or mow them down and martyr them. They made like that Martin Luther King motherfucker. They put out passive resistance and popped the little putzes into paddy wagons. Pedro Pimentel's successor would subsidize their rigorous reeducation.

They succumbed to Sinatra in one magic moment of misplaced identity. They couldn't sustain their subversion without him.

I said *vaya con dios* to the Vauxhall van and freed Frank's lilac Lincoln. I hit the hip whorehouses and the jai alai games and buzzed by the bullfight ring. I saw Sambo and the Savior at the Salamander Club and dipped by on disingenuous instinct.

Frank looked freon-fresh and crisply non-Christlike. His gracious greeting: "Getchell, you cocksucker, what are you doing here?"

Sammy marched me into the men's room and revealed the reverse metamorphosis.

Frank collapsed cold on Mink Mountain. He woke up wigged out and wondered where he was. His lost days lapped back to L.A. and the snuff snafu. He did not recall his re-resurrection and his acid-induced atavism. He was pissed at my piece on the payola probe—properly so. Sammy said he propagandized the prick. Bygones as bygones—let's bop back to L.A.

Sammy's pulverizing punch line:

"He *is* the Christ, Danny. I know you think it's all some kind dope fluke, but it's not. I'm back with him now, and I'll always be with him, and thank God he doesn't know that I betrayed him."

We buzzed up to the border. We quaffed Cuervo from the bottle and bit bitter limes. Re-Sambofied Sammy chauffeured and shucked and jived. I daydreamed and disdained his Christ crap.

Fuck Frank the Freewheeling Freak. I had the 3/9/53 fuck film and four more. I had Governor Goodwin J. Knight and his nigger nurse. I had Diana Dors and a dipshit who delivered her pizza. I had Dan Dailey in a daisy chain and Mickey Mantle and Marilyn Monroe in the men's room at the Mocambo. That meant MONEY in my tote tucked in the trunk.

Frank tippled tequila and licked lime and blue-eye blitzed me. It rankled and roughed up my ego. I bored back with my beady browns. Our brainwaves bristled and telescoped telepathically.

Frank hopped in my head. He crept around my cranial crevices and crisscrossed my crazily wired wig. He verbally vandalized me. He thumped me with a thick thesaurus and alliterated with alacrity. Literal lightning flares flew between our foreheads and threw out huge thuds of thunder. Synaptic syncopation singed the seats we sat on. We communicated in capsulized containment. Samboized Sammy sat there and didn't see or hear shit.

Frank Freud-frappéed me and undid my unconscious. I shared my chickenshit childhood in Chillicothe, Ohio. We commiserated. He communicated *his* kid conundrums contrapuntally. I sunk down syncophantic. We negotiated a nonaggression pact. I said I'd never hurl him hurt in *Hush-Hush*. Frank Freud-frappéed and freed himself. He conflagratingly confessed his love for non-barbaric Barbara Graham.

He was addlepatedly and adoringly in love with awful Ava Gardner. Ava liked to lez once in a soft sapphic moon. Hubert Humphrey hipped them to thrilling three-way thrush Barb. The triad trick went down on 3/9/53. The soft siren syphoned his soul off Ava as they all linked limbs on luscious lilac sheets.

He capitulated. He commandeered himself into captivity. La Graham graced him with three grateful months. He left avid Ava in the lilac lurch. The scandal rags read it wrong and said *she* spun out for Splitsville. The cops mistakenly made Boss Barb for the Mabel Monahan murder. Sinatra stormed out to straighten her strait. Boss Barb interceded and interdicted him. She said his alibi would annihilate him and annex him from the world he wowed and rang ring-a-ding. Her death would not diminish them. She possessed preternatural powers. She could dip into them dispensationally and deify him beyond his catastrophically cool charisma.

Dig:

She died and did it.

Doubt ditzed me. Scandal-scribe skepticism scrawled itself out in telltale telepathy. Frank scrolled a resounding response: "Don't you dig me, Dad?" I screwed up and scrawled back: "Jesus, I'm not sure."

Frank snapped his fingers. The trunk door trembled and leaped off the lilac Lincoln. My tote bag tipped out and popped to the pavement. Two mangy muchachos materialized and moseyed up to it.

Frank said, "It's my world. Even God knows that."

L.A. paled pallid next to torrid T.J. I loped by Linda Lansing's lair and let myself in with Liz Scott's key.

No blood. No maggot mounds. No cool corpus delicti. No living room ratched and wrecked past recognition.

Dot Rothstein wrapped in a man-sized muumuu. The NEW Joi Lansing lez-locked on her lap.

A headline hopping off a heap of *Herald*s chucked by their chair:

SINGER LANSING FOUND IN HOLLYWOOD HILLS. CORONER CITES DECOMPOSITION AND RULES CAUSE OF DEATH UNKNOWN.

The girls giggled. They looked me over looooooong. The live Lansing licked crumbs off her lips.

I said, "I don't have the fifty Gs. Things went bad down in Mexico."

Dot dipped into an ice-cream dish and chomped some chocolate chips.

"Frank squared it for you. He called Miller Leavy and told him you were kosher. Miller called off the BHPD and told them to hang the fur job on Al Teitelbaum. And as far as they're concerned, those heist guys you killed didn't exist."

The REAL Linda Lansing toyed with a toll-house cookie. She'd popped on some porky pounds to portray her pudgy sister. The coffee table was covered with candy cartons and cruller crusts and doughnut debris.

I said, "You killed Joi. You were in way too deep with way too many people, and you needed a way out. You rented this place to set up your murder scene. You trashed it to make it look like the killers were looking for something. Then I came along and saw the body, so you decided to dump it in the hills to queer the cause of death."

Dot dive-bombed a devil's-food doughnut. "Mention money, Danny. We've been expecting you, and we know you didn't come up here to moralize."

I said, "Money."

Dot drowned her doughnut in Drambuie-drenched coffee. "He said 'money.'"

Lansing lanced a ladyfinger and sunk it into Sambuca. "He certainly did."

I said, "Cut the comedy, cuties." I framed the line à la Frigidaire Frank at his frostbitten best.

Dot pulled a packet of pix from her purse and popped them my way. I snared the snapshots out of the air and snagged myself in a snafu.

Danny Getchell—film-fucked forever.

I'm humping the *Hush-Hush*–hated Helen Gahagan Douglas—the Lewd Lady of the L.A. Left. I'm jabbing some jailbait in the gym at Hollywood High. I'm ecstatically entwined with Ethel Rosenberg—somewhere in Sedition City. I'm holed up with Hattie McDaniel at the height of my fatty phase. I'm liquored up and looking longingly at Lassie and her luscious littermate. I'm skunk drunk in a skid-row dive. I'm passed out on a putrid pallet. A filthy filly is fellating me. FUCK—it's a dreg-like drag queen draped dramatically!

Dot dunked her doughnut and doused me with John Donne: "Send not to know for whom the bell tolls. It tolls for thee."

I hit my knees hard. I concentrated on a karmic counterattack. I couldn't cough one up.

I whimpered. I wailed. I keened and keeled over. I cried and cringed, and crawled into an abyss of abasement.

White light wafted in. I shot to my feet on a shimmering shaft. His voice vibrated off an old Victrola vaulted in my head. It vipped through me victoriously.

I vowed to roll with the punch and reign on ring-a-ding.

February, March 1999

PART THREE

CONTINO

Half-buried memories speak to me. Their origin remains fixed: L.A., my hometown, in the '50s. Most are just brief synaptic blips, soon mentally discarded. A few transmogrify into fiction: I sense their dramatic potential and exploit it in my novels, memory to moonshine in a hot second.

Memory: a symbiotic melding of *then* and *now*. For me, the spark-point of harrowing curiosities.

A man gyrating with an accordion—pumping his "stomach Steinway" for all it's worth.

My father pointing to the TV. "That guy's no good. He's a draft dodger."

The accordion man in a grade-Z movie, clinching with the blonde from the Mark C. Bloome tire ads.

The accordion man is named Dick Contino.

"Draft dodger" is a bum rap—he served honorably during the Korean War.

The grade-Z flick is *Daddy-O*—a music/hot-rod/romance stinkeroo.

Memory: the juxtaposition of large events and snappy minutiae.

In June 1958, my mother was murdered; the killing went unsolved. I saw Dick Contino belt "Bumble Boogie" on TV, noted my father's opinion of him, and caught *Daddy-O* at the Admiral Theater a year or so later. Synapses snapped: A memory was formed and placed in context. Its historical perspective loomed dark: Women were strangled and spent eternity unavenged.

I was 10 and 11 years old then; literary instincts simmered inchoately in me. My curiosities centered on crime: I wanted to know the WHY? behind hellish events. As time passed, contemporaneous malfeasance left me bored—the sanguinary '60s and '70s passed in a blur of hectic self-destruction.

I drank, used drugs, and did a slew of ten-, twenty-, and thirty-day county-jail stints for preposterous and pathetic misdemeanors. I shoplifted, broke into houses, and sniffed women's undergarments. I jimmied hinges off Laundromat washers and stole the coins inside. I holed up in cheap pads and read hundreds of crime novels. My life was chaos, but my intellectual focus never wavered: L.A. in the '50s/corruption/crime. A '50s sound track accompanied my musings: golden oldies, Dick Contino on the accordion.

In 1977, I got sober and segued into hyper-focus: *writing* crime novels. Dick Contino back-burner brain boogied as I attempted to replicate Los Angeles in the 1950s.

In 1980, I wrote *Clandestine*—a thinly disguised, chronologically altered account of my mother's murder. The novel is set in 1951; the hero is a draft dodger whose life is derailed by the Red Scare.

In 1987, I wrote *The Big Nowhere*. Set in 1950, the book details an anticommunist pogrom leveled at the entertainment biz.

In 1990, I wrote *White Jazz*. A major subplot features a grade-Z movie being filmed in the same Griffith Park locales as *Daddy-O*.

Jung wrote: "What is not brought to consciousness comes to us as fate."

I should have seen Dick Contino coming a long time ago.

I didn't. Fate intervened, via photograph and black-and-white videocassette.

A friend sent me the photo. Dig: It's me, age 10, on June 22, 1958. An L.A. *Times* photographer snapped the pic five minutes after a police detective told me my mother had been murdered.

I'm in minor-league shock: My eyes are wide, but my gaze is blank. My fly is at half-mast; my hands look shaky. The day was hot: The melting Brylcreem in my hair picks up flashbulb light.

The photo held me transfixed; its force transcended my many attempts to exploit my past for book sales. An underlying truth zapped me: My bereavement, even in that moment, was ambiguous. I'm already calculating potential advantages, regrouping as the officious men surrounding me defer to the perceived grief of a little boy.

I had the photograph framed and spent a good deal of time staring at it. Spark-point: late-'50s memories reignited. I saw *Daddy-O* listed in a video catalogue and ordered it. It arrived a week later; I popped it in the VCR.

Fuel-injected *zooom* . . .

The story revolves around truckdriver/drag racer/singer Phil "Daddy-O" Sandifer's attempts to solve the murder of his best friend while laboring under the weight of a suspended driver's license. Phil's pals Peg and Duke want to help, but they're ineffectual—addled by too many late nights at the Rainbow Gardens, a post-teenage doo-wop spot where Phil croons gratis on request. No matter: Daddy-O meets slinky Jana Ryan, a rich girl with a valid driver's license and a '57 T-Bird ragtop. Mutual resentment segues into a sex vibe; Phil and Jana team up and infiltrate a nightclub owned by sinister fat man Sidney Chillas. Singer Daddy-O, cigarette girl Jana; a comely and unstoppable duo. They quickly surmise that Chillas is pushing Big H, entrap him, and nail the endomorph for the murder of Phil's best friend. A hot-rod finale; a burning question left unanswered: Will Daddy-O's derring-do get him back his driver's license?

Who knows?

Who cares?

It took me three viewings to get the plot down, anyway. Because Dick Contino held me spellbound. Because I knew—instinctively—that he held important answers. Because I knew that he hovered elliptically in my L.A.-in-the-'50s novels, a phantom waiting to speak.

Contino onscreen: a handsome Italian guy, late twenties, big biceps from weights or making love to his accordion. Dreamboat attributes: shiny teeth; dark, curly hair; engaging smile. He looks good, and he can sing; he's straining on "Rock Candy Baby"—the lyrics suck, and you can tell this up-tempo rebop isn't his style—but he croons the wah-wah ballad "Angel Act" achingly, full of baritone tremolos, quintessentially the pussy-whipped loser in lust with the "noir" goddess who's out to trash his life.

The man oozes charisma.

He's the flip side, subtext and missing link between my conscious and unconscious fixations.

I decided to find Dick Contino.

I located a half-dozen of his albums and listened to them, reveling in pure *Entertainment.*

"Live at the Fabulous Flamingo," "Squeeze Me," "Something for the Girls"—standards arranged to spotlight accordion virtuosity. Main-theme bombardments; sentiment so pure and timeless that it could sound-track every moment of transcendent schmaltz that Hollywood has ever produced. Dick Contino, showstopper on wax: tapping two keyboards, improvising cadenzas, shaking thunderstorms from bellows compression. Going from whisper to sigh to roar and back again in the length of time it takes to think: Tell me what this man's life means and how it connects to my life.

I called my researcher friend Alan Marks. He caught my pitch on the first bounce. "The accordion guy? I think he used to play Vegas."

"Find out everything you can about him. Find out if he's still alive, and if he is, locate him."

"What's this about?"

"Narrative detail."

I should have said *containable* narrative detail—because I wanted Dick Contino to be a pad-prowling/car-crashing/moon-howling/womanizing quasi-psychopath akin to the heroes of my books. I should have said, "Bring me information that I can control and exploit." I should have said, "Bring me a life that can be compartmentalized into the pitch-dark vision of my first ten novels."

"What is not brought to consciousness comes to us as fate."

I should have seen the *real* Dick Contino coming.

Richard Joseph Contino was born in Fresno, California, on January 17, 1930. His father was a Sicilian immigrant who owned a successful butcher shop; his mother was first-generation Italian American. Dick had two younger brothers and a sister; a maternal uncle, Ralph Giordano, a.k.a. Young Corbett, was a former professional welterweight fighter.

The family was tight-knit, Catholic. Dick grew up shy, beset by wicked bad fears: the kind you recognize as irrational even as they rip you up.

Athletics and music allowed him to front a fearless persona. High-school fullback, five years of accordion study—good with the pigskin, superb with the squeeze box. Dick Contino, age 17, ready for a hot date with history; a strapping six-foot *gavonne* with his fears held in check by a smile.

Horace Heidt was passing through Fresno looking for amateur talent. His *Youth Opportunity* radio program was about to debut— yet another studio-audience/applause-meter show, three contestants competing for weekly prize money and the chance to sing, play, dance, or clown their way through to the grand finals, a five-thou payoff and a dubious shot at fame. One of Heidt's flunkies had heard about Dick and had arranged an audition; Dick wowed him with a keyboard-zipping/bellows-shaking/mike-stand–bumping medley. The flunky told Horace Heidt: "You've got to see this kid. I know the accordion's from Squaresville, but you've got to see this kid."

December 7, 1947: Horace Heidt slotted Dick Contino on his first radio contest. Dick played "Lady of Spain," "Tico-Tico," and "Bumble Boogie" and burned the house down. He won $250; horny bobby-soxers swarmed him backstage. Horace Heidt hit first-strike pay dirt.

Dick Contino continued to win: week after week, traveling with the Heidt show, defeating singers, dancers, trombone players, comics, and a blind vibraphonist. He won straight through to the grand finals in December '48; he became a national celebrity while still technically an amateur contestant.

He now had 500 fan clubs nationwide—and averaged 5,000 fan letters a week.

Teenage girls thronged his appearances, chanting "Dick-kie Cont-ino, we love you" to the tune of "Lady of Spain."

Horace Heidt said years later, "You should have *seen* Dick play. If my show had been on television, Dick Contino would have been bigger than Elvis Presley."

A Heidt tour followed the grand-finals victory. Other performers appeared with Contino—crypto lounge acts backstopping the newly anointed "Mr. Accordion." Heidt had his cash cow yoked to a punk twenty-five-grand-a-year, seven-year contract; Dick sued him and cut himself loose. Mr. Accordion flying high: record contracts, screen tests, top-liner status at the BIG ROOMS— Ciro's and the Mocambo in L.A.; the El Rancho Vegas; the Chez Paree in Chicago. Dick Contino, age 19, 20, 21: soaking up the spoils of momentum, making the Squaresville accordion hip, unaware that public love is ephemeral. Too callow to know that idols who admit their fear will fall.

Nineteen fifty-one: the Korean War heating up. Dick Contino goes from "Valentino of the Accordion" to draft bait. A selective-service notice arrives; he begs off his army induction, citing minor physical maladies. He's scared, but not of losing his BIG-ROOM status, big paydays, and big poontang potential.

He's scared of all the baaad juju that could happen to you, might happen to you, *will* happen to you—shit like blindness, cancer, passing out onstage, your dog getting dognapped by vivisectionists. The army looms—claustrophobia coming on like a steam-heated shroud. Fear—BIG-ROOM fear—crazy stuff, big-time diffuse. Crazy stuff he might have outgrown if he hadn't been too busy on the Heartthrob Tour, jump-starting adolescent libidos.

Fear owned him now.

Three army psychiatrists examined him at the induction center and declared him psychologically unfit. The assessment letter was "lost"; Richard Contino was processed in anyway.

April 1951—Fort Ord, California. Dick's fear becomes panic— he bolts the reception-station barracks and catches a bus to San Francisco. Now AWOL and a federal fugitive, he trains down to his parents' new house outside L.A. He confers with friends and a lawyer, gets up some guts, and turns himself in to the Feds.

The incident got front-page publicity. The papers harped on the BIG-ROOM pay Dick Contino would be giving up if forced to serve as an army private. Dick's response: Then take away my accordion for five years.

The Feds didn't buy it. Dick Contino went to trial for desertion; he fought his case with psychiatric testimony. Fear on trial, fear convicted—the judge hit Dick Contino with a $10,000 fine and six months in the federal joint at McNeil Island, Washington.

He did five months of the sentence, shaving four weeks off for good behavior. It could have been worse: He hauled pipes, did gardening work, and put on a prisoners' Christmas show. Inside, the big fears seemed to subside: The business of day-to-day survival kiboshed that part of his imagination where terror flourished. Five months in, out, the ironic kicker: He got drafted and sent to Korea.

Where he served with distinction. Korea proved to be a mixed psychological bag: Dick's draft-trial notoriety won him friends, enemies, and a shitload of invitations to play the accordion. Duty with a Seoul-attached outfit, back to the States early in '54. Richard Contino: honorably discharged as a staff sergeant; while overseas, the recipient of an unsolicited presidential pardon signed by Harry S Truman.

Dick Contino: back in the U.S.A.

Back to derailed career momentum, a long transit of day-to-day survival behind him.

The BIG-ROOM gigs were kaput. Momentum is at least 50 percent hype: It requires nurturing and frequent infusions of bullshit. Dick Contino couldn't play the game from McNeil Island and Korea. A bum-publicity taint stuck to him: "coward" and "draft dodger" throbbing in Red Scare neon.

He worked smaller rooms and ignored catcalls; he cut records and learned to sing. A few journalists befriended him, but the basic show-biz take on Dick Contino was *This guy is poison.* Justifying yourself to the public gets old quick—"coward" may be the toughest American bullet to dodge.

Dick Contino learned to sing, but rock and roll cut him off at the pass. He learned to act, top-lined a few B-films, and faded in the wake of heartthrobs with underailed momentum. In 1956, he married actress Leigh Snowden, had three kids with her, and settled down in Las Vegas—close to his hotel-lounge bread and butter. He continued to get small-room gigs and played Italian festas in Chicago, Milwaukee, Philly, and other paisano-packed venues.

Leigh Snowden Contino died of cancer in 1982. The Contino kids would now be 35, 32, and 30.

My researcher's notes tapped out in '89. He said an obituary check turned up negative—he was certain that Dick Contino was still alive. A week later, I got confirmation. "I found him. He's still living in Las Vegas, and he says he'll talk to you."

Before making contact, I charted the arc of two lives. A specific design was becoming clear—I wanted to write a novella featuring Dick Contino and the filming of *Daddy-O*, but a symbiotic pull was blunting my urge to get down to business, extract information, and get out. I felt a recognition of my own fears binding me to this man: fear of failure, specific in nature and surmountable through hard work, and the very large fear that induces claustrophobic suffocation and causes golden young men to run from army barracks—the terror that anything might happen, could happen, *will* happen.

A merging in fear; a divergence in action.

I joined the army just as the Vietnam War started to percolate. My father was dying; I didn't want to stick around and watch. The army terrified me—I calculated plausible means of escape. James

Ellroy, age 17, fledgling dramatist: pulling off a frantic stuttering act designed to spotlight his unsuitability for military service.

It was a bravura performance. It got me a quick discharge and a return trip to L.A. and my passions: booze, dope, pantie-sniffing.

Nobody ever called me a coward or a draft dodger—the Vietnam War was reviled from close to the get-go, and extricating yourself from its clutches was held as laudable.

I *calculated* my way out—and of course my fears remained unacknowledged. And I wasn't a golden young man sky-high on momentum and ripe for a public hanging.

I've led a colorful and media-exploitable life; my take on it has been picaresque—a stratagem that keeps my search for deeper meaning channeled solely into my books, which keeps my momentum building, which keeps my wolves of nothingness locked out of sight. Dick Contino didn't use my methods: He was a man of music, not of words, and he embraced his fears from the start. And he *continued:* The musicianship on his post-army beef albums dwarfs the sides he cut pre-'51. He continued, and so far as I could tell, the only thing that diminished was his audience.

I called Contino and told him I wanted to write about him. We had an affable conversation; he said, "Come to Vegas."

Contino met me at the airport. He looked great: lean and fit at 63. His *Daddy-O* grin remained intact; he confirmed that his *Daddy-O* biceps came from humping his accordion.

We went to a restaurant and shot the shit. Our conversation was full of jump cuts—Las Vegas to the Mob to serving jail time to L.A. in the '50s, fear and what you do when the audience dwindles.

I told him that the best novels are often not the best-selling novels; that complex styles and ambiguous stories perplex many readers. I said that while my own books sell quite well, they are considered too dark, too densely plotted, and too relentlessly violent to be chart-toppers.

Dick asked me if I would change the type of book I write to

achieve greater sales—I said no. He asked me if I'd change the type of book I write if I knew that I'd taken a given style or theme as far as it could go—I said yes. He asked me if the real-life characters in my books ever surprise me—I said, "No, because my relationship to them is exploitative."

I asked him if he consciously changed musical directions after his career got diverted, post-Korea. He said yes and no—he'd kept trying to cash in on trends until he'd realized that, at best, he'd be performing music he didn't love and at worst he'd be playing to an audience he didn't respect.

I said, "The work is the thing." He said, yes, but you can't cop an attitude behind some self-limiting vision of your own integrity. You can't cut the audience out of its essential enjoyment—you have to give them some schmaltz to hold on to.

I asked Dick how he arrived at that. He said his old fears taught him to like people more. He said fear thrives on isolation, and when you cut down the wall between you and the audience, your whole vision goes wide.

I checked in at my hotel and shadowboxed with the day's revelations. It felt like my world had tilted toward a new understanding of my past. I kept picturing myself in front of an expanding audience, armed with new literary ammunition: the knowledge that Dick Contino would be the hero of the sequel to the book I'm writing now.

Dick and I met for dinner the next night. It was my forty-fifth birthday; I felt like I was standing at the bedrock center of my life.

Dick played me a bebop "Happy Birthday" on his accordion. The old chops were still there—he zipped on and off the main theme *rápidamente*.

We split for the restaurant. I asked Dick if he would consent to appear as the hero of my next novel.

He said yes and asked what the book would be about. I said, "Fear, courage, and heavily compromised redemptions."

He said, "Good, I think I've been there."

We hit the Tillerman's—a surf-and-turf palace outside Vegas. The food was good, but my brain was schizophrenic while I ate. I listened to Dick talk; I plotted my Contino novella full-speed. By the time the pecan pie arrived, I had *Dick Contino's Blues*—a picaresque tale of '58 L.A.—fully mapped out.

Dick said, "Penny for your thoughts?"

I said, "You're my ticket back and my ticket out, but I'm not sure where to."

November 1993

HOLLYWOOD SHAKEDOWN

I

Every time and place hides secrets that only one person can spill. History is recorded by hacks who don't know the real secret shit.

L.A. History is subterfuge and lies. Outrageousness is passed off as full disclosure. Nobody has connected all the celebrated players and defined the moment that L.A. was won and lost.

On March 23, 1954, I killed a rogue cop and a stick-up man and sealed the fate of a great city.

I

My flight landed ten minutes early. I bribed a stewardess to let me off first.

I wanted to disembark *sloooooow*. I wanted the newsmen to dig my stripes and campaign ribbons.

The plane taxied up to the gate. The steps locked into the door. I shoved my way to the front of the aisle. A fat nun ate my elbows.

The door slid open.

I stepped into the sun.

I saw my agent, Howard Wormser. I saw two newsmen and counted five picket signs.

DICK CONTINO, RED PAWN and DICK CONTINO, AMERICAN. TRAITOR, GO HOME and WE LOVE OUR DICK. A poster depicting me in the electric chair. I'm perched between the recently smoked Ethel and Julius Rosenberg.

I walked into it.

Howard grabbed me. We skirted some ground-crew guys and found a spot under the right-front propellers. Passengers filed off the plane. The nun shot me the bird. Three picket punks shouted, "Draft dodger!"

Howard hugged me. His hands danced down my back to my ass.

I said, "I need some tail. I need it *baaaad*."

Howard dropped his hands. I smiled. The stewardess I bribed walked by and blew me a kiss.

Howard's a fag. He got drunk once and made a dive for my dong. Tail talk and pussy patter keep him in line. It's our sex semaphore.

He slipped me a pawnshop tag. "I had to hock your accordion. I needed money to get the booze for the loyalty-oath gig. Dick, Dick, Dick, don't look at me that way."

My heartbeat went atomic. My body heaved. A combat ribbon popped off my pecs.

Ransomed:

My rhinestone-wrapped/pearl-patterned/candy-cane ax!

The picket factions faced off. "Draft dodger!" and "Go, Dick!" nullified each other. Howard cupped his hands around my left ear.

"Dick, you don't serve Ward Bond and Adolphe Menjou anything less than top-shelf liquor. Those guys are prepared to call you 100 percent American, and you can't stiff them with off-brand shit."

Howard's tongue shot into my ear. I stepped back and shook it dry.

"They're coming to the gig?"

"That's right. A buddy of mine set it up. We've got the booze and cold cuts from your old man's store, and thirty American Legion guys at five bucks a head."

My blood pressure depressurized. "What do I play with?"

"I got a loaner off a kid at Belmont High. You have to take the bitter with the sweet, Dick. I promised him three personal lessons."

Two newsmen bucked the picket line and waved to me. I knew them: Morty Bendish and Sid Hughes from the *Mirror* and the *Herald-Express*.

I joined them. Howard joined the picket clowns. He passed out accordion ashtrays. We bought them bulk at a child sweatshop in Pacoima.

Sid Hughes said, "You're back, Dick. You did your time and did your duty. What's next?"

I laid out my precanned pitch. "I'm going directly to the Lieutenant Colonel Sam DeRienzo American Legion Post in Glendale. I'm going to voluntarily sign a loyalty oath that declares me as 110% American. I'm back to let the world know that I can bang that stomach Steinway better than ever."

Sid laughed and hummed the "Tico Tico" finale. Morty said, "Harry Truman pardoned you—and that's good. But you've also gotten support from some pretty unsavory quarters."

I said, "Keep going. That last stuff is all fresh to me."

Morty checked his notepad. "Oscar Levant was on *Jukebox Jury*. He said, 'Dick Contino has more to fear than fear itself. He has the accordion.'"

Oscar, you hump. Oscar, you rubber-room raconteur.

Oscar's wife signed him into the Mount Sinai nut ward. His agent signed him out for local TV gigs. Michael Curtiz signed him out for cultural kicks and took him down to watch wetbacks fuck in a skid-row hotel.

I said, "If that's 'support,' put me back on that airplane. I'd rather fight the Red Army than go up against Oscar's mouth."

Sid laughed. Morty checked his notebook. "There's a pinko lawyer named L. Trent Woodard. He's said some pretty raw things about the LAPD, and he's gone on to call you a 'gallant young man who had the courage to acknowledge his rational and understandable fear and implicitly address the absurdity of the war in Korea.'"

My blood pressure went presto-prestissimo. "I'm 100% American. And Ward Bond and Adolphe Menjou will verify that."

Howard walked up. He grabbed me and lip-locked my ear.

"Dick, we've got to go. I've got you a quick gig on the way out to Glendale."

"What are you talking about?"

"You're going to serenade a young lady. She's in an iron lung at Queen of Angels."

Howard drove me downtown. I stretched out in the backseat and skimmed my recent clips.

CONTINO BACK IN SOUTHLAND was good. The guy stressed my presidential pardon and soft-pedaled all the fear stuff that deep-sixed me. ACCORDION KING RETURNS took a tragic tack. The guy ran down my run on *The Horace Heidt Show* and said I "hipster-ized" the squeeze box. I "beat out vocal groups, a Negro trom-bone, and a blind vibraphone virtuoso" and "sent applause meters haywire for fifty-two weeks straight." I had "4,000 fan clubs nationwide" and "almost got signed to play Rudolph Valentino" in a "big bio-epic at Fox." The guy implied that I had the world by the ass and that I got more ass than a toilet seat. Too bad I "cravenly exposed a fearful nature," "crybabyingly tried to avoid Korean service," and "cringingly ran from basic training at Ford Ord, California." Too bad I "shakily served six months at the McNeil Island pen" and "shadily segued back to the army as a hardened con."

Hush-Hush magazine called me "CONtino." They said my "destiny was deliriously and dolorously determined by deep-seated demons dramatically and detrimentally defined as debili-tating FEAR." They ran a sidebar with Oscar Levant and some dope-clinic quack. The quack said I was badly breast-fed and tem-peramentally toilet trained. Oscar said I should dump my box and exploit my weak pipes like a dozen famous guinea crooners.

A picture ran next to the sidebar. There's Oscar and me at the Shrine. We're flying on some high-end shit that I copped from Bob Mitchum. Oscar's banging out Prokofiev. I'm winging a ditty that's half Brahms and half "Lady of Spain."

I skimmed the rest of the rag. I caught some sin-sational bits that played like prime Oscar.

Johnnie Ray honked a vice cop at the Vine Street Derby. The pull-quote was pure Levant: "He took the law into his own hands." LEZabeth Scott frequented a sapphic whorehouse. Matchhead-hot James Dean was a mumble-mouthed masochist known as the "Human Ashtray." George Burns liked it dark and dusky. He was spotted at a browntown motel with two large congo cuties.

People told Oscar things. They overestimated his dope habit and dumped their shameful shit wholesale. They underestimated his memory.

Oscar heard all, remembered all, and told all. People looked at Oscar and saw all their sinful stuff personified and multiplied. They overestimated his empathy. They underestimated his guile. They flocked to the nut ward. They sought Oscar out. Oscar fed their secret shit to an L.A. cop named Freddy Otash. Otash paid him off in dope and shot the shit straight to *Hush-Hush*.

I skimmed the rest of my clips. L. Trent Woodard sunk his hooks under my skin.

The L.A. *Herald*, 12/19/53:

Woodard calls Chief William H. Parker "the führer of the LAPD." He calls me a "sacrificial lamb" two columns down.

The L.A. *Times*, 1/8/54:

Woodard calls the LAPD "an occupation force." He calls me a "Police-State Victim" three columns down.

The L.A. *Mirror*, 2/20/54:

Woodard boohoos "the forces that condemned Dick Contino." He rags the LAPD and the L.A. County Sheriff's for a botched robbery job.

The city cops and the county cops were working a joint gig. They had the Scrivner's Drive-In at Ivar and Sunset nailed down tight. They got the drop on four bad Negroes.

A cop popped his piece premature. Six cops and four stick-up men threw fire. Three Negroes and two carhops went down dead.

The LAPD blamed the Sheriff's. The Sheriff's blamed the LAPD. Chief Parker blamed Sheriff Biscailuz. Sheriff Biscailuz blamed Chief Parker. A heist guy named Rudy "Playboy" Wells escaped. A city cop named Cal Dinkins caught the blame.

Three pix ran with the piece. Dinkins wore a lot of fat and a tall flattop. Wells wore dark skin and a big boogie conk.

They ran a Fed mug shot of me. I wore tear tracks and a grimace.

I dumped the clips in the front seat. Howard turned around. His hands flew off the wheel. A truck almost blitzed us.

"Dick, Jesus Christ. I had them in chronological order. You can't just—"

"That Woodard guy is putting me in shit up to my ears. He's making me look like a fellow traveler."

We slid into oncoming traffic. Howard grabbed the wheel and slid us out. "We'll work around it. We'll get you to snitch off some left-wing types and boost your credentials that way."

"I don't know any left-wing types."

Howard smiled. "We'll work around it. There's a guy at Metro I'd love to put the screws to."

The iron lung was 6' by 8' and weighed two tons. The lung girl was pale and skinny.

She was propped up inside the thing lengthwise. Her head poked out the top. She saw me and got choked up. Her tears hit the lung ledge and sizzled. The thing ran twice as hot as a clothes dryer.

A kid brought my loaner.

The keys jammed. The buttons stuck. The bellows creaked bad. The strap gouged a zit on my back.

The kid brought half the Belmont High wind section. A boss blonde blew lead tenor. She buzzed around me. I told Howard to check her ID and note the date she turned legal.

Howard promised me reporters. He delivered. The kiddie press showed up en masse. Six high school papers sent scribes. The lung ward ran SRO.

I strapped in and played to the lung girl. I pounded my pelvis and humped my hips and socked my sockets out at right angles. I played "Sabre Dance," "The Beer Barrel Polka," and "Cherry Pink and Apple Blossom White."

I strutted. I writhed. I sprayed sweat laced with Old Spice

cologne. My Tiger Wax melted. My pompadour dropped into my eyes. I bent back and resurrected it. I pressed my eighty-pound ax out to arm's length and played from a full-arch position. My spine shook, shuddered, and held. Applause eclipsed my crescendo.

I bent back to a normal stance. I bowed to the lung girl. Her tears spattered off the lung ledge.

Howard shot me a look:

Quit while they love you/Fuck these kids/No encores and no good-byes.

I dumped the ax and pulled a fast exit. A big ovation blew me out the door. The sax slipped me an envelope. I stepped into the hallway and opened it.

Her note:

> *Dear Dick*,
> I will reach the age-of-consent at 10:49 P.M. on Thursday, March 29, 1954, which is only 6 days from now. Please call me at 10:50 P.M. (Dunkirk 4-5882) to arrange a rendezvous. I know that we will make beautiful music together.
> xxxxxxxxx!!!!!!
> Linda Jane Sidwell (Contino?)

I felt a little heft in the envelope. I looked in and saw a fat reefer.

We drove out to Glendale. Howard wanted to toke the reefer en route. I said no. Maryjane always flipped his switch. I didn't want him hopped-up and horny.

I shut my eyes and daydreamed. Linda Jane Sidwell—six days to love.

I'd form a combo and take it to Vegas. Linda would quit school and blow sax for me. We'd work up a patriotic shtick. We'd suck up to professional patriots. We'd play lounges and move to main rooms. Linda's parents would hate me. I'd buy their love with Cadillacs and introductions to Sinatra.

Howard nudged me. "Wake up. We're here."

I opened my eyes. We pulled up in front of the Legion Hall. Howard said, "Shit."

No banners. No reporters. No Ward Bond, no Adolphe Menjou, no Legionnaires. A table full of cold cuts rotting in the sun.

I jumped out of the car. An old guy walked out of the hall and snagged some cheese puffs.

He saw me. He drooped. He said, "Dick, I'm sorry."

I kicked the table over. Delicatessen delights hit the sidewalk. Two dogs caught the scent and leaped from a moving car.

The Legion guy said, "Dick, I'm sorry." The dogs snouted up salami and sun-ripe cheese.

I said, "What happened?"

The guy took off his Legion cap and wiped his face with it. "Duke Wayne called the post commander. He said, 'Lou, I hate to ask you for this, but you see how it looks. Contino paid his dues, but that Red cocksucker Woodard's screwing up his public perception. I hate to exert pressure, but you know I always buy three pages in your book every Christmas.'"

I shut my eyes. I tried to blot it out. I saw the Duke in my revised *Fort Apache*. A redskin keestered him and snatched his wig for a scalp.

I opened my eyes. The dogs attacked a three-pound *capo-collo*. I said, "Where's the liquor? I want to take it back and get a refund."

The guy pointed to the door. "Your buddy took most of it, and he said he'd be back for the rest."

"What buddy?"

"I don't know. He said he was your buddy, and he said you went way back."

I ran inside. I saw the stuff that Wayne and Woodard fucked me out of.

The lectern draped in red, white, and blue. The prepaid seats and party hats. A wall-mounted flag and a cue-card gizmo to feed me the words to my oath.

I ran back to the storeroom. I saw a pile of flattened cartons five feet high.

Johnnie Black and Hennessy XO. Bonded bourbon, Ballantine's and Bacardi.

Stacked on a shelf.

A box of rubbers and a six-pack of Brew 102.

The back door opened. Danny Getchell walked in.

The *Hush-Hush* guy.

Who:

Called me a "pretty-boy pantywaist" and a "pusillanimous punk."

Who:

Called my mom a "maladroit madonna" and my pop the "punk's paterfamilias."

I saw Danny. Danny saw me. He grabbed the rubbers and ran.

He cut through the parking lot and jumped into a blue Merc coupe. I chased him. He gunned the engine. He yelled, "Commie castrato Contino can't run for shit!"

I ran harder. I gained ground. Danny put the car in gear and goosed it out of reach.

He yelled, "Lefty loser less than lethal at Legion loyaltyfest!"

I ran harder. I gained ground. Danny goosed the car out of reach.

He yelled, "Ballsy bandit burgles boffo batch of brand-name booze! Less-than-lethal loser left in lurch!"

I ran harder. I gained ground. I hooked around to the front of the hall and hauled ass.

Danny goosed the car out of reach. I slipped on a pile of my dad's cold cuts. I hit the street ass-over-elbows and ate hot exhaust fumes.

2

Howard refused to front me the coin for a room. I moved into my dad's bomb shelter.

I treated my elbows and knees. I climbed into a bongo shirt and peggers. I called Linda Sidwell's house and left a message with her mom.

Tell Linda to pack for ground zero. Make an atom-bomb sound. Tell her we'll head for Hiroshima and level the town with our love.

I was desperate. I was walking the lonely streets of Shit City. The bad guys dug me. The good guys feared me. The lung gig was my welcome-home highlight. Howard said we could sell the lung-ward kids accordion lessons and spring my ax from the hock shop. My comeback would boom from there.

I didn't buy it. I felt one of my Patented Post-Passive Rages poised to pop. I lashed out once in a billion blue moons. I imploded all my impacted shit inward and outward and took it out on inanimate objects.

The bomb shelter smelled like a catbox. I taped some nudie pix to the ceiling above my cot and stretched out to slam the ham.

I noticed two envelopes on the nightstand. My mom must have brought them in. They were perfume dipped and pale blue linen.

I picked them up. I sniffed them. I saw my name and address. The back flaps were stained at the edge. Prison mail was steamed open, read, and resealed. This looked like the same thing.

The postmarks read 2/18 and 2/20/54. The return-address stickers read:

Vivian Woodard, 348 South Muirfield Road, Los Angeles, 4, California.

"Woodard"—as in "L. Trent." Swank Hancock Park.

I opened the envelopes. I read the letters inside. Passionate passages pounced on me.

"Your art is dubious and derivative, but you play with an astounding sensual conviction." "My husband admires your struggle and your blunt and wrenching admissions of your fear, and is concurrently vexed by your power over me." "You cannot be socially enlightened without acknowledging Dick Contino as a symbol of candor and transcendent vulnerability." "I want you inside me. I want to swing off the axis where our loins meet in wetness and tumescence." "Your music is my anthem. Your seed is the hot ink that courses through my veins and my pen as I write these words."

Ooooooooooh, Daddy-o!!!!!

I read the letters four times. I circled the sex stuff. I taped the letters to the ceiling above my cot and formed an erotic collage.

Somebody banged on my door. My mom yelled, "Dick! Oscar's on the phone!"

Oscar Levant said, "You're a schmuck. You're also a schmendrick, a schlemiel, and a schlemazel."

Oscar was pissed. Freddy Otash cut down his dope dose. Oscar said Freddy extorted the shit out of *schvartze* jazz musicians. Freddy didn't want Oscar to overdose and die. *Hush-Hush* couldn't fly without his sinful and sincere sinuendo.

I tilted my chair back. I scoped out the nut ward. Oscar tilted his chair back and tracked my eyes.

The rec room was chock-full of nuts. An orderly was marching an old man around. The old man was talking non-stop and drooling into a cup.

Oscar said, "Pops is a Wall Street trader. He recites nursery rhymes, with some insider stock tips laced into the flow. The orderly is Freddy O's watchdog. He keeps an eye on me, pumps the old guy for stock tips, and feeds them to Freddy."

Gail Russell and Barbara Payton were playing dominoes. Barbara ran her right foot up Gail's leg sapphically *slooooow*. Gail swatted it away.

Oscar said, "They're both dipsos. The boss at Paramount told them to dry out or else. Babs always goes lez in stir. Gail's pining for Rock Hudson. Rock's playing skin-flute on a bartender at Don the Beachcomber's. The bartender snorts Big 'H' and moonlights at an all-male cathouse."

A geek was twisting his hair in knots and doodling on a scratch pad. A dozen nuts stood around and watched him draw.

Oscar said, "He's an animator for *The Webster Webfoot Show*. He makes animated smut flicks on the side and sells them down in T.J. He thinks he's Webster Webfoot. His wife shows up once a week and throws popcorn at him."

I laughed. The orderly noticed me and sized me up. Oscar lit a cigarette and blew smoke in my face.

I said, "You want something. You're playing some kind of angle here."

Oscar blew concentric smoke rings. "I want to contemporize you. I want to revitalize your career and end your days as a schmuck, a schmendrick, a schlemiel, and a schlemazel."

"What's in it for you?"

"You check me out on a pass, right this goddamn instant. You take me down to Darktown and get me what I need to survive."

He was headed for Shake City. He sucked that cigarette down to a stub in sixteen seconds.

He started twitching. He started shaking. His eyes started begging me.

I said, "Let's go."

We drove south and smoked Linda's reefer. Life lapsed into slow motion. We were bebop bwanas on the Dark Continent. My dad's '50 Ford was a barge on the River Styx.

Dig the jazz clubs! Dig that drive-in mosque! Dig the unkink-your-hair parlors and the chopped-and-channeled chariots in cool coon maroon!

We cruised Central Avenue. A voodoo moon beamed down and lit the way. Oscar found Rachmaninoff on the radio. We rolled our windows down and shared him with our wild-ass world.

The weed unkinked Oscar. He stopped twitching and abusing me. I steered the barge with one finger. Water lapped under my feet.

Oscar said, "The Pharaoh Club. They've got a steam room, and all the hip junkies sweat themselves out there before their Nalline tests. Freddy O jacks them up and steals their stuff."

My life lapsed out of slow motion. Oscar wrecked my reverie. He sounded like a 45 single spun at 78.

I spoke *slooow* and easy. "Freddy O is a cop. He can flash his badge and pull that kind of thing off."

Oscar lit a cigarette and sucked it down to a cinder in one drag. He flicked the butt out the window and flashed two little gold stars.

Toy badges.

"Junior Deputy" at the bottom. "Sheriff John's Lunch Brigade" at the top.

I blinked. The Belgian Congo disappeared and cohered as Darktown L.A. A bazaboo bipped in front of the car. I missed him by a snatch-hair margin.

Oscar said, "You can't pass this up. It's too sweet. You'll do anything to prove you're not a crap-your-pants crybaby."

I gulped. I popped a sweat. I saw the Pharaoh Club three doors down and pulled to the curb.

I wore a babaloo bongo shirt and peg pants. Oscar wore a nutward robe and pj's. Hepcats, hipsters, and hopheads knew our faces.

Oscar said, "Fearful *faigeleh* fiddle-faddles while—"

I jumped out of the car. Oscar jumped out. We squared off on the sidewalk. Oscar passed me my badge. I concocted an intro line and pushed the door open.

We entered Pharaoh's Tomb. A big *schvartze* in Egyptian threads materialized. I caught the layout behind him.

Black crepe walls. Tables shaped like scarabs going sixty-nine. A bandstand inlaid with a gold-embossed Ramses II holding crossed scepters. A jazz combo decked out in fezzes—blasting to an all-sepia crowd.

Steam seeped through some ceiling cracks. The spa was upstairs.

The *schvartze* eyeballed Oscar's pajamas. "You lookin' for a bed, or you come for some milk and cookies?"

Oscar flashed his badge and said, "Fuck you, King Tut."

The *schvartze* laughed.

I reached for my intro line. I lost it in the flight path of Marijuana Airways. I said the first thing that hit my head:

"My name's Friday. I carry a badge."

Fuck—straight out of *Dragnet*.

The *schvartze* laughed. He leaned back and howled. His sheik shirt rolled above his sheik pants. He packed a beavertail sap in his waistband.

Oscar grabbed the sap and cracked him in the head. The

schvartze hit the side wall and knocked a liquor license loose. I grabbed him by his conk and bent his head back. Oscar cracked him again.

He spit out some denture debris and a slice of his tongue. Oscar said, "Who's holding? Who's got the stuff to feed the monkey on my back?"

The *schvartze* quaked and quivered. I dropped his head. Oscar propped it up with the sap.

"I asked you, 'Who's holding?' Who's got the doughnuts, the strudel, the *shit*?"

The *schvartze* stammered, stuttered, and pointed upstairs. He got out a string of popped *P*'s and the single word "Playboy."

Go, Oscar!

The *schvartze* stammered and stuttered. He got out more popped *P*'s and the words "Please don't hit me!"

I looked at Oscar. Oscar looked at me. We tore through the Pharaoh Club.

People laughed. People snickered. People ducked and dove under their tables. Oscar's robe billowed. It snagged on chair backs and chicken-and-waffle plates. We distracted the combo. They blew their beat. "Bumble Boogie" bent off-key.

We ran up the backstairs. We kicked down a door marked Private. Black faces poked out of a steam cloud. Dissipating dope drifted through it. Oscar sucked the shit into his lungs and swung his sap blind.

A black blip blipped into black-and-red. Blood spritzed through the cloud. I heard bones crack. I heard a man scream. Oscar yelled, "Where's Playboy?"

A black face yelled, "Out back!" A black face yelled, "The parking lot!" A black face yelled, "Out back with some white guy!"

We ran downstairs. We kicked down an exit door. That voodoo moon lit up the parking lot. I saw a white man and a Negro man huddled by a '49 Olds.

They had their backs to us. I tapped Oscar and made the *ssssshhh* sigh. Oscar nodded and zipped his lips shut.

We tiptoed up. I heard every word they said.

The white man said, "You weren't supposed to pull heists. That was part of our deal."

The Negro man said, "*Sheeit.*"

The white man said, "You were supposed to recruit colored tail for the movie gig and chauffeur the girls out of Sybil Brand, and that's fucking all you were supposed to do."

The Negro man said, "I didn't like the way that Harvey creep was lookin' at my bitch."

The white man said, "He's harmless. All he wants to do is take pictures."

Oscar held up his badge and said, "Freeze, shitbirds."

The men turned around. I made them from the *Mirror-News*. Cal Dinkins—LAPD bull. Rudy "Playboy" Wells—robber.

Dinkins laughed. Wells laughed. I dug my feet into the ground and reinforced my spastic sphincter. Dinkins said, "Holy shit! Oscar Levant and Dick Contino."

Oscar said, "We just look like those punks. It's part of our cover. Cough up the dope, Playboy."

The word "Playboy" tripped Playboy's trigger. He looked at Dinkins. The look said, "They know us." Dinkins said, "Kill them."

Oscar twitched and dropped his sap. Playboy pulled a shiv and flicked his tongue down the blade. Blood trickled over his lips. He licked it off and giggled.

I kicked him in the balls. He jackknifed. I pried the shiv out of his hand and jammed it in his right eye. Oscar picked up the sap and whacked Dinkins in the knees.

Dinkins yelped. Playboy screamed. I pulled the shiv out of his eye and lashed it across Dinkins's throat. It snagged on his windpipe. I pulled it out loose and ripped Dinkins down to the breastbone.

They gurgled. They spat blood. They hit their knees in one big convulsion. I picked them up and tossed them in the '49 Olds. Oscar picked their pockets.

They gurgled. They spat blood. They moaned. I saw a hunk of hose on the seat beside them. I got a fuck-their-ID-up idea.

I popped the gas cap and stuck the hose in the tank. I siphoned six inches of ethyl and spat it in their two gasping gullets. They choked. They gasped. They opened up *wiiiide*.

I pulled the gun off Dinkins's hip. I popped the clip. I dropped four slugs in his mouth and fed three to Playboy. I chased them with two matches.

The bullets blew up. I heard dental work destroyed and saw detective work deconstructed. They shot mouth flames. They scorched the upholstery. The Olds went up like Cinder City.

Oscar shook and twitched. He lit a cigarette off the car flames and killed it in a third of a drag.

I picked him up. I threw him over my shoulder and ran.

3

I opened my eyes. I saw the mash notes and the girls taped to my ceiling.

It all came back. I almost pissed in my pajamas.

I got Oscar back to Mount Sinai. We tossed Playboy's billfold en route. I kept Cal Dinkins's address book. I wanted to know who he knew. Maybe I could frame some freak for my murders.

I was hung over from Maryjane and mayhem. I made up for the men I didn't kill in Korea. They sheltered me in Seoul. They didn't know that candid cowards could kill with correct provocation.

I was scared.

I showed my face at 83rd and Central. Oscar showed his face and shot off his dope-deprived mouth. People knew us. We were penny-ante public personas. Oscar played piano and portrayed pissants in a dozen flicks in constant rerun. A Pharaoh Club patron might see *Humoresque* and buzz the fuzz. My career might soar and plant my puss in a million memory banks. I might fall from cloud nine to the gas chamber.

I stared at my ceiling. I strafed words and pix. I lingered on "I want you" and a blonde with a heat rash.

Yesterday and today. The tightrope and the abyss.

I rolled off my cot. I cooked up some coffee and skimmed the radio dial. I caught the morning news on six stations. Nobody mentioned the Pharaoh Club inferno.

I went through the address book. I saw a bunch of no-names listed in alphabetical order and some names and numbers listed at the back.

Two name-names/one familiar name/one no-name.

The no-name:

Harvey Glatman (Harvey's TV Repair, HO-49236). $2,000.

The familiar name:

Johnny Stompanato, CR-28609. $4,000.

Johnny Stomp: ex-Mickey Cohen goon.

I knew Mickey at McNeil Island. He said Johnny poured the pork to Donna Reed and Rita Hayworth. Orson Welles filmed the trysts through a 2-way mirror and screened them at a stag night at the Cannes filmfest.

The name-names:

Ida Lupino/CR-62211/$6,000. Steve Cochran/OL-65189/ $6,000.

Ida Lupino: Mrs. Howard Duff. Film star and director. Steve Cochran: B-movie stud.

I kicked the names around. I retrieved two things that Wells and Dinkins said:

"You were supposed to recruit colored tail for the *movie* gig." / "I didn't like the way that *Harvey* creep was lookin' at my bitch."

Dinkins: rogue cop. Wells: heist man. They colluded on the drive-in job. The "movie gig" had to be something else.

I ran out to my parents' porch and picked up the *Herald*. On page two: NIGHTCLUB NIGHTMARE.

They tagged the victims John Doe #1 and #2. The *schvartze* described his assailants: "Big guys—they'd have to be to mess with me." Two sketches ran on page three. The sketch artist did not draw Oscar and me. He drew two bullet-headed pachucos.

I laughed. I roared. I did an impromptu shimmy. We took two Gs off the stiffs. My half would spring my ax and rent me a slick little love shack.

A big man stepped out of a shadow. He held out a badge and blocked out my brand-new sunshine. He said, "You silly cock-sucker."

The badge was real. The man was all muscle. He pulled out a claim tag and flicked it on my nose. He said, "You silly fuck."

He wore a gold watch and a gold-plated .45. He wore a gold ID link. The "F.O." ID'd him.

Fred Otash—the big-time Big O.

I twitched. I shook. I popped a Popsicle sweat. A van pulled into the driveway. Dig the side panels: HARVEY'S TV REPAIR.

A creep stared out the windshield. He picked his nose. Otash flicked the claim tag on *my* nose.

"You dropped it by the car you torched, and that orderly saw you check Oscar out of Mount Sinai. He called Danny Getchell. Danny tailed you down to niggertown and lost you. He figured you went down there for some smoky meat, and he thought he might nail you coming out of some coon whorehouse."

I shook. I shivered. I shrugged like I didn't give a shit. A gyro-scope popped out of the van and spun on the roof. The next-door-neighbor lady walked out on her porch and picked up her morning paper. The creep ogled her.

I looked at Otash. Otash looked at me. It hit me hard:

A fix was in. The cops John Doe'd Wells and Dinkins deliber-ately. Otash did not know that I knew that. Otash did not know that I knew my victims' names. I did not tell Oscar their names. I had to hold it all back from Oscar and Otash.

Otash yawned. "Let's wrap this up before your folks get back. First, quit shaking and lay out last night for me."

I laid out a condensed version. "Oscar Levant and I got in some trouble at the Pharaoh Club. We tried to cop some dope, and a white guy and a colored guy attacked us. I killed them in self-defense."

Otash smiled. The creep smiled back. Otash nodded. The

creep hit a switch on his dashboard. My voice boomed off the gyroscope and covered the whole block:

"Oscar Levant and I got in some trouble at the Pharaoh Club. We tried to cop some dope, and—"

Otash nodded. The creep hit a switch. My voice died out.

I shook. I weaved. My legs went. I fell back and hit a porch post. Otash pulled his gun and pinned me to it.

"Did you take anything off the bodies?"

I lied big. "We took the money out of their wallets and tossed the wallets down a sewer grate."

"Did you find an address book on the white guy?"

"No."

"Are you sure?"

"Sure I'm sure. Do you think I'd—"

Otash slapped me. A big gold ring raked my nose.

"Here's the question, paisan. Do you want to burn for this? Do you want me to sweat Oscar cold turkey until he gives you up to corroborate your confession, or do you want to get some middle-aged pussy and make friends in the LAPD?"

My head spun six ways. My tongue tripped over six ways to express acquiescence. I stammered. I stuttered. Otash slapped me. Blood burst out of my nose.

"I'll take that response as a yes and lay it out for you. One, the Feds intercepted some letters that a certain pink lady wrote to you and shared them with us. Two, the pink lady's husband has said some entirely unacceptable things about the LAPD and has to be punished. Your job is to meet the pink lady at a bash at the Wilshire-Ebell tonight, fuck her silly, and get her to admit that her pinko husband is a member of the various Commie-front organizations that we suspect he is. Do you understand your job, paisan?"

I said, "Yes." My voice sounded too deep and overamplified. It *wah-wahhed* off the van.

Otash glared at the creep. The creep hit a switch. My voice *wah-wahhed* and died.

Otash tapped his gun on my chest. "That's Harvey Glatman.

He's a genius, but he likes to play with his toys too much. You meet him at his shop at 5:30. He'll wire you up for the job."

The neighbor woman walked out again. Glatman ogled her. He panted and fogged up his windshield.

Otash slapped me. I tasted his ring.

"Stay scared, Dick."

I had to act like I still had a future. I had to tap the shallow show-must-go-on part of my soul and dig up some desperate ego to pass off for courage. I had to sort out the shit I stepped into and get up the guts to shaft L. Trent Woodard for the shit he slung my way.

I repo'd my accordion. I called Linda and outlined her birth-control options.

I called Howard. He said I was poison. No booking agent or casting boss would touch me. I was poison. I was contagious. I was the syph and the clap. L. Trent Woodard lavishly lauded me in the morning *Mirror.* He smeared me and slathered me pink.

I called Oscar at Mount Sinai. He sounded bombed. He didn't remember the Pharaoh Club and our double homicide. He thought we drove to T.J. We caught the mule act and played Gershwin for the mule and a queer matador. We drove back to L.A. at dawn.

I pumped him for dope on Fred O. He said Freddy ran a string of snitches for *Hush-Hush.* He kept the secret dirt stash that was too hot for *Hush-Hush* to handle and had every fag bathhouse in the swish alps wired for sound.

Freddy beat up Japs at Manzanar. Freddy killed Japs on Saipan. Freddy broke the strike at the Ford plant in Pico Rivera. Freddy popped a Mickey Cohen punk named Hooky Rothman. Jack Dragna paid him ten grand. Freddy popped a Dragna punk. Mickey paid him ten grand.

I dropped the address-book names. Oscar didn't know Johnny Stomp or Harvey the Creep. He said Steve Cochran packed the biggest *schvantz* in Tinseltown. He said Ida Lupino dried out at Mount Sinai last year. Freddy O snuck her Turpenhydrate. Ida loved Freddy. Ida feared Freddy. She fed him bits for *Hush-Hush.*

Ida and the Schvantz were making a picture right now—some lox called *Private Hell 36*.

I hung up and called a guy at *Variety*. He said *Private Hell 36* was shooting nights out in Duarte. Howard Duff costarred with Ida and the Schvantz.

I drove downtown and skulked around the main library. I pulled old clips and new clips and rolled microfilm. I came up with insinuating shit.

The drive-in heist was hot. Cal Dinkins took heat for Playboy. He bopped away from his stakeout post. Playboy plowed a barricade and skedaddled.

I saw a shot of Dinkins and Jack Webb. The *Times* called them "tight-knit." Dinkins taught Webb how to play his part on *Dragnet*.

The *Times* ran heist copy. The *Herald* ran context.

The stakeout was covertly co-op: the LAPD and L.A. Sheriff's. The stakeout was steeped in interagency grief. It went way back.

The Sheriff's sanctioned Mickey Cohen's Sunset Strip incursion. The LAPD hated Mickey. Mickey was bushwhacked on Sheriff's turf in July '49. He took two .12-gauge pellets and walked. His pal Neddie Herbert took a spread in the face. The case was unsolved. The LAPD was suspected. The key suspect was Officer Fred Otash.

Chief Parker hated Sheriff Biscailuz. Biscailuz hated Parker. The LAPD and Sheriff's were knocking noggins now. The state legislature had their budgets up for review. Both agencies wanted more money. Both agencies wanted a cut of the other guys' coin. The LAPD got more money now. Biscailuz wanted that money and more.

I skimmed a piece on Johnny Stompanato.

Johnny made bail on an extortion bounce. The *Herald* hinted at horny housewives and naughty snapshots. The D.A. declined to file charges.

The *Herald* ran a picture. Johnny looked like me. He was one handsome guinea side of beef.

I found a piece on Viv and Trent Woodard. Viv wrote poetry. Viv took colored kids to the Civic Light Opera. Trent lived off a trust fund. He filed suits for drunks and derelicts pistol-whipped and pounded by the LAPD.

I saw a shot of Viv. She's doing a curtsy at some debutante ball. It's '47. She's dark haired, rangy, and busty. She's coming up on 45 fast.

The picture goosed my gonads. I wanted to rip it off the microfilm roll and tape it to my bomb-shelter ceiling.

I found a piece on *Private Hell 36*. It said the Schvantz disrupted the shoot with two dates in court. It implied Mickey Mouse misdemeanors.

I walked to a pay phone and called Oscar. I ran it by him. He said the Schvantz beat up a hooker and got caught with a fat bag of boo. Ida Lupino told him. She said the judge shot the Schvantz a suspended sentence in exchange for a part in his next picture.

My head buzzed like a bumblebee on Benzedrine. My names bopped in a tight spread.

I pressed Oscar. I wanted more dirt. Oscar said he couldn't think. The doctors deregulated his daily dope drip.

He wanted Demerol. They gave him Dilantin. He wanted to duck down to Darktown and dig up some Dilaudid.

I pressed harder. Oscar said he talked to Barbara Payton. Babs said she had a thing with the Schvantz. She said the Schvantz measured in at 12.4 inches.

Harvey Glatman shaved my chest and taped on a microphone. I looked around his back room.

TV tubes dumped on chairs and a dusty old couch. A six-slat shelf packed with diodes and diagnostic devices. Four walls of perverted pinup pulchritude.

Women trussed with rope. Women spread-eagled. Women gagged with black rubber balls. Chaste shots of Joi Lansing on the *Dragnet* set.

I lingered on Joi. Harvey caught it.

"She just broke up with Jack Webb. Jack's torching. Joi's working the line at Ciro's, and Jack sits ringside every night."

Cal Dinkins knew Jack Webb. Webb was LAPD Shill #1.

"Did you take those pictures of her?"

Harvey twisted three wires and taped them above my right nipple. "I used to be Jack's unit photographer."

I took a big whiff of Harvey. I took in his peeper pix and his panty-sniffer paraphernalia. I smelled ex-con. I smelled snitch. I smelled rabid Rottweiler.

"Let me guess. Jack heard you served time. He cut you loose, and Freddy O picked up your option."

Harvey deadpanned me. "You should stand away from electrical appliances. They screw up the sound quality."

I said, "Jack's tight with Chief Parker. I heard the LAPD runs R & I checks on the *Dragnet* crew, and I'll bet they turned up a rap sheet on you."

Harvey pulled a wild hair off my chest. I yelped. Harvey dabbed a styptic pencil on the raw spot.

"I'm a certified genius. I can broadcast TV pictures from any installation to any individual TV set, which means I don't have to sit still for your insinuations."

I looked at the bondage pix. I saw yellow bands on the girls' wrists. Sybil Brand inmates wore yellow wristbands.

Cal Dinkins to Playboy:

"Recruit colored tail for the movie gig" / "Chauffeur the girls out of Sybil Brand" / "All he wants to do is take pictures."

"What did you go up for, Harvey? Statch rape? Flimflam? Some weenie-wagger beef? I think you—"

Harvey pinched a tuft of hair and ripped it off my chest. I yelped. Harvey said, "Be nice, Dick. You're an ex-convict yourself."

4

My chest stubble itched. My tape wrap stung. My tuxedo smelled like mothballs.

I parked outside the Wilshire-Ebell. I saw a sign by the door: SISTER KENNY FOUNDATION GALA. I saw the nut-ward orderly and a strapping goon parked in a tow-away zone.

I walked inside. They watched me. I flashed my invitation to a hostess and zoomed straight back to the bar.

I was early. The ballroom was almost empty. Two nuns and a priest were blasting scotch at a bar-side table. The nuns looked half-gassed. They saw me and giggled.

I ordered a quadruple martini. I told the barman to put it in a pail or a dog dish. He brought me a pitcher and a glass and cleared out fast.

I drank. I kept my back to the ballroom and heard it fill up behind me. I heard people at the bar whisper, "That's Dick Contino."

I kept my snout in my glass. The booze sparked political conversions and apostasies. I moved left and denounced Joe McCarthy. I moved right and shot Alger Hiss 2,000 volts. I freed the Scottsboro Boys and beat Helen Gahagan Douglas to death with my accordion.

The booze enlightened. The booze obfuscated. I figured I'd see Viv and respond to stimuli like Pavlov's fucking dog.

I heard a familiar voice. I recognized it. I glanced two stools down.

Gene Biscailuz plucked the fruit off an old-fashioned. L. Trent Woodard sucked a cherry out of his Manhattan.

I saw Woodard. He didn't see me. I eavesdropped.

Biscailuz made small talk. Polio and Sister Kenny—blah, blah, blah. Woodard said, "Sheriff, let's talk turkey. You can't let Bill Parker and the city cops bootjack all that money. You can't—"

Woodard saw me. He dropped the Sheriff in midspiel and slid two stools down. I slid to the far right and got right up in his face.

"Back off, baby doll. I'm a pistol-packing white man, and I don't like your leanings. And don't blast the LAPD and invoke me in the same breath. Those guys are the thin blue line between freedom and the fifth column."

Woodard dropped his glass. A priest spun off his stool and spilled scotch in my lap. I shouted my declaration. My chest mike must have caught every word.

I locked orbs with Woodard. An eyeball duel ensued. I broke it

⁻off and barged into the crowd. A little bit of my soul broke loose and bopped off unbidden.

People watched me pass. I heard a dozen "Dick Continos." Tuxedos and taffeta swirled around me. I caught a split-second blip of Chief William H. Parker in dress blues.

I walked out to a palm-lined portico. It was private and peaceful. I figured she'd find me and pounce.

I leaned on a railing and watched cars bomb down Wilshire. I counted up from zero. She pounced at twenty-two.

"I thought you'd at least send me an autographed picture."

I pulled a perfect pivot and spun around close enough to kiss her. I said, "I knew you'd be here."

She smiled. She smelled like Tweed or Jungle Gardenia. She was 49 or 50 and looked it. She wore a tight black gown. Her right breast was half again as large as her left. Her cleavage dipped proportionately. Her right nipple was half-exposed. It was dark and pebbled up from cold air or excitement.

I wanted to fuck her. My heart lurched to the left.

"How did you know I'd be here?"

Freddy O briefed me. He said to cite Harrison Carroll's column.

I stepped closer. Viv reached up and tossed her hair off her right shoulder. I saw a razor nick under her arm.

I said, "I read about the Sister Kenny thing, and I saw your name mentioned."

Viv stepped back. Her heels snagged on her floor-length hemline. She tottered and caught herself. My heart lurched. I wanted her to reach for me.

I looked over her shoulder. Her husband slid through the ballroom. He had one arm around a young man.

Viv said, "Can I tell you why I came on so strong?"

I nodded. I jammed my hands in my pockets. I didn't want to touch her too soon.

She said, "To begin with, I acknowledged our age difference and decided to risk the chance that you'd find me elderly, then I thought you might be lonely and vulnerable after all that time in prison and Korea, then I thought I owed you something for the injudicious way my husband has expressed his admiration for you, then I thought that anyone who's been as candid about their fear as you've been would appreciate my candor and not judge me as desperate, and then I figured I'd better act fast before I hit menopause and get indifferent to sex."

My heartbeat escalated. My chest expanded. A strip of Harvey Glatman's tape popped loose.

Viv said, "Say something. I had that speech prepared, and you're just looking at me."

I said, "Your husband's in the next room."

She said, "He's a homosexual, and he wants me to be with you."

I said, "What?"

She said, "You're an artist, so don't pretend you don't understand."

I backed into the railing. L. Trent Woodard walked by the doorway and winked at me. His young man blew me a kiss.

I said, "Jesus fucking Christ."

Viv said, "Be less vulgar, and follow me home. I'll be in the Packard Caribbean."

Viv led the way. I followed. The nut-ward guy and the goon tailed me.

We caravanned to 3rd and Muirfield. The nut-ward guy and the goon goosed my tailpipes. Viv stopped in front of her house. She pointed me into the driveway and pulled up behind me.

She boxed my dad's car in. She didn't want me to rabbit.

The pad backed up to the Wilshire Country Club. Viv walked in ahead of me and turned on some lights. The nut-ward guy and the goon disappeared down the block.

The house was big and salmon pink Spanish. I walked up and peeped the peephole. Smoked glass smeared my view. My martini-mottled mind went wild.

I saw a Commie commissar corps. I saw my mom strapped to a rack. Trent Woodard brandished a branding tool. Dig that hot hammer and sickle.

I blinked. I saw a dozen old women. They were dowager demons and sex-starved succubi. They craved my seed. They bared their geriatric genitalia.

Viv was their siren and shill. Trent couldn't get hard and hose women. They needed ME.

I blinked. A car pulled up to the curb. Somebody whispered, "Ring the bell, shithead."

I yipped and cringed. I turned around. I saw the nut-ward guy and the goon in the goonmobile.

I rang the bell. Viv opened the door. My peephole panorama went poof!

I stepped inside. Viv handed me a martini. I sniffed it for Spanish fly or knockout drops.

Viv shut the door. My drink looked kosher. I chugalugged it and ate the olive.

The living room was king-sized and leftist primitive chic.

Labor posters. Furniture fabrics finished in gold filigree. Atavistic statues with fat phalluses and pointy pudenda.

Viv tracked my eyes. "I'm eclectic. And the fertility gods are special to me."

I said, "You married a fag, so I guess you needed all the help you could get."

Viv walked to a sideboard and mixed herself a martini. My martini sent me mixed messages:

Fuck her/Don't fuck her/Fuck her rich Red pawn of a husband. Fuck the LAPD for the way they fucked you/Fuck everyone and fuck no one at all.

Viv said, "You shouldn't underestimate my husband. He has some powerful allies."

"I know. I saw him talking to Sheriff Biscailuz."

Viv dropped an olive in her drink. "Gene's a friend, yes. He kept Trent out of the papers when he—"

"Got picked up during a fruit roust at some joint in West Hollywood?"

Viv smiled. "You're correct. He saved Trent from a great deal of embarrassment and turned him into quite a resource."

"What do you mean?"

"That's Trent's a good lawyer, and Gene Biscailuz isn't so blinded by a hatred of homosexuals that he can't utilize his talent."

I said, "Too bad the LAPD doesn't feel that way."

Viv sipped her drink. "Yes and no. For one, Trent hates them too much to work with them. Gene hates them, too, and Trent's been working with him on this budget contretemps that the Sheriff's and the LAPD are embroiled in."

"On the Q.T., you mean."

"That's correct. Gene doesn't want it known that Trent's working with him, and Trent doesn't ever want the LAPD to learn that he's quite fond of young men. He's quite sure that the LAPD is out to compromise him any way they can, so of course he's remained quite discreet."

I looked around the room. The labor posters were laid out in gold-lacquered frames.

"Is Trent an actual Communist?"

Viv laughed. "Nobody with brains and a soul is a *real* Communist."

"What about Commie front groups?"

"For instance?"

I pulled names off Freddy O's crib sheet. "The People's Committee for a Free Philippines, the Free-the-Rosenbergs Defense Fund, the National Alliance for Social Justice, the—"

Viv cut me off. "It sounds like you have those names memorized."

I shuddered. My chest mike shifted and settled off to the left.

Viv said, "Fixate on me. Don't fixate on my husband."

I got pissed. I got wild-hair-up-the-ass pissed.

"I can't get work because of your husband. He's run a big, goddamn guilt-by-association number on me."

Viv shrugged. "Then work for social justice. Teach underprivileged Negro children to play the accordion, and I'll pay you what Las Vegas entertainers earn."

Don't blow your cool/Don't blast your cork/Don't—

"Really, Dick, you must overlook the few injudicious comments my husband has made about you. Look to the real historical source of your troubles and try to understand the big picture."

I tamped my temper down. "For instance?"

"For instance, my husband is involved in big issues."

"For instance?"

"For instance, a woman came to Trent recently. Trent wouldn't tell me her name, but he told me she broke up with her boyfriend, and she knew something about a horribly draconian LAPD plot to initiate some truly Fascistic measures, all of it tied in to TV propaganda. You see, Dick, those are the types of issues my husband deals with."

My skin prickled. My hackles hopped. The pitch tweaked and tantalized me.

"What else did your husband say about the woman?"

Viv said, "That she was a big, busty blonde."

My synapses snapped and snagged a connection.

Joi Lansing was a big, busty blonde. Harvey Glatman said she just dumped Jack Webb. Webb: LAPD lapdog. TV propaganda. *Dragnet:* top-rated TV fare and the LAPD's PR lightning rod.

Viv said, "Dick, what is it? You look abstracted all of a sudden."

I moved in on her. I mixed a martini and guzzled it for guts. Viv ran a *sloooow* hand down my cheek.

"I'm tired of talking about my husband, and I'm tired of talking in general. Let me duck into the loo for a moment."

I kissed her hand. I made her as musk as Matchabelli's Midnight Madness. She smiled and popped into a powder room by the door.

I popped to the front window. I pulled the drapes. I doused a light behind me and looked out. A breeze blew in. I peeped and perked my ears.

Two cars at the curb. A curbside confab. The nut-ward guy and the goon. Danny Getchell and the kid who cozied up to Woodard at the gala.

Standing and smoking and staring into a book.

The goon said, "What's that?" The kid said, "It's a fucking thesaurus." Danny said, "Limp-wristed lawyer lollygags at lavender lovefest! Pinko plutocrat paralyzed as cops cop preadult playmate!" The kid said, "Cute, but remember—a C-note down and no ass action."

"Come here, Dick."

I pulled the drapes. I turned around *slooooow.*

Vivid Viv in a sheer peach peignoir. Embroidered: crossed cocks and pointy pudenda and fierce fertility gods.

"Come here, Dick."

She wanted to siphon my seed. SHE was the succubus!!!

I panicked. I tore through my pockets for garlic cloves or wolfsbane. Viv jumped on me.

She tore at my jacket. She tore at my shirt. She tore at the power pack packed on my pectoral muscles.

She stopped. My microphone flopped free and dropped down to my cummerbund. She saw the wires and the tangled-up tape.

The succubus shrieked. She clawed my chest and kicked me in the balls.

The succubus went for my eyes.

I blocked her hands. I judo-chopped her. I caught her on the neck and dumped her flat. I ran—

I got out the door. The nut-ward guy and the goon counterattacked. They jumped in their car and blocked off the driveway.

I went for my car keys. They were gone. I lost them when I grabbed for garlic cloves or wolfsbane.

Somebody whispered, "Get back in there and fuck her!" Danny Getchell whispered, "Don't run!" Somebody whispered, "Quiet— or she'll hear us!"

I ran to the Packard Caribbean. I found the keys in the dash. I hit the gas and rammed my dad's car.

It spun into the big backyard. It spun off wet grass and spun into a swimming pool. It sunk down to its tailpipes.

I hit my headlights. I saw a trellised fence and a dark golf course. I punched the gas and plowed through the fence and spun fishtails and wild figure 8's.

5

I made it up to the Strip. I leveled nine golf holes and left three miles of grassy tire tracks behind me.

The Packard was mud mottled and stained grass green. I ditched it with the valet outside Ciro's. I walked in and caught three bars of "You Belong to Me."

It tremolo'd and trickled through the foyer. I stepped into the main room and caught it full on. Joi Lansing held the room hostage. Blonde hair and spray-painted spangles in a hot spotlight.

I stood at the back and scoped the room long-distance. Harvey Glatman stood behind some drapes draping off a side exit. He stared at la Lansing. He had his hands full.

He held out a little camera. The drapes popped and puckered off his pelvis. Harvey was pounding his pud.

I looked left. I looked right. The room rocked to a torch-song tempo. Jack Webb sat ringside. He wept into a Rob Roy and tossed red roses onstage. Joi ignored him. Two toady types consoled him.

They screamed "LAPD." The scene outside the Woodard house screamed "BACKUP SHAKEDOWN." I was set to crucify a Commie. *Hush-Hush* was set to humble him as a homo. The package screamed "LAPD."

Joi whispered. Joi warbled. Joi torched Jack Webb's heart and tossed it away.

I couldn't brace her yet. I got the Packard and laid tracks for the San Gabriel Valley.

I found the location. I watched *Private Hell 36* wrap. The shoot *had* to shoot into my whole web of intrigue.

They shot at a trailer park in downscale Duarte. I parked in a vacant lot across the street. I found binoculars in the backseat and freeze-framed my focus. Arc lights gave me added eyeball oomph.

The trailers were beat-up and slapped down in rows sans tow hooks and cars. They looked empty. The crew stood on a pavement patch off to the left. They looked itchy.

They dispersed at 12:01 A.M. They peeled out in individual cars. They left their arc lights up. Two people stayed behind and paced the pavement.

Ida Lupino. Steve "the Schvantz" Cochran.

Ida smoked and sucked on a hip flask. The Schvantz sniffed a dress rack. It was standing by a trailer marked #36.

I waited. I watched.

12:08 A.M.:

A car pulls up. Freddy O and Johnny Stompanato get out.

Ida shoots Freddy a tongue kiss. Johnny Stomp shoots the Schvantz a mean look. Stomp enters #36 and exits with a small movie camera. The Schvantz dumps it in Freddy O's car.

12:13 A.M.:

An LAPD van pulls up. Six women hop out. They're dressed in jail denims. The driver hops out. He's dressed in LAPD blue.

The girls hit the dress rack. The girls hit #36. The girls exit looking vampy and dressed va-va-voom. The Schvantz licks his chops.

12:26 A.M.:

The girls get back in the van. Ida and the Schvantz hop in

Freddy O's car. Freddy and Johnny Stomp hop in. The LAPD man pulls down the arc lights and straps them to the roof of the van.

12:34 A.M.:

The car pulls out. The van pulls out. I pull out behind them.

We drive three blocks east. The car and the van pull into a courtyard motel. I pull into a vacant lot fifty yards east.

The Larkcrest Motel. Abandoned. One light in one room lit. A long string of dark doorways and windows.

I grabbed my binoculars. I crept into the courtyard. I peeped the scene perspiringly close.

12:46 A.M.:

The girls hit the lit-up room. The cop hauls the camera and arc lights in. Ida and the Schvantz hit the room.

12:50 A.M.:

Johnny Stomp walks around the courtyard. He opens the doors and turns on the lights in every other room.

Six rooms are now lit. Six rooms remain dark.

12:59 A.M.:

Freddy O hauls a box from his car. He circuits the six lit-up rooms. He drops a bottle of booze and two paper cups on six bright blue bedspreads.

1:04 A.M.:

The cop climbs in his van. He unloads a dolly. It holds six movie cameras. The cop circuits the six dark rooms. He dumps six cameras on six bright blue bedspreads. He shuts the doors behind him.

I got the picture. I got it in SIN-emascope.

The cop climbed back in his van. I snuck *way* into the court-yard. I hunkered down and entered a dark room on his blind side.

I flicked a light on. I flicked it off fast. I saw a 2-way peek built into the wall. I fumbled in darkness and bumbled into a door.

I opened it. I entered a lit-up love room. The 2-way looked out on the bed. I pulled the microphone and power pack off my chest and taped it to the bottom of the mattress.

I snuck back to the vacant lot *slooooooooooow*. I grabbed my binoculars. I waited. I watched. I patiently peeped the courtyard. I listened to grunts and groans in Ida Lupino's room.

1:36 A.M.:

Ida's door opens. Johnny Stomp walks out. I get a two-second tantalization.

Ida's got her camera in tight. A blonde's got the Schvantz trapped in her tonsils.

He's huge. He's a pineapple impaled on a pipe threader.

Stompanato shut the door and lit a cigarette. I waited. I watched. I patiently peeped the courtyard.

2:08 A.M.:

Six cars pull in. Six middle-aged men jump out. They've got smirks on their lips and guns on their hips. They whoop. They holler. Johnny Stomp greets them.

I zoomed in on their cars. I latched my lenses on their license plates and memorized them.

I ran to my car. I peeled out. I heard Ida Lupino yell, "Cut! That's a take!"

3:26 A.M.:

I peeled into the alley behind Ciro's. There's Joi Lansing.

She's dressed in a Girl Scout getup. She's dumping red roses in a trash bin.

She blinked into my headlights. I doused them. She said, "Jack, Jesus Christ."

I got out of the car. A flashlight flashed me. Joi said, "Jesus, Dick Contino."

I didn't know what to say. I hummed three bars from "Lady of Spain."

Joi laughed. "I don't know what you're doing here, but at least I know that Jack didn't send you."

I leaned on the trash bin. Joi flipped off her flashlight. A late moon lit the alley low and languorous.

"How do you know Jack didn't send me?"

"Sergeant Joe Friday and *you*?"

I laughed. "You haven't asked me what I'm doing here."

Joi lit a cigarette and looked me over. "You're wearing a tuxedo, and you look like you've been crawling in dirt. Your shirt's unbuttoned, and it looks like you've shaved your chest. I couldn't begin to guess, and as long as Jack didn't send you, I don't care."

I laughed. I coughed away a cloud of Joi's smoke and tossed her a teaser.

"I heard you and Jack broke up. I think I read it in *Hush-Hush*."

Ba-boom, bam, bingo:

Joi went bug-eyed and choked on a chestful of Chesterfield.

I let her cough up some composure. She came back strong.

"Over's over. Jack didn't want to get married and have kids, and I did. I wouldn't be playing den mother to a bunch of Mexican brats in Boyle Heights if I didn't. Jesus, I mean, look at this outfit."

I tossed Teaser #2. "Politics had nothing to do with it?"

Joi dropped her cigarette and stepped on it. "I'm an actress, a chorus dancer, and an occasional singer. I've got about as much interest in politics as you do."

"You'd be surprised."

"Try me."

Try this:

"You went to L. Trent Woodard last year. You told him you had inside information on an LAPD plot to put out propaganda on TV. I'm betting Jack Webb was in on it, and I'm betting you had second thoughts and just dropped the whole thing, and I'm betting Woodard can't put any more of the plot together."

Joi said, "Jesus, Mr. Accordion." She said it breathless and *very* Hush-Hushed.

I said, "I nailed it?"

Joi lit a cigarette and flicked ash off her Girl Scout sash. "I got ahold of some *Dragnet* scripts that Jack and Chief Parker wrote. They had Joe Friday running speeches on how the LAPD needed to round up all the bums in Los Angeles and deport them to Cuba permanently, and how they needed to establish debtors' prisons and work farms to take all the deadbeats off the streets. I told Jack,

'You and Bill Parker can't possibly be serious about proposing this sick shit,' and Jack said, 'It isn't sick, and we'll shoot those scripts when the time is right.'"

Puzzle pieces popped into place. I said, "Does Jack know you approached Woodard? Does he know that this sick shit convinced you to leave him?"

Joi shook her head. "No. He thinks the marriage issue queered things, and wait, it gets sicker."

I sniffed Jack Webb's red roses. Joi shut the trash bin and smothered the smell.

"I overheard Jack and Parker talking a few times. Their plan was to shoot the scripts and air them on *Dragnet*, to soften the public up. Then they'd get up a public petition to deport the bums and build the debtors' prisons and work farms. Now, dig this. Jack and Freddy Otash own a big construction firm under the table, and Parker's tight with that Cuban dictator, Fulgencio Batista. The plan was for the LAPD to sell the bums to Batista, so he could use them as slaves in his sugarcane fields, and Jack's construction firm would get the contract to build the debtors' prisons and work farms, and once they were built, the inmates would build the sets for all the movies Jack wanted to make. The only thing holding all this back was seed money. They needed a few quick million to get things going."

More pieces popped into place. I said, "The LAPD's tangling over money with the Sheriff's right now. Parker wants to get his hands on that seed dough."

Joi shivered. "William H. Parker is the devil with horns."

I said, "Freddy O's right up there."

"He is. He's got a big dirt dossier on all of Parker and the LAPD's enemies, and he's got this sick twist Harvey who does bug work and phone taps for him. Harvey's got this sick thing for me. He used to follow me around the set when I visited Jack."

Pieces PERCOLATINGLY popping into place—

"And Cal Dinkins was—I mean is—tight with Jack and Freddy?"

"Yes. Dick, how do you know all—"

"And the LAPD dirt dossier is sort of like the big *Hush-Hush* master file that Freddy O's supposedly got?"

"Yes, but it's all one file, and Parker and Otash decide who gets smeared, and it's all so ugly that I wish I didn't know about it, and . . . and . . . and . . ."

Joi ran out of breath and lit a cigarette. I said, "I need a tape recorder, and I need to get some license-plate information."

Joi squawked like a squad-car squawkbox. She popped out a parcel of penal-code numbers, *Dragnet*-style.

"I know how to do things like that. Jack taught me. And I've got a tape gizmo inside."

I pulled a pen from my pocket. Joi pulled some paper from her Girl Scout skirt. She leaned over. I used her back for a blotter and jotted down my vehicle dope.

She ran into the club. I bayed at the big bright moon.

Pieces PALPITATINGLY popping into place. A bonaroo blonde to rescue and redeem me.

Joi jumped into the alley. She handed me a tape rig and a scratch-pad sheet.

"I got the vehicle information and ran an employment cross-check. The six registered owners are all members of the L.A. County Sheriff's Department."

I bayed at the moon. I grabbed Joi and kissed her. She kissed me back hard. I tasted tobacco and sweet vermouth on her tongue.

We broke the clinch. Joi said, "Be brave and stupid. I go for guys like that."

I drove back to Duarte. I hit the Larkcrest Motel at 5:33 A.M. The courtyard was deserted and dead quiet.

I hit Love Hut #9 and pulled my power pack off the mattress. I pulled the tape spool out of the pack and popped it in Joi's tape rig.

I sat on the bed. I hit the Play button. I heard bits of the Wilshire-Ebell bash and my clash with the succubus. I heard tape hiss and fuck sounds and a real male and a fake female climax.

I heard voices.

Male voice: "Sweetie, that was . . . Jesus."

Female voice: "I could tell it's been a while for you."

Male voice: "Yeah, well . . . the old lady's the old lady, but I guess that doesn't count."

Female voice: "Look, it's been a while for me too. I've been out of circulation."

Male voice: "What do you mean? I thought you got bit roles at M-G-M and lived here in L.A."

Female voice: "Yeah, I do. It . . . was . . . well, just a figure of speech."

Male voice: "I'm glad Stompanato sets up these stag nights. We all work hard, and we need to blow off some steam from time to time."

Female voice: "You must be really busy. Didn't it say 'Captain' on that badge you showed me."

Male voice: "That's right, Sweetie. I'm a captain on the inspector's list."

Female voice: "Tell me what you do. I just love to hear men talk about their work."

Male voice: "Well, I run the West Hollywood Substation."

Female voice: "That's my old stomping grounds. I used to work at a call house on Havenhurst, and the West Hollywood deputies were good to all us girls."

Male voice: "Well, you know how it is. One hand washes the other."

Female voice: "I think I know what you mean, but tell me more."

Male voice: "Well, on the q.t., all the call houses in the county kick loose donations to the Sheriff's Annual Rodeo Fund, so the money gets laundered that way. See, Gene Biscailuz is a good guy. He's not like that prick Bill Parker, and he knows a lot of deputies have drinking problems, so he shoots some of the rodeo money to a hospital where they can dry out. I've dried out there six or seven times myself. Pass me that bottle, will you, Sweetie?"

Female voice: "Tell me more."

I heard footsteps. I tossed the tap shit out a back window. The door blew off its hinges and landed on my lap. Two men charged me and beat me blank with big black saps.

I woke up chained to a chair. I saw a dress rack and an arc light. I recognized the dark little room.

Trailer #36 on the *Private Hell 36* set.

Fred O and Johnny Stompanato stomped in front of me. They tapped black leather saps on their knees. I heard voices outside.

Jack Webb and Ida Lupino.

My head hurt. I felt woozy. My teeth felt loose. I saw tooth marks on the two saps.

Otash said, "Why'd you ditch out on Viv Woodard?"

Stomp said, "Why did you steal her car?"

Otash said, "Where's the bug apparatus?"

Stomp said, "What did you and that Commie cooze discuss?"

I played it brave and stupid. I said, "Bah fungoo," with full Italian inflection.

Stomp sapped me. I spat two teeth on his Sy Devore suit. Fred O flashed a newspaper. I caught a headline: PROMINENT LAWYER A SUICIDE.

Otash dropped the paper. "Our vice guys caught Woodard with his pants down. He bailed out and drank some Drāno. The kid they caught him with gave *Hush-Hush* a statement. The story's going on the May cover, unless you convince the widow to sit on everything she might know about a certain police agency."

I said, "Fuck you, Fritz."

Otash sapped me. I spat two teeth on his Sy Devore suit. Otash sapped me again.

"Woodard's dead, Dick. You're not much use to us anymore, and you just might prove to be a liability. You killed a valuable buddy of ours, and brave and stupid guys like you are always better off dead."

"Brave" and "stupid" clicked with "dead" and cleared my clogged head. I screamed like a scared little baby.

Otash clamped down on my arms. Johnny Stomp rolled up my

shirtsleeves. Harvey Glatman and the nut-ward guy popped in my periphery.

Somebody stuck a spike in my arm. I whooshed into ecstasy and darkness.

Light and dark came and went. Hypodermic needles slipped in and out of my arms.

I went wonderful places. I returned to Private Hell 36. I fucked the mermaid from the Chicken of the Sea tuna can.

Harvey Glatman photographed my arms. Ida Lupino shot me up and shot my needle tracks with 3-D film. My bladder burst. Somebody said, "Oh, shit."

I flew to Mars. The succubus siphoned my python and gave birth to trident-tailed twins. I apologized to her husband. He condemned my cowardice and deplored the damage I did. Howard dove for my dong. Linda Sidwell jumped on Jack Webb. Joi Lansing saw the Lupino loop and left me for the Schvantz.

I heard voices or ventriloquistic voodoo.

"We've got to move the master file tonight. Stash it someplace safe at your studio."

"Yeah, boss."

"Dump Contino someplace."

"Levant scares me."

"You never know what he knows."

"He's a hophead. Those guys crap out all the time, and nobody thinks twice."

"Torture him and find out what he knows, then kill him."

I flew to Pluto. I asked Mickey Mouse why they named a planet after his dog.

"You've got to move him or move the fucking trailer. He's starting to smell, and our location permit expired."

I flew to Neptune. I flew back to Private Hell 36. Joe Friday said, "Hitch the trailer." A spike went in my arm. I flew to Venus. It looked like Las Vegas. I wondered how that could be so.

. . .

White.

White plastic. White Naugahyde. Maybe white leather. Tucked and tufted. Sticky. Stuck against my cheek.

White.

Stiff-starched. Mummifyingly tight.

I blinked. I yawned. I tried to rub my eyes. My hands didn't move. My arms didn't move. I had myself in a bear hug.

A big bug bounced my way. He bopped over white tucks and tufts. He got close. I tried to swat him. I couldn't break the bear hug.

I rolled away. I slid on sticky white webs. I saw white-webbed walls and a white-webbed ceiling.

My head hurt. My body throbbed. My white world wiggled and wobbled.

It hit me.

Padded cell/straitjacket/voices or ventriloquistic voodoo:

"Torture him."/"Kill him."/"Dump Contino someplace."

I remembered Mars and the mermaid. I remembered my trident-tailed twins. I remembered the hypo hits that hopped me up on Big H. I diagnosed my dilemma.

I was hooked on Horse.

I shook. I shuddered. I shivered. I decided to probe my prognosis.

I rubbed my cheek against white rubber. I felt a sticky two-day stubble. I couldn't be a junkie yet.

I *still* hurt. I *still* throbbed. My white world *still* wiggled and wobbled. I was *still* mummified and dope-doctored.

I scanned my white world. I saw a small black square cut into one wall about a foot above floor level.

I rolled up to it. Heat hit me. I saw metal grates set six inches in. I tried to jam my ass and my rear restraint straps up against them. I couldn't get close.

I rolled over and faced the wall. I bit at white plastic. I snapped three times and got a good tooth hold. I burrowed, bit and spat, burrowed, bit and spat, burrowed, bit and spat. I chewed a big hole around the grates and slammed my ass against them.

Heat.

It warmed me and singed me and scorched my ass. I bit the floor to staunch my pain and stifle incipient screams. I smelled toasted white cotton and burning flesh.

I slammed my ass in tighter. The pain accelerated. I felt little ass hairs sizzle. I bit down harder and almost choked on a chunk of white plastic.

My armlock went limp. My bear hug broke. I rolled away from the grates and rolled out of my straitjacket.

I stood up. I stumbled and fell. My circulation started to circulate. I crawled to a waffle-webbed white door.

I crouched. I rubbed my ass. I counted the waffle webs on the walls to stay calm. The door opened at 4,806.

A man stepped in. I grabbed his ankles and pulled. He hit the floor facedown. I kicked the door shut and jumped on his back.

I pressed his face into white plastic. Tucks and tufts muffled his screams. I knee-dropped him nine times. I came down on his kidneys full force.

Blood blew out of his mouth. It spritzed and sprayed and trickled through little white troughs.

He was dead.

I pulled a key ring off his belt and stumbled to the door. I looked out. I saw an empty hall. I saw a door marked "Pharmacy/Restricted."

I shook. I shivered. I braced myself into the door. My hands hopped to heavy rpms.

I needed a fix.

I looked down the hallway. I recognized the pink walls. I thought I heard a screech two doors down.

Mount Sinai. The locked ward.

I stumbled to the pharmacy door. I fumbled and bumbled my keys. My hands hopped. I stabbed keys at the keyhole. The fourth key let me in.

I shut the door. I turned on a light. I dumped three drawers of dope into a sink. I dug through Digitalis, Desoxyn, and Dilantin. I tossed Tuinal and Terpin Hydrate and shoved Seconal aside. I grabbed four vials of Methedrine Hydrochloride and dumped every drawer in the room.

I sifted through morphine Syrettes and pawed through pills. I found a portable spike and jabbed up a big jolt of Meth. I tied off my arm with my black lizard belt and mainlined my way back to Mars.

I strafed the stratosphere in six seconds. I returned to Earth and ran toward that screech two doors down.

I kicked the door in. I entered another white world.

Oscar Levant was strapped to a king-size dartboard. A dozen darts dotted his chest. The nut-ward guy held jumper cables and a squirt gun. The cable cord was socked into a wall switch.

He saw me. He squirt-gunned me. He charged at me with his cables. I slipped on wet white plastic and hit the floor.

He stabbed at me. He caught me. Voltage bounced off my chest. I rolled into the dartboard. It capsized. Oscar hit the floor and slipped free.

I stood up. The nut-ward guy charged me. Oscar pulled a dart off his chest and let fly. He nailed the nut-ward guy in the neck.

It stunned him. He dropped the squirt gun. I grabbed it and squirted him. Oscar lobbed two darts at his face.

They stunned him. He dropped his cables. I grabbed them and clamped them down on his balls.

He screamed. I slipped Oscar the squirt gun. He shot him in the balls and electrocuted him.

6

Joi Lansing hid us out. We turned her house into a kick pad.

I kicked Big H. Joi knew a dope doc and a Chinese herbalist. They collaborated and cooked up compounds to cleanse me. I popped their portions and felt all the poison pour out of my pores.

Oscar kicked cold turkey. He played Joi's piano twenty hours a day. He played himself into and way past exhaustion. He played blistering Bartók and soft Brahms ballades. He perched on Joi's balcony and played for the Hollywood Hills. People stood on their rooftops and listened.

Busy hands can't shake. Busy brains don't dwell on dope deprivation.

I kicked Horse. I didn't know if I could kick my homicide habit. Murder was a monkey on my back now. I found a context to make mayhem mine. Most men found it in war. I attracted it with my fear and put myself in peril to perpetrate it. I was a murder magnet. I'd continue to kill as long as it felt justifiable and erotic.

I wanted to juke Jack Webb and Johnny Stomp and hang their hides out to dry. I wanted to fry Freddy Otash in hot oil and pulverize William H. Parker. I didn't know if I wanted to avenge Trent Woodard or go on another kill spree. My murder motives were convoluted and ego-polluted. I didn't know if I wanted to save L.A. or annihilate it and go down behind a big ovation.

I ran it by Joi. She told me to relax and let things play out hush-hush. Dinkins and Wells were still John Doe'd in the papers and on TV. The Mount Sinai massacre never made print. The LAPD plot was huge and unverifiable. Oscar was a hophead. I was a draft dodger. Jack Webb was Joe Friday. Let it go. It was all too big to fuck with.

I couldn't let it go. My murder-mangled memory said no. Joi took me to bed and tried to induce amnesia.

We made love to Bartók and Brahms. We slept to soft Schubert and Schumann. Oscar played to our passion. His music molded my memories of murder and sparked my lust for more of the same.

We made love and slept for a week. A Rachmaninoff opus 32 prelude pushed me over the edge.

I called my parents and told them to hide in their bomb shelter. I told Joi to call Harvey Glatman and suggest some publicity pix.

7

Voices or ventriloquistic voodoo:

"We've got to move the master file tonight. Stash it someplace safe at your studio."

"Yeah, boss."

I heard those words in a hop haze. I was half-ass sure that Freddy O and Harvey Glatman said them. I had a hunch that Harvey took his pervert pix in some sick sanctum sanctorum.

Joi walked into his repair shop. Oscar and I watched. We were staked out in Joi's Jag coupe.

We watched the door. We waited. Joi went in wired.

Oscar hooked her up. We bought a "Sergeant Joe Friday Surveillance Kit" at a toy store and went wild. Joi packed a "Jill Friday Purse Pistol" and a signal device. Oscar held the "Trap-Your-Man Transmitter." We parked two doors down from the shop. Joi was set to signal us to the sanctum sanctorum.

We watched the door. Oscar sucked cigarettes. I fought the homicide heebie-jeebies.

I wanted to hurl some hurt on Harvey. I wanted to kick my homicide habit and reembrace my accordion.

Seconds slogged by. Minutes meandered. We watched the door.

Our beep device beeped.

We jumped out of the car. We ran into the shop. We shut the door and threw up the Closed sign. We followed the beeps. We beeped through the back room. We beeped up to a big green door.

BEEP BEEP BEEP BEEP—

Oscar kicked the door. It stayed upright. Oscar grabbed his foot and yelled, "Shit!" I kicked the door. It stayed upright. Oscar picked up a TV set and threw it at the door. The door blew off the doorway.

We ran into a little green room. It looked like the gas chamber up at San Quentin. Joi held Harvey hostage. He sat in a gas-chamber chair. Joi held her toy gun on him.

I smelled stale gas. I pried open a floor vent. I smelled it stronger there. I saw cardboard boxes stacked in a hidey-hole. I saw a crawl space behind them.

Oscar grabbed a box. Joi pistol-slapped Harvey. Her toy gun decomposed in her hand.

Harvey yelped. Joi said, "He tried to tie me up, the sick shit."

I eyeballed the room. It had a feral feel and an abattoir air. Oscar opened a box and skimmed some carbon paper. He said, "It's the big *Hush-Hush* file."

Harvey yipped and yelped. Joi jammed a high heel down on his foot. Oscar spieled scandal-rag skank:

"Otto Preminger sniffs coke and H speedballs. Mayor Bowron's got a Filipino love child. Randy Randolph Scott wrangles with a Mexican middleweight. Dean Martin moves Mob money direct to Pope Pius at the Vatican. Dick Powell delivers dope to—"

I cut him off. "Talk, Harvey."

Harvey squirmed. I sniffed more stale gas. I caught a bitter-almond subscent and felt my hackles hop.

Harvey said, "What do you want to know?"

I said, "All of it. Off-the-record, on the q.t., and *very* hush-hush."

Harvey talked. Harvey laid out the whole ball of wax. I sniffed bitter almond and shivered as he spritzed it.

He was Freddy O and Johnny Stomp's Einstein. He ran their "Subscription TV" scam. They sold smut-film subscriptions to pervs and the Great White Priapic all over L.A. Harvey could beam film from his shop to any Joe Blow's TV set. The pervs paid prime prices for home pornography.

Cal Dinkins and Playboy Wells provided inmate actors. LAPD goons transported them to the fuck-film set in Duarte. Freddy O coerced Ida Lupino into director duty. Freddy fixed her manslaughter beef. Ida plowed a car full of wetbacks dead drunk and killed all four passengers. Freddy forced the Schvantz to star in her films. The Schvantz had three reefer-roust priors and a current case pending. The Schvantz skin-popped White Horse and loved jungle-bred jailbait hot off a slave boat from Zanzibar. The Schvantz was viably pliable.

Freddy O was Chief Parker's pet pit dog. Parker wanted to shaft the Sheriff's Department and take a fat share of its budget. Freddy concocted a covert operation. He coopted Johnny Stomp's stag-night racket and put six ranking Sheriff's men in bed with six inmate hookers. The men shot their mouths off. They shamelessly shared Sheriff's Department secrets. Ida Lupino filmed their philandering.

Parker needed money. He wanted to build debtors' prisons and work farms. He wanted to wipe the winos and strong-arm the stumblebums off the streets of L.A. and sell them to spic dictators.

It was all working well-oiled and wonderful. Until Playboy pulled an unpermitted heist with Cal Dinkins right there. Until Oscar Levant and Dick Contino bumbled down to Darktown.

Harvey stopped talking. Joi blew cigarette smoke in his face and said, "Creep." Oscar tossed a dozen film cans out of the hidey-hole.

I looked in the hole. I saw pipes pointing up to the hot seat. I caught a biting blast of bitter almond.

Oscar said, "I've been through six boxes. There's enough dirt in them to outextort the gross national product. Bing Crosby bangs underage tail in an archdiocesan ark moored in San Pedro! Dave Garroway checks out the chicken in—"

I jumped into the hole. I bent down and followed a shaft of light. The cyanide scent went south. I smelled something worse.

The hole expanded into a tunnel. Wood walls shut out dirt and foundation debris. I saw a pile of bones and smelled mothballs mixed with decomposed flesh.

Skulls. Arm bones. Leg bones. Wide female pelvic bones flecked with red gristle.

I ran out of the hole. I ran up to Harvey Glatman.

Harvey smiled. Harvey said, "Seventeen. But then, who's counting?"

The terror trove went telepathic. Time stood still.

Joi dropped her cigarette. Oscar dropped a scandal skank sheet.
Nobody said a word. We all let IT sink in.

Nobody talked. Nobody breathed. We all looked at the hole.
Harvey read my mind.

"I know you want to kill me, Dick. I know how it is when timid
men smell blood."

Nobody talked. Nobody breathed. We all looked at Harvey.

He said, "Don't be hasty. I'm the only one who can help you
out of this scrape you're in."

He explained.

I granted him a stay of execution.

8

I hogged a booth at Ollie Hammond's Steakhouse. I held a cross
and a big garlic bulb.

The succubus was late.

Oscar and Joi guarded the gas chamber. They barricaded the
shop and held my dad's shotgun on Harvey. Harvey hammered
away at my Home-TV Show. He thought he could buy me out of
the shit I slid into and slide on his seventeen snuffs.

He was wrong. I passed sentence. Oscar and Joi played public
defenders and petitioned me for a pardon. I said no. They said
they were glad and conceded their collusion in Contino's kangaroo court. I said Harvey's death would be a real gas. Oscar and Joi
laughed. We drew straws to pick who'd drop the pellets. Joi won.
Oscar dipped down to Western Costume. He bought her a boss
black death robe.

I felt righteously righteous and smilingly smug. I ratified my
rationale a dozen times and reveled in its logic. Harvey was a free-
lance freak. The LAPD did not know he killed women. The
LAPD could not be trusted to rein in their rabid Rottweiler. I
could gas Harvey and give up gore for good.

The succubus was late.

I felt valiantly virile. I felt spectacularly spiritual and alluringly alive. I had the big *Hush-Hush* file. I had dirt. I knew who fucked and sucked and licked and dicked and boozed and coozed and injected and elected to genuflect to their basest desires. I could wreck careers and resurrect my own. I could shake down booking agents and casting agents and columnists. I could run a prime portion of the press and have them castrate my competitors. I could regulate my rise to Mount Olympus. I could humble those who humbled me in the spirit of *Hush-Hush* hegemony.

The succubus walked in.

I shook. I shivered. I squeezed my garlic bulb.

She sat down at the table. She wore her widow's weeds witchingly well.

Vivid Viv.

She said, "Jesus, Dick. You smell."

I dropped my garlic. I picked up my cross. I aimed it at her crotch under the table. I said, "You're probably wondering why I called."

She nodded. "I'm wondering where you found the audacity."

I said, "I've been having an audacious time lately."

"That's an evasion, and it's not a suitable answer."

Vicious Viv.

I said, "I'm sorry about your husband."

Viv flicked some tobacco off her tongue. "That's a craven response, and it's what you should have said first."

Vindictive Viv.

I tamped my temper down. I made a neutral and nut-neutered statement. "I didn't have a choice. The LAPD was squeezing me."

Viv laughed. "You had a choice. Your options were suicide or direct action."

I laughed. Viv laughed. It was shitty laughless laughter.

"You blew your most immediate options and your chance to father my child. I suspect that you'll blow whatever else comes your way."

I popped a few tears. Wicked words and garlic fumes sucked them out of me. A waiter walked up. Viv waved him away.

"You never returned my car, Dick."

I shrugged.

"I found another handsome Italian man to impregnate me. He's much more famous than you, and I'm sure that he has a larger penis."

I said, "Who?"

Viv said, "Dean Martin."

I dropped my cross. It hit the floor. It made a *wop!* sound.

I said, "Fuck Dino. He moves Mob money to the Vatican."

"Yes, and my husband was a homosexual. If you're trying to shock me or titillate me, you're employing the wrong tactics."

I wiped my eyes. I wiped my nose. Viv tossed me her napkin.

"Tell me what you want, Dick. I'm meeting Dean at Chasen's, and I don't want to be late."

I blew my beak on white linen. "I want direct action, and I need to talk to Sheriff Biscailuz."

Viv stood up. "I'll arrange it in the spirit of what we could have had."

I smelled her perfume. I recognized it. Joi said she wore it to funerals.

Matchabelli's Mourning Madness.

Viv said, "Wash my car before you return it."

9

I walked in on the Sheriff's arm. Chief Parker almost shit on his living-room floor.

I said, "What's shakin', Daddy-O?"

Daddy-O went raging red and pulmonary purple. His veins bulged blue and vibrated violet.

The Sheriff sat him down in front of his TV set. He drilled me with Draculean eyes and hexed me from the heart. I knew he couldn't talk. I knew a catatonic cat captured his tongue.

I shut the door. I said, "Nice pad, baby doll. Those plaid drapes and that wall flag are so you."

Parker sputtered and spit split syllables. His tortured tongue and paralyzed palate could not connect.

The Sheriff said, "This won't be fun, Bill. But I can promise you we won't prolong things."

I grabbed a spot by the TV set. The Sheriff stood beside me. Parker sat two feet behind us.

I checked my watch. I counted down. The TV blipped on, black-magic-style.

Jack Webb in close-up. Duh-duh-duh-duh/duh-duh-duh-duh-duuuuh—the *Dragnet* theme on the sound track. Jack's toking a big stick of tea. He's giggling and goofing on his *craaaaazy* existence.

He says, "My name's Friday. I carry a badge. I use it to coerce hookers into blow jobs. My name used to be Webb, but I got lucky and met this tight-assed chump Bill Parker, who got laid once in 1924, decided he preferred power to pussy, and took over the Los Angeles Police Department. Duh-duh-duh-duh!"

I turned around. I looked at Parker. I couldn't count the colors he turned.

Jack says, "Bill hitched his badge to me, or maybe it's the other way around, but who gives a shit when you're making all this money? And if you think *Dragnet* is all that I'm talking about, you're wrong, 'cause we've got some *biiiiiiiig* plans with a Cuban guy names Batista—off-the-record, on the q.t., and very hush-hush, and Bill's the number one cop in America, not that faggot Gay Edgar Hoover, and boy do we have some dirt to fuck him with if he ever gets uppity! Duh-duh-duh-duh. Duh-duh-duh-duh-duuuuh!"

I turned around. I looked at Parker. I couldn't peg all the pastel pallors he passed through.

Jack Webb laughed. A man laughed offscreen. It sounded like Fred O. Jack Webb flipped out a fat middle finger.

"Hey, Bill, fuck you! This is for that time you humiliated me at the Jonathan Club, you frigid cocksucker! Hey, Bill, your mother fucks the mule down in T.J.! Hey, Bill, you better be nice to me or

I'll tell Mayor Bowron your boys set him up with that Filipino whore! Hey, Bill—"

I heard a shot. The TV screen imploded. Glass blew out the back of the set and took out the window behind it.

Diodes decomposed. Wires whipped and wiggled. The console cracked and popped into pieces.

I turned around. I looked at Parker. I kicked the gun out of his hand.

The Sheriff said, "No slaves. No work farms and no debtors' prisons. No reprisals on Contino, Levant, or their families. No shakedowns on my men and no more attempts to steal money off my budget."

Parker couldn't talk. The catatonic cat had his tongue. The Sheriff said, "We're hooked into J. Edgar Hoover and Mayor Bowron's set, and 8,000 random sets in Los Angeles. Nod to signal your compliance."

Parker nervously-nellingly nodded and turned six sheets of seraphim white.

The TV debris ignited. It sparked and sputtered and metamorphosed into a mushroom cloud.

I drove back to Harvey's repair shop. I found the whole block leveled and torched to a trash-heap hell.

Fire trucks. Rubberneckers. Cop cars.

Soot. Smoke. Ash-afflicted air. A wiped-out wasteland with a single scorched skeleton standing.

The gas-chamber chair.

I saw Oscar and Joi. I ditched my car and ran up to them. They wore black executioner's robes. They lit cigarettes off a piece of red timber and looked at me.

I said, "What the fuck happened?"

Joi said, "Harvey tricked us. He crossed three or four wires and blew himself out a fake wall panel. One of the arson cops said he probably created a sonic boom and controlled the downdraft. The fire started about a minute later."

I yelled, "He's gone?"

Joi nodded. "We underestimated a genius."

Oscar said, "And we overestimated you."

I kicked a rubble pile. My tennis shoe ignited. I hopped on one foot and swatted out the flames.

"What about the files? I've got plans. Those files can make me!"

Joi said, "They burned up. Tough luck, Dick. I was hoping they could help you mount a comeback."

I threw a tantrum. I stamped my feet and kicked at hot rubble. My shoes caught fire. I let them burn.

Oscar said, "Dick, you're fucked."

43 years, 6 months, 26 days. A twisting twirl of time to now.

Covert connections. Contaminations cataloged in conflagrated carbon paper. Secrets lost in smoke.

The contamination that I witnessed. The collusion that I tried to contain. The rampaging ramifications that still ram L.A.

History hidden and sooooooooo *hush-hushed.*

The Sheriff sheltered me for three years. I lived in exile on the Sunset Strip. Joi dumped me. I married an actress named Leigh Snowden.

Parker kept his promise. He did not visit violence upon me or mine. He did not sell slaves to Bad-Boy Batista. He did not imprison the impecunious. He did not juke Jack Webb in any public manner and did not drag Dragnet *into the dirt. He dramatically drove Fred Otash out of the LAPD.* Dragnet *dragged on for five more seasons.*

Fred O became a private eye. He shagged shit and skimmed skinny from a thousand insider informants. He brokered abortions. He set up dry outs and dope cures. He sold pictures of Rock Hudson with a dick in his mouth. He doped a racehorse in '59 and almost did time. He died old and rich in 1992.

Heart attack.

Johnny Stompanato ran sex shakedowns and took up with Lana Turner. Lana's daughter shanked him in April '58. Fred O made a mint on morgue memorabilia. Slab shots sold for a C-note. Marilyn Monroe bought Johnny's hair. A pederast purchased his penis.

The Schvantz died in '65.

On his yacht. Alone with five women.

Heart attack.

He lived fast, loved hard, died hung.

Ida Lupino died in '95.

Cigarettes and booze and attrition.

Sheriff Biscailuz died in '69.

Old age.

I went to his wake. I got drunk with some robbery cops and joined them on a liquor-store stakeout. I told them the REAL Harvey Glatman story. They didn't believe me.

Harvey disappeared for three years. He resurfaced in L.A. in '57. He snuffed three women and dumped them in the desert. A pinup model dumped Harvey. She disarmed him and dropped him with a flesh wound. The cops grabbed him. He copped out to his three recent killings and no more. He was tried and convicted. He sucked cyanide in September '59.

The three women weigh on me. The unidentified dead undermine my sleep and own me at odd moments. Harvey escaped on my watch. He killed his last three victims and other women under my imprimatur. I exploited his genius. It saved my life. I sold him a death-house reprieve. He exploited the time and bought himself five years and untold victims.

Time.

Oscar and Joi died in '72. They put in a million showbiz miles and burned out every part of their bodies.

I miss them.

Viv Woodard died in '61.

Suicide.

She never hatched her half-guinea love child.

Jack Webb died in '82. Heart attack. He promulgated police propaganda with other tuna TV shows and tapped out to the tune of authority. His malevolent mentor William H. Parker died in '66.

A heart attack hastened by his brief blast of me.

He passed on as one pissed-off patriarch. I derailed his most demonic designs and forced him to settle for second-class methods of suppression. He stepped up his stern measures in indirect defiance of me. I destroyed his dystopia and devastated his most darkly held dreams. I fragged his frazzled and fragile ego. He suppressed the suppressible underclass and dicked the disenfranchised as dickable Dick Contino surrogates.

His boys kicked black ass and brown ass and poor-white ass. Parker paternalistically popped his rocks along with them. He left a lethal legacy. He left his suppression-minded successors the unlearned lesson that suppression has a price.

Rodney King. The '92 riots. The repellent and radically race-ratified O.J. Simpson verdict.

The twisting twirl of time.

Back to 1954.

And me.

I never resurrected my career. I banged my box and made maintenance money and raised three kids. My draft-dodger drama dogged me and diverted my audience. My wife died in '82.

Cancer.

I'm 67 now. I'm healthy. I live in Las Vegas and work lounge gigs. I chase women. Women chase me. I chase the twisting twirl back to THEN.

My fear flared and flowed THEN to NOW. My Patented Post-Passive Rages popped once in a billion blue moons. I mainlined my way into madness and meandered out with more mini-myths.

I've mentioned this aforetold myth to a million myth-hungry people. They don't accept my secret history. They tell me the players are dead and unable to confirm or refute. They point to my genetic link to Alzheimer's disease.

They tell me I'm lying. They say I'm wrong. They say it's a fever dream. They get frenetically frustrated and say no no no.

I get righteously righteous and smilingly smug. I point to L.A. and claim credit for the nightmare.

November, December 1997

PART FOUR

L.A.

SEX, GLITZ, AND GREED

THE SEDUCTION OF O. J. SIMPSON

The Simpson-Goldman snuffs are recognizably prosaic. Subtract the accused killer's celebrity and showbiz milieu and you've got a spur-of-the-moment whack-out equally indigenous to Watts, Pacoima and Dogdick, Delaware. The intersection of fame, extreme good looks, and pervasive media coverage has blasted a common double slash-job to the top of the pantheonic police blotter of our minds. The Leopold-Loeb, Wylie-Hoffert, and Manson Family cases—replete with complex investigations and psychological underpinnings emblematic of their time—cannot compete with the Simpson Trinity. A botched hack-and-run caper has become the Crime of the Century.

On Sunday, June 12, 1994, O.J. Simpson did or did not drive to his ex-wife Nicole Brown Simpson's pad and slaughter her and a young man named Ronald Goldman. He did or did not wear gloves and a ski mask; he did or did not butcher his victims with a bone-handled knife, a bayonet, or an entrenching tool. He did or did not split the scene and drive to his own home, a few minutes away.

Nicole Brown Simpson was or was not a devoted mother, a cocaine addict, and an airheaded party girl. She was or was not an

(This piece was written prior to the verdict in the O.J. Simpson trial.)

anorexic, a bulimic, or a nymphomaniac given to picking up men at a Brentwood espresso pit. The minutiae of her life can be compiled and collated to conform to almost any sleazy thesis. She is most unambiguously defined by this heavily documented fact: O.J. Simpson beat the shit out of her over the last five years of her life.

Ron Goldman was either a waiter who wanted to be an actor or an actor working as a waiter—a very common L.A. job euphemism. He was or was not Nicole Simpson's lover. He did or did not borrow Nicole's Ferrari on occasion—which did or did not piss off O.J. no end. Forensic evidence indicates that Goldman fought very hard for his life.

Forensic evidence is utilized to supersede interpretation and conjecture through the application of impartial, empirically valid scientific methods. Forensic evidence is used to place suspected felons at crime scenes. Forensic evidence is a counterweight to gooey pleas for mitigation.

The gathering of forensic evidence is a conscious search for the truth. So are legitimate attempts to debunk scientific fallacies and sloppy applications of long-established forensic procedures. The analysis of forensic evidence may prove to be the adjudicating bottom line in the O.J. Simpson case. The flip side might be logical chaos—a verdict or the absence of a verdict spawned by the numbingly protracted cross-media extravaganza that has deluged all would-be jurors and indeed the entire American public with an accretion of contradictory details both densely pertinent and superfluous—a huge shitstorm of information, misinformation, innuendo, and disingenuously reported rebop that backs you into a corner like a date rapist you can never escape until you shut down your electronic and printed-page access to the world, move to the South Pole, and start fucking penguins.

O.J. did or did not shed his own blood outside Nicole's pad. He returned from an overnight trip to Chicago sporting a fresh cut— which might have been caused by his slamming down a glass upon hearing the news of his ex-wife's death or might have been caused by his slashing at the woman a bit too close to his free hand. Blood trajectories are primarily matters of forensic and hard legal concern. They lack the mass-market appeal inherent to hearsay accounts of an attractive woman's sex life and attempts to portray a career misogynist as a lost brother to the Scottsboro Boys, and until the blood-oozing interactive O.J. CD-ROM hits stores, we just might have to view where that blood was spilled as a literal indication of Mr. Simpson's guilt or innocence—a niggling restriction to keep us tenuously open-minded as data rains down and inundates us.

The O.J. Simpson case is a gigantic Russian novel set in L.A. The extravaganza occurred in L.A. because the major characters wanted to suck the giant poison cock off the Entertainment Industry. It's a novel of metamorphoses—because L.A. is where you go when you want to be somebody else. It happened in L.A. because it's the best place on earth to get breast and penis enlargements. It happened in the Brentwood part of L.A. because homelessness, crack addiction, and other outward signs of despair appear at a minimum there.

O.J. Simpson wanted to be White. Ron Goldman wanted to be an actor—an equally ridiculous ambition. Nicole wanted a groovy fast lane and the secondhand celebrity that comes with fucking famous men.

Her second-tier status extended to her death. She became the blank page that pundits used to explicate her husband's long journey of suppression.

Nicole bought a ticket to ride. The price was nakedly apparent long before she died. Her face was pinched and crimped at the edges—too-pert features held too taut and compressed by too many bouts with cocaine, too many compulsive gym workouts, and too much time given over to maintaining a cosmetic front. Her beauty was not the beach-bunny perfection revered by stupid young men and the man who may or may not have murdered her. The physical force of Nicole Brown Simpson is the glaze of desiccation writ large on her face. The lines starting to form might have been caused by inchoate inner struggles, or the simple process of aging, or a growingly articulate sense that she had boxed herself into an inescapable corner of obsessive male desire, random male desire, and a life of indebtedness to things meretricious and shallow.

Nicole's relationship with O.J. was deceptive and collusive from the start. He bought the hot blonde that fifty years of pop culture told him he should groove on, and an unformed psyche that adapted to his policy of one-way monogamy. She bought a rich, handsome, famous man possessed of infantile characteristics, which led her to believe that she could control him.

He bought a trip through his unconscious and a preordained mandate for horror. She abdicated to an inner drama that would ultimately destroy her.

They both bought a trip to Hollywood. O.J.'s athletic career was phasing out at the time they met; he sensed that he could continue his nice-guy impersonation and ease himself into plum acting roles with his long-perfected chameleon aplomb. He had made a second career out of disarming people with smiles and self-effacing gestures, and if he failed to hit the level of transposition that quality acting required, he could always play his familiar old ingratiating self, lower his cloning-sights from Laurence Olivier to Sly Stallone, get a mojo going as an action-flick hero, make big bucks, and score beaucoup poontang in the process. He knew a shitload of wimps and tough-guy wanna-bes in the Biz—geeks who subscribed to the ruthlessness-as-strength-of-character ethic that pervades Hollywood but had never been in a fistfight and loved to tell jokes about their wives leaving them for well-endowed *shvartzes*. He knew these guys; they knew him; he got a symbiotic groove going with guys like that. Guys like that could make him a *biiiiig* movie star.

O.J. miscalculated. His powers of sociopathic seduction were best exposited in five-second sound bites and best received by callow young women. It should be noted that O.J. Simpson is not the smartest motherfucker ever to walk the earth. He is a man of great physical gifts, superficial charm, and limited cunning, who segued from football to Hollywood with an impressionable girl in tow. He nested in a place where marriage is a shuck and a smoke screen for hidden sexual agendas; he brought a woman into the Inside

World that the Outside World has been brainwashed into believing is the World Most to Be Coveted. He got her hooked on celebrity the way pimps get whores hooked on dope.

O.J. brought Nicole into a world where he was a second-class citizen. He got small roles in doofus comedies—but the tough-guy wanna-bes had no serious use for him. He would never be a movie star because he possessed the expressive range of a turtle. He'd transformed himself into a confirmed ass-kisser who could never appear truly heroic or dangerous onscreen.

Nicole witnessed O.J.'s long downward slide. She saw the essential bifurcation of his fame: He was a big cheese to the outside world and small potatoes to the world he sucked up to. She came of age in lavish surroundings and reveled in insider perks. She had a front-row view of her husband cracking under the weight of his emptiness.

O.J. got his racial-identity wires crossed up a long time ago. He must have figured his choices narrowed down to White man's shill or glowering rape-o. He never figured out that the vast majority of Black men do not fall into either camp. His appeal transcended race because he was an equal-opportunity con artist capable of snow-jobbing Blacks and Whites alike. He fit into Hollywood because he had looks and name value, fawned and joked to the correct degree, and zinged some pseudo-egalitarian heartstrings. If his trial becomes a referendum on African-American rage and its inevitable consequences, a minute cause-and-effect examination of his life will reveal no overt instances of personality-forming trauma directly attributable to specific acts of White racism. To offer the historic oppression of Blacks as a salient factor of mitigation in an adrenaline-fueled double lust homicide is preposterous. O.J. Simpson will have *truly* transcended race at that moment when Blacks and Whites get together and recognize him as a cowardly piece of shit who may or may not have murdered two innocent people and left two Black *and* White children devastated for the rest of their lives.

. . .

Of course, it won't go down that simply. This is one gigantic L.A.-set Russian novel that exceeds the most extreme visions of Los Angeles as a bottomless black hole of depravity. This is a bottomless meditation on celebrity that will not eclipse until someone more famous than O.J. Simpson is accused of murdering two people sexier than Nicole Brown Simpson and Ron Goldman in a considerably more outré manner. This is a story told in a thousand voices—one of those microcosmic, kaleidoscopic, multiviewpoint jobs that sum up a time and place with interlocking subplots that go on forever.

This novel teems with grotesque characters and roils with unhinged incidents. The multimedia creators of this novel are grateful for the opportunity to regroup in the wake of a major disappointment: The Michael Jackson scandal diminuendoed before they got the chance to exploit its full sleaze potential and work up a hypocritical load of bile over the plight of butt-fucked children. They've got their teeth in the O.J. case now—they're pit bulls with a standing order for more, more, more—and verisimilitude and dramatic viability outgun outright veracity as the criteria for determining the thrust of their reportage. Thus a longtime informant who says he heard two White men do the snuffs gets screaming national coverage before being dismissed with footnote-like shrugs; thus A.C. Cowlings cavorting at a porno-industry wingding militates against O.J. with an inference of "check this lowlife jungle bunny out"; thus Valley-girl model Tiffany Starr pitching a boo-hoo number about her two-date relationship with Ron Goldman implies that any man who'd pour the pork to this bimbo deserved to get whacked.

Thus freedom of speech has given us a hybrid extravaganza that rests somewhere between haphazardly proffered obfuscation and willfully evolved fiction. The exploitability of the case intersected with the ascendance of tabloid television and created a phenomenon of great magnitude, and to censor it or attempt to curtail it in any manner would be unconscionable. The O.J. Simpson case is a collective work of performance art that has to play itself out before it can be assessed, structured, deconstructed, and dissected for moral meaning.

It may boil down to issues of public disclosure and legal ethics. It may boil down to an outcry for journalistic circumspection and objectivity at all costs.

The art of fiction hinges on subjective thinking. Novelists must assume the perspectives of many different characters. Some months ago, the Simpson defense team assumed O.J.'s perspective and realized that their client was flubbing his performance as an innocent man unjustly accused. O.J. never screamed, "Let's nail the shitbird who killed my wife!"

The defense team worked up some belated damage control. They took their strand of this gigantic Russian novel interactive via a toll-free tip hot line. O.J. offered a fat reward for information leading to the apprehension of the real snuff artists—cash he might or might not have after his lawyers bleed him dry. The Los Angeles Police Department canvassed the area surrounding Nicole Simpson's town house in a search for witnesses to confirm or refute O.J.'s guilt, and got nowhere. The defense team, eager to cast the LAPD as both incompetent and racist, put out their public appeal—in case potential witnesses missed the canvassing cops and the media coverage attending the most publicized crime of all time. This was a move of epic disingenuousness—specious in its logical structuring and wholly cynical in its application.

The post–Rodney King LAPD would prefer not to hassle high-profile Blacks. Popping a low-profile White killer for the job would vibrate their vindaloos no end. The Simpson defense team understands the tortured history of the LAPD and Los Angeles Blacks—both its historical validity and the level of justified and irrational paranoia that it has produced. They put out a magnet to attract misinformation, fear, and outright madness—and some of the more presentable bits they receive may show up in court as fodder to further confuse an already informationally swamped jury.

And the LAPD will be exhorted to check out "leads" that they

know will lead nowhere, or risk a barrage of courtroom recrimi-
nations that will further obscure the facts of the case, serve to
excite racial tension, and contribute to the cause of general divi-
sive bad juju.

The defense team's probably thinking they can sell the hot-line
tapes for big bucks. The LAPD's probably wishing they framed
some random pervert for the job.

If O.J. is guilty, he should cop a plea behind exhaustion. His
2,033 yards in one season rate bupkis when compared to his post-
football sprint.

Second-rate acclaim and the pursuit of empty pleasures wear a
guy out. Beating up women is a young man's game. Attrition nar-
rows your choices down to changing your life or ending it.

Change takes time. It's not as instantaneous as a few lines of
coke or some fresh pussy.

Suicide takes imagination. You've got to be able to conjure up
an afterlife or visions of rest—or be in such unbreachable pain
that anything is preferable to your suffering.

O.J. went out behind a chickenshit end run. He didn't have the
soul or the balls to utilize his first two options.

December 1994

THE TOOTH OF CRIME

Captain Dan Burt looks and talks like an enlightened fast-track Republican. He's midsized, tan, and groomed. If he wasn't running the Los Angeles County Sheriff's Homicide Bureau he'd be saving America from both Bill Clinton and right-wing yahoos within his own party. He knows how to talk, inspire loyalty, and wear a dark-blue suit.

Today he's riffing on the Simpson case and its lessons for homicide detectives. Six team heads and two administrative aides pack his office SRO.

Burt says: "We can cop an attitude behind the O.J. thing or we can learn from it. I'm glad it wasn't our case, but I want to make damn sure we all go to school on it."

He's got seven lieutenants and one sergeant by the short hairs. He lays out a dizzying spiel on crime-scene containment, evidence chains, and the need to recognize the media magnitude of celebrity murders at the outset, think them through from an adversarial attorney's perspective, and evaluate and define every investigatory aspect as they progress. The pitch is tight and inside, with a slow-breaking kicker: The LAPD took the grief on this one, and *we* reaped the benefit.

A handsomely crafted ceramic bulldog sits on a table beside the captain's desk, replete with a Sheriff's Homicide baseball cap and a rubber turd behind its ass. Burt pats the beast and wraps up the briefing.

"This unit has flourished because we've made an effort to stay open-minded and learn from our mistakes. We've never let our reputation turn us arrogant. If we continue to assess the Simpson case and incorporate what we learn into our procedures, we'll make something good out of one big goddamn mess."

Murder is a big, continuous twenty-four-hour-a-day mess. Murder spawns a numbingly protracted investigatory process that is rarely direct and linear—chiefly because it overlaps with more and more murder, taxing the resources of the investigative agencies involved and inundating detectives with interviews, courtroom appearances, reports to be written, and next-of-kin to be mollified and cajoled into intimate revelations. Murder seldom slows down and never stops; murder stays true to its Motivational Trinity: dope/sex/money.

The L.A. Sheriff's Department investigates all murders, suicides, industrial-accident fatalities, and miscellaneous sudden deaths within the confines of Los Angeles County—the vast, unincorporated area in and around the L.A. city limits. The LAPD's jurisdiction snakes inside, outside, and through the LASD's turf—city/county borders are sometimes hard to distinguish. The county consists mainly of lower-middle-class suburbs and rat's ass towns stretching out ninety-odd miles. This is the big bad sprawl visible from low-flying airplanes: cheap stucco, smog, and freeway grids going on forever.

The LASD Homicide Bureau is housed in a courtyard industrial park in the city of Commerce—six miles from downtown L.A. Sheriff's Homicide is individually subcontracted by numerous police departments inside the county—if you get whacked in Norwalk or Rosemead, the LASD will work your case.

Sheriff's Homicide investigates about 500 snuffs a year. The L.A. District Attorney's office has publicly acknowledged its investigators as the best in southern California. Police departments nationwide send their prospective homicide dicks to the

LASD for two-week training programs. LASD detectives teach well because theirs is regarded as the pinnacle assignment—one bestowed after a minimum of ten years in jail work, patrol, and other Detective Division jobs. The mid-forties median age says it all: These people have put the rowdier aspects of police work behind them and have matured behind the gravity of murder.

Former sheriff Peter Pitchess dubbed his homicide crew "the Bulldogs"—a nod to their tenacity and salutary solved-case rate. In truth, bulldogs are lazy creatures prone to breathing disorders and hip dysplasia. The vulture should replace the bulldog as Homicide's mascot.

Vultures wait for people to die. So do homicide cops. Vultures swoop down on the recently dead and guard the surrounding area with sharp claws and beaks. Homicide cops seal crime scenes and kick off their investigations with the evidence culled within.

Sheriff's Homicide is a centralized division. Its basic makeup is six teams of fourteen detectives apiece, bossed by lieutenants Derry Benedict, Don Bear, Joe Brown, Dave Dietrich, Ray Peavy, and Bill Sieber. Two adjunct units—Unsolved and Missing Persons—work out of the same facility. The teams handle incoming murders on a rotating, forty-eight-hour on-call basis.

On-call detectives carry beepers and sleep very poorly, if at all. Beeper chirps signify death and additions to their already strained caseloads. Late-night beeps are only marginally preferable to what the old-timers called "trash runs": call-outs for obvious suicides and pro forma viewings of the poor fucker who got decapitated by an exploding boiler.

The bureau is furnished in the white-walled, metal-desked, policework moderne style. All incoming calls originate in the "Barrel," a desk counter rigged with telephones, memo baskets, and boards for charting murders and assigned personnel. The Barrel adjoins the main squad room—ninety desks arranged in lengthwise rows. The team lieutenants' desks sit crosswise at the far end, next to a shelf jammed with Sergeant Don Garcia's bulldog trinkets.

You can purchase bulldog watches and T-shirts at Sergeant

Garcia's cost. A bulldog wall clock will set you back $39.95. Dig the bulldog lapel pin—the giant tongue and spiked collar detailing are worthy of Walt Disney on angel dust. Don's been running the concession for years. He buys the stuff bulk from various manufacturers. He's just acquired a new item: a bulldog neon sign to light up your wet bar!

The Unsolved and Missing Persons units reside in separate rooms off the squad bay. The sign on Unsolved's door reads "UNLOVED." Unsolved is charged with periodically reviewing cold cases and investigating any new leads pertaining to them. The crew—Dale Christiansen, Rey Verdugo, Louie "the Hat" Danoff, John Yarbrough, and Freddy Castro—is the faculty of the College of Unresolved Justice. Their curriculum is the file library that Louie the Hat has lovingly preserved. Louie says the files talk to him. He's on a spiritual trip and runs his "no body" cases by psychics once in a while.

A corridor links Unsolved to a room lined with computers. A dozen screens glow green all day every day—dig the dozen clerks running record checks on permanent overdrive. The clerks— mostly women—hog the lunchroom from noon to 2 P.M. daily. They watch soap operas and pine for the candy-ass male stars— right down the hall from the ugly bulldog wall plaque.

Note to Sheriff Sherman Block: Vultures are more charismatic than bulldogs.

It's early December. Deputies Gil Carrillo and Frank Gonzales have tickets for the annual Sheriff's/LAPD fistfest. They're primed for an evening of charity boxing—until Lieutenant Brown tells them they're the first on-call team up.

It's a given: Some geek will get murdered tonight and fuck up their fun.

Carrillo and Gonzales decide to stay home and rest. Gil lays some comedy on the deskman, Sergeant Mike Lee: I want a good night's sleep and an indoor crime scene near my pad about 10 A.M. tomorrow. Joe Brown says he'll place the order, ha! ha! ha!

Gil and Frank retire to their cribs. Gil's about six foot three and massively broad. The earth shakes whenever he walks. He co-bossed the LASD's end of the Richard Ramirez "Night Stalker" serial killer task force back in the eighties, ran against Sherman Block in the last sheriff's election, and glommed 17 percent of the vote. Frank's picture should appear in every dictionary on earth, next to the words "Latin lover." He is one handsome mother-fucker. Carrillo and Gonzales bring vulture charisma to every case they work—but they're pissed that they blew the fights off for nothing.

Because Gil's wish comes true. His beeper beeps at 10 A.M.—it's an indoor crime scene ten minutes from his pad.

The victim is Donna Lee Meyers, female Caucasian, age 37. She's dead at her house in Valinda, a downscale San Gabriel Valley town.

She's facedown on a green shag rug in the bathroom. She's nude. She's been stabbed between twenty and forty times. Defensive wounds on her hands and arms indicate an extended struggle with her killer.

Patrol deputies responded to the 911 call. The informant was Donna Lee Meyers's father. He came to pick up his 3-year-old grandson and found the back door unlocked and the house filled with gas fumes.

The boy coughed and led him to the body. Every gas burner in the kitchen had been turned on and left unignited.

Carrillo and Gonzales arrive at the scene and get a rundown from the deputies. Their first collective hypothesis: The killer didn't have the stones to ice a little child up front, so he juiced up the gas before he split. Their first collective instinct: The murder was unpremeditated, with a sharp instrument used as a weapon of opportunity. Their first collective decision: Stay outside and let the criminalists do their work first—don't risk contaminating the crime scene.

The serologist takes blood samples off the rug and the surrounding area. The print man dusts and comes up with smudges and smears. A technician prowls with an Electrostatic Dust Lifter—a vacuum sealer–like device that transfers the outline of footprints to a cellophane dust-catching sheet. The coroner remains on hold—to remove the body when Carillo and Gonzales give the word.

Carillo and Gonzales canvass the neighborhood. The word on the street: Donna Lee Meyers did cocaine—and used to deal small quantities of it. Carillo and Gonzales take notes, write down names for backup interviews and compile a list of Donna Lee Meyers's known associates. A friend of the victim's shows up at the house—and appears to be genuinely shocked that Donna Lee is dead. Carillo and Gonzales take the man to a nearby sheriff's sub-station and question him.

He tells them that he dropped by to pay Donna Lee back some coin, and cops to being a casual coke user. The man vibes totally innocent. Carillo and Gonzales let him go and hotfoot it back to the crime scene.

They view the body. A deputy tells them that the killer left the TV on for the kid. Coroner's assistants take Donna Lee Meyers to the L.A. County Morgue.

The follow-up begins.

Carillo and Gonzales attend the autopsy and hear the cause of death confirmed. They locate the father of Donna Lee Meyers's son and dismiss him as a suspect. A psychologist assists them in their dealings with Donna Lee's little boy. The boy's memories of that day are hellishly distorted. Gentle questioning elicits ambiguous responses.

Early December becomes mid-December. Carrillo and Gonzales interview Donna Lee Meyers's known associates and come up short on hard suspects. It's becoming a long, hard one—the kind you solve or don't solve while other cases accumulate.

It's creeping up on Christmastime. The bureau lunchroom is draped with red and green banners and packed with an assortment of sugar-soaked treats.

Bulldog-vultures swoop by and chow down—pecan pies and toffee clusters hook you on the first bite.

Talk flows. Food disappears. Nineteen ninety-four is winding down in a swirl of rapid-fire conversation.

Bill Sieber's midway through his standard epic pitch: how a friend's daughter was murdered in Olympia, Washington, and boy did the cops screw up the case! Bill's a primo monologuist. He's got his audience hooked—even though every detective has heard the story six dozen times. Lieutenant Frank Merriman's interjecting punch lines, smiling his standard shit-eating grin. Frank grins 96 percent of the time. Somebody should transpose his brain waves to TV, so the whole world could cut in on the laughs.

Cheryl Lyons zips by. She's got electric turquoise eyes—or she's wearing electric turquoise contact lenses. The late Jack Hoffenberg bootjacked Cheryl's persona for the female lead in his novel *The Desperate Adversaries*. Cheryl the 1973 narc became Cheryl of the Paperback Pantheon. Cheryl's pensive today—will the county notch in eight more murders and top its all-time yearly high of 537?

Ike Sabean thinks it's a lock. Ike works Juvenile Missing Persons—and must be considered a certified genius.

You've seen his work on milk cartons—the photos of missing kids and the number to call if you spot them. Ike developed the idea in cahoots with a Chicago dairyman. He got a total of sixty-seven dairies and industrial firms to display the pix—and ran up a 70 percent local found rate until the public became inured to the photos. Ike's also a board-licensed mortician. He explains the allure of his moonlighting job thusly: "I like to work with people."

Jerome Beck lingers by the chocolate-chip-cookie plate. Beck was the technical adviser on the flick *Dead Bang*. He also wrote the story. Guess what? The director of that movie named the Don Johnson–portrayed lead character "Jerry Beck."

Big Gil Carrillo walks in. The floor shakes; a serving bowl full of Jell-O jiggles. Gil buttonholes Louie the Hat and runs the Donna Lee Meyers crime-scene pix by him.

They discuss defensive wounds and blood-spatter trajectories.

Louie's got a spaced-out woman in tow—a psychic he consults every so often.

They call him "the Hat" because he always wears a Tyrolean porkpie with a feather in the band. If you fuck with Louie's hat, Louie will fuck with you. A few years ago, some LAPD clown snatched Louie's hat and goofed on Louie's shaved head. Louie unhesitatingly popped him in the chops.

Big Gil walks off. Louie hobnobs with his psychic. Don Garcia tacks a notice to the bulletin board: Bulldog wristwatches make wonderful Christmas gifts!

The computer women look pissed. All this holiday bonhomie is drowning out the volume on their soap opera.

The boss is teething on the Guevara case. His ceramic bulldog is teething at the fur ball on the tip of his Santa Claus cap—Dan Burt likes to dress the beast in seasonal headwear.

Ray Peavy's crew got the job—a double abduction/murder way the hell out in Lancaster. Deputy Liova Anderson and Sergeant Joe Guzman caught the first squeal—one baffling whodunit.

Peavy's laying out a chronology for Dan Burt. It's an informal captain's office confab—and the open door encourages kibitzers.

Anderson got the initial call on Wednesday, November 30: a body dump out in the desert. Liova drives up to Palmdale/Lancaster and views the stiff: a male Latin with his hands, face, and crotch scorched.

The victim was wrapped in a baby blanket, doused with a flammable agent, and burned. Liova picks up a strong vibe: The genital scalding indicates some sort of sex murder.

Liova has to work solo for the first seventy-two hours—Joe Guzman, a nationally known expert on gang violence, is off giving a lecture in Texas. She knuckles down and *hauls*.

She attends the postmortem on Friday. The doctor pulls a bullet out of the dead man's head and tags the cause of death as a "gunshot wound." He cuts the dead man's fingers off, rehydrates them, and rolls a clean set of prints.

On Sunday, Liova hears a radio news broadcast. A Latin couple named Carlos and Delia Guevara have been reported missing in Lancaster. She gets another strong vibe: Her dead man is Carlos Guevara.

She calls the Antelope Valley Sheriff's Missing Persons unit. An officer tells her that Sergeant Jim Sears and Deputy Jerry Burks of Sheriff's Homicide have already been assigned to the case—because a bullet hole was found in Carlos and Delia Guevara's living-room wall.

Joe Guzman returns from Texas. Liova drives him up to Lancaster and explains the case en route. The team meets up with Burks and Sears at the Guevara house. Sears drops a belated bomb: Delia Guevara's body was discovered in Yermo over the weekend.

The woman had been shot and similarly dumped—in San Bernardino County, sixty miles from the spot where Guzman and Anderson's body was found.

Liova checks the Guevaras' family records stash and finds a fingerprint ID card on Carlos. She takes it to the L.A. County crime lab and has a technician compare it to the rehydrated digits cut off her victim.

The prints match.

Burks and Sears work the Delia side of the case. Anderson and Guzman stick with Carlos.

Liova's original vibe simmers: This is a sex or sexual-revenge killing. She begins an extensive background check on the Guevaras.

She learns that Delia worked at a local Burger King and Carlos worked at a local appliance store. She learns that the couple had emigrated from Mexico illegally and were living above their means. She learns that Delia had been receiving menacing phone calls at work and that Carlos loved to talk lewd in mixed company—even though it made his friends and neighbors uncomfortable. Carlos was also known for chasing women outright.

Joe Guzman finds numerous toys in a sealed-off bedroom at the Guevara house. It is a striking anomaly. The Guevaras were childless and had often told friends they did not intend to have children. The motive takes circumstantial shape.

Two killings. Vengeance perpetrated by a cuckolded lover or the parents of an abused child.

Ray Peavy wraps his account up. Anderson and Guzman, Burks and Sears are *still* on the case—which remains one baffling whodunit.

Sergeant Jacque Franco pokes her head in the door and eavesdrops. Deputy Rick Graves sidles by for a listen; Dan Burt shoots him an attaboy for his work on that drowning case off Catalina Island.

Ray Peavy says, "It never ends."

Jacque Franco says, "We're still six short of breaking the record."

Dan Burt pats his fat ceramic bulldog.

Sergeant Bob Perry and Deputy Ruben "B.J." Bejarano get called out on Christmas Eve. It's cold, dark, and rainy—good indoor mayhem conditions.

They roll to a video store near the Century Sheriff's Station. A Taiwanese woman named Li Mei Wu lies dead on the floor behind the counter.

The weather has kept rubberneckers to a minimum. Patrol deputies have rounded up eyewitnesses and sequestered them at the station. A sergeant lays things out for Bejarano and Perry.

Three black teenagers entered the store around closing time. They gave the victim some verbal grief, split, and returned a few minutes later. One of them shot Li Mei Wu with a rifle. They ran outside and disappeared on foot.

The victim is positioned faceup. There's a live .22-caliber round and a .22 ejected casing behind the counter. A coroner's assistant lifts the body, notes the exit wound, and points to a projectile tangled up in Li Mei Wu's clothes. He says the shot probably tore out the woman's aorta.

The assistant finds $300 in Li Mei Wu's pockets. Perry and Bejarano note the untouched money and the full cash register and tentatively scratch robbery as a motive. The patrol sergeant tells them what eyeball witnesses told him: The perpetrators bopped to a coin laundry a few doors down before they bopped back and bopped Li Mei Wu.

The body is hustled off to the county morgue. B.J. diagrams the video store in his notebook, zooms down to the laundry, and quick-sketches the floor plan. A deputy from the crime lab arrives. He begins snapping crime-scene shots and dusting both the video store and the coin laundry.

Bob and B.J. secure the location and drive to Century Station. Two witnesses are waiting; three have signed preliminary statements, left their phone numbers, and gone home.

B.J. and Bob conduct interviews. They go over minute points of perspective and indoor and outdoor lighting repeatedly. Questions are phrased and rephrased; answers are cross-checked against the three preliminary statements. A single short narrative emerges.

At 8:20 P.M., three black teenagers enter the video store. They behave in a raucous fashion; Li Mei Wu tells them to leave. The kids peruse the skin-flick section and touch numerous *fingerprint-sustaining surfaces*. They walk to the laundry, behave in a raucous fashion, return to the video store and approach Li Mei Wu. One boy says, "Give me your money, bitch!" One boy pulls a rifle from under his clothes and shoots Li Mei Wu—just like that.

It's Christmas morning now. Yuletide greetings, Bulldogs—your new case is senseless blasphemy on this day of peace and joyous celebration.

Days pass. Bejarano and Perry work the Li Mei Wu snuff.

They interview four more witnesses and get their basic scenario confirmed. They run mug shots by the witnesses and come up empty. They run a previous-incident check on the video store—and hit just a little bit lucky.

The place was robbed in November, while Li Mei Wu was working the counter. The perpetrators: three black teenagers.

The same kids robbed a nearby pizza joint that same November night. Li Mei Wu ID's one boy as the grandson of one of her customers. Deputies went by the family pad to grab him—but Junior was long gone.

B.J. and Bob think the December incident report through. One fact stands out: Li Mei Wu hit the silent alarm when she was robbed in November—but did not rush for it on the night of her death. *She obviously did not recognize the kids as the kids who robbed her the previous month.* Bejarano and Perry get their gut feeling confirmed: The murder was committed by local punks. The killers ran away on a rainy night—they didn't have a car and got soaked dispersing back to their pads. One robbery threesome; one trio of killers. Word would be out in the neighborhood—and loose talk would give them a good shot at solving the case.

While other cases accumulate.

There's a big post-Christmas murder lull. Entire on-call shifts are rotating through sans killings. The lunchroom tree is wilting under the weight of decomposed fake snow.

Bulldog eyes are bloodshot. Bulldog waistlines have expanded. High-octane coffee can't jolt Bulldog talk out of a desultory ripple.

Rey Verdugo's recalling other murder lulls. A few years ago the County of Los Angeles went nine days without a single murder. One of Rey's buddies put a sign reading KILL! in the squad-room window. Sheriff's Homicide notched twelve righteous whack-outs over the next twenty-four hours.

Dave Dietrich's showing off some threads he got for Christmas. His wife reads men's fashion mags and shops for him accordingly. You'd call him "Dave the Dude"—if he didn't look so much like a college professor.

Bill Sieber's drinking Slim-Fast in anticipation of his New Year's diet. He's monologuing between sips—in an uncharacteristically subdued fashion. Ray Peavy and Derry Benedict are discussing the Christmas party at Stevens Steak House. Ray worked the bash as a disc jockey—between his regular off-duty deejay gigs.

Talk shifts to famous unsolved murders. Derry brings up his favorite: the 1944 Georgette Bauerdorf job. When he retires he's going to write a novel about the case.

Louie Danoff and Rey Verdugo compare shaved heads. Gary Miller pokes at a cookie like it's a hot turd.

The killers of Carlos and Delia Guevara, Donna Lee Meyers, and Li Mei Wu are still at large. Soon the year's murder tally will stop—and a new list will begin.

Nineteen ninety-four winds up three short of the all-time murder high. Gunfire rings in 1995—celebratory shots all over the county.

Gunshots and firecracker pops start to sound alike. The locals get used to the noise but expect it to diminish before January 2.

Five shots explode at 6:45 New Year's night. The location is California and Hill, in the city of Huntington Park.

The shots are very loud. The shots in no way, shape, matter, or form sound like anything short of heavy-duty gunfire.

The shots have a gang-killing timbre—maybe the H.P. Brats and H.P. Locos are at it again. A dozen people on Hill Street call the Huntington Park PD.

Huntington Park rolls a unit over. Patrolmen find the body of Joseph Romero, male Latin, DOB 5/11/69. He's dead behind the wheel of his car, ripped through the torso by five AK-47 rounds.

Spent shells rest near the curb. One round blew straight through Romero and out the driver's-side door.

Sheriff's Homicide is alerted. Lieutenant Peavy, Deputy Bob Carr, and Sergeant Stu Reed make the scene.

Carr and Reed are short, heavyset, and fiftyish. They joined the department back in the '60s. Reed's an expert wood-carver; Carr sports the world's coolest handlebar mustache. Both men talk as slow and flat as tombstones.

A crowd forms. Huntington Park cops seal the people out with yellow perimeter tape. Coroner's assistants remove the body; a sheriff's tow truck hauls Romero's car off to the crime lab.

Reed and Carr eyeball the scene. They hit on a hypothesis fast.

Romero was sitting in the car by himself. He was parked six doors down from his pad. He was waiting for somebody.

The passenger-side window was down. "Somebody" walked up, stuck the gun in, and vaporized him.

The crime vibes "gang vengeance" or "dope intrigue," or somebody fucking somebody's girlfriend or sister. The cops have got some witnesses on ice—just dying to offer their interpretations.

Reed and Carr interview them at the H.P. station. Three solid-citizen types tell similar stories: shots fired and two male Latins running off in divergent directions. One man was short; one man was tall—their descriptions match straight down the line. Reed and Carr go over their statements from every conceivable angle.

It's an exercise in spatial logic and a master's course in the plumbing of subjective viewpoints. It's the culling of minutiae as an art form—and Carr and Reed are brilliant cullers.

It's starting to look like another neighborhood crime. The shooter and his accomplice fled on foot and were probably safe at home within minutes.

Reed and Carr interview a Mexican kid named Paulino. Paulino denies being a gang member and states that he hasn't done dope since he got out of rehab. He says he saw the tall male Latin fifteen minutes after the shooting. The guy was waving to a babe leaning out a window in that beige apartment house on Salt Lake Avenue.

A fifth witness independently corroborates the story. He saw the tall man running toward that same building moments after the shooting.

It's coming together. Reed and Carr decide to wait and not hit the building tonight—too many things could go wrong. They agree: Let's check with the HPPD Gang Squad when they come on duty. We'll find out who lives in that building and move accordingly.

Three non-eyewitnesses remain: Joseph Romero's uncle, aunt, and brother. Carr and Reed talk to them gently, and phrase all intimate questions in a deferential tone. The family responds. They say Joe was a nice kid trying to put dope and gang life behind him. They supply names: Joe was tight with a dozen male Latins in the neighborhood.

Reed and Carr do not mention the beige apartment house. They do not know who the family knows and might feel compelled to protect.

The family leaves. Reed and Carr drive home to get a few hours' sleep. They look old and cumulatively exhausted—like they never had a chance to get caught up while murders accumulate.

The holidays are over. Bob Perry and Jacque Franco are bullshitting at their desks.

Bob says he just notched a score on the Li Mei Wu case. The kids arrested turn out to be the punks who robbed the video store a month before the murder. The suspects are 13, 13, and 16.

Stu Reed sidles by. Jacque asks him how the Romero job is going. Stu says they've got one shooter ID'd but can't find him. Jacque says, "Don't worry—he'll come back to the neighborhood to brag."

Gil Carrillo sits down. He straightens a mimeographed sheet of paper he keeps pressed to his desk blotter.

"The Homicide Investigator" jumps out in bold black print. A single paragraph is inscribed below it:

"No greater honor will ever be bestowed on an officer or a more profound duty imposed on him than when he is entrusted with the investigation of the death of a human being. It is his duty to find the facts, regardless of color or creed, without prejudice, and to let no power on earth deter him from presenting these facts to the court without regard to personality."

Gil blows the motto a kiss. His eyes take on that "Don't mess with me, I'm deep in a reverie" look. You see why people voted for the man. He cares way past the official boundaries of the job. Jacque says, "This job is still Disneyland to you, isn't it?"

Gil tilts his chair back. "It's not Disneyland when you get called out at 3 A.M., but when you get to the murder scene it's like you're coming up on Disneyland and you can see the Matterhorn ride in the distance. It's not Disneyland when you see all the ugliness, but it's Disneyland at the trial when the jury foreman says 'Guilty' and you break down crying just like the victim's family."

The holidays are long gone.

Dan Burt's bulldog has gone back to his baseball cap.

Burt tosses a gun catalogue in his wastebasket. He's a lifelong gun fancier pushed to the point of apostasy.

"My gun collection sickens me now," he says. "It makes me feel like I'm part of some mass illness."

Ray Peavy coughs. "We found Carlos Guevara's car at the Greyhound Terminal downtown. The crime lab's got it."

Burt points to a sheet of paper on his desk blotter—a mock-up of the condolence letter the bureau sends to murder victims' families.

"We can't send that to Guevara's wife, because she's dead too. I guess all we can do is pray and work the case."

While other cases accumulate.

July 1995

BAD BOYS IN TINSELTOWN

"L.A. Come on vacation; go home on probation."

Somebody dropped that line on me twenty-five years ago. The line dropper was not an academic or a media pundit. A street freak or a honor-farm bunkmate probably shot me those words. He probably heard them on an old Mort Sahl or Lenny Bruce record and passed them off as original wisdom. It's a throwaway line with a rich historical subtext and snappy implications. It's a travelogue ad for the hip, the hung, and the damned.

That line implies that L.A. is a magnetic field and that all L.A. migrations are suspect. That line indicts *your* desire to come to L.A. and categorizes you as an opportunist with a hidden sexual agenda. That line is a cliché and a prophecy. It foretells your brief sensual riches and your grindingly protracted fall and retreat.

You can reinvent yourself en route. You can assume your desired identity and make attitude count for a thousand times its hometown value. You can live in a community of people who came to L.A. to be somebody else and envy the few who make money at it and blow you off as a loser. You can blame your fall and retreat on the city that magnetized you and duck the issue of your own failure.

People will understand and empathize. They know that L.A. is big, bad, and beautiful and full of the power to mortify. That power carries a built-in escape clause. L.A. rejects can cite it with-

out the appearance of unseemly self-pity. The clause grants for-
giveness through mitigation and holds L.A. up as a city beyond
any individual's control. There's enough truth in the clause to
keep anyone from questioning his desire to come to L.A. in the
first place.

I'm *from* L.A. My parents made the migration and spared me the
grief of making the jaunt on my own. I possess certain L.A. migra-
tor tendencies. I migrated east to enact them. I'm sure that my
parents would have understood the move.

My father arrived in the mid-'30s. He was a tall, handsome guy
with a gigantic *schvantz* and an inspired line of bullshit. He had
won a few medals during World War I and hyperbolically embellished his exploits. He jumped on every woman who'd let him and
firmly believed that every woman who didn't let him was a lesbian. He landed in L.A. with a flash roll and some snazzy threads
and gravitated toward the movie biz. His career as a Hollywood
bottom feeder topped out in the late '40s. He got a gig as Rita
Hayworth's business manager and allegedly poured the pork to
Rita on many auspicious occasions.

My mother won a beauty contest and flew to L.A. in December
of '38. She was a 23-year-old registered nurse from the Wisconsin
boonies and the Elmo Beauty Products' newly crowned "America's Most Charming Redhead." She toured L.A. with the most
charming blonde, brunette, and gray-haired winners, took a
screen test, and flew back to her job in Chicago with $1,000 in
prize money. L.A. kicked around in her head. She learned she was
pregnant, aborted herself, and hemorrhaged. A doctor acquain-
tance fixed her up. She got the urge to start over in a sexy, new
locale. She took a train back to L.A., found a pad and a job and
met a schmuck who may or may not have been an heir to the
Spalding sporting-goods fortune. She married the guy and
divorced him within a few months. She met my father in '40 and
fell for his good looks and line of bullshit. My father deserted his
wife and shacked up with my mother. They were married six years
into their shack job and seven months before my birth.

They told me stories, took me to movies, and encouraged me to read books. They force-fed me narrative lines. I grew up in the film noir era in the film noir epicenter. I read *Confidential, Whisper,* and *Lowdown* magazines before I learned to ride a two-wheel bike. My father called Rita Hayworth a nympho. My mother wet-nursed dipsomaniacal film stars. My father pointed out the two-way mirrors at the Hollywood Ranch Market and told me they were spy holes to entrap shoplifters and disrupt homosexual assignations. I saw *Plunder Road* and *The Killing* and learned that perfectly planned heists go bad because daring heist men are self-destructive losers playing out their parts in a preordained endgame with authority.

Johnnie Ray was a fruit. Lizabeth Scott was a dyke. All jazz musicians here hopheads. Tom Neal beat Franchot Tone half-dead over a blonde cooze named Barbara Payton. The Algiers Hotel was a glorified "fuck pad." A pint-size punk named Mickey Cohen ran the L.A. rackets from his cell at McNeil Island. Rin Tin Tin was really a girl dog. Lassie was really a boy dog. L.A. was a smog-shrouded netherworld orbiting under a dark star and blinded by the glare of scandal-rag flashbulbs. Every third person was a peeper, prowler, pederast, poon stalker, panty sniffer, prostitute, pillhead, pothead, or pimp. The other two-thirds of the population were tight-assed squares resisting the urge to peep, prowl, poon stalk, pederastically indulge, pop pills, and panty sniff. This mass self-denial created a seismic dislocation that skewed L.A. about six degrees off the central axis of planet Earth.

I knew an inchoate version of this at age 9. I knew it because I came from L.A. and my parents told me stories and lies. I knew it because I read books and went to movies and eschewed the gospel of the Lutheran Church in favor of a scandal-rag concordance. I knew it because my mother was murdered on June 22, 1958, and they never got the guy who did it.

My mother's death corrupted my imagination and reinforced my sense that there were really two L.A.'s. They existed concurrently. I bebopped around in the cosmetically wholesome Outer

L.A. I conjured the Secret L.A. as a hedge against Outer L.A. boredom.

The Secret L.A. was all SEX. It was the shock and titillation of a child slamming up against the fact that his life began with fucking. It was my father's profane laughter and scandal-sheet deconstructionism. The sheets rendered beautiful people frail and somehow available. Common lusts shaped and drove them. Their pizzazz and good looks made them more and less than you. If the wind blew a certain way on a certain night, you could get lucky and have them.

The Secret L.A. was all CRIME. It was Stephen Nash and the kid he slashed under the Santa Monica Pier. It was Harvey Glatman and the cheesecake models he strangled. It was Johnny Stompanato shanked by Lana Turner's daughter two months before my mother's death.

CRIME merged with SEX on 6/22/58. My Secret L.A. obliterated the Outer L.A.

I've been living in it for thirty-nine years. I've reconstructed L.A. in the '50s in my head and on paper. I did not come on vacation or go home on probation. I lived in the literal L.A. and dreamed my own private L.A. I left the literal L.A. sixteen years ago. It was simply too familiar. I left the Secret L.A. one book and one memoir ago. I made a conscious decision to drop L.A. as a fictional locale. I had taken it as far as I could.

I've been jerked back to L.A. '53. A man made a movie and reinstated my L.A. life sentence.

Curtis Hanson is serving life himself. His sentence carries binding permanent-residence clause and a work-furlough waiver. He's got ten five-year hash marks on his jail denims and the beach pad characteristic of all successful L.A. lifers. He splits town to make films and comes back to L.A. rejuvenated. He's serving his life sentence voluntarily.

He made *Losin' It* in Calexico, California, and Mexicali, Mexico. He made *The Bedroom Window* in Baltimore and *The Hand That Rocks the Cradle* in Seattle. He made *The River Wild* in Montana and Oregon, and *Bad Influence* in present-day L.A. It's the Faust tale retold for yuppies and hipsters and a symphony in bold colors and smog-kissed pastels. It doesn't look like any other L.A. film.

Hanson has provocative L.A. roots. He's second-generation L.A. stock. His birth certificate is stamped "Reno, Nevada." His father, Wilbur, was working on a government road crew there when Curtis was born.

Wilbur Hanson was a conscientious objector. He refused to fight in World War II and served out his draft commitment with a pick and shovel. The Hanson family moved back to L.A. in '46. Curtis and his older brother banged around a big, run-down house at Fifth and Hobart. His mother rented out their spare rooms. His father taught at the Harvard Military School and chauffeured rich kids to school for extra money.

Wilbur Hanson was a gifted and thoroughly dedicated teacher. He took his students on field trips and gave them more time than he gave his own sons. The Harvard School was an upscale dump site for the sons of the Hollywood elite. Darryl F. Zanuck's son matriculated there. Old Man Zanuck got a hard-on for Wilbur Hanson. He didn't want no fucking CO teaching at his kid's school. He applied the big squeeze and had Wilbur Hanson bounced from Harvard.

Wilbur Hanson caught a Red-scare bullet but dodged another one. He got certified to teach in the L.A. city school system. He was not excluded on the basis of his expressed pacifism or his documented CO status. The family moved out to the San Fernando Valley. Wilbur Hanson began teaching at a school in Reseda.

Wilbur and Beverly June Hanson encouraged their sons to read. Beverly June loved movies and dragged Curtis and his brother to bargain matinees all over the Valley. He had seen dozens of film noir flicks before he knew the term "film noir." He watched *Dragnet*, *M Squad*, *The Lineup*, *Racket Squad*, and *Mike Hammer* every week. School bored him. His real curriculum was films, novels, and TV shows. His major course of study was narrative. His minor course of study was crime.

He wrote a story called "The Man Who Wanted Money" and read it to his fifth-grade class. His teacher found the story and Curtis's general crime fixation disturbing and ratted him off to his parents.

Curtis had a dual-world thing going. He had his family/school world and his film/book/TV-show world. He figured he'd grow up, become a screenwriter and director, and pull off a two-world merger.

He developed a dual-L.A. thing. It grew out of a dual thing with his dad and his uncle Jack.

Wilbur Hanson was a morally committed schoolteacher with $1.98 in the bank. Jack Hanson was a morally desiccated rag merchant who sucked up to movie stars and showbiz players.

Dad had a shack in the Valley. Uncle Jack had a big pad in Beverly Hills. Dad spent most of his time with schoolkids. Uncle Jack hobnobbed with Hollywood swingers. Dad took kids on uplifting field trips. Uncle Jack owned Jax—the grooviest, sexiest, most altogether bonaroo boutique on Rodeo Drive.

Curtis spent weekdays in the Valley and weekends in Beverly Hills. Uncle Jack loved having him around as a companion for his son. Curtis's two worlds were regulated by his school duties and divided by the Hollywood Hills. Uncle Jack gave him access to a world within his world. It was the fast-lane world of aggressive people out to get all they could and fuck the cost. That world-within-a-world dovetailed with Curtis Hanson's crime fixation. Uncle Jack's movie-biz fixation dovetailed with Curtis's ambition to grow up and become a filmmaker.

Jack Hanson was noir personified. He was a movie-biz toady straight out of *The Big Knife*. He hoarded money and paid his people the minimum wage. He was arguably the cheapest cocksucker who ever walked the face of the earth. He opened up the Daisy in the mid-'60s. It was the first members-only dance club in Beverly Hills. Jack sold memberships to showbiz hipsters and employed it as his vehicle to suck his way further into the in crowd.

Curtis watched. Curtis took mental notes. Curtis finished school and got a chump job with *Cinema* magazine. He drove copy to the typesetters and film to the photo lab. The magazine started to go belly-up. Curtis convinced Uncle Jack to take over the operating costs and let *him* do all the work.

He did it. He wrote the critical pieces and feature interviews and took the photographs. He took some shots of Faye Dunaway and was paid with a plane ticket. He flew to Texas and watched the filming of *Bonnie and Clyde*.

It was a period film and a crime film. Curtis Hanson wrote it up in *Cinema* magazine. He prophetically called it "the most exciting American film in years."

I read that issue of *Cinema* magazine thirty years ago. I was 19 and strung out on pills and Thunderbird wine. I was breaking into houses in a ritzy L.A. enclave and stealing things that wouldn't be missed. I was shoplifting and reading crime novels and going to crime movies.

Hanson got me hot to see *Bonnie and Clyde*. I saw it and wigged out on it. I stole the money that paid for my ticket.

A year ago, I drove out to Lincoln Heights to watch a day's filming of *L.A. Confidential*. It was mid-August and very hot and humid.

A northeast-L.A. street was doubling for a street in south L.A. Nineteen ninety-six was doubling for 1953.

Period cars lined the curb. A dozen equipment trucks and trailers were parked just out of camera view. Twenty-odd technicians and gofers were standing near a catering van. They were snarfing cookies and ice-cream bars in the hundred-degree heat.

The focal point was a shabby wood-frame house. It was a near perfect match to the house I'd described in my novel. I visualized the scene I wrote in 1989.

A cop vaults a backyard fence and walks up a flight of outside stairs in broad daylight. He slips the catch on a second-story door and enters a cramped apartment. He sees a woman gagged and tied to a bed with neckties. He walks into the living room and shoots her presumed assailant in cold blood.

My cop was named Bud White. He was a huge man with a

football-injury limp and a gray flattop. The movie Bud White is an actor named Russell Crowe. He is a compact and muscular man with dark hair and a quasi-flattop.

I watched Crowe nosh an ice-cream bar and bullshit with extras in cop uniforms. The actors playing Lieutenant Ed Exley and Captain Dudley Smith were standing across the street. My Exley was tall and blond. Guy Pearce, the film Exley, is medium size and dark haired. My Smith was burly and red-faced. James Cromwell, the film Smith, is pale and imperiously tall.

I felt like I was entering a brand-new L.A. world and a multi-media extravaganza. Period snapshots and scandal-rag headlines formed the visual borders. The audio track was the sound of my written words spoken by the actors around me. My mother's ghost was somewhere in the mix. She was eating popcorn with a spoon and humming Kay Starr's 1952 hit, "Wheel of Fortune."

I reeled behind a jolt of heat and a thousand quick-cut blips of my own private L.A. I had written *L.A. Confidential* as an epic hometown elegy. It was established fact and half-heard scandal and whispered innuendo. It was the world of horror I had first glimpsed the day my mother died.

It was Mickey Cohen and his henchman Johnny Stompanato. It was *Hush-Hush* magazine, my stand-in for *Confidential*. It was sex shakedowns and perverts modeled on Stephen Nash and Harvey Glatman. It was the "Bloody Christmas" police-brutality scandal and the twisted story of a theme park disingenuously disguised to remind readers of Disneyland.

L.A. Confidential was conceived and executed as a large-scale novel. It was not written with an eye toward movie adaptation. I did not expect it to bushwhack me six years after its publication.

I read the screenplay. Two writers had taken my milieu, my characters, and a good deal of my dialogue and fashioned their L.A. world within my L.A. worlds.

I walked into the wood-frame house. I was entering their visual world now. I passed the bedroom where the woman would be gagged and bound with neckties. I found Curtis Hanson framing a shot in the living room.

He saw me and smiled. He said, "What do you think?"

I said, "It looks inspired."

I had dinner with Hanson that night. We met at our mutual favorite restaurant.

The Pacific Dining Car is a swanky steak pit on the edge of downtown L.A. It's been there since 1921. It's dark and wood paneled. It's a self-contained time warp in a city of time warps and dark continuums.

Hanson's uncle Jack brought him to the Car for steak dinners that his father couldn't afford. My father brought me to the Car on my tenth birthday, in 1958. I met my wife at the Car. A minister married us a few yards from my favorite booth.

I sat down in the booth and stretched my legs. I was exhausted.

I'd watched Bud White shoot the rape-o two dozen times. I'd watched Hanson refine and perfect the scene. I felt dispersed. I was losing track of all my L.A.'s.

Hanson showed up a few minutes later. A waiter brought us our drinks automatically.

We discussed the day's shooting and the thematic shifts between my novel and his film. Our conversation drifted back to L.A. in the '50s and the dark corners we had peered into as children.

I said, "There's a phrase that puts it nicely."

Hanson said, "Tell me."

I said, "'L.A.: Come on vacation; go home on probation.'"

Hanson laughed and said, "It's inspired."

October 1997

LET'S TWIST AGAIN

Seasons of grace come and go. People never designate them in the moment. They look back individually or en masse and impose narrative lines. It all comes down to what you had and what you lost.

The lines apply to nations, cities, and people. Kodachrome snapshots offset them. Faded colors send out a glow. Gooey music fills in the rest of the picture and tells you what to think.

It was better then. We were better then. I was younger then.

It's specious stuff all the way. It's schmaltzy hindsight built from verisimilitude. It obfuscates more than it enlightens. There's just enough hard truth in it to keep it running strong.

One season defines the whole mind-set. A formal name denotes it. Knights and maidens in a savage time. A three-hanky weeper on stage, screen, and CD.

A corny musical and a worn-out media concept. With a three-point intersection running soft and sure in my head.

I had my own Camelot. It ran concurrent with the Broadway show and Jack Kennedy's spin in the White House. I lived in a dive apartment with my pussy-hound father and our unhousebroken dog. I had a fancifully corrupted mind and poor social skills. I had a Schwinn Corvette with gooseneck handlebars, chrome fenders, rhinestone-studded mud flaps, fringed saddlebags, and a speedometer that topped out at 150 miles per hour. I had a great city to roam and a shitload of kid lore to assimilate.

Our pad straddled Hancock Park and lower Hollywood. To the south and southwest: Tudor castles, French châteaus, and Spanish haciendas. To the north: small houses and studio back lots. To the east: wood-frame cribs and apartment dumps on a hilly plumb line downtown.

My beat covered Hollywood to Darktown. The southern border was a race line that white kids never crossed. It was pre-riot L.A. L.A. was pre-hysteric. Parents told their kids not to stray south of Pico and let the little fuckers roam.

I started roaming at age 11. It was summer '59. I had to start junior high in September. It scared the shit out of me.

I bike-roamed. I shoplifted books and candy bars. I ran into strange kids in bike cliques and picked up information.

How this girl popped some Spanish fly and impaled herself on a shift knob. How Hitler was still alive. The word on aspirin and Coke. The word on Liberace and Rock Hudson. The word on your local junior high schools.

Le Conte Junior High, AKA "Le Cunt": Coool guys. Fast girls. Partyville, U.S.A. A breeding ground for studs in the "Lochinvars" and "Celts." Be cool or stay out.

Virgil Junior High: Full of cholos with Sir Guy shirts and slit-bottomed khakis.

King Junior High: Full of Japs and creeps from Silverlake—the "Swish Alps." Lots of homos who wore green on Thursdays.

Louis Pasteur Junior High: Full of uppity spooks who thought they were white.

Berendo Junior High: Danger zone. Pachuco rumbles. Full of Catholic girls who smoked Maryjane and had babies out of wedlock.

Mount Vernon Junior High, AKA "Mount Vermin," AKA "Mau-Maunt Vernon": Niggerland, U.S.A. Beware! Beware! Frequent homicides and race riots on campus.

I was slated to attend John Burroughs Junior High, AKA "J.B." I asked about it. Nobody had a riff down pat.

I spent three years at J.B. It was the buffer zone between my dark childhood and bleak postadolescence. J.B. was Camelot writ small and contained and unimpaired by hokey images of lost innocence to come. It was my taste of earned privilege and potent destiny and the unacknowledged secret pulse of my wild L.A. trip.

J.B. stood at 6th and McCadden. It was the southwest edge of Hancock Park. Kosher Canyon kicked in a few blocks away. J.B. divided two diverse and significant hunks of Central L.A.

Pedigreed goys and big-ass homes to the east. Hard-scrabbling Jews in duplex pads and stucco huts to the west. A legacy of entrenchment and a prophecy of powerful emergence. A contentious demographic. Two gene pools programmed to spawn swift kids.

J.B. was red brick and built to last. The main building and north building were contiguous and joined at an L-shaped juncture. Offices and classrooms covered two floors linked by wide stairwells.

The main building adjoined a large auditorium. A blacktop athletic field stretched south to Wilshire. Shop bungalows and two gyms abutted the main and north buildings perpendicularly. They enclosed the "Lunch Court"—a paved space dotted with benches and green-and-gold trash cans.

J.B. was named after a dead guy who fucked around with plants or soybeans. Nobody stressed his accomplishments or gave him much play as an icon. He was stale bread.

The student body was 80% Jewish. I didn't know from Jews. My father called them "Pork Dodgers." My Lutheran pastor called them complicit in the famous Jesus Christ homicide.

Fifteen percent of the kids hailed from Hancock Park. Their parents preferred J.B. to prestigious prep schools. My guess: they wanted their kids to compete with Jews so they'd grow up tough and kick ass in business.

The final component: Gentile riffraff and a few Negro kids who escaped restrictive housing laws and certain death at Mount Vermin.

There's J.B., '59. I storm Camelot on my steed—a two-wheel taco wagon.

I'm tall. My dog shits on my living-room floor. I pick my nose with gusto. I stick pencils in my ears and excavate wax in full view of other kids.

I'm afraid of all living things. I pull crazy-man stunts to attract attention and deter kid predators. My psycho act is now in its third or fourth school year. The performance lines are starting to blur. I can't tell when I'm putting people on and when I'm not.

It's '59. Performance Art has not been conceptualized. I'm prescient and avant-garde and unaware that I just got lucky. Art requires an audience. Camelots play out on stages—large and small. I hit the one place that would tolerate and occasionally laud my amped-up and wholly pathetic act.

I didn't know it going in. J.B. was regimented and rule-bound.

A dress and appearance code was strictly enforced. Jeans, Capri pants, and T-shirts were banned. Boys kept their hair neatly trimmed—under threat of swats on the ass. Girls wore oxford shoes and maintained low hemlines.

The boys' vice-principal ran J.B. His name was John Hunt. He was a short, blustery man. He had bloodshot eyes and ruptured veins and strutted like a low-rent Il Duce.

Hunt stressed hard work, hard play, and physical reprisals for fuckups. He addressed Boy's League assemblies and got border-line bawdy. He said shit like "You're young men now, soon you'll discover that broads should be broad where they ought to be broad," and "I know you're studying hormones in science class. You know how you make a hormone? Don't pay her."

Hunt dispensed swats with a space-age paddle. Air shot through holes on the downswing. He made you drop trou. The aftermath exceeded the impact. The welts, blood dots, and sting lingered loooooong.

Hunt had a teacher/goon named Arthur Shapero. Hunt was 5'6". Shapero was 6'4". He looked like Lurch and Renfield from *Dracula*. I kept waiting for him to say, "Master, I come!"

Shapero hulked around the lunch court. Hunt kept him on a

long choke chain. He ran the Space Cadets, Space Legion, and Solarons—kiddie cops empowered to cite other kids for littering and dress-code infractions.

The little shits abused their power. Hunt and Shapero backed them up. It was minidrama worthy of a mini-Camelot—and as futile as JFK's attempts to suppress Fidel Castro.

You couldn't quash the exuberance of the J.B. rank-and-file kid. You could infiltrate his imagination and hope your lessons took. The J.B. rank-and-file teacher knew this. He knew he was up against a big ego and a spongelike mind eager to soak up the latest and greatest knowledge—if it was sold in a boredom-proof package. He learned to digress off his basic curriculum and work in topical angles. He never played down to his kid audience.

I had my act. The teachers had theirs. We shared the same audience.

I infiltrated it as a J.B. student. I stood apart from it as a grand-standing leper afraid of his peers.

It's fall '59. I hit J.B. I scope out the turf and rule out assimilation. I'm a stranger in a strange fucking land. Ike is still in the White House. I don't know from Camelot. I don't know that I'm about to embark on my first and most formative season of discourse.

With:

Little sharpsters with hungry eyes and paperbound copies of *Exodus* in their hip pockets. Jokesters who said, "Did you know Abraham Lincoln was Jewish? He was shot in the temple." Twelve-year-olds who'd read more books than I had and could recite baseball stats back to the time the Nazis ran Mom and Dad out of Poland. Hancock Park surfers who dry-surfed the main building on slick-soled penny loafers. Girls with stunning big features die-cast for sex appeal generations back in the shtetl. Girls bred breathtakingly blonde and raised refined by the back nine at Wilshire C.C. Kids with their own acts. Kids who could spiel, spritz, run shtick, and perform without hocking their soles.

I settled in.

I listened. I learned. I performed.

I *observed*.

Formal learning came easy. I read fast and retained well. My father did my math homework and supplied me with crib sheets. I gave oral reports on real books and books that I concocted extemporaneously. I hipped a few kids to my ruse and watched them howl. No teacher ever busted me for book-report fraud.

J.B. had some *très* hip teachers. Lepska Verzeano was Henry Miller's ex. I asked my father what this meant. He waggled his eyebrows at me.

Walt Macintosh killed Reds in Korea. His gun barrel melted during a Red death charge. He doped out the '60 campaign and held a classroom election. The Jewish kids backed JFK. The Hancock Park kids backed Nixon. I backed Tricky Dick—because my father said that JFK took his orders from Rome.

Laurence Nelson got me hooked on classical music. Beethoven wrote the sound track for my J.B. years.

I fell for an English teacher named Margaret Pieschel. The kids called her Miss "Pie-Shell." She was dark-haired and slender. She had bad acne. The J.B. boys considered her a dog. I sensed her inner torment and caught her sex vibe full on. It was Beethovian. I stared at her and tried to zap her telepathically. I tried to tell her, I know who you are. I looked at her and knew what it was like to love a lonely woman to death.

J.B. teachers were classifiable and divisible by two. Call them the Quick and the Dead.

The Quick contingent swung hip. They dug the Peace Corps, cool jazz, and Mort Sahl. The Dead contingent swung limp—as in elderly and sincere and content to rest on J.B.'s hot rep. The Deads were a needle stuck in the groove of a looooong-play record. The Quicks faced a Camelotian dilemma: whether to toil for chump change in the L.A. school system or strike out and try to make it in the real world.

J.B. kids were classifiable and divisible by two. Call them the Naked and the Dead.

The Dead contingent swung square—as in no spiel, spritz, shtick, or performance capability and no sexy angst. The Deads did not know from discourse. The Deads accepted J.B.'s social stratification—regardless of their status. The Naked contingent swung hungry—as in voluble, argumentative, hormonally unhinged, and hip to the fact that the world rocked to a Rat Pack beat and lots of people got fucked in the ass. The Nakeds faced a Camelotian dilemma: whether to accede to the realities of social stratification and capitulate to appearances as *everything* and deny your own hunger and seek contentment in conformity and tone down your spiel, spritz, shtick, and performance capability and rework it to suit a mainstream audience—or go iconoclastic all the way and fuck this overweening adolescent urge to BELONG.

The Nakeds formed the bulk of the J.B. student body. I was an uber-Naked. I was genetically programmed for self-destructive kid iconoclasm. I expressed it in a buffoonish manner that marked me as harmless. My antics amused on occasion. My antics reminded the rank and file that they weren't as whacked-out as I was. I made them feel secure. They rewarded me with tolerance and a few pats on the back. I listened to their spiels, spritzes, and shticks. I performed impromptu or on command. My three-year J.B. discourse was rarely interactive.

I went for my own jugular. I trashed liberal pieties and ragged JFK. I trashed Jewish pieties and yelled, "Free Adolf Eichmann!" I listened to sincerely fevered classroom debates, measured their value, and voiced ridiculously reasoned opinions calculated to agitate and spawn belly laughs. I inspired a few sad-assed guys with no riffs of their own. We became friends. We dissected the J.B. boys and stalked the J.B. girls that we craved.

I bopped around the lunch court with my stooge, Jack Lift. We lurked, loitered, listened, and leched.

There's David Friedman. He pulled in a bundle for his bar mitzvah and laid it down on blue-chip stocks. There's Bad John and his fat sidekick, "Hefty." The word: they pour glue and glass shards on cats and blow them up with cherry bombs. There's Tony Blankley—a weird kid with a British accent. He's some kind of child actor—catch him in that Bogart flick, *The Harder They*

Fall. There's Jamie Osborne. Check *his* British accent. He says he's James Mason's nephew.

There's Leona Walters. She's a tall Negro girl. I danced with her at "Co-Ed": the mandatory gym class hoedown held on Friday mornings. Negro kids are accepted magnanimously. They rate high on the Coolometer. Teachers and kids dig their victim status and try not to act condescending. I told my father that I danced with Leona and blushed the whole time. He said, "Once you've had black, you can't go back."

Howard Swancy is the alpha dog in J.B.'s black litter. He's abrupt and outspoken and a great athlete. He's always scoping out weakness in white kids. He's a dancing motherfucker. He did the Twist with Miss Byers—this redheaded English teacher with wheels like Cyd Charisse. The other twisters froze and watched. The boys' gym dance was never the same.

Steve Price is a little Lenny Bruce manqué. He's the spritz personified. He's always trawling for straight men. He knows how to mine current events for big yocks.

Jay Jaffe is any doppelgänger. He's a popular kid with edgy nerves and some kind of wild hunger. He's socially deft and a great baseball player. He's got the stuff to get by on laced in with some crazy shit. I observe him obsessively. If I could bite his neck and mix his DNA with mine, I could remake myself and not cede my own essence.

Lizz Gill is a pixielike Hancock Park girl. She works for wholesome laughs. She knows the Big J.B. Kid Truth: Sex is the ridiculous, consuming thing that life is all about. There's something subversive in her pedigree. She probably wouldn't judge me for the dog shit on my living-room floor.

Richard Berkowitz refers to himself in the third-person. He says, "I, the Great Berko have decreed" and "The Exalted Berko welcomes you" routinely. He doesn't talk much beyond that. He's a restrained shtickmeister in a frenetic crowd. His stated ambition: to serve as the towel boy in the girls' gym forever.

The girls' gym adjoined the boys' gym. There were no secret

passageways between them. They were separate outposts of Camelot. The boys' gym was a comedy club. Monomania reigned. The one joke was sex and the breathlessly close proximity of the girls' gym. One shtick lasted three whole years. Boys fluffed out their pubic hair and crooned, "Kookie, Kookie, lend me your comb!"

The standard J.B. romantic form was the serial crush. Love affairs came and went sans physical contact or mutual acknowledgment. Crush objects rarely knew that they were crushed on. It was all decorous and voyeuristic and abetted by intermediaries.

Crushers crushed on crushees and detailed their lust to their crush confidantes. I cranked my crushes and confidant duty up to sustained surveillance.

There's Leslie Jacobson. She's willowy. Her black bouffant bounces and shines. My stooge, Dave, loves her. He tracks her across the lunch court. I run point and linger near her in food lines. She's the quintessential Teen Fox. Dave can't get it up to address her. We discuss her and beat every aspect of her into the ground. Dave's crush fizzles out and reignites on a new girl. He carves her initials on his right arm and gets up the guts to show her. She flees in horror.

I torched my way through Camelot. I burned flames for Jill Warner, Cynthia Gardner, Donna Weiss, and Kathy Montgomery.

Jill's an in-your-face little blonde. She'll talk a blue streak to anyone. Her accessibility marks her as fatally flawed and thus a kindred spirit. She's hard to stalk. She keeps spotting me. She starts intimidating conversations and forces me to respond. Jill rates high on spunk and low on hauteur. I crave mystery and elusiveness in my women. It flips my fantasy switch and gives me groovy shit to talk about with my stalking buddies.

Cynthia, Donna, and Kathy radiated wholesome beauty and hinted at stern character. I stalked them inside and outside of school and across a big patch of L.A.

Jack Lift backstopped my surveillance. He lived across the street from Cynthia's pad at 6th and Crescent Heights. We shined shoes around the corner at the Royal Market and used it as our stakeout point. We tailed Cynthia around on our bikes the whole Summer of '61.

I knew my love was doomed. I knew the Berlin Wall thing would escalate to World War III at any moment. L.A. was scared. J.B. kids stocked up on goods at the Royal Market. We discussed the crisis and concluded that our time was running out. I told the kids that I was hot for Armageddon. They said I was nuts. Jack and I fucked up their shoes under the guise of free shines.

The world survived. My crush on Cynthia Gardner didn't. I entered crush monogamy with Donna and Kathy and torched my J.B. days down to an ember.

Donna had big eyes and a pageboy hairdo. She lived at Beverly and Gardner—the heart of Kosher Canyon. I set up a voyeur spot by the Pan Pacific Theater and surveilled her after school and on weekends.

I watched her front door. I watched people enter the synagogues on Beverly. Jack said they were war refugees. I perched by the Pan Pacific and watched the parade go by. I time-tripped back to World War II. I saved the people with the funny beanies and top hats. Donna loved me for it—until I left her for Kathy.

I traded up to a freckled brunette and a big house at 2nd and Plymouth. I boosted some Ivy League clothes to look more Hancock Park. The makeover thrilled me. JFK never looked so good. I hit a growth spurt, popped over six feet, and rendered my new threads obsolete. My pincord pants bottomed out at my ankles and drew jeers at 2nd and Plymouth. I never got up the stones to play Jack to Kathy's Jackie.

I was starting to get the picture:

Camelot was a private club and an inside joke—and I didn't know the password or the punchline.

I went to the J.B. graduation dance on 6/14/62. I wore my father's 1940-vintage gray flannel suit and drank some T-Bird with a neighbor kid en route.

I sweltered in gray flannel. I squeaked across the dance floor in brown canvas shoes. I asked Cynthia Gardner to dance. She accepted in the manner of nice girls worldwide. I sweated all over her and breathed Thunderbird wine in her face.

The class of Summer '62 passed into history. The 400-odd members dispersed to three local high schools. My season of craaazy discourse ended.

I didn't know what I walked away from. I left J.B. with no fanfare and no friendships intact. I didn't know what I'd learned about myself or other people. I didn't know that the inexorably destructive course of my life had been diverted and subsumed by a magical time and place. I didn't know that the seeds of a gift were nourished then and there or that the raucous spirit I carried away would influence my ultimate survival.

My life went waaay bad. I gave up fifteen years to booze, dope, petty crime, and insanity. I rarely thought about John Burroughs Junior High School. I stumbled past it and never acknowledged it with affection. I never thought about my stooges or Jay Jaffe and the Great Berko. I carried snapshots of the girls in my head and loved them in place of real women.

I almost died in '75 and cleaned up in '77. The act was reflexive and instinctive and tweaked by ambiguous forces that I didn't comprehend in the moment. It was a blessed non sequitur. I didn't dissect the act or question its componentry. I didn't want to look back. I wanted to write books and look forward.

I did it. I moved east to expedite my forward momentum. I shut my unacknowledged Camelot in a time-locked vault and forgot the combination.

A series of external events clicked into place and inspired me to reinvestigate my mother's 1958 murder. I spent fifteen months in L.A. and wrote a book about the investigation. It forced me to walk backward in time and linger in Camelot.

My time lock blew. All the old players flew out of the vault.

There's Howard Swancy. There's Berko and Jaffe. There's the girls I stalked and all the Naked and the Dead in a jumble of faces and voices.

My memoir was published in November '96. I spent ten days in

L.A. on the publicity tour. Kosher Canyon and Hancock Park took on a wild new sheen. I drove by J.B. every chance I got. I sent up prayers for the faces and voices every time.

I designated J.B. as a formal phenomenon. I developed narrative lines on the players and began to view them as kids *and* middle-aged men and women. They wore interchangeable masks. They moved between then and now in unpredictable ways. I fashioned their masks from memory and flattered them with their present-day faces. I did not know what they looked like now. I granted them beauty as a way to say, Thanks for the ride.

A year passed. My memoir was published in paperback. A toll-free number and e-mail address were listed at the back of the text. They were there to solicit leads on my mother's murder.

An old J.B. classmate read the book and contacted me. His name was Steve Horvitz. I didn't recall him. He remembered me vividly. He ran down a list of my antics and detailed his own life then to now.

His parents were L.A. kids. His old man came out of Boyle Heights, and his old lady went to Le Conte and Hollywood High. They broke up in '55—the same year my folks split the sheets. Steve lived at Olympic and Cochran. He hung out with Ron Stillman, Ron Papell, and Jay Jaffe—all lawyers now. Jaffe moonlighted as a TV pundit. He worked the O.J. Simpson trial for KCBS.

Steve went to San Francisco State. He stalked Jill Warner in Frisco—more successfully than I stalked her in L.A. He graduated and sold insurance. He went into his old man's wholesale candy and tobacco biz. He made a mint off high-interest CDs in the go-go years and bought a car wash and a marketing business. He did custom framing for model homes and design work for restaurants and coffee shops. He went into the sports lithograph field and lost a mint in the Bush recession. He was working on Mint #2 now. Credit card processing was hot, hot, hot. He had two sons—one from Wife #1 and one from Wife #2. Wife #2 had a son from Husband #1. Wives, kids, mints—life could be worse.

Steve and I became friends. We shared a similar take on Camelot and rehashed the time and place in two-hour phone talks. We debated John Hunt as sadist or man-on-moral-mission. We dissected "Kampus King" Tony Shultz and Tony Blankley—now a big cheese with Newt Gingrich. Steve stayed in L.A. He didn't lock J.B. in a time-vault. He retained a few friendships and had a handhold on the slender J.B. grapevine. He provided rumors and facts and a necrology.

Howard Swancy—allegedly a cop. Jamie Osborne—dead in Vietnam. Mark Schwartz—dead—possibly a dope-related homicide. Eric Hendrickson—murdered in Frisco. Laurie Maullin—dead of cancer. Steve Schwartz—heroin O.D. Steve Siegel and Ken Greene—dead.

Lots of attorneys—the law attracted bright kids who didn't know what else to do with their lives. Josh Trabulus—doctor. Lizz Gill—TV writer. The Great Berko—Berko'd out somewhere unknown. Cynthia Gardner—last seen as a Mormon housewife. Leslie Jacobson—allegedly a shrink.

Steve lent me his "Burr" yearbooks. The photos served as synaptic triggers. My backlog of faces and events expanded fiftyfold.

Howard Swancy almost trades blows with Big Guy Huber. Leslie Jacobson twirls to the "Peppermint Twist." Jay Jaffe wins a penny stomp that leaves a half-dozen kids bloody. Herb Steiner rags the folk song craze at the Burr Frolics. I disrupt a classroom postmortem on the Bay of Pigs invasion. I contend that JFK should A-bomb Havana. Kids bomb me with wadded-up paper. I dig the attention and launch a counterattack. The teacher laughs. The same teacher laughed when Caryl Chessman got fried.

Steve and I deconstructed Camelot. We conceded the predictable nature of fifty-year-olds looking back. We traced the known arc of J.B. lives and the mass reconstellation at Berkeley in the late '60's. We tagged it as predictably emblematic and explored it as a cliché and an issue of enduring ideals. We questioned J.B. as a substantive endeavor or a freeze-frame from some ditzy teen flick. I categorized it as an auspicious L.A. lounge act.

We opened strong. The curtain went down before we had to take it any further.

Steve said, "Let's get some motherfuckers together."

I said, "I'll fly out."

The Pacific Dining Car defines my L.A. continuum.

It's a swank steak house west of the downtown freeway loop. It's been there since 1921. It's open twenty-four hours, every day of the year. It's dark, cavelike, and lushly contained in the middle of a poverty zone. I was born in the hospital half a block south. I met my wife at the Dining Car and married her there.

Steve found most of the people. A private eye found the rest. The RSVP list tallied in at 99%. One dinner turned into three.

Steve and I attended them all. The Dining Car fed groups of thirteen, twelve, and nine. We convened at the same long table in the same dark room. I can't break down the specific guest lists. The whirl of laughter and reminiscence ran seamless over three nights.

Camelot redux.

There's Berko and Jaffe. There's Donna Weiss in a new page-boy. Howard Swancy—a preacher instead of a cop. Helen Katzoff, Lorraine Biller, Joanne Brossman—bright faces out of a big crowd thirty-six years back. Lizz Gill and Penny Hunt from Hancock Park. A big Kosher Kanyon kontingent that I knew by name and yearbook photo only. Josh Trabulus—a small boy, a tall man. More lawyers than an ABA convention. Jill Warner, in your face à la 1960. Steve Price with the same fucking grin. Tony Shultz in saddle shoes. Leslie Jacobson sans bouffant and the Peppermint Twist.

We toasted the dead and the missing. Wallet photos went around. Nobody asked the childless people why they didn't breed. We all agreed that J.B. was a blast. Anecdotes passed as insight into why. We decided to throw a mass reunion early next year and elected a steering committee.

One person in ten remembered me. I recalled every name and

face and could have picked half the people out of a thousand slot lineup. It told me how hungry and lonely I was then. It confirmed everything I'd come to believe about my cut-rate Camelot.

We agreed that we were *all* observers. We *all* superimposed our shaky psyches against the boss bods we wanted and wished we had and came up way short. We punted then. We conformed or got raucous to cut the edge off the pain.

Everyone came off prosperous and well cared for. We looked like a prophecy of affluence fulfilled. I didn't detect much smugness. The braggarts boasted too hard and vibed Naked more than middle-aged Dead. I picked out two functioning drunks. I judged as I laughed and observed. It didn't mar my enjoyment or subvert my affection one bit.

I listened more than I talked. I table-hopped and found the people I carried around in my head. They told me their stories and filled in that big gap in time.

Jay Jaffe played baseball at USC and went to the College World Series. He batted .306 and had a three-night tryout with the San Diego Padres. They expressed interest and never called him back. He went to law school and gravitated to the criminal defense field. He liked the combat and the mix of people in trouble. He liked to explore motive and mitigation. He'd handled some big cases. He won the celebrated "Burrito Murder Case." The LAPD tried to shaft an innocent Mexican kid. Jay got him off.

He was still hungry. He loved his work the way he loved baseball.

Lizz Gill wrote TV movies. She fell into it. People told her she was funny and urged her to get her shit down on paper. She had a bad run with booze and cleaned up in '75.

She knew the Big Joke then. She still knew it. Other people sensed her gift and pointed her on her way.

Berko Berkowitz went to Vietnam. He defecated in his pants quite a few times. He returned to the States and got strung out on booze and dope. He ran a string of businesses into the ground and cleaned up twelve years ago. He made a big wad in real estate and watched it grow. He works as a homeless advocate and digs on his wife and two kids.

Jill Warner was a teacher up in Oakland. She had a daughter with her ex-husband. I told her I used to stalk her. She applauded my good taste and asked me if I defaced her house in 1963. I said, No. Jill laughed and got up in my face like she did at J.B.

Howard Swancy played all-city sports at L.A. High School. He tried to get on the LAPD and Sheriff's Department and flunked the screening process. He sold TV ad time for seventeen years and became a minister. He had a congregation in Carson.

Howard looked hungry. He still had alpha dog eyes. He liked to run the show. The raw language at the table torqued him the wrong way.

I spent some time with Donna Weiss. I described the Big Stake-out of 1961 and the unrequited crush that inspired it. Donna praised my stalking prowess. She never spotted me—a 6-foot, 13-year-old boy—on a candy-apple bike.

I was invisible then. The world was out to ignore me.

Donna spent time in Spain and studied at the University of Madrid. She learned the language and came back to L.A. She taught in the city school system and spent three years down in South Central. Some Chicano kids were stranded in an all-black school with no English language skills. Donna got the little fuckers fluent.

She quit teaching and went into real estate. She's been at it twenty years. Her husband's a voice coach and the locally lauded "Cantor to the Stars."

My crush burned out thirty-seven years ago. Donna's presence did not resurrect it. I was irrevocably in love with my wife.

Tony Shultz starred in the first New York stage run of *Grease*. He worked as an actor for twenty-plus years and burned out behind the inherent frustrations. He sold real estate now. His turf bordered Donna's.

Leslie Jacobson went to Berkeley and lived two blocks down from Tony. She became an antiwar activist and street agitator. She got a teaching credential.

She married Husband #1. She entered the mental-health field. A colleague got raped. Leslie viewed the brutal aftermath and took it as a signal. She studied rape and post-rape trauma. She ran a rape crisis hotline and an innovative antirape program. She went out on rape calls with the Huntington Park PD and trained cops in rape awareness. She ditched Husband #1 and married Husband #2. He was a doctor.

Leslie became a psychotherapist. She built up a practice. She studied breast cancer and its ramifications and counseled afflicted women. She and her husband collaborate and stage breast-cancer seminars.

I listened to my old classmates. I felt the restrained warmth that you feel for decent people you shared a past with and don't really know. I observed thirty-four individuals over three nights. I detected one significant difference between them and me.

They came to reconnect with specific people and dig on a collective nostalgia. I came to honor them and acknowledge their part in my debt.

The debt was large. J.B. was my first testing ground. I learned to compete there. I nurtured a perverse self-sufficiency. My warped little world meshed with the real world—for "one brief shining moment."

L.A. was hot and smoggy. I was wiped out behind all my time travel and the clash of old/new people. I took a ride with Tony Shultz.

It felt like my seven-millionth hot L.A. day. Tony was digging it. He ran a riff on the NEW L.A.—immigrant cultures and wild cuisines and big rejuvenation.

We drove down to Howard Swancy's church. We made the noon service ten minutes early. The joint was jumping jubilantly high.

A six-piece combo backed up the choir. Sixty loud voices praised God. They soared over loud air-conditioner blasts and woke me up like six cups of coffee.

The church was SRO. Howard saved two pew slots near the altar. The congregation was 99.9 percent Black. The people were snazzily dressed and ran toward the plump side.

I hit the Pause button on my life. Fast-Forward and Rewind clicked off. I got choked up behind a big blast of gratitude.

The service commenced. I sang hymns for the first time since First Dutch Lutheran and shared smiles with Tony. I felt intractably Protestant and unassailably un-Christian. I grooved on John Osborne's Luther. He slayed the Papist beast because he was constipated and wanted to get laid.

The collection plate went around. Tony and I fed the kitty. Howard hit the altar and introduced us. We stood up and waved to the people. They waved back.

Howard launched into his sermon. He was main-room talent in a southside carpet joint.

He strutted. He stalked. He banged the pulpit and shouted over a four-octave range. The crowd went nuts.

He sustained a half-hour roar. He sweated up his vestments and blew out his lungs with the word on salvation.

Go, Howard, go!

It was a New Testament Greatest Hits medley. It was a deftly etched exposition of your alternatives: embrace Jesus or fry in Hell forever. It proclaimed the restrictive housing law in Heaven.

I wouldn't want to buy a tract in that development. They wouldn't sell to pork dodgers or skeptics or that Moslem guy at my favorite falafel stand. They'd exclude the bulk of the J.B. class of 1962.

Howard cranked it out. My mind wandered. I dipped thirty-six years back and thirty-six years into the future. I wondered how many bonds would rekindle and flourish in the wake of three effusive evenings. I thought about a survivors' bash in 2034. A collective senescence might color the proceedings and distort recollections for better or worse.

Let's Twist again, like we did that summer.

It's a teen dance party at the Mount Sinai Nursing Home. A boss combo rules the bandstand. It features all my old heartthrobs on skin-flute.

Jack and Jackie appear. The kids go nuts. Jack nuked Castro just last week. He's on a fucking roll.

Jack cuts a rug with Leslie Jacobson. He eyeballs Donna Weiss and Jill Warner. He can't commit to an image. He doesn't know whether to shit or go blind.

Somebody slips LSD in the punch. The J.B. dead resurrect. Jackie goes down on the Great Berko.

Howard cranked it out. I looked around the pews. I locked eyes with a tall black kid. He looked bored and agitated.

I winked. He smiled. The Apostolic Church of Peace turned into the Peppermint Lounge.

I sent up a prayer for the kid. I wished him imagination and a stern will and lots of raucous laughs. I wished him a wild mix of people to breeze through and linger with over time.

November 1998